I0742681

THE LIGHT HEART OF STONE

TOR ROXBURGH

IMPRINT PAGE

First published in 2012 by Curious Crow Books

This revised edition published in 2025 by Curious Crow Books

Curious Crow Books

PO Box 433

Ballan Victoria 3342 Australia

Copyright © Tor Roxburgh 2012

Copyright in this revised edition © Tor Roxburgh 2025

The moral right of the author has been asserted.

All rights reserved. Any person or organisation wanting to copy, store, or transmit material in this book needs permission in writing from Tor Roxburgh.

ISBN 978-0-9805249-9-4

Cover design by Stuart Bache Design

www.torroxburgh.com

JOIN MY READING COMMUNITY

Welcome to The Light Heart of Stone. My reading community is always the first to hear about giveaways and new releases. Please stay in touch by joining my email list at www.torroxburgh.com.

N
E
S
KOMEY
OAK
NEW LYTALIA
KELP
KELP OCEAN
KOMIC SEA
COTTON SEA
A MAP OF THE STONE BODY
Gifted By The Oak Companion
To The People Of Kelp Province
(On The Occasion Of Their 1st Successful Crossover)

1

WINTER

Fox Oak thought she could smell the past, the world beyond the city. She closed her eyes, lifted her face to the sky, and inhaled.

Just a hint of brine. Just today. Surely, that wasn't too much to ask?

She reached for the longed-for smell and the wind picked up, slapping her face with grit and dust. Just dirt, yet the memories it brought of the provinces beyond the city lifted goose bumps on her arms, tied a knot in her belly, and made her throat ache for home.

'Are you helping or are you helping?' Willie, the Oak House cook, bumped his barrow into the back of her legs, rattling the jars of preserved peaches.

'Of course.'

She stepped back, leant a hand to settle the barrow on the gravel path. Willie waved his kitchen staff forward, arranged his helpers in a line, and they began handing out provisions to the impoverished Companionari families and the starving Beranish men who'd arrived in the Oak House kitchen garden. The charity was mainly olives, onions and dates. The few jars of preserved peaches were disappearing fast.

The housekeeper sidled up, eyeing the remaining jars. He was careful to avoid the dirty edge of the barrow as he leant over and counted them. 'I've written to the Oak Companion. I keep her apprised.'

'You and half of the household,' Willie muttered, re-tying his apron strings into an elaborate bow.

'She's opposed to charity,' the housekeeper said.

In response, Willie raised his voice and spoke to the dwindling crowd, 'Pull a few weeds on your way out. The Oak Companion favours tit for tat, labour for bounty. No charity here.'

'You think you're helping people, but you're not,' the house-keeper said. 'I don't know how you imagine we can sustain this. Oak House has a responsibility to its own. Two hundred and seventy people live in our house here in the city—'

'It's actually two hundred and sixty-eight,' Willie said. 'I know because I feed them every day.'

'Fine. But the point remains: we must husband our resources.'

Willie turned to face the housekeeper. 'And yet you haven't bothered asking me who paid for this bounty. Have you considered that Persica House might have donated the peaches?'

'I can't imagine Persica...'

Something interrupted Fox's concentration. Her name. Spoken in an undertone. A sound more welcome than the smell of brine and the taste of earth. Mica. Well fed. Looking nothing like a Beran in need. No one seemed to notice the incongruity of his presence. He didn't speak again. Nor did she. She didn't acknowledge him, but noticed he left with a bag of olives and a jar of peaches. The knot in her belly shifted into something different. A beautiful shape. A shape full of the past and touched with hope for the future.

Fox headed into the garden, following the direction Mica had taken. Behind her, she could hear Willie shooing the kitchen hands towards the house. She didn't need her rock skin to re-emerge to feel the cook had half an eye on her, longing to ask where she was going. She glanced back at the housekeeper and saw him staring at her. That one would add a note about her in his next letter to the Oak Companion. Fox didn't acknowledge him. She turned away and lifted her head. He would need to be careful. The Oak Companion still favoured Fox. It was partly guilt, but there was genuine affection between them. Still, the housekeeper's gaze was uncomfortable, as though he could sense her intentions, knew she was about to ignore the rules. She smoothed her lapels, touching the knotted lace pictures of fox cubs, twenty-one of them running riot over her shoulders and down the front of her coat. A birthday gift from Aikin, her adopted father.

Ahead of her, the path split. She turned left and found herself between two long lines of fig trees. They never really fruited for the Oak family, but their branches offered a thick leafy wall to hide her. She ran, didn't stop until she reached the next fork. She turned and there he was: Mica. Sitting on a garden seat under the eaves of one of the Oak House garden walls. She came to a halt and hesitated.

'It's safe,' he said. 'There's no one about.' He rested his arms on the back of the seat. The movement pulled his sleeves back from his wrists. The rock skin on the backs of his hands refracted the sunlight, scattered colour across the weathered seat. He frowned. 'What's the matter?'

'It's nothing. I'm fine.'

He gave her a worried look. 'Don't lie. Not when I can rock sense what you're feeling. And you were happy a second ago, but now you're not. Talk to me. Are you homesick?'

'Always.'

'You missed me?'

She smiled. 'Of course. You're the only one who visits me.' She felt like kicking herself as soon as the words left her mouth. So self-pitiful. And she wasn't self-pitiful about her life, never had been. She owed Mica better. He was her only friend from before. 'It's just... I caught sight of your rock skin.'

He stood up, walked over, and she thought he wanted to embrace her. She took a step back, but he reached for her hands and lifted them, exposing her arms and the faint marks, the slight and scarcely detectable irregularities in her pigmentation. Her olive skin was as healthy as any other 21-year-old's, but touched with faded patterns.

'Can you still feel it, your rock skin? Is it still hidden in there?' He touched a faded mark on her arm. 'Like we agreed?'

Her gaze went past him to the cork oak beyond the wall. Anywhere to hide her eyes. 'Yes.'

'So there's nothing to feel sad about. You're still you.'

But he didn't know how it felt. She couldn't feel people approaching. She couldn't rock sense emotions. If she ever got the chance to walk out one of Komey's city gates, she'd probably get lost. Certainly she'd lose her footing if she tried it in the dark. He was wrong. She wasn't who she had been. She turned, ready to reject his pity or argue with his pigheadedness, but he was smiling. A broad grin that made him look younger and reminded her of when they'd first met and they'd decided she should cheat the Companionaris.

'It's still there, Fox.' He patted her arm. 'You're still Beranish and you'll be ready for change when it comes.'

'Nothing will change,' she said.

'Everything will change,' he insisted.

His boyish faith made her laugh. She braced for bitterness, but there was nothing bitter about it. That was Mica. He could produce a better future from any story, and a better version of Fox to stand in it. Soon she was sitting beside him on the garden bench, giving him anecdotes for his story collection, not short of words for once. Mica listened as though the stories of her sewing circle and her work in the Department of Beranish Affairs contained everything he'd ever wanted to know.

'I should go,' she said, realising more than an hour must have passed. 'I'm having a birthday lunch with Aikin. Can't be late. There isn't much time, but one mustn't hurry.'

'You're still keeping my obsidian with you wherever you go?'

She put her hand into her pocket and pulled out an embroidered cloth purse. She loosened the ribbons and slipped Mica's stone into her palm. 'Did it call you? Is that why you came today? I'm fine. Really.'

'No.' He shook his head. 'That rock child hasn't called since I left it with you.' His hand had crept closer to the stone, and she didn't need her lost senses to know he longed to take it back.

'You can. Take it.'

He withdrew his hand. 'No. It loves me, but it wants to stay with you.'

'You think that's what it wants, or you know that's what it wants?'

'I can feel that's what it wants. Needs.'

Fox nodded and slipped the rock child back into her purse, tightening the ribbons. She didn't say she was glad to keep it, that the obsidian was a comfort. No need to tell him. He was a Beran. He could rock sense her feelings. 'Where are you headed now?'

'I thought I might try to get some news of home. Your home.'

She caught her breath and then the words tumbled out, 'You're going to visit Kelp? Visit my family?'

He nodded.

'But you mustn't tell any of them you've seen me. They mustn't know we've broken the treaty. Not my grandmother, and especially not Saury. My sister's too young to be burdened with that sort of secret.'

'I won't tell anyone. You know that.'

'And you need to be careful around my father,' she said.

'It's not my first visit.'

'I know but—'

He interrupted her, 'I won't go if you don't want me to.'

'I want you to.'

'I thought it could be my birthday gift,' he said, 'getting news for you.'

She suspected he'd forgotten to bring something, but she didn't mind. News from home would be the best gift. She leant forward and kissed his cheek. 'Thank you.'

'Getting back may take months.'

'I have months, but please don't let it be years.'

Despite the late hour, Fox sat alone for a while after he departed. There were catkins on the ground, and acorns, and both young and autumnal leaves. It was late winter, but the garden sisters' minor talents could overcome any season. She bent down, cleared the litter away. In its place she made a pattern, something pleasing. With another sharp gust of chilly wind, the pattern was gone.

The cavernous Oak House trading room felt chilly after the sunny garden. Fox pulled her coat closer and loosened her hair over her collar. She kept to the centre of the room as she traversed its length. The day workers and traders didn't need her getting in their way.

Evidently, a trainload of white oak had arrived from the province that morning. Dozens of workers in worn leather tunics were dragging hand carts down the length of the hall. Others were unloading the bark to bark slabs from parked carts and were stacking the timber along the walls. Some of it still sported small branches and leaves, filling the room with a pleasant, faint vanilla scent.

Fox entered the house proper, then hesitated on the far side of the threshold.

She'd forgotten to pick flowers for Wren. The kitchen garden didn't have many blooms. The Oak talent didn't excel at growing flowers, but the garden always had nasturtiums. She liked to take a posy when she visited Wren. But it would mean hurrying if she didn't want to be late for lunch with her father. And it would be impossible to hurry without being noticed. There were too many people about. She could see Acacia, one of the rising stars in the household, officially still just an associate in household records, but already a leader of an influential sewing circle. She was poring over an account book with an elderly sister. Acacia was all right. She wouldn't gossip, but the old woman beside her was another story entirely. That one belonged to an old-fashioned sewing circle. Fox couldn't risk gossip. You didn't hurry in front of women like that. Then, out of the corner of Fox's eye, she spotted the answer. Oak leaves.

A neat, shoulder-high stack of timber stood just inside the trading room, leafy twigs still attached. She walked over and snapped off three of them, held them posy-like in front of her face. Why not? Wren was unlikely to have enough clarity to know the difference between oak leaves and flowers.

'Hey you!' a day worker shouted, heading in Fox's direction. 'Put that down. That's not meant for housegirls to play with.' The woman's footsteps faltered as she saw Fox's eyes. 'Back and path!' she hissed. 'A piss-eye.'

Fox didn't move. She belonged here. She hadn't chosen her life, but she was a daughter in this house. The day worker wasn't a household member. Fox could have her thrown out. Everyone in the hall had fallen silent. And still. Mostly still. But there was some movement. Acacia was already halfway across the hall with the elderly sister at her heels and three soldiersisters were heading in Fox's direction.

'It's okay.' Fox held up her hand. 'I don't need help.'

The worker glanced back, then returned her attention to Fox. 'You're right,' Fox said to her. 'I wasn't born a Companionari, but you shouldn't assume I have no rights here just because my eyes are golden.'

The woman muttered, 'Rock wild Beran.'

'Believe me, I would be delighted to be a rock wild Beran and I certainly wouldn't be standing here if I were. Sadly, I'm not. I am Companionari. I am an Oak House daughter and I can have this stack of timber carried up to my rooms if I want to.' Fox knew she was being unkind, boastful, but the insult hurt.

Acacia appeared at the day worker's shoulder, but her attention was on Fox. 'That might be a slight exaggeration.'

Then the old sewing sister pushed between Acacia and the day worker. She poked the day worker's chest with an arthritic finger. 'Out. We don't want rude girls in our hall.'

Acacia touched the old woman's arm. 'I don't doubt that you're right, Sister. But I think... Perhaps, what's really needed is a little ribbon for Fox's posy.' Acacia pointed at the branches in Fox's hand. 'Then Fox can be on her way and we can get back to work. Would you have something suitable in your purse or in your pockets? I'm afraid I've nothing apart from pencils and paper. And a bit of string, but string isn't good enough. An oak leaf posy deserves something more.'

The old woman felt her pockets and then opened her satin purse. 'I have something. Might suffice.' She pulled out a lengthy piece of red velvet ribbon. 'And I'll write to Oria and tell her about this. Not about her,' she nodded her head at the worker, 'but she'll love hearing about the posy. The Oak Companion does so love the trees. She'll enjoy hearing they're venerated in the city.'

'How sweet,' Acacia said. 'What a lovely thought.'

The old woman took the posy from Fox. Within moments, she'd pulled a pair of secateurs from her belt and had trimmed the stems. Then she cut the ribbon into three and dexterously worked an elaborate plait down the stems. She tied it off at the bottom, leaving three elegant lengths of red ribbon trailing the posy. The day worker had disappeared.

'Is it for your father?' Acacia asked.

'Not for Aikin, no,' Fox said. 'It's for Wren.'

'Ah... Poor Wren. That is kind.'

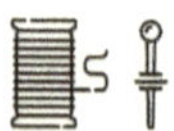

Fox could appreciate why Oria had chosen the first floor for Wren's suite, but it didn't make visiting easy. Too many eyes. Too much judgement about one adopted Beran-born talent visiting the other less successful adoptee.

Oria housed Wren on the first floor because it made Wren noticeable. The early colonists had intended the first floor to be used for important sewing circles, for reading in the afternoons, for sitting at secretaires to write in day books or illustrate journals. It was the floor of grand parleys, of wide corridors filled with conversations and ostentatious displays. No one apart from Wren slept there, but the Oak Companion had a stubborn, almost mean, streak. Fox could tell that Oria didn't like her city house sisters forgetting the treaty or the provinces or the gritty origins of Komey's wealth.

The best way to reach Wren's door was ostentatiously. She almost always brought flowers and normally began calling out to houseboys for vases and teas and cakes before she'd taken her second step on the eight oak-themed rugs that led to Wren's door. Today she let her routine slip. Today, she walked straight to the suite, unlocked the door and stepped inside.

Fox said hello but didn't get an answer. Sometimes it took time before Wren realised there was anyone in the room. She paced in front of the window, and Fox let her be. Fox put the room in order and then threw out the old flowers and left the oak leaf posy on the table beside the rocking chair. At some stage, Wren would sit. The rocking chair, its movement, always called to her, soothed her. Not surprising that sitting brought the poor woman comfort. Too much time on one's feet would tire anyone in late pregnancy, especially someone who paced all day.

Wren muttered something.

'What was that?' Fox asked. 'I didn't catch what you said.'

Wren didn't seem to hear, but she spoke again, whispered under her breath, 'The moon.' She pointed at the sky with one hand and the other flapped.

Fox didn't correct her, didn't bother trying to explain to Wren that the day's orb was called the sun. Explanations didn't help. When Wren registered Fox's presence, she would talk to Fox, but it wouldn't be a conversation. Sometimes the scent of flowers brought Wren closer to the world and conversation, but mostly not. Often, Fox wondered why she came. Well, to keep an eye on Wren, make sure her care was kind. Fox wrote of it when she wrote to the Oak Companion. She hoped her heartfelt letters meant more than all the other missives that journeyed from Komey to Oria's desk in the manor.

Wren moaned. It was a tiny sound, easy to miss. She rubbed her sides, rubbed the place where her pregnant belly met her lean frame. Fox called to her and set the rocking chair in motion. Wren turned and watched the chair as it slowed. Her hands left her sides and moved with the rocking motion.

'Come and sit. It's lovely.'

Wren took a deep breath, as if preparing for a long-awaited speech. Only she didn't speak. She walked over to the chair and sat. Fox put the posy in her hands. Wren closed her eyes and inhaled.

The price of ensuring adoptees had bare Companionari-looking arms was too high. Fox felt grateful that Oria had taught her how to clear the dust bush toxins from her system. What was Aikin's favourite saying? *If you swallow a fate chosen by others, be prepared for a hungry life.* She hadn't wanted that hunger, so she'd forced herself to listen and to learn the Companionari way. Maybe Wren hadn't tried hard enough. Maybe Oria hadn't helped enough. But it was wrong. No one should suffer the way Wren suffered.

'It's my birthday,' she told Wren. 'My novitiate is complete. I can ask my father for a birthday boon. I'm going to ask him to make them stop giving you dust bush tea.' She would do it too. She was ready. Aikin would likely sympathise, but she didn't imagine he would, or could, create the change Wren deserved. But the request might start a conversation about a different future.

Fox picked up a hairbrush and began brushing Wren's hair, careful to keep the strokes even and gentle. The woman sighed with pleasure. Soon the posy slipped from her hands into her lap. Soon she was asleep.

Fox let herself out of Wren's suite. She paused in the hall, her stomach tight. She was only slightly late, but her feelings were too fiery for an encounter with Aikin. She relaxed, settled her emotions. As she started down the corridor, she found she could smile and accept the birthday greetings from the sisters she passed, feign the calm that the city so admired.

○ ○

2

Mica walked through the Oak camp, heading for the manor house. The welcome smell of the province enveloped him, still fresh to his senses even though he'd been home for weeks. He sighed. The loveliness of the day wasn't quite enough to lift his spirits. His mission to visit Fox's family was yet to begin, but it wouldn't be the easy trip he'd planned.

He was supposed to be travelling alone and travelling at a leisurely pace. Instead, he needed to beg the Oak Companion for the loan of two Companionari horses so he could take his nephew with him, so he could hurry.

He passed the last Beranish tent and quickened his step, crossing the flax meadow and walking the path through the twist trees. Standing before the manor's front door, a feeling of urgency pressed him. The uncomfortable heaviness of a stone calling had caught him unawares less than an hour ago. Somewhere, in Kelp's direction, a rock child needed his presence. He felt like a fool in a fireside fourth story.

The day had begun with a lie, and the lie had become the truth.

He'd told his former master, Quartz, that a rock child was calling from the southeast. A lie. But he couldn't share the real reason he needed to go to Kelp. But, when he spoke the lie, that familiar itchy feeling rose in his chest. A stone pulled at him. Or maybe it had already been calling and he hadn't realised. Sometimes, it was hard to know. All he knew, was the stone wanted him and needed him to hurry, so hurry he must.

He knocked at the manor door. Bronda, the Companion's ancient handmaid, let him in and led him to the receiving room where Oria sat working at the desk. His heart sank when he saw the open ledger and realised she was doing the accounts. Course she was. It had been that kind of day.

'Busy,' she said without looking up and he rock sensed her readiness to be rid of him.

'It's Mica,' Bronda said. 'He's asked to see you. You remember him: Quartz's apprentice.' Then she turned to Mica. 'But you're not an apprentice anymore, are you? A wanderer now.'

'That's right,' Mica said.

'Still busy.' Oria didn't look up from her ledger.

Mica found he'd closed his mouth on the explanation he'd intended to offer for his presence. He would wait until she met his eye. The woman had a nerve, treating him like a nuisance.

'Well?' Oria said, glancing up. 'I said I was busy. What is it you want?'

'A rock child is calling me—'

'Yes? And? That concerns the manor how? Why?'

'It feels urgent. The stone needs me to hurry.'

There was a slight shift in the old woman's expression. Mica felt something buried in her emotions, some shadow of a past warmth. 'Urgent, you say? You'll be after one of my horses?'

'Two.'

'Two? Why?'

'I need to take my nephew with me. There's no one to mind him.'

'Ridiculous,' she said. 'There's an entire camp full of people who can mind children.' She waved a thin, claw-like hand in the camp's direction, a gesture full of dismissal.

Mica stiffened. Oria had no idea about what was going on beyond her ledger. No one in the camp wanted to look after Doubt. And the orphan's latest escapade had made him even less popular. Disappearing for two nights, telling no one where he was going.

'Everyone in the camp is working. They're scattering acorns for next season's oaks. For you.'

'For us,' she corrected him. 'And they can still take care of a boy. There are always jobs for children in the field.'

'He's been causing trouble,' Mica said. It felt like a betrayal. It was a betrayal, but he needed those horses.

'Not my problem.'

'I am asking you as a wanderer. Would you prefer Quartz to ask you? Should I fetch him? Would you like him to recite the treaty and the four grand stories that founded it?'

She clicked her tongue, 'Spare me. I don't have time for Quartz today.' Oria spoke to her handmaid, 'Tell my lazy, stable sister to prepare two horses.' She turned back to Mica, gave him her full attention. He felt the depth of her. Old. Complex. Hungry for something. Worried. Selfish. Sad. Longing. Fearful. Too much emotion for such a shrivelled frame. Then she tucked it all away. Used the Companionari mindful practice to hide her signature. 'Perhaps you could bring me back some stories.'

'For your entertainment?' he asked. 'Or are you seeking knowledge?'

She stared at him, a look of need in her gaze that told him she wouldn't dissemble. 'I want knowledge. Ask for news of the other provinces. Any of them. All of them. Ask everyone you meet. The news I get from that useless sister, Grevillea, is absolute drivel. And the rest of my city sorority is worse. I need to know how the other provinces are doing.'

He nodded. 'Those are the terms, then? Stories for horses? Is that what you're suggesting? How very transactional.'

She lifted her chin as she answered, 'As must be the way now. For all our sakes. The stories are valuable, so I won't add the horses to the camp's debt.'

He wondered if she expected him to thank her. He wouldn't. Never. Not another word. Behind him, Bronda's emotional signature was loud. Mica's arms were full of the handmaid's embarrassment.

'Give Mica Canción,' Oria told Bronda. Then she tapped her teeth with her pencil. 'And let the boy ride El Embaucador.' She looked at Mica and smiled. He didn't need his rock skin to parse her amusement.

'The Caballo Companion insists she can sense the nature of every foal her province breeds and that's how she names them. I've chosen Canción for you. It means song, an allusion to the stories you will hear and then sing to me. Your nephew, the boy whose troublesome nature isn't news to me, gets El Embaucador, the trickster. Let's hope they can teach each other a few lessons.'

Mica led the two horses back to the camp, one a rangy bay, the other a stocky grey pony. He had half a mind to take El Embaucador for himself, but the trickster was too small. The pony would never carry a man. Mica wasn't sure how he felt about the morning. He loathed the Oak Companion for indenturing the camp and her manner was infuriating. Yet, he would leave the province well provisioned. His saddle bags were full at her command, and the horses Oria had provided were two of the best-looking animals in the stable. And he hadn't compounded the camp's debt. He just hoped that this complicated trip would be uneventful.

The ride across the provinces was straightforward. For Mica. Doubt had a little more trouble. El Embaucador had a gift for getting rid of the boy. On the way out of Oak province, he trotted under low-growing trees and raced through hazelnut bushes. In the rocky country in Aries province, the pony scraped Doubt's legs against boulders. When they entered Rice province, the pony concentrated on bucking, but Doubt had the beast's measure. The boy clung on and the pony finally settled as they rode across the brittle dirt of the failed rice paddies.

By the time they rode into Kelp province, Doubt had resumed his constant chatter and Mica found himself once again answering endless questions about why. But it wasn't onerous. The boy was cheerful company and the soft coastal grasses, and the smell of the ocean, were a balm after the bleak ground and whistling emptiness of Rice.

They were about a day away from the Kelp camp, riding a trail that ran parallel to the beach, when Mica began sensing the presence of people at the water's edge. The stone's call urged him on, but he'd committed himself to the Oak Companion's exchange and he was a man of honour. He'd promised her stories of provinces and that meant stopping and listening. The people were likely fishers or kelp gatherers from Kelp's camp. And they might have the news the Oak Companion was looking for. He wouldn't stay longer than was necessary, but he would stop and see.

Mica and Doubt turned aside and made their way over the dunes toward the water. Soon Mica's nebulous awareness that there were people ahead sharpened, and he began sensing individual emotions. Dark feelings: sorrow, despair, anger. Strong enough to make him shiver. El Embaucador snorted. Mica leant over and caught the pony's reins to stop Doubt rushing ahead. 'I need you to keep him quiet,' he said. 'Ride behind me.'

'Why?'

Mica nodded his head towards the dunes. 'Just until we know who they are.'

Doubt lowered his voice to a whisper, 'They're Berans.'

'But do they feel right when you rock sense them?' Mica said.

Doubt concentrated for a moment and then shook his head. 'What's wrong with them?'

'I don't know.'

Mica kept hold of the boy's reins and soon he and Doubt were looking down at a camp, a full camp with pitched tents. There were babies and children, old people, and women and men, and there were multiple smoky fires, not the single cook's fire that would normally be the core of any camp. Paintings of fish, water, and nets adorned the tents. Several people glanced up from tending the fires. They acknowledged Mica and Doubt with a nod, but turned back to their tasks.

Doubt stood in his stirrups to get a better look and then pointed at the nearest tent. 'They're not from Kelp. The fish on the tents are bass.' He looked at Mica, brow wrinkled. 'This must be the Bass province's camp. Kelp's emblem is garfish, so it's not Kelp.' He sat back in the saddle, frowned at the beach. 'I know all the emblems and talents for the thirty-seven provinces. The Kelp Companion has a talent for kelp and garfish and daisies, and garfish are long and thin. This must be the Bass camp. But what are they doing here? Bass is further south, beyond the Winter province.'

Mica shivered, realising what he was seeing. He found there were tears in his eyes.

'Has Bass province failed?' Doubt sounded frightened.

Mica nodded. He let go of the pony's rein and set his own horse in motion. 'When we get down to the beach, you need to let me ask the questions. They don't need a seven-year-old interrogating them when they've lost their home.'

'I'm eight.'

'You are seven.'

'I am almost eight.'

'Then you're old enough to know that sometimes you should listen, not talk.'

'Canis province,' Doubt whispered, 'Linum, Taurine, Murasia, Rice...'

'Don't,' Mica said.

'And now Bass. That's not too many,' Doubt said. 'Is it? Is it too many?'

'It's far too many,' Mica said.

'But it won't happen to us. The Oak Companion is strong. She's a good companion.'

That brought a bitter laugh. 'She might be strong, Doubt, but she isn't good. Never think that. The Companionaris are not good. They are conquerors, enslavers, child thieves and they are not our friends.'

The winter afternoon had turned to evening by the time Mica led Doubt to the last campfire on the beach. The wanderer drew his coat more tightly against the cold, smoky air. He glanced back to check the boy was warm enough. His nephew looked pale and tired, but his coat was thick and his scarf was wound around his neck. Mica turned his attention back to the last fire, a part of him still busy resisting the rock child's call to hurry, leave this beach and the stories of its sorry people.

Ahead, he counted five people huddled near a fire. They glanced up but returned their tired gazes to the embers. Only one, a woman, seemed to care that strangers were present. She was standing in front of a rickety wooden frame, turning salted fish over the coals. It was garfish. Mica already knew from visiting the other hearths on the beach the fish was a good riddance gift from the Kelp camp. The sight made him sad, the fish and the rickety wooden frame.

The part of Mica that had a feel for the right way to do things longed to rework the frame so that the strips of kelp that hung from the driftwood racks above the turning garfish would dry more effectively. Least of their needs. What they'd done was good enough for preparing rations. The camp was preparing to turn inland and walk to Komey. Mica thought about the reception they'd receive in the city. The families would camp outside the city walls. Then the Companionaris would let the men into Komey to beg for charity.

Not for the first time, Mica thought about his home province. These people would reach Oak before they reached the city. Could they settle there? Their presence would stretch Oak's resources. It was a keeper's decision, but Oak's keeper was dead. The decision would fall to Quartz, but Quartz wasn't on the beach, listening to the stories.

The woman nodded at Mica, and Mica introduced himself. He offered her a story from his collection. 'I'll try to think of one to warm the heart,' he suggested.

'Nothing could.'

'Then perhaps you would give me one of yours.'

She turned back to the fire. 'Mine will make you weep. Besides, you already have mine. It's the same as everyone else's.' She waved at the tents surrounding them without looking up from her work. 'But it's yours if you want it.'

'I do.'

'Bass bounty failed. The Bass Companion fled with her sorority. Took the train and abandoned us. Now we are hungry and our camp no longer has a home on the Stone Body. We're adrift.'

'And your reception in the Kelp camp? Would you tell me about that?' As though the stone that called him sensed Mica's words, it renewed its pull. He pressed back, mentally, emotionally and the pressure in his chest eased.

The woman was talking again, 'We should have walked inland to the Winter province. The Brassica camp would have taken us. We went to Kelp because of the kinship of fish. The keeper refused us asylum. "How many neighbours are we expected to feed," that's what he said, and then he complained he was already feeding the Berans from Rice.'

'What do you make of it?' Mica asked.

'Of him? Kelp's keeper? A sharp and cruel man, leading a brittle camp. Still bitter about the Rice refugees living on the edge of his camp and that's been more than a decade now.'

Mica thought of Fox. He wouldn't tell her this. She already knew her biological father wasn't a kind man. He turned his attention back to the woman in front of him. 'I meant the new bounty failures. The companionships that have ceased in the past couple of years. The provinces being abandoned?' He wondered whether he'd misspoken because she stiffened at his words.

She jabbed at the fire and then turned to Mica, the burning stick in her hand. 'You should watch your words. We didn't abandon Bass. Bass is home. We... We... We are just seeking shelter until a new Bass Companion is born. Then we'll return.'

Doubt stirred, but Mica held up his hand to stop the boy from speaking. This woman didn't need to be reminded that the Linum and the Canis companions had died in the past year, their crossover rituals failing to produce new companions. Something was wrong. What had felt like a vague unease, a niggling worry about the health of the Stone Body, was solidifying into dread. He needed to talk to Quartz. And to the Oak Companion; much as he disliked her.

'I'm sorry,' he said.

'We're all sorry,' she said.

Mica tried again. 'Let me give you a fourth story. Something to ease your heart.'

She pointed her stick at the miserable camp. 'Give us shelter or food, Wanderer. We don't need stories. Get on your way, if you have nothing but tales to offer.'

Mica hesitated and then spoke in a rush, 'Come to Oak. We'll give you asylum. Tell them Mica promised you refuge.' The woman stared at him, the stick loose in her hand. She watched his face. He repeated the promise. 'There's enough for you in Oak. We'll manage.'

She laughed and dropped the stick, and then she stepped forward and embraced him. He held her, patted her awkwardly, but he wondered what he'd done. The Oak camp would honour his word, but what about the companion? Yes, Oria had lent him horses without compounding the camp's debt, but that was nothing compared to this. Oria would extract a bitter fee. Mica told himself that he would make sure the debt was his alone. He would offer her his life's labour, his stories, his time, but he wasn't sure it would be enough.

He spent another hour on the beach sharing the details of the best route to Oak and who they should ask for when they arrived. The people's gratitude left him feeling empty and awkward, and he was glad he had the rock child's call to excuse his departure.

Doubt waited until they'd climbed the dune before he spoke, 'You are going to be in so much trouble.'

'Just concentrate on El Embaucador. We'll be riding all night and I don't want any broken bones.'

Mica urged Canción on, set a pace that made conversation difficult. Doubt stopped asking questions, leaving Mica to worry about what he'd done, picking over his decision, looking for better options, and finding none. Soon, the rising urgency in his chest overtook his worries. The rock child was somewhere ahead of him, and it needed him to hurry.

I t was not yet morning when Mica dismounted at the edge of the Kelp camp and motioned for Doubt to do the same. They tethered their horses to a windswept tree and walked into the canvas village, Mica in front, Doubt on his heels.

Fox's home was quiet in the faint pre-dawn light. The air smelt fresh: part river mouth, part marsh, part ocean. The quiet wouldn't last. Already birds were calling. The voices of the fishing folk would soon follow. Mica wanted to locate the stone before the camp woke. It felt as though the end of dawn's twilight posed some sort of deadline. As they passed each tent, Mica felt the sleepers' flickering emotions as the occupants responded to the last of their dreams.

Then the stone call intensified, clamoured, and he broke into a run. For once, Doubt's questions failed to reach his lips as he struggled to keep pace. The two of them jumped over guy-wires and rounded the curves of the circular tents, closing in on the source of the call. Mica's heart sank when he realised where they were heading. He'd assumed the stone would call from the river's mouth or the beach, that the urgency was just the imminent risk of being washed out to sea. Claiming a stone in a hostile camp like Kelp would be difficult, and it was clear now the rock child was in the very centre.

The dark was thinning as they reached the circle of tents surrounding the cook's fire. The cook, a strong young man, was feeding kindling into the embers, coaxing fresh flames. He looked up and smiled a welcome, which gave Mica some hope that all might be well despite the camp's reputation. The wanderer scanned the surrounding tents, locating the source of the call: the keeper's tent; the home of Fox's birth family. His heart sank, but he knew his duty.

There was a free-standing stone arch in front of the laced door. Mica was glad the rock child wasn't buried in the arch. He wouldn't relish telling Pace, Fox's father, that he needed to dismantle it. The call was coming from inside the tent. Mica licked his lips, wondering how best to approach this. Behind him, Doubt had already introduced himself to the cook and was busy asking him what he was making for breakfast.

'... I'm quite hungry. We've ridden all night.'

'Ah well, that makes a person hungry,' the cook said. 'Horses though... You're not refugees, then. Are you here with a message for us or for our companion?'

In front of Mica, there was a grunt. The laced door of the keeper's tent bulged, then fell still. He felt someone's fear, and another's anger, and then someone gasped and a girl shouted. There was a small yelp and the sound of a struggle.

Mica bent down, felt for the ends of the door ties. The door bulged again and someone stood on his probing fingers. He pulled his hands back, then tried again, began unlacing the door.

'I wouldn't,' the cook spoke. 'Family matter. Little girl doesn't want to be apprenticed to Aries and they're setting out this morning. I would have taken her if Pace had asked. But the keeper probably knows best. Saury is a handful. And Aries isn't a terrible place. At least it's on the coast.'

Mica didn't stop working the laces on the door, but knowing helped. Saury. Fox's little sister. And the rock child...? The girl's distress would have triggered the call. That meant it was hers, which meant Mica was about to take on his first apprentice.

Doubt spoke up, 'Why doesn't she want to be a cook? Cooks can eat whatever they want.'

The cook didn't answer, just repeated his advice to Mica to come away.

With the door partly unlaced, Mica could see, but not well. He rock sensed Pace's fury, Saury's fearful determination, and he could tell that there was an old woman in there too. She felt unfazed. Probably the grandmother.

He pulled his head back just in time as a girl burst through the gap and slammed into him. Stared at him for less than a second and then started clambering over him as though he were a boulder in her path. He stood up, held her, stepped back. Just in time, because Pace was right behind her. Mica wished Quartz was with him. He'd never taken an apprentice, was scarcely out of his own apprenticeship, and the circumstances weren't exactly auspicious.

Pace roared at Saury, ignoring Mica, and reached out to grab her. Mica stepped back again, edging his way toward the cook's fire, keeping out of reach as Pace followed. The grandmother had appeared now, and there were other people about too. A small crowd had gathered. Mica rock sensed them: some worried, some curious, and some relieved. And Doubt. Scared. Fighting the urge to run.

'Put my daughter down.' Pace had stopped moving, but Mica's arms thrummed with the heat of the man's anger.

Saury's grandmother coughed and then pointed the stem of her clay pipe at Mica. 'We've company, Son. A wanderer by his cloak. I think I've seen him in our camp before. Lurking about.' She stepped forward, peered at Mica. 'Hum, but you've not presented yourself to the keeper, have you? Rude. Well, you've got your chance now. You'd best introduce yourself.'

Mica didn't want to let go of Saury, but he needed his arms free for the traditional greeting.

'Put her down,' the old woman said. 'She can sit by the fire with your boy. Give them some tea,' she told the cook.

Pace glared but nodded, and Mica set Saury down. He waited a moment for the two children to sit and then introduced himself with a sweeping gesture, one hand open toward the ground, the other to the sky.

Pace stared, chin thrust forward. He waited a good minute before offering a truncated version of the keeper's welcome, '...and I take it the boy is your apprentice?'

'My nephew, Doubt.'

'Since when did wanderers travel with family?'

'Are you asking for the four stories?' Mica raised an eyebrow.

'Spare me. Well, you're here now so you can sit down, eat, and then get on with your work.' Pace waved his hand at their surrounds. 'There are stories here, as many as you could want. You can talk to that lot from Rice. They love telling their tales of hunger while they eat our garfish.' The keeper stepped closer to the campfire . Mica could feel that the only reason Saury hadn't taken off again was that the fire was between the girl and her father. The cook handed Pace a cup of tea. Mica joined the circle and the cook gave him a cup. He sipped it before speaking to the keeper, 'Your daughter needs to be apprenticed.'

'And will be.' There was a threatening edge to the man's words.

Mica set his cup down on the ground and then stood up, and faced Pace. 'To me.'

There was a moment's silence, and then Pace laughed. 'You're a one, aren't you? Wandering with family in tow; claiming other people's daughters as apprentices. The world upside down, is that it?'

'You're asking for the world upside down stories?' Mica asked. 'Because I've plenty.'

'No. *I am not!*' Pace's voice hardened. 'We have no use for a wanderer's knowledge— or ignorance, more like. I run my province simply. I run it the way it should be run: and that goes for my family too. So you had better be on your way.'

Mica shook his head. 'Your daughter has a stone, and it's called me all the way from Oak. I'm to apprentice her.'

Pace's face hardened as he turned to look at his daughter. 'Is this true? Have you got a rock child?'

Saury was standing now, looked ready to run. 'No... I don't. I...'

'Have you, or have you not, got a rock child?'

'Likely, she doesn't know.' Mica stepped towards her, crouched down, faced her. 'But you have got a stone, haven't you? A rock or a pebble that you're fond of?'

Saury nodded.

'And you keep it with you always?'

She nodded again.

'Give it to me,' her father said. 'Right now.'

'She can't,' Mica looked up at the man. 'That's the point. It called her and claimed her. She would die before giving it to you or me or to anyone.'

Pace began moving, heading for Saury, and the girl leapt up and started backing away.

'Stop!' the old woman held up her hand.

The keeper halted, his face and rock skin flushed.

'You know the law,' she said. 'When a wanderer recognises his apprentice, none may stand between them: not father, not mother, not companion, not keeper, not husband, not wife, not even child. None. You risk your own death, and dishonour for us, for Kelp.'

Pace rocked on the balls of his feet. Then he stepped back, spat on the ground. 'Have her. Another daughter gone. Take her and get out of my province. But if I see you in my province again... If I see any of you useless parasites, you wanderers, you're dead. And that goes for you too,' he pointed a gnarled finger at Saury. Then he turned, faced the onlookers, his people. 'You hear me? You hear what I'm saying? My daughters must not set foot in this camp again. I won't have wanderers either. And I won't have any more refugees in Kelp. Never again.'

Mica stood up and looked across at Saury's grandmother. 'And you, old woman? Would you come with us?'

'I'll stay here.' The old woman picked up her tea and took a sip with a loud slurp before speaking again, 'Me, I don't fancy traipsing about after smart alecs. Wouldn't suit me. Besides, there's my son to take care of. But take the little one. She's not a good fit here. Not surprised she's a wanderer in the making. She'll enjoy the life: collecting rocks and stories.'

3

Aikin rolled out of bed with particular care, for Whilomena, the Wheat Companion, slept beside him. It was rare that she agreed to sleep the night in his suite; a compliment reserved for husbands, not lovers, and most particularly not secret lovers. He would have liked to stay beside her and wait for her to awaken. He might have tempted her to lie on top of him. But he had heard a soft tap on his bedroom door from his houseboy and knew that something important awaited.

The boy handed Aikin a tiny ball of paper. Something ripped from a journal and rolled between rough palms. It was enough. Aikin knew what it meant, what it symbolised: a rock child found and taken. A message from Captain Birch.

Soon he was outdoors in the city's landscape, stepping off the Oak House path onto the rutted track the domestic staff used in the mornings and evenings on their walk between the Mint Gazette and Oak house. While it was still early, the workers were already at their posts and Aikin had the track to himself. A cold sharp wind blew from the south and chilling rain made the moment he'd planned to savour into a hurried rush.

He bent low against the wind, and it was a relief when he spotted the broken ridge of the old warehouse. Aikin left the track, entering the shelter of the cork trees. He hoped Birch wasn't wasting his time. Aikin wouldn't appreciate being called out for an admission of failure or some counterfeit stone. But Birch wouldn't dare cheat him.

Aikin shook his head and let the idea go. He and the soldier had traded many a taboo item, and the woman took pride in her work.

No, the real problem was knowing what to do with the stone when he had it in his possession.

He'd discovered something. He hoped he'd discovered the sort of secret that could change life on the Stone Body, but it might be little more than a scribe's decision to make use of the end pages of a book. And what a book it was!

Calling *The Book of Kinesis* a book felt wrong, never mind the fact the word *book* formed part of the title. It was a philosophy, a treatise on power, forgotten or lost to Companionari culture. When he'd first found the anonymous work, he'd been so dazzled by it he'd scarcely heeded the ledger entries on the end pages. Even now, he wasn't certain that its columns itemising marriages, alliances involving payments and receipts, were anything more than bookkeeping. It wasn't unthinkable that the genius philosopher writing on power might also be the bureaucrat who was interested in the prosaic nature of accounting.

The first column listed candidates for marriage and was full of names of eligible Galean settler women. A second listed payments, money changing hands between settler families. A third listed receipts for gifts. At first glance, he'd imagined these were ordinary wedding gifts. It was the sameness of the gifts that caught his attention. Azurite, carnelian, sunstone and turquoise, with each stone's weight noted. He'd imagined jewellery, but there had been nothing but stones: no gold rings, no silver earrings. So, he'd re-examined the ledger, noticed that beneath the words *Gifts Received* in the column's heading there were some curious notations: *Wndr. Stns.* and *d.w.*, He suspected *Wndr. Stns.* were rock children and *d.w.* was dry weight and the marriages were... Well, companionships. It made sense. It was not unheard of for companions to refer to their relationship with their plants or animals as a marriage.

But creating one of those marriages remained a mystery.

He wished he had someone to share his nascent ideas with. Birch would never do. The soldiersister was only interested in herself. While his darling Whilomena would appreciate his ambitions, she wasn't discreet. If the Berans got wind of his plans to experiment on rock children, there'd be violence. Besides, he wanted to complete his research and offer the results to Whilomena as a dowry when he proposed. For he was sick of the secrecy she imposed on their relationship and longed for the public state of marriage.

The only other person he'd ever considered sharing his secrets with was Fox, and her Beranish origins ruled her out. And she'd been impossible in recent weeks.

Thank the Back she'd started her working life as a departmental junior and was out of his hair. He hadn't had a moment to himself during the month of the interregnum that had followed her birthday. She'd trailed after him, hampering his work, harping on about Wren and her birthday boon. Fox had too much time on her hands. She needed a regime. He'd given her the biography of Astoria Caballo, the first equine companion, whose daily journal was a lesson for anyone in need of discipline. Fox hadn't grasped it. Thought the book was about persisting when it was about the power of regimes. Who knew fatherhood could be so irritating? Even now, at this crucial moment in his destiny, his adopted daughter was cluttering his head.

He wasn't adept at the Companionari meditative practice, but he didn't need more than a sliver of attention to disperse his emotions, settle his heart rate, and return his focus to the task at hand. He was here for Birch and the stone.

The soldier looked up when Aikin emerged from the cork grove. She started towards him through a swathe of wheat that had sprung up in front of an abandoned warehouse. The woman held a wooden box, lifting it high to keep it away from the wet stalks, and the sight made Aikin smile. That part of the ledger had been clear enough. His ancestors had presented the gifts in oak boxes lined with silver. It was possible those gift boxes were simply fashionable items at settler weddings, but Aikin suspected they shielded the stones' distress, hid them from Beranish wanderers. Unlikely, it was a coincidence that the gift boxes resembled crossover coffins. So he had bypassed the Oak House workshop and had some boxes made in Galea.

That Birch was here, unhindered and uninjured, suggested that the box had done its job.

... a companion mother is only ever born of a ruthless mind.

Dastrium Lintel's advice. And somehow, for everyone's sake, he hoped he'd create not one but many new companions. Life on the Stone Body would be impossible without them. And breeding them wasn't working properly anymore. But if Aikin could create them...? The Stone Body would gain powerful new companions who would breed generations of powerful daughters, gifting everyone another thousand years of plenty. An astounding and noble ambition, but one that had a price.

'You've got one?' Aikin asked Birch when the two of them were in touching distance.

'Four.'

'Four!' Aikin moved closer. Reached for the box. Felt a flash of fear that at the last minute Birch would be difficult. But the soldier just smiled, a long slow grin that was all pride and pleasure, and handed over the box. Aikin found he was stroking the timber as though the soldier had handed him a milk-sweet puppy or a beautiful curly-hair child.

'And there's also a chip in there. Don't think it's a rock child. A miserable-looking thing. Must have got caught up in the wanderer's pouch when he rolled it up one night. It's a bit of talc. Soft. I wasn't sure whether you'd want it, but—'

'No, you did well to bring it,' Aikin said. 'Thank you. So that's four, maybe five. And you kept the box closed?'

Birch nodded. 'Followed your instructions to the letter.'

'And you asked first? Asked the wanderer to give you the stones?' That was important. It was something Aikin had learned from the political section of *The Book of Kinesis*:

Leave room in your plans for the act of the Other. When the Other acts, your reaction will carry greater kinetic energy.

Birch sniffed. 'Yes, for all the good it did. Could have got me killed. Could have.'

'And how many wanderers died for these?' Aikin looked down at the box.

'Just the one. Those were everything he was carrying.'

'Well, Captain Birch—'

The soldiersister stilled at the change in her rank. 'Captain? Not Lieutenant then?'

'No. Captain. I've seen to it. And I have a purse for you to pay for a new suite in the Oak House compound. I put a little extra in for new furniture.' Aikin met the woman's eye. 'I hope the new level of comfort doesn't tempt you to leave off foraging.'

Birch shook her head. 'Not when there are more rungs on the ladder.'

By the time Aikin returned to his suite, Whilomena had left. Probably for the best, because it meant there were no awkward questions about the box. He resisted the temptation to look inside. He locked it away and went down to the library. Aikin knew the ledger by heart, but he still fetched *The Book of Kinesis* from its hiding place and re-read those last few pages. It was no help. A woman married the Stone Body? But what was the marriage process? How did a rock alter an ordinary woman? Make her into a companion capable of flourishing plants and animals? There had to be a way to find out.

Aikin intended to start with a least harm approach. He'd begin by steeping one stone in water and another in alcohol and he'd give the resulting teas to a couple of his more impoverished cousins. If that didn't work, he'd be ready. He had a back-up plan. His long wait to acquire a rock child had given him time to think, and he'd invested in something, a device that could transform a rock child into a product that one could describe in terms of its dry weight.

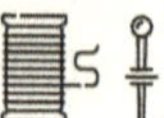

The ordinary obligations, the duties of a respectable man in Oak House were hard to maintain, had been since Aikin took possession of the rock children less than a week earlier. And now there was even more to do. His new toy had arrived. Shouldn't call it that. His noble device, more like. His back-up plan. Not for the first time he wished he was free to concentrate on unlocking the rock children's secret, but he had other obligations. He had to get to the first floor parley room in time to argue for Fox's need for a good quality birthfather for her embryo. Because what happened to Fox would always be a reflection on him. He realised he was rushing when he almost tripped on the edge of a rug in the long first floor hallway. He glanced around, but there was no one to see the poverty of his hurried gesture. Wonderful moment to remember the famous biographer's dictum:

Greatness can be recognised. Consider a great woman's slow footsteps, her careful gestures, and her resonant voice. She is rich in time and her deportment speaks of it.

Course the idea was nonsense, but if a writer like Dastrium Lintel thought you could judge someone by their movements and the sound of their voice, there was little doubt lesser people would believe the same.

And the parley would be full of lesser people. He didn't respect them, didn't like them at all, but that didn't mean he could be reckless with his reputation. Likewise, Fox's reputation. He stopped to admire a ghastly Companionari weaving depicting a wanderer standing in front of a sunset. Awful, but it gave him time to compose himself.

He could hear the parley. Noisy. Already. He was glad he'd stopped. It had given him a chance to think about the need for balance in a life and in Oak's domestic economy. Yes, the birthfather for Fox's baby shouldn't be cheap, but if the man was too expensive, Aikin would never hear the end of it from Oria. The woman was obsessed with the manor's accounts.

When he reached the parley room, he was glad to see he hadn't missed the start. The parley bed was still empty. Fox had saved him a seat in the middle of the room, and he joined her just as Grevillea, that haughty old crone, made her way to the parley bed. Bent over her walking stick. Almost breathless with age. Aikin wondered what Dastrium Lintel would think of her movements. Nothing good.

Fox leant in, kept her voice low, 'It's terrible, isn't it?'

For a second he imagined she was talking about Grevillea, but he caught himself before he said anything careless. He gave his adopted daughter a questioning look.

'The news from Oak.'

'What news?'

'Oria's letter. The winter logging. It failed.'

'What do you mean? How can logging fail?'

'The trees were riddled with fungus. All the wood was spongy, punky. We can't salvage any of the timber. They're burning it and felling the surrounding stands so the fungus won't spread. They hope. The consensus is we'll have to leave the ground fallow in that part of the province.'

Grevillea clapped her hands, and the room fell silent. She spoke a welcome that went on longer than it needed to. Very busy reminding everyone about the importance of parleys during a crisis, '... choosing a cause together, revering the gift of God's Turning by taking responsibility...'

Aikin thought about the news from the province, turned it over and over while Grevillea droned on, looked for the best way to use it. It was a tragedy, yes, but not unexpected. The companionships were failing, so the entire agricultural system was going to fall apart. No point gossiping about it. Still, that propensity could be useful. Oak House would be busy, consumed. His new device would be noticed, but not noted. With more important things to talk about, the household's curiosity about his sudden benevolence in donating equipment to the furniture workshop would be fleeting. Yes, this was the right moment. He would go down to the river port tomorrow, hasten the paperwork, organise the team to haul the press.

The noise in the room increased as people began making suggestions. Not about a suitable father for Fox's embryo. It was still the crisis in Oak province.

'Let's rally around Oria,' a gate sister suggested. 'Let's send a delegation to offer our support.'

'Waste of time,' a gardener spoke up.

'Well, we aren't short of time, are we?' the gate sister said. 'I don't believe the Oak Mother's letter mentioned anything about time. Just a shortage of timber.'

'But is it temporary?' this time it was one of the younger gardeners who spoke up. 'Or is our province failing?'

Several people jumped in with their opinions and then the viander of rooms made a disparaging comment about parleys and good causes. Grevillea admonished him for not appreciating the humble act of love all good causes represented. 'Leave effects to fate, Viander. All else is vanity. We're adults, yes, but not gods.'

Aikin realised he'd begun jiggling his foot, irritated with the drift into old-fashioned Companionari dogma. Time to bring the focus back to the cause that concerned him, then he'd be free to go down to the river.

'I am not a lace maker,' he spoke up, clearing his throat, 'and my needlework would never elicit an invitation to a sewing circle even if I was lucky enough to be born a woman.' Several women smiled at that. 'And while I am not a woman—'

'Surely, we should talk about the problem with the timber,' the housekeeper complained, 'not listen to this scholar's ramblings. The garden girl was right to ask whether Oak is failing. Is that what we're facing? Because I provision this household and without an income that will be impossible.'

Aikin smiled. 'Esteemed housekeeper, esteemed sisters and brothers, the province's welfare is the question that grips us all. How could it not?' He turned toward the parley bed, addressed the senior sister, 'Grevillea, you reminded us to focus our efforts on good causes and leave effects to fate. There is just such a cause. We are due to choose a birthfather for my adopted daughter's first child.' He gestured to Fox.

An old woman in a wheeled parley chair interrupted, 'Really? You think this is the time and place? We need to focus on our province's problems, not your daughter.'

'I don't mind waiting,' Fox said. 'We can talk about this later.'

'My daughter is too kind,' Aikin said. 'However, I think we should recall that we brought her to Komey, claimed her under the treaty, because of her potential to give birth to a new companion. Companions sustain provinces. Choosing a father for her child is therefore vital in this crisis.'

There were rumbles of agreement, even though many wanted to continue discussing the news from the province. Then Grevillea reminded the room that it had been Oria herself who had tested Fox for talent, who'd tussled with the other families for the right to adopt her. And that got the parley's attention. Anything related to their *dear Mother Oak* always did.

Someone suggested Costa Bass as a birthfather, an idea scarcely voiced before being discarded. No one trusted the Bass family's blood now that its companion had returned to live in Komey with the news her province had failed. A few daughters with minor gifts for flourishing plants and animals amounted to nothing in the face of such a failure. Besides, several women had heard that Costa was too old to salute a woman, let alone fertilise an egg. There was also talk of the Caballo family's Andreas. Even though he was modestly, blandly, uninterestingly priced, the crisis in the province made him look expensive.

'We must be frugal,' the gate sister said. 'Careful of Oak House resources. Oria would want us to be careful.'

Aikin nodded. The ground had shifted. Now there was honour in frugality.

'Then we should consider an older man,' Grevillea said. 'Not Costa, but someone like him.'

'He needs to be capable,' the viander of rooms said.

'If he isn't, we'll just get our money back.' The gate sister shrugged and several people nodded.

'Then why not try Louis Oak?' the housekeeper suggested. 'He's an Oak House man and several of his daughters have been talented. Louis' on his last legs, but what's the harm in trying a few cycles? He was a great birthfather in his time and he'll be inexpensive.'

'We could get a quote from him,' Grevillea said. 'And use him for Wren, too. When is her baby due?'

Fox elbowed Aikin, and he felt his irritation with the parley return, along with a dose of irritation with his daughter and his own foolishness. He hadn't thought there'd be much risk to agreeing to advocate for Wren when Fox asked for that as her birthday boon. But he'd no intention of doing so in a parley. Risk his reputation for something pointless? There wasn't a parley on the Stone Body that would allow a Beranish adoptee to re-grow her rock skin. No, Wren would have to live with her medicinal tea for the rest of her life, and all the madness it entailed.

'You promised,' Fox whispered. She elbowed him again, sharper this time. He leant over and whispered in her ear. 'Not here. This is not the way. We need to lobby. It will be a slow process.'

'We have to try,' she whispered back. 'You promised.'

'Speak up,' Grevillea said. 'This is a public forum, not a kitchen table.'

'It's nothing,' Aikin said.

'It's not nothing,' Fox said. 'I have a cause. It would be a good thing and a kind thing to let Wren's rock skin re-grow so that she can walk a Holy Path. She could consent to the choice of birthfather. Ride her own fate.'

There was a momentary silence. Then several people laughed. Aikin felt his skin crawl. Stupid girl.

Grevillea frowned. 'It's understandable that you'd feel for her, given your origins. But she had the same chance you had to use her mind to manage her body. She didn't take that chance, so she is already riding her fate on her Holy Path. I don't need to count the room to know that we are agreed.'

Aikin felt Fox stir, saw the flush of heat on her neck. He wasn't above elbowing her if he thought it would keep her quiet, but he knew it would only make things worse. For several agonising moments, he watched her wrestle with herself and then she sighed and nodded. He credited his influence, but knew the issue wasn't over and done with. The sorority and Oria would be on the receiving end of Fox's pleading letters. She was headstrong and full of notions that would never amount to anything, but he had educated her, spent time with her. He had taught her the principles of power, which included knowing when to restrain oneself and when to press an advantage. If he needed any proof of that, he got it after the parley broke up. She reminded him of the terms of a birthday boon. He had failed to speak up, failed to deliver, so she would ask for a different boon.

He returned to his suite in a lighter mood. Her persistence was a credit to him. He'd taken an unruly ten-year-old, filled with grief, and he'd turned her into a mind. Not a mind like his. Not as good, but a pleasant reflection that did him credit.

Two days after the parley, Aikin hovered at the edge of the crowd of men and women pushing the trolley that carried his new metal press toward the Oak House furniture workshop. The thing was heavy and had come all the way across the Komic Sea from Galea, compliments of Aikin's private purse. Even with four burly riverhood haulers, the trolley beneath the press was slow to respond. As the head of the Department of Beranish Affairs, Aikin was about as far from a riverhood labourer as one could get, but he was itching to get his hands on the lovely device. He spotted a gap between two of the burly haulers and was about to add his weight to the momentum when he felt a tap on his shoulder.

'A fine machine,' a woman's voice spoke, a little too close to his ear for his liking. 'And again, thank you so much Aikin. So generous.'

He turned and smiled. The senior joinery sister was tall and muscular, a powerful, attractive woman, a woman he'd been hoping to avoid. She was a little too flattered by his donation to her workshop and had misunderstood his sudden interest in furniture making. Understandable. He had been at great pains to keep his true purpose to himself. He took a step back, putting some distance between them. 'It's a beauty, isn't it?' He nodded. 'I'm pleased to see it here. Finally. I've always felt our furniture deserves the very best ornamentation your metalworkers can devise. The screw press was limiting their options. This steam powered press is a different story.'

She nodded, a look of passionate agreement on her face, and he was glad to see her focus had shifted to her furniture. 'The parleys just don't understand the need for a diverse economy. Half of them think we should give up furniture making. All I hear is talk about the need to concentrate on lumber, that Komey prefers Galean furniture anyway, so we shouldn't bother making our own.'

'Well, that's the point, isn't it?' He nodded at the new machine. 'Having the capacity to express our own aesthetic.' He resumed his pursuit of the trolley, speaking over his shoulder as he walked, 'We couldn't compete and now we can.'

She caught up with him again, not easily shaken. 'Yes, and we're already designing. Brass strips for metal galleries on tables and desks but other ornamentation too. So much is possible now: brackets, escutcheons, decorative strapping. This press will be transformational.' She touched his arm and he resisted the urge to jerk it away, 'Aikin, I want you to come and visit the workshop at any time...' She caught up his hand and he felt a key pressed into his palm. He almost shivered with revulsion at the intimacy, but the key offered easy access to the press. A key was what he needed but how to accept it and use it without her getting the wrong idea.

The next half hour gave him some reprieve from the woman's attentions because the trolley had crossed the lip of the workshop and was making slow progress over the workshop floor. The joinery sister directed its path, seeing to the exact positioning. Then there was the ceremony.

Aikin stood with the metal workers as the joinery sister spoke about prizing the Stone Body's arts and crafts. Then the metal workers gave Aikin a gift, an antique copper bookplate, etched with a Beranish version of the Oak family motif and the department's Ex Libris inscription. His lips twitched. He couldn't keep the smile from his face. They couldn't have found a better gift.

'This plate,' he held it up for all to see, 'will be busy. I can assure you of that. Its productive life will recommence. Our esteemed senior joinery sister has thought of everything. She's given the Beranish Affairs' library this exquisite etching plate, and she has given me the workshop key and, with it, access to the new press. My department will put both to good use, printing new bookplates for the collection. Don't worry,' he held up his hand to the metalworkers as though they had objected, 'we'll use this beauty after hours. We won't get in your way. I imagine we will rebind some of the more valuable books in our modern collection. What a lovely use of time.' He turned to the joinery sister. 'Thank you.' He looked to the metalworkers. 'And thank you. The Department of Beranish Affairs is touched. We are touched.'

Aikin spent the afternoon in the workshop learning how to use the press, admiring the chugging thumping steam engine that powered it, and touring the woodworking area. He left feeling elevated, as though the task ahead of him was something to be savoured rather than regretted for its destructiveness.

It took him several weeks to habituate those in and around the workshop to periodic visits by various library staffers. By then, the joinery sister had quite given up on him and his staffers had lost interest in the novelty of printing their own bookplates. He admired his own patience. There weren't many men of ambition who could lay such delicate plans and hold off from surveilling them.

When the time came, he crushed all four stones and the dubious-looking talc chip. He worked quickly, minimising the exposure of the stones, and the crushed residual, to the open air. Afterwards, he put the dust from each one into its own container and hid them among his toiletries.

The following week he fed one cousin a water-based stone paste and another an alcohol-based version. Both died. His original failures, the teas he made before crushing the stones, had been disappointing, but the failure of his pastes was a terrible blow. It set him back, left him feeling despondent. Worse than that, it left him feeling weak. He'd expected success. He hadn't given up by any means. Not when the welfare of everyone on the Stone Body was at stake. But the two remaining stones and the talc chip would have to remain idle until he worked out what had gone wrong.

4

Oria gripped her stick more firmly and continued toward the door. The manor cats swarmed around her, running ahead and then doubling back in chaotic fashion, their sleek bodies flashing in and out of her line of vision as she concentrated on the uneven stone floor.

Bronda hurried forward. 'Let me help you.'

Oria slapped the woman's hand away. Didn't mean to. She stopped, intending to apologise, but somehow the wrong words emerged, 'I don't need your help. I'm not dead yet.'

'No Mother Oak,' Bronda agreed, 'but let's not hasten things.'

It still galled, being called Mother. And Bronda knew it better than anyone. She'd been with Oria for eighty-two of Oria's ninety-four years and had witnessed Oria's pregnancies falter and slip beyond her grip. Sometimes Oria thought her handmaid called her *Mother* in some ill-conceived effort to soften her, remind her of her sorrow. Fool. The last thing the province needed was a companion wallowing in sorrow.

Oria continued her slow progress. She reached the open door, then made her way over the portico and started down the broad stone steps. On the fourth step, her foot slipped, and she reached out. An oak tree sprung up to meet her hand.

Bronda spoke from the top of the steps, 'That tree you rushed has broken the tread.'

'Blame the sister who let an acorn drop in the wrong place,' Oria huffed. 'And ask around for a mason when I'm speaking with Quartz. Maybe you'll find a refugee who works stone.'

'If you'd let me help you, you wouldn't have needed to call up the tree and you wouldn't have broken the step.'

'Then you'd better get down here because you can't help me from up there.' Oria glared at Bronda, had to turn her head to do it because the woman was at the top of the stairs. The effort hurt Oria's neck. 'Well! Come on, woman. I need you here.'

They descended the remaining steps together, Bronda's hand on Oria's elbow. The ancient wheelchair waited on the gravel, the sturdy stable sister manoeuvring it so that Oria could lower herself into it with some level of ease.

'Who's looking after the horses while you're standing about in my driveway?' Oria asked the woman.

'Those four Berans you employed. We're over staffed.'

Oria sniffed. 'Then you'd better get back there to direct everyone. Bronda can manage from here.'

'No,' Bronda said. 'I can't. I'm too old to manage your chair. I warned you it was too much for me on my own. We should have prepared the carriage.'

Oria shook her head. 'You want me to turn up at the camp in a carriage? And with that lovely impression still lingering, I'll just get down to business and announce that I'm moving the Bass refugees on? Brilliant idea Bronda. That will ease tensions between camp and manor.'

'You can't move them on. Under the treaty—'

'Thank you, yes. I know what the treaty says. The land is theirs and they can live as they want. I know. But move them on, I will. Hopefully, with some level of diplomacy. I'll call it something else, but excuse me if I speak the truth in my own driveway. You won't begrudge me that?' Oria waited, but Bronda was keeping quiet now. Oria knew she should have stopped, but Mica's idiocy in accepting the refugees had been eating at her all morning. 'Yes, Bronda, the camp can welcome whomever they please, but I am feeding the camp. Still feeding them. Don't forget, they needed those timber profits as much as we did. The indenture obliges me to feed them, and I want to do that, but I have no obligation to Bass' Berans. Komey can take care of them. Besides, we should make the Bass Companion face up to her responsibilities. Enough.' Oria waved at the path. 'Let's get on with it.'

They rolled past the twist trees, ignoring the leering branches, past the delicate beauty of the wild flax meadow, and into the camp.

The scene that met them was disturbing. The camp's neat concentric formation looked at least twice its normal circumference, the outer rings frayed and haphazard. There were cooking fires in odd places and the air smelt of charred fish.

Oria held her side, doing her best to manage the discomfort, as the wheelchair left the path and began crossing the cloddy ground. She suspected a broken rib. Last week she'd reached over her desk to grab a pen and she'd felt something snap. Age. Nothing could stop it, but the same couldn't be said about this mud. Some idiot had put sawdust on the wet ground. Only made things worse. Likely, a fish Beran. No oak-loving Beran would make that mistake.

Word of her presence must have spread because Quartz appeared when they were about halfway into the camp. He and the stable sister lifted the chair and carried Oria to the cook's fireside. The Oak Companion protested, but no one listened. That wouldn't have happened a decade ago. But a decade ago, the keeper was still alive. Virtue Remains had been a consummate diplomat. He would have come to Oria before accepting the refugees. They would have found a better way to keep those poor people alive than this disaster in the making.

'Where is he, then? This idiot wanderer you trained? I lend the man two horses and he comes back with all these people for me to feed.'

'I know.' Quartz nodded. 'I wasn't pleased, either. And with a new apprentice, which is at least something we can be grateful for.' Quartz explained about the girl and the stone. It took Oria a minute to realise the senior wanderer was talking about a child who was probably Fox's sister. 'Wonderful,' Oria snapped. 'The Kelp keeper's daughter. Here. Perfect. Now Fox won't be able to visit the manor without breaking the treaty. Send Mica to live somewhere else. Or maybe give his apprentice to a different camp. We can't have her here.'

'We can, and we will, have her here,' Quartz said. 'And I'd ask you to mind your mouth. We aren't chattels to move around. This is Mica's home.'

Oria sighed. 'Yes, I know. I know. But this makes things complicated. Having that girl here.'

Quartz looked confused. 'Were you thinking of bringing Fox to live in Oak? That would be... unusual to say the least.'

'Don't be an idiot. An adoptee living in a province? Pure folly. No, no. Just that after I die. If her daughter inherits my gravity. For the health of the newborn. There have been sororities that have allowed adopted birthmothers to visit manors to nurse their babies. Just a temporary arrangement. I would want that for the baby's welfare...' She frowned, dropped a finger of attention down into her body and tucked away the unexpected emotion. She returned her attention to Quartz, waved the conversation away. 'Off topic. Where is Mica? I want to speak with him. Now.'

'Not here, but he asked me to tell you he accepts full responsibility for the changes in the camp...'

Oria almost lost her grip on her feelings. Rage this time. 'What do you mean, not here?'

'He is training Saury. They have gone to find her first story cycle.'

Oria inhaled. She pushed her anger down, tucked it away, but not fast enough to stop herself from speaking, 'He has burdened my purse. He has forced me to treat these refugees as though they were Oak's Berans. He must pay. I will extend his indenture. For life. Mine to direct. And he won't be wandering anywhere without my express permission. In writing. He stays here, in this camp and he does what I ask.'

Quartz looked aghast. Bronda and the stable sister, too. Even Oria was shocked by what she'd said. A Beran's freedom, a wanderer's freedom... Taken for life. It was impossible. She had planned to move the refugees along. Gently. Something subtle. Instead, she'd demanded all of Mica's time. A person's most precious belonging. She had no right. It was servitude, nothing like the short indentures she'd negotiated in return for feeding the camp. Yes, she'd extended and extended them, but they'd been necessary and they would end. Eventually. This was wrong. Only she wasn't sure how to retract it.

Quartz looked angry. 'This is beneath you.'

For a moment, no one spoke. Oria told herself to retract her demand, but couldn't quite make herself speak. Then Quartz spoke instead: 'I imagine Mica will agree even though I will advise him not to. He wants us to help these people. I will ask him to call on you when he gets back,' Quartz hesitated and when he spoke again, he looked Oria in the eye. 'This is punishment. You know that, don't you? It's wilful. It has nothing to do with fair trade, with the tradition of companion and camp negotiations.'

'Is it fair that I feed these people as though they were Oak's Berans?' Oria couldn't seem to stop herself even though every word further committed her to her folly, 'Fair, that I shoulder the Bass Companion's burden? Fair that you are in my debt? I didn't want your debt. Never wanted it.'

'And yet you have it,' Quartz said, 'and the fault is yours. It is your failing gravity that has led us to this. If those trees we cut down had been healthy, the indenture could have ended. You should end it now.'

She shook her head. 'And continue feeding you? No. Charity beggars the soul.'

'Servitude beggars the soul,' he said.

'Then we must hope our fortunes change, that I die soon, that an infant companion emerges after the crossover, that she is a stronger talent.'

Her head pounded on the way back to the manor. She thought she might die. Right there in the chair. It would have been better for all concerned if she had. But she didn't die. She lay down on a parley room couch and Bronda brought her a bone tea to ease her discomfort. It helped, but nothing helped her work out how to extricate herself and her province from this mess.

O ria had planned to receive Mica in the formal sewing room, the downstairs room that Oria's grandmother used to favour. It was light filled, had to be for fine needlework, but it was uncomfortable. The chairs were hard and there was something odd about the painted acorns adorning the walls. Somehow, the scales on the cupules brought furrowed brows to mind. Combined with the nuts they crowned, the effect was scowling acorn-ish faces. Oria had thought it might suit the tone of their conversation, but now that she was in the room, she changed her mind. It would be a mistake to bring Mica here. Better to be outdoors. She decided on the stables. Sheltered from the wind but airy and light, and it would be a not-so-subtle reminder of the man's debt. A struggle to reach them, but Oria was feeling slightly more mobile today.

The stables were busy. Horses were being moved in and out of stalls as the hands mucked out straw and manure. The smell was earthy but not unpleasant and Oria felt a pang of envy for the hands' simple life.

She met Mica at the large double doors. He'd arrived with his nephew. No sign of Fox's sister, for which Oria was grateful. Mica sent the boy off to pet the horses and Oria and Mica walked the cobbled aisle to the tack room in silence.

Polished saddles and bridles lined the walls of the room and there was a pleasant scent of dubbin in the air. Bronda insisted on helping Oria into a worn wooden chair, and the stable sister found a stool for Mica.

Oria waved her handmaid away after she'd tucked a travel rug over the companion's knees. 'All right, all right. I'm fine. Don't fuss.'

'Can I get you anything?' the stable sister asked them.

'Privacy,' Oria says, then regretted her sharp tone. Everything was hard now that her body was failing.

Mica declined the woman's hospitality more graciously, and then they were alone. Already she felt weary. The morning felt like a circus and Oria wondered why it had become so hard for her to do something simple like conduct a conversation.

'So Wanderer, you owe me news of the provinces.'

'Ah yes. A cycle.'

'It needn't be formal.'

'Then it won't be knowledge. You said you wanted knowledge.'

Oria tamped down her impatience. 'Yes. I did. You're right. Go on.'

He began in the traditional way, introducing himself, speaking about all he brought to the cycle, '...so the first story is about me as a man. I am here resentfully, speaking with a woman I consider an enemy.'

She couldn't help interrupting, 'The feeling isn't reciprocated. You are not my enemy.'

'A good listener listens in silence,' he said.

She bit back a response, tied her emotions more tightly, and nodded for him to continue.

'The second story comes from one of the younger women who was on the beach when we found the Bass camp on the move. Apparently, Mother Bass was never very talented with freshwater fish, but she could flourish salmon and perch and she kept the province's lakes and rivers full. Flourished them until a few years ago when a mass death event killed off the freshwater bounty. The young woman I spoke with was still a child at the time, but she remembered the stink. The companion wouldn't speak about it. Tried to forbid the camp to speak about it. Then in recent months the camp began noticing problems in the ocean.' Mica described skin lesions and gill rot, behavioural changes in the fish, low-quality eggs and shoals that kept shrinking. 'And eventually the boats came back empty and Mother Bass fled.'

Oria was listening, but found she'd fixated on the mention of rot. Her trees had been rotten. That had been a fungus. She wondered whether the coincidence meant anything. She would have liked to ask, but she didn't. Strange to be speculating about mechanical causes for the provincial failures. Common wisdom had it that the companionships were spiritual gifts from the time of the Turning. But the two notions were not incompatible. If the gifts failed, then the ordinary processes, which had made the Stone Body such a barren continent prior to the Companionaris' arrival, would re-emerge.

She realised she had stopped listening, that Mica had begun the divergent account, the third story. 'There was a wanderer I met when Doubt and I were on the beach. He told me a stone called him to his home province, to Bass, called him down to the seabed. He dived—'

'Wait,' Oria held up a withered hand. 'Dived into the water, swam down? You're telling me a wanderer dived to the seabed? You said this is the third story. It sounds more like a fourth, like a folktale. A wanderer wouldn't break the taboo and penetrate the stone body. *Plant and reap,*' she voiced the familiar saying, '*but don't delve too far into the Stone Body's depths without consent.* He must have been talking about putting his head underwater, diving in the shallows. Even then...'

'No,' Mica said. 'Deep water. He swam down from a boat. He

penetrated the Stone Body's depths in Bass province, just like the lover in the fable, the one who raped the Stone Body.'

'And I suppose he thinks the collapse of the province is punishment?'

'Yes. He said the shoals curled away from him in disgust. He said he rock sensed the horror of the fish, felt them recoiling.'

Oria was about to tell Mica that fish were wild, and it was natural that they would recoil from a man, but the stable sister barged in, breathless and flushed.

'Your boy,' she said to Mica. 'Hurry. He's taken El Embaucador. He told the hand he had permission, that he was going to be the cook's apprentice in Aries.'

Mica protested, insisting the boy wouldn't dare, but the wanderer was already moving, following the stable sister. 'He's not a thief. He's just young and lonely.'

Oria called out after him as he left, 'Back and Path Wanderer, this nephew of yours is no end of trouble.'

Alone, she struggled out of her chair and had almost made her way to the door when she caught sight of movement through the window. A boy on a bolting pony, heading for the twist trees. She felt a jolt of fear. Better to break a bone in a fall than get trapped in a carnivorous tree. She reached for the ground around the horse and boy, felt for acorns, found them. She called them up, created a corral of oaks, laced their limbs. El Embaucador slid to a halt, and Mica's nephew fell from the saddle.

They took him to the nursing sister. Nothing broken. Oria and Mica stood near the door and watched while the sister treated the boy's cuts and bruises. Mica was silent. She didn't need rock skin to know the knowledge that his debt was large and growing burdened him. He'd already pledged his life's service to Oria, and she was at a loss to know how best to manage his responsibility for the boy's theft of the horse. She was about to propose the boy muck out the stables for a month as repayment when Mica spoke, 'I didn't tell you the fourth story.'

'True.' She touched his arm. 'Come. Let's sit and you can finish the cycle. The sister will find us when you're needed.'

Oria led Mica upstairs. This time to the smaller, more welcoming sewing room. Once they'd settled into a sunny corner under the window, the companion opened the nearest sewing basket. Someone had been working on a handkerchief, embroidering a wild flax flower. Luckily, the sister had left a threaded needle. She couldn't thread her own without calling for Bronda's help. But now she set to stitching.

The wanderer began the fourth story with all its traditional flourishes. Oria had little faith in the illuminating power of folktales, but she had a soft spot for fourth stories. She'd been listening to them since childhood and they were so familiar now they almost felt as though they were part of her own culture, not a Beranish institution. This time it was the story of the weathered pole, but Mica had chosen a version that Oria hadn't heard before. In the more familiar version, Wife forgot to prepare a promised wedding gift and as she ran to the wedding, she snatched up a weathered pole. Today Mica claimed she grasped an adder stone.

'... a glassy rock with a hole in the centre, an ugly thing. Coughed up by a serpent or a dragon, but Wife didn't have time to look for something prettier. She reached for the first thing that caught her eye. The rock was heavy, and she carried it with both hands, held firm despite the grit and bite of the thing. Wife hefted it up, intending to set it onto the gift table. As she went to set it down, she tripped on Husband's shoe. The rock flew out of her grip and over-shot the table. It spun in the air and sunlight bounced off its glassy facets. Then it fell. Down into the foundations of the newlyweds' fireplace. Down into the very depths of the Stone Body.

The camp laughed. Wife blushed. Husband fell silent. Then Husband remembered all the children Wife had borne and the work she had done and the stories she had told and the love she had given him. "Look here, you fools," he cried out to the camp. "Can't you see the rock is a talisman for Bride and Groom? Look how it longed to sit beneath their hearth… It wants to make their home a home. It wants to make their food plentiful and their family flourish." The camp's brow furrowed. And the camp's certainty wavered. And the camp withheld its judgement. When time told the last story, the newlyweds' pot was indeed plentiful, and each birth brought twins. Soon each hearth had a stone, and life on the Stone Body flourished.'

Oria looked up as Mica fell silent. 'Fascinating. It must have originated before the taboo became widespread and when tents had fireplaces. I must share it with the archivist in the Beranish Affairs department in Komey and with Aikin. Those two will be interested.' She set down the embroidery. 'Now, if you don't mind, I need some rest. Take your nephew and go. He can muck out the stables. I won't add his foolishness to your debt. Besides, you have nothing left to give. I have all your time.'

She closed her eyes, waved him away.

'A fourth story should be discussed,' he said. 'That's what turns a cycle into knowledge. You said that was what you wanted. It's what led me to that beach. At the very least, a discussion would show some respect for me as the storyteller.'

She didn't open her eyes. 'I'm not being disrespectful, but I need to rest. I'll send Bronda to fetch you when I'm ready.' She could feel sleep calling her, demanding her attention, but he hadn't moved. There'd been no shifting of his chair, no carpeted footsteps. She opened her eyes, irritated now.

He met her gaze. 'I won't be able to come back later. Another stone is calling me. I felt it when we were in the stables. I still have my duties as a wanderer. You can't take that away from me. The Stone Body doesn't care about your indenture. You need to let me go.' He stared at her, waiting, the tension in his jaw speaking volumes about his feelings. She couldn't help thinking that it was always like this with Mica: insisting on his rights but asking for her aid.

'Another stone?' she said, unable to keep the resentment from her voice. 'And now it's three horses you'll be asking for? Perhaps you'd like to take the Bass refugees with you and you'll want horses for them too?'

'No. Just me this time. I'll find someone to care for the children. I'll go on foot. I don't want your horses. I can't afford them. I've nothing left to give. You've taken everything I have, even my freedom.'

That galled. She'd wanted nothing from him. He'd forced her hand. 'But I'm yet to feel any benefit from all these gifts,' she said. 'You say I have your time, but you're already asking for it back. And you're proposing to leave those children and what...? Be away for weeks? Months? I'm afraid not. You stay right here. You deal with that nephew of yours, stop him causing so much trouble. And when Quartz tells me the boy is back under control, come and see me again and we can discuss you leaving to chase stones.'

The wanderer stared at her, cheeks flushed. She had gone too far. She knew it. Diplomacy had never been a strength, and this one tried her patience.

She gave the youngster a moment, waited for him to argue, acknowledge she had a point, and then persuade her that the trouble he'd been causing was over. She would have given way, but he said nothing. He sat there staring at her, and then he stood up and left the room. Left without a word as though they weren't in the middle of a negotiation.

Oria stayed in her chair. She needed to lie down, but she was too tired to call for Bronda. Her joints ached and her head felt light. She felt self-pitiful and sorrowful even though she knew she'd been the one who'd made most of the mistakes. She thought about her death. It would be best for everyone if her life ended, if she stopped making a mess of things, but she didn't want to go. When she fell asleep, it was a restless sleep full of adder stones and angry Berans and rotting trees.

5

ox stared at Louis. The man rested on the carved and canopied bed like a pile of kelp. Though he could still walk several paces, his age and poor health made the trip from his house to Fox's rooms impossible. Any other man would have and should have knocked on the door of her suite and waited until she let him inside, but this man couldn't make it up the Oak House stairs to knock on anyone's door. It had taken six gardeners to carry him here, to one of the garden houses. The unexpected privacy was a relief. Louis was worse than Fox had imagined and he gave off a fetid, sweet smell. At least here there was no one to see her reaction. Except the man himself. She knew she should feel compassion, but compassion was difficult in the face of unwanted intimacy.

She made herself speak, 'Thank you so much for accepting my contract. It's good to meet you.' She tried not to look at his ageing body, but failed. 'Would you like something to drink? Or some food? We've missed dinner but perhaps some supper, if you're hungry...?'

He smiled at the suggestion. 'What a sweet little poppet you are. Yes. Yes, why not? Boost the energy, so to speak.'

Fox turned away, but not before she'd caught the unwelcome sight of the damp, sweaty grey hair on his vast chest. She gathered herself, turned and walked over to the tasselled bell pull, tugged it. He was worse, worse than she'd ever imagined. But it didn't matter. It didn't matter what he was like. She would sleep with him. It had nothing to do with liking or loving. And she'd only need to do it once if her control over her eggs was any good. She found she was holding Mica's stone for comfort. That had been happening recently. She had too much on her mind. It wasn't just her own worries. It was also her worry for Wren.

Wren's baby was due any day now, and Fox hadn't found a way to force the house to free Wren's mind. There was still a little time yet. Oak House would wait a month or two after the birth of the baby, but soon enough it would be Wren in this house, with this man.

They ate in silence, Fox picking at her plate, Louis giving the supper the attention it deserved. She waited until after they'd finished before she spoke again, 'Should we begin...'

'Course dear, course...' he hefted himself up onto his elbow. 'I can hardly wait, but if you don't mind, I've only just finished supper. I know you're eager, but I might just take a nap first. Young ones like you are always so eager to be ready for a crossover, but I'm not as young as I used to be— or as fit. Hold yourself, my dear. We've time enough.' He smiled. 'Just fifteen minutes' sleep and then I'll be ready for you.' He leant back against the pillows, closed his eyes, held up a hand as though she needed fending off.

He fell asleep almost immediately. She left their trays outside the door and then cast about, looking for something to do. There was nothing. The housekeeper had readied the room for one purpose only. There were no books on the tables and no games on the shelves, and she hadn't even brought her embroidery. Not that she enjoyed doing handiwork, but it would have given her something to pass the time. She wished she could go for a walk, but there'd be talk if she did. She moved over to the open casement window and leant out, her hips hard against the sill. The window looked out on a secluded fernery, fenced off from the rest of the gardens. Better to wait under the stars than watch Louis sleep. She climbed out the window and settled herself on the grass. Behind her, Louis snored.

When he woke again some two hours later, she climbed back in and smiled at him. It was hard to make herself do it, but she did it. She'd hardly set both feet on the ornamental carpet when he announced he was famished, needed a little more supper, and began listing his preferred menu.

'Oh, and mind you don't let anyone see you looking like that when you order the food.' He rolled over onto his side and peered at her, frowning.

'What do you mean?'

'Well, you don't look like we've touched each other, do you, dear? Not that we won't just as soon as I've eaten and rested… because the journey was hard on me, terribly hard. But we can't have them out there poking about asking questions. For them it's all money, money, money, babies, babies, babies, as though love has a timetable.' He shook his head. 'No, my dear, we'll take this affair of ours at a fitting slow pace. A Companionari pace. So take off that tunic of yours, dear one, so the wretched houseboy doesn't catch sight of you looking all buttoned up, so to speak. And pull out those virginal braids.' He pointed at her hair. 'Muss up that fine mane and put a little sparkle in those lovely golden eyes.'

Fox stared at Louis, understanding that this inexpensive prospective birthfather was inexpensive for a reason. So it would all be for nothing then, the money already outlaid, the effort of getting him here, the evening spent in his company. The family would have to spend more if they were going to get someone else at such short notice. She turned toward the tasselled bell pull. 'I'm sorry, but I think I'd best call my father,' she spoke over her shoulder. 'This won't work, will it?'

'No… please,' Louis cried out, his voice quite different from its earlier droll tones. 'Don't. Don't complain about me. Not when you haven't given me a chance.'

'I'm sorry,' she paused, 'truly. But I need to get pregnant. If you can't...'

'Not can't. Just have a little trouble sometimes now that I'm older. Just a little trouble. It isn't easy when you're a mature man and then... well... it isn't easy when you're tired.' And then he began crying. Great, loud sobbing sounds.

She hesitated and then came back to the bed. Sat on the edge. 'Shush. The houseboy is probably nearby. He'll come running if you keep on like that. Look, maybe we can try. If we try now before you eat anything, you might manage.' She stood up, lifted her tunic, preparing to undress.

'No. It's no good,' he sobbed. 'You were right. It won't work. Truth is, I can't. Not for anyone, not even a little peach like you. I'm done... Finished... Set to starve.'

'Surely not.' She dropped her tunic back down. 'You must have some sort of income. You don't look as though you're starving.'

'Charity. Charity from those who are grateful to me for the love and happiness... Damn it, for the pleasure I've provided. Oh, if only you'd known me then...' He smiled. 'But I'm not the man I was,' he sighed. 'I need this fee. You'll have other opportunities. Take pity on an old man.'

His plea moved her. Life in Komey wasn't easy when you were poor. Fox had run enough errands in the city to know that. And Louis' life would be hard now that he could no longer father children. She closed her eyes and dropped into her body, feeling for her egg. It was in the gap between ovary and fallopian tube: graceful, slow, exquisite. She could feel its ripe presence: its surface so ready. It had no consciousness, no intention. There was no feeling or seeking, but Fox felt for it, felt on its behalf. She longed for it to enclose sperm and tumble chromosomes. She didn't know if she could wait now the egg had departed its ovary.

Fox withdrew her mind from her body and it became easier. The pressing feeling was gone, that sense of ripeness disappeared.

She looked at Louis. What did a small waste of money and a

delay of a month matter? The Oak Mother could live a few more years. Because that was the companionship Fox wanted for her daughter embryo. She could never go home to Kelp, but Oak was her house province, and Mica's home. Could she delay this chance of getting pregnant? What if Aunt Oria died in the meantime? She looked at Louis and he smiled at her, already grateful even though she hadn't decided. To her surprise, she saw a flash of sweetness in his broad face, a hint of the man who had been.

'There you are, pet. I can see you've got a kind heart for an old man like me,' he said. 'I can see you won't turn on me, make me lose my service fee. A lovely girl like you? No, not likely. And if you're not turning me in, could you just mess up your hair a little and take off that tunic and then ask that nice young boy to fetch us another supper...?'

Against her better judgement, Fox began pulling out her braids, loosening her hair. 'But I'm not taking off my tunic.'

'All right,' he frowned, 'but the shoes have to go.'

They carried on the charade for two days: Fox sleeping outside in the sheltered garden; Louis alone in the bed.

On the third night, Fox climbed out the window with her blanket and pillow to make her bed under the stars, but found she wasn't tired and couldn't sleep. She was missing her long walks in Komey and missing the library and the house and the constant movement of people. She tried going within to nudge sleep forward, but it didn't work. Eventually, she accepted that the night would be restless and lay on her back and looked up at the sky. The stars were diamond bright. She could hear the click and rasp of crickets and the creeping sounds of the night. She frowned... Something felt out of place. Not an extra noise, just a thickening in the air.

Her arms almost ached with her need to rock sense. She sat up, looked around, wishing her remnant rock skin was strong enough to parse the world beyond her immediate surrounds. There it was again. Stronger now. She stood up. It should have felt dangerous, someone moving about in the night, but perhaps her rock skin worked well enough to know it wasn't. Because the thickening in the air felt welcome.

The ferns moved, parted, and Mica stepped into the grass circle. A dark silhouette but immediately recognisable. She wondered if he was in trouble and the thought set her heart racing. Her life was so constrained it would be almost impossible to help him unless it was something she could write to Oria about or something simple she could sort out in Komey.

'What's wrong?' she spoke first. 'What are you doing here?'

'Don't worry,' he sounded confident, although he was whispering. 'I got here with no one seeing me, although I wouldn't have made it if the Oak Companion had her way. Things in Oak have become complicated... But that's not important.' He came closer, put his hand on her shoulder, and drew her into a quick embrace. 'So? Tell me,' he said. 'I assume we're safe to talk, here?'

It was good to see him. Beyond good. She'd been alone with her worries for too long, but his words didn't quite make sense. 'Safe? Well, no one will see you here, if that's what you mean.' She kept her voice low, but didn't whisper. 'There's someone in the room behind us, but he's sleeping.'

'I was worried they had hurt you,' he said. 'What's wrong? Why did you call?'

'I didn't. But it's... It's good to see you.'

'But you needed me. The obsidian wouldn't have called me otherwise. And it was urgent too. The stone started calling me about a week ago. So strong. I would have been here earlier, but Oria tried to stop me.'

'She what?'

He glanced about as though someone might listen, then drew her further away from the garden house, deeper into the shadows, his warm hand in hers. 'It's not important. But are you sure you're all right because something disturbed the rock child? And what are you doing out here?' He looked around the tiny, grassed fernery and then glanced back at the window before turning back to stare at her. 'Is this your house? Do you have your own house now? But why don't you sleep inside?'

Fox looked at him. Even in shadow, with worry written all over his face, his features held the humour and determination that she remembered from their first meeting. It had been a mild winter's night, just like this one. Fox had been alone in the abandoned rice paddy. She'd stolen away from Oria and the other Companionaris, stepped out of the travelling tent she'd slept in since being taken from her camp and her family. Mica had also been alone, but his solitude wasn't full of grief like Fox's. He was consumed with rebellious energy and optimism, a freshly minted wanderer on his first solo journey to collect stories. They'd made promises and pledges. She would hide some remnant of her rock skin and he would visit her and help her. But he couldn't help her now. That he was trying, stirred something in her arms. Mica was warmth and love and everything that was missing from her life. But she let go of his hand.

'It's complicated. Traditions in Komey aren't like our traditions.'

He snorted. 'I'm not going anywhere until you tell me what you're doing out here and why the obsidian thinks you're in trouble.' He walked over to the window and looked inside the lamplit room. Louis chose that moment to resume snoring. Mica stilled. Then, Louis must have shifted because a moment or two later, his snoring settled into a soft snuffle.

Mica turned away from the window and looked at her. He knew. He understood. When he walked back to her, he told her he was sorry. 'How stupid of me. I should have realised you'd be making your daughter embryo.' He shook his head. 'I guess the obsidian didn't like the choice of birthfather, but I suppose that's beside the point now. Are you pregnant already?'

She sighed and shook her head. 'No. I should be. But the man they chose for me hasn't been able to—'

'Really?' Mica sounded pleased. He caught up her hands. 'Then the obsidian was right to call me. I can sleep with you. We'll make your daughter embryo together. I want to. Besides, it's another act of rebellion!'

Fox felt longing at the touch of his hands: her own longing and his. She pulled away, furious with herself for reacting to him when she knew she must only sleep with a talented Companionari man. She fumbled to find the obsidian in her pocket, no longer wanting it. He needed to go, take the rock child with him; not come here and unsettle everything when she was coping. She reached into her pocket and brought out the embroidered pouch. She slipped the stone from the pouch, held it out to him. But instead of taking it, he put his hand around hers and closed it, making a double fist around the sentient rock. And as though the rock child had the power to amplify everything, she felt her hunger for Mica return. She leant forward and her mouth met his. He put his arms around her. She drew him closer.

Then she remembered herself. 'I can't just do whatever I want. Our baby wouldn't be talented. It would fail in the crossover and then I'd have a Beranish child to hide in a city where there aren't any secrets. Do you want that? I'd have to feed our daughter dust bush tea, suppress her identity. She might lose her mind like Wren. Is that what you want?'

Mica sat back, looked up at the night sky, and sighed. 'No, but there must be something right about this, otherwise the rock child wouldn't have called me. The Stone Body wants me here.'

'What does the Stone Body know about Companionari life? We're not in a fourth story,' Fox said. 'If you had Companionari talent, it would be different. It would be worth the risk.'

'Maybe I do,' he said.

'Don't be silly.'

He reached for her hand again and she let him take it. 'I'm serious. Maybe you should test me and see.'

'Don't be silly,' she repeated.

'Could you tell if I did? Could you test me like Oria tested you? Blood to blood?'

'I suppose so. In theory, any Companionari who can master her body can test a Beranish talent. But Mica,' she frowned, 'Beranish men aren't talented.'

'How do you know?'

'Because they're never tested.'

'That's not why they're not tested.' He shook his head. 'The Companionaris don't need men, don't value them, so they don't bother testing them.'

'That's wishful thinking,' she argued.

'Then there's no harm in trying, is there?' he countered.

'I guess.' She thought for a minute. 'We'd need a pin and I don't have one.'

'I've got a knife.' He reached into his belt and drew it out.

'Okay.' She nodded. 'We'll try.'

They sat down on her bedding. Mica pricked his right thumb and held it up, offering the knife to her with his other hand. Fox stared at the blade and then licked her lips, only hesitated for a moment before taking it. She told herself that this was foolishness, but she pressed the tip of the knife against her right thumb until it bit. Who knew what a talent felt like? How would she recognise Mica's talent if he had any? And yet, there was no harm in trying. She would ride her blood to where it touched his, discover whether there was anything to be discovered.

'Hold up your hand and keep quiet while I do this,' she instructed him.

He nodded without speaking. She gripped his hand, locking her fingers around his, pressing her thumb to his. Fox closed her eyes and flew within, navigating her bloodstream, letting it carry her down into her hand. She hurried forward and found the tiny wound where she'd pricked her skin. She hesitated, uncertain about moving beyond her body. Was it dangerous? Perhaps she would get lost. Perhaps it was possible she would die. She moved carefully, using smaller and smaller increments until she reached the foremost blood cells in the wound. Then she paused. She was far from the usual comfort of her body. There was nothing more than a thin membrane between her blood and Mica's blood. Then she did it. She stepped across and felt a sudden burst of heat as the face of her consciousness met the inner life of Mica's body. The feeling was electric. His cells recognised her, strained to embrace her.

She gasped and withdrew, letting go of his hand.

'Fox?' he sounded worried. 'Are you all right?'

She opened her eyes and smiled. 'Yes.'

'So?'

'I don't know Mica. I've got nothing to compare it to.'

'But you felt something because I heard you gasp in surprise.'

'But I don't know what it meant. It might mean nothing.'

'So tell me what you felt,' he insisted.

She looked at him and wondered whether her physical and emotional desire for him could be trusted. 'It might just be an attraction.'

'So, I felt attractive?' He sounded pleased.

'Kind of electric. Maybe all people feel like that.'

'How did it feel when Oria tested you? When you were a child?'

'There was heat.'

'And with me?'

She nodded. 'Yes, with you too.'

He lay back down on the blanket and looked up at the night sky without speaking.

Fox took up one of his hands and recognised a softer version of the warmth she'd felt in his blood. 'I think you've got talent, but how can I know?'

'You're right. You can't. Not without testing a few other Beranish men to compare. So you'll just have to weigh up the risks and decide.'

Fox looked up and drank in the stars. She realised she'd decided. 'Mica, if the crossover fails and our daughter can't capture a companionship, you need to come and take her away from Komey. I'll have to find some excuse: fake her death. I don't want her to grow up here. So promise me...'

'I promise.'

They undressed and lay close. Afterwards, she dropped into her body and called out to those sperm that carried Mica's daughter potential. She hurried them forward so that the journey that would have taken them hours took minutes. And that same warm hunger that she'd felt for Mica remained with her as she watched his daughter sperm reach her ovum. They crowded it until it spun with a dense aura of lashing tails. Then she urged her egg to open, to admit one coded head. It obeyed and then shut itself off from the rest.

The beginnings of her child drifted, and she nudged it forward. It buckled and rippled, and divided. Then it doubled, trebled, quadru-pled... She drew it down into her womb so that what took days happened in seconds. Fox felt a shiver as the conceptus touched her womb's soft, rich wall. She drew herself around it like a cloak, saw the implantation and marvelled at the colours of her blood swooning about the mulberry button of cells.

She opened her eyes to find Mica watching her. 'It's done?' he asked.

She nodded. 'We have a daughter: a Beranish daughter embryo.'

He smiled.

'But what if our plan doesn't work? What if she comes to grief here in Komey and I can't protect her?'

He was silent for a moment and then began speaking. 'I'll come for her. I promised I would and I will. And nothing will go wrong...' He hesitated. 'There's a fourth story I want to tell you. Maybe it will help. It's an odd story, but somehow... Well, you be the judge.' He smiled again and covered them with the blanket, their heads resting on a single pillow. Then he began the story, 'Wife and Husband lived together under the rock eaves on the northern edge of Oak province,' he said, his voice warm against her ear. 'In the beginning they were happy with all they had: Husband hunted boar; Wife cooked boar. Wife's boar pot seemed generous and full; Husband's spears seemed sharp and swift. But as the years passed, Husband and Wife grew weary of their lives and wished that the Stone Body would do something different for a change. Husband complained that the sun kept rising in the east; Wife found it irritating that the river flowed downstream. After a while, neither of them could bear to live another day under the eaves of the province and so they set out across the Stone Body in search of change. They travelled for a year and a day, visiting every part of the world, but everywhere they went they found the same story: rain fell from the sky; the sun set in the west; wind carried clouds; rocks lay on the ground. When at last they arrived back at the eaves of Oak province, they sat down in despair and wept. Husband lay flat on the ground and let his tears fall into the river. Wife lifted her face to the sky and wailed. Husband's tears flowed into the river. The river swelled until its banks broke and the pressure of the water was so great it flowed backwards. Wife cried. The sound was so loud that the ground rumbled, sending rocks dancing into the air. When Husband and Wife saw what they had done, they laughed. They fell asleep laughing and when they awoke the next morning, they discovered the Stone Body had changed. The sun that woke them rose in the west; rocks drifted across the sky; and the river wound its way upstream.' He paused then. 'So, I guess I'm saying that change is possible. Maybe the obsidian brought me here because the Stone Body is going to help us effect change.'

'I hope so.' She shivered, and he drew the blankets more closely around them.

She slept then. And when she awoke, she opened her eyes to find Louis framed by the window. He was staring down at them. With some sort of instinct, he must have known what was going on, because he'd lifted himself off the bed and walked to the window with no help.

Louis let out a long, delighted laugh that woke Mica. 'Solves our problem. Looks like I'll be getting that pregnancy bonus after all. Well, thank you, my dear.' He smiled at Fox. 'I am grateful. You're a lovely lass, you are. And thank you too, young man.'

Fox felt her spirits lift. Then she remembered Wren. 'The other contract. Her name's Wren. Be nice to her. She's lost, consumed by dust bush tea. She won't understand what's going on. Brush her hair when she's upset and tell them you fulfilled the contract.'

'And when she doesn't fall pregnant?'

'They won't blame you, will they? Not with my easy success.'

Mica stayed for the remaining days of the six-day service that the Oaks had brought from Louis. On the last morning, Fox suppressed their daughter embryo. Gently and carefully, she increased the surrounding pressure until she felt it fall into the long, suspended state that would last until she released it again during a crossover.

It was one of the happiest times in Fox's life. Even Louis enjoyed himself. Mica spent hours with him, collecting his stories of the sex trade in Komey and telling him counterpoint tales about marriage and love and infidelity among Berans. It would have been the happiest time in Fox's life, only something awful happened just as Mica was leaving. They were in the secluded fernery and had just said goodbye. Mica went to leave and then hesitated. When he turned back, he was frowning.

'What?' she asked.

'It's odd, but the obsidian doesn't want to stay here.'

'Here in Komey?'

'No.' He shook his head. 'It doesn't want to stay with you.'

Fox felt hurt. She'd almost given the stone back to Mica on that first night, but that didn't mean she wanted it to go. She'd spent her life in Komey carrying it, grown used to it; it was a comfort to her. It wasn't just that it could call Mica: the stone symbolised her connection with her own people. But now it wanted to leave her. She reached into her pocket and pulled it out, handing it back to Mica. 'But how will we communicate? I can't write to you.'

Mica spoke as he put the obsidian back into his pouch. 'Don't worry. I've four others...' He paused, frowning again.

'What?'

He looked up at Fox, almost embarrassed. 'I don't know how to say this, but none of them will stay with you.'

Fox felt cold. Not fearful for now, but fearful for their daughter embryo. Betrayed by the fickle rock children. She'd relied on them. She wouldn't have risked sleeping with Mica if she'd known she'd be without means to call for help. But in the end, there was nothing she and Mica could do. It wasn't the Beranish way to keep hold of rock children when the stones wanted to depart with a wanderer. Fox wasn't the only one who was worried. Mica looked stunned by the rock children's refusal to stay. In the end, they agreed that he'd remain alert to the news of any crossover and that he'd seek Fox out at the time of their daughter's birth. It was worrying, but they had no other choice.

The setting sun had too much bite for Oria's liking, but she was as comfortable as she could be beneath the poplar. A nice tree. One of only two in the grove that weren't cork oaks. Course Oria couldn't look up into the branches without hurting her neck, but some of the foliage was low enough for her to enjoy the breeze shifting the leaves, turning them from silver to green and back again.

'We shouldn't sit here,' Bronda said. 'We should sit under one of our own trees.'

Oria opened her fan and gave it a couple of flaps, setting the warm air moving. 'This is the best spot to view the ceremony. Mother Salix said that's why she wanted them planted here. A gift for my benefit. So I could enjoy Harvest Night in comfort.'

'She planted them here to annoy you. Slap bang in the middle of our corks.'

Oria shushed Bronda, waved her comments away. The Oak Companion hadn't expected to be part of another harvest ceremony, but somehow she was still alive. Her Companionari sisters, the members of the Oak sorority, were meant to be here sitting beside her, but she'd ordered them to stay in the manor and listen to the festivities through the open windows.

It was petty and unkind of her to have denied them the pleasure of the evening, but her stomach had burned all day and they hadn't let her rest. One minute it would be her opinion about which bit of lace to put on a collar, then it would be some unimportant piece of news about whether the manor cook had begun the baking on time. She'd lost her temper with them. The only person who seemed to know what she needed was Bronda, and Bronda was almost as irritating.

The sound of laughter brought her back to the present. The camp's children were racing around, ducking under feast tables as they chased each other about, waiting for the ceremony to begin. She spotted Mica's nephew and Fox's sister, playing like little ones. She couldn't see Mica, but Quartz was there, filling his plate, licking his fingers. Oria smiled. Course he was. Who didn't love a harvest feast when everything felt touched with summer's glow? She snorted, pulling herself up. Sentimental nonsense.

She turned her attention to the arrangements for tonight. The manor kitchen had supplied three-quarters of the food. It didn't do to have a lean table on Harvest Night. The evening set the tone for the coming year and the tone needed to be one of generosity. The Berans needed her to be a firm Oak Companion, but a generous Oak Mother.

A group of men, the ceremonial harvesters, waited beneath the cork oaks that surrounded the glade. Some leant against their trees, others rested their hands against the stocks of their axes. Then it began. Almost as one, they picked up their tools and started cutting lines to mark out panels of bark. They worked the fan-shaped blades, never hesitating, never breaching the precious membrane beneath the cork that ensured each tree's continued survival. The sound of metal against tree trunk and the grunt of effort filled the air. Oria and the rest of the camp watched their progress. Then one man turned his machete around, using the handle to lever the cork away from the trunk. Others followed. Soon the trees looked like women preparing for bed: the top of their pinafores hanging down from their waists, revealing their soft pink under things.

Oria's stomach burnt, spoiling everything. The pain had been worsening. She closed her eyes. *Breathe in. Breathe out. Sunlight against oak leaves. Feel the pain pass away.* The nursing sister's mantric poem seemed to have some power in this setting because the sensation eased. She opened her eyes again, looked at the men. They were working their way around the trees, creating more panels. Their movement made their loose, red cotton trousers dance against the backdrop of the landscape. One man stopped and wiped the sweat from his brow. A child ran forward and handed him a drink in a cork cup made from the elbow of a branch. How Oria cherished these traditions. How she loved the virility of these Beranish men. She had never slept with any of these. Her lovers were old or dead now, but it felt good to remember.

Behind the cork cutters, deeper into the grove, a separate gang worked at a project to re-build the stone arch and wall that surrounded the grove's lone white oak, the province's foundation oak. The crew had the same festive red trousers but also wore caps. Oria couldn't remember why. A superstition of some sort.

The first Oak Companion had built the arch, but it had toppled a few days ago: a bad omen. Oria had insisted it be re-built. She was paying for the work out of her own purse, ignoring her right to free labour under the current indenture. She didn't want to die with the arch scattered about on the ground: not the sort of legacy she wished to leave for the little girl who'd follow. Everything should be in order when she left; everything complete. The repair, the work continuing during the harvest ceremony, was the source of some anger in the camp, but Oria knew from the unrelenting pain in her stomach and the buzzing in her head, she didn't have long. Oak's Berans had refused point blank to do the job. They wouldn't work through the harvest ceremony nor dig to the depth Oria needed. But Bass' Berans would to do anything for coin. They hadn't seemed worried about offending the Stone Body.

Oria shook her head. She should have let them pause during the ceremony. Never mind that the stone arch and its stubby ornamental walls were important to her: she had wider duties.

'My father always said that wall building was a genuine homage to God's Back,' Oria said.

Her handmaid jerked awake and shifted in her chair. '… a good man.'

'A wall gives God something to lean against,' Oria said.

Bronda picked up her embroidery. 'For Berans, it's just work.'

'*We* know God can rest against it. Never mind Berans don't.' Oria realised she meant it. 'You never know,' she laughed, 'I might lean against it myself when I turn away and head down the Path.' For a while, there was silence as the two of them watched the harvest. When Oria began speaking again, she talked about what was really ailing her. 'A young man stepped off Wanderers' Cliff last night. His cousin found him this morning. Dead, of course.'

The handmaid's breath caught. 'Another?'

'I've written it down in the manor records as an accident. I didn't even know him. Hope Appears,' Oria gave a grim laugh. 'You couldn't think of a worse name under the circumstance.'

Bronda frowned over her embroidery. 'Why do they keep killing themselves?'

'When there's no hope in a person's heart—'

'Then the indenture is to blame,' Bronda spoke in a rush. 'Your doing.'

It didn't help that Oria could feel her handmaid waiting to be reprimanded. If only it were that simple: lift the indenture. But it wasn't. The suicides had been worse this year, yes, but the Oak's older men were in better health than those in other provinces.

Oria drew Bronda's attention back to the men working on the new arch. 'I don't think they'll be placing any stones today. The footings need to be deep and it will take at least another day before they can rebuild.'

The cork harvesters had finished the inner circle of trees and had lowered their axes. Oria watched them unbend from their labours. The songs were about to begin. It always began this way: with the downing of tools. The singer opened his mouth and uttered a long, low note. Then the sound of the traditional treaty song filled the clearing. Oria closed her eyes, forced herself to let go of her worries and enjoy the moment. She didn't need to sing out loud, not yet. Instead, she joined in with a whisper, mouthing the words. It was effortless, automatic. The lyrics slipped through her lips, more comforting than the nursing sister's poem. Soon, she stopped speaking and just thought her responses. Perhaps dying wouldn't be too hard. Perhaps she could let go.

She woke to her handmaid's insistent nudge. For a moment, she wasn't sure where she was. Her tongue felt dry in her mouth, her stomach burned. Birdsong had replaced the song. They were waiting for her ritual words. The clearing was in twilight, the grove in shadow. It was time. She straightened her back, concentrated, and waited.

The same man, who had begun the singing, turned to her, calling, 'Welcome Companion Oria. Welcome to the Stone Body.'

Oria stood up to speak. She felt the pain in her belly intensify. Bronda slipped a steadying arm around her waist.

'Thank you for your welcome,' Oria let her handmaid support her weight. 'I have brought within my Very Body companionship for the oaks.'

'We thank you!' the men called in unison.

'I have brought within my Very Body the Gifts that are minor expressions of goodwill from my family: olive, onion, poppy, eagle, snake, rose, lesser flax, wild flax.'

'We thank you!'

'All this I give you in accordance with the treaty. In return, I sit at your feet as a guest, in gratitude, with respect, and I thank you.' Oria smiled, nodded, waved, then moved to take her seat.

'Parasite!' a single male voice shouted.

Oria paused and felt for the mood in the clearing, looking for something sharp, looking for the first signs of trouble, but the atmosphere still seemed balmy, festive. Trouble was coming, she knew it was coming, but she still couldn't sense its timing. She leant more heavily against her handmaid, again focusing on retaking her seat. The pain in her stomach was strong, and she felt a rushing in her head.

A second shout went up, but this time the call was different, more urgent. Oria experienced a jolt of fear that she'd misread the situation, that her strategy to steady the province until the new companion could create a decent bounty, hadn't been effective. She gripped Bronda's arm and peered into the grove. The Bass refugees, the workers. They'd fallen back from the footings of the stone arch.

'There's something here, Mother Oak,' one of them called out. 'Something you need to see.'

Oria felt a surge of irritation. She fumbled for her stick and brushed away Bronda's cautioning hand. 'No. You stay here. I don't want you trailing around after me.'

She stepped away from Bronda and made her way toward the excavation. 'Nothing to see. Nothing to see,' Oria called out to the harvesters. 'Enjoy yourselves.' She made herself smile and wave at the families seated on the grass in front of the tables. Quartz caught her eye, moving to join her, but she held up her hand. 'I'll deal with this. Don't spoil your evening.'

The camp relaxed at her words. She'd always been able to convey certainty and confidence. Oria's command to ignore whatever had disturbed the refugee workers had been a welcome instruction: no one wanted to look into the opening in the earth, into the Stone Body's privacy. Thank the Back this hadn't happened mid-ritual.

She made her way over to the labourers with the help of her stick. The men stood on the eastern edge of the hole. The foreman's face was closed, and the others watched Oria's approach, sneaking downward glances into the trench. As soon as she was near enough, she looked down, too. A shovel had exposed the corner of what looked like an elaborately decorated wooden plank.

She didn't ask about what had happened. She didn't want to give them an excuse to call for Quartz and have him weave a ponderous story cycle. Instead, she directed two of the younger men into the diggings, and watched while they cleared away more soil, exposing something large and long. Somehow, it was no surprise when the object was free from the clutches of the earth, it turned out to be a coffin. On a day when it felt as though death was everywhere, it seemed only fitting. It couldn't stay beneath the foundations of the new arch, that was certain, so it would have to be moved.

'Take it to the greenhouse. And then you can join in the festivities,' she told the workers. 'Finish the foundations tomorrow.'

She almost waved for Bronda to help her walk to the greenhouse, but she didn't. She would examine this thing on her own.

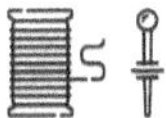

Oria found a slightly unsteady seat at the back of the greenhouse and rested. The distant sounds of Harvest Night still filtered through the aged panes of glass, but the emptiness and silence of the building felt peaceful.

The men had set the coffin to rest on a potting bench. Its pale wooden panels looked luminous in the shadowy dusk, highlighting its dark inlay. As she looked at it, her head filled with the old stories of vigils that hadn't been practised since the last great age before her ancestors had left their Galean homeland and crossed the Komic Sea. She imagined the setup was similar: everything quiet, nothing to focus on except the death of a loved one.

It wouldn't be like that when her life ended. They would sweep her rooms clean, her walls washed down, her objects scoured, her clothes laundered, her body bundled off to Komey. The idea was unpleasant. She wondered whether she might hide something of herself where they couldn't find it.

Oria lifted herself out of the chair and came forward, leant against the bench that supported the coffin. She reached out and touched it, brushing soil away from the surface. Hard to tell how long it had been in the ground, but obviously interred before they built the arch. She wondered if her forbears knew they were erecting an arch over the dead. And whose dead? Probably a Companionari corpse. The Beranish taboo about digging meant that they opted for cremation.

Oak would have been the obvious choice for the box, but this timber looked more like the exotic golden pine that used to grow in Caballo before it became extinct. Now the place just grew onions: bred horses and grew onions. Oria ran her fingers over the silver strap work on the side and felt some engraving. She bent down and saw a single word: *Promise*. A Beranish name. Strange to find it here; strange that it was unfinished. Normally it would be *Promise Delivered* or *Promise Offered* or even *Promise Given*. Perhaps Promise had died before finding a second name.

She supposed she should return to the manor. Bronda would be back at the house organising the sisters' supper and worrying about Oria. Wondering whether to come and look for her, but too scared to try. Oria was glad that she hadn't brought her handmaid.

She hobbled over to the racks of tools and gardening mixtures, her legs tired after the walk from the grove. She'd be lucky to find a candle: her people rarely used the place at night. Oria moved aside pots and gloves and small hand tools, brushing away cobwebs, but couldn't locate any stubs. Turning away, she caught sight of a lamp. That would do if it worked. She lifted the lamp up onto a nearby bench. No matches. Bronda would have some, but Oria carried nothing herself. Irritating: stupid to have so many pointless rules.

She stood in front of the unlit lamp. The light would be gone soon. She'd have to make her way back to the manor in the dark. She'd best get moving. It was time to farewell the coffin and leave.

She moved back to the casket, used her hand to brush away the last of the soil. Two large straps circled the box, forming hinges on the far side and latches on the near. As soon as her eyes rested on the clasps, she knew she would open them.

She lifted the lid, expecting it to be heavy, but it rose easily and fell away as it swung back on its hinges. The body was Beranish, a young woman, resting on her stomach. There was no decay. It was almost as though she were sleeping, like so many coffined young women in the telltales and fourth stories.

It looked as though they had placed the girl face down, looking into the Stone Body. But the bolster supporting her head had shifted, and her head had turned so that now she faced Oria. She seemed about sixteen or seventeen and wore some sort of ceremonial hunting costume. Oria didn't recognise it, but it was sufficiently close to today's hunting attire for her to understand what it meant: the girl was hunting something in the afterlife. Or so her friends and relatives had thought. A reckless death then... Or a suicide. Oria's heart sank at the thought.

The girl had long black hair and the rock skin on the back of her hands and arms seemed larger than normal. It began as small ridges on the backs of her fingers and then rose like rough-cut stone on the backs of her hands, running all the way up her arms. The formations were dark but threaded with scarlet lines, bright as silk twisted into a skein of wool. Her eyes were almost closed, but not quite. Her hands made fists and in one, she clasped a leather pouch. Oria reached out and touched her cheek and suddenly there was nothing but darkness.

7

As the sun drifted lower, Mica moved cautiously. He held up his hand and the soft footfalls of his followers fell silent. The meadow looked empty, but dusk could be deceptive so he relied on his rock sense, feeling for danger. There was nothing, no hint of the emotional signature of people, nothing to warn them against proceeding, so he continued and the others followed. He felt for the men behind him, sorting through the tangle of emotion: adrenaline, hope, fear, excitement... and anger. He glanced back at Rush. The man would need to be watched. Mica hadn't wanted to bring him at all, but Rush's cousin had been indiscreet about the plan to snatch and hold the Oak Companion.

They moved through the wild flax without incident, but Mica still felt uneasy. As he had done repeatedly since devising the plan, he weighed this enterprise and knew it was wrong. While he didn't like the companion, his intention to use her to bargain with the Oak family in Komey was a violence against her person. It was abhorrent and he wouldn't pretend differently, especially not to himself. But he'd run out of options. He could live with the loss of his own freedom. Almost. But yesterday's death had proved that not everyone in the camp could survive the endless indenture.

Oria would die soon. From what he'd seen of her, it would be a matter of weeks, if not days, and the camp couldn't afford the consequences. The next companion, the infant Mother Oak, would inherit Oria's indenture rights. If Mica didn't act, the camp would have another eighteen years or more of despair as it waited for the new Mother Oak to grow up and make her own decisions. Even then, there were no guarantees. Mica's plan was wrong, but it was the lesser evil. He reminded himself that they wouldn't hurt Oria. They would wrest a promise from Oria's city sisters to lift the indenture and then return the old woman to her sisters. And Mica would accept responsibility. Imprisonment in Komey would complicate things with Fox, but he had little choice.

Ahead, the twist trees cast a dense shadow in the fading light. He shivered at the sight. Hard to believe that some Companionaris thought a sleep in their branches could cure as well as kill.

Behind him, sounds of the harvest song had ceased, but there was still plenty of time to secure the manor before the crowd broke apart and Oria headed home. They were lucky that Oria had confined the sisters to the manor. Mica and his men wouldn't have to contend with the sorority entering the house at the same time as Oria. By the time the rebels reached the kitchen, the sisters would be in their rooms, dressing for their supper. By the time the men had secured the ground floor, the sisters would be checking their reflections in the mirror. Then each man would take a door; each man would speak calmly and courteously; and each sister would be led down to the basement and locked inside for as short a period as possible. Easy.

Mica grimaced, knowing it was neither easy nor courteous. All the same, it had to be done.

A branch reached for Mica as he entered the grove of twist trees. He moved into the centre of the dark track and waved at his followers, motioning that they should do the same. There was no real danger, but anyone could make mistakes under pressure. He felt for his men's emotions again. They were quieter now, focused on the need to proceed carefully as they passed the waving branches. Good.

That was good. Still, it was a relief when they reached the manor's kitchen garden.

He sent an advance of four men into the kitchen and waited, counting off, allowing them time to subdue the skeleton staff that had remained behind to set the sisters' supper. At a signal from the advance party, Mica led the rest of the rebels into the kitchen. A single lamp and a fire lit the room, casting long shadows. Two of his men had hold of the cook and her assistant, covering their mouths. The other two were busy binding their feet. The cook had been looking after the sisters for over twenty-five years and her assistant had spent at least ten years in the companion's service. They were Berans all right, but Berans with divided allegiance, and Mica didn't want to take any risks that could endanger lives.

'Gag them,' he whispered. 'Tie them to that.' He pointed to one of the sturdy square posts that supported the kitchen's exposed roof beams. 'Make them secure: comfortable, but secure.'

The kitchen staff emanated waves of outrage and alarm. He felt it coursing under his rock skin. They'd give him plenty of grief once they were free again. Well, he hoped he'd be able to answer them with a better deal for the camp.

They moved on, checking the ground-floor rooms in a pre-arranged pattern. Mica stood in the foyer and, one by one, his men returned. No one spoke now, but each signalled their section of the house was clear. Mica looked up the staircase to the first floor, where the sisters were dressing in their rooms. All was quiet, but it was time to move.

They started up the sweeping staircase that led from the foyer to the sewing rooms, studies, and bedrooms. They moved with no sound at all; rock sensing where to place each foot with infinite precision. Mica opened his senses, feeling the mood of the timber structure of the staircase: the tensions and strains in the wood.

They reached the landing, and the men spread out and swept down the corridors like ghosts, heading for the doors to the sisters' rooms. Rush and a rebel named Cast waited beside Mica. He was keeping them close. Cast was young and Rush was a stranger and Mica wasn't taking any chances.

He'd planned for the sisters' bedrooms to be breached as he and Cast and Rush secured Oria's study and its adjoining sitting room and sewing room. Those rooms would be empty, but it was sensible to be careful.

Progressively, his men reached their designated doors and turned, waiting for his signal. He raised his arm, watching the last two men falling into place. Then, before he could set everyone in motion, a sister opened her door and caught sight of the rebels and screamed.

Mica flung down his arm, and everyone whirled into action.

Cast opened the study door in front of Mica and stepped inside, with Rush right behind him. Mica hesitated for a second or two. He glanced in both directions, checking that his men were managing. Then he heard a thud and a grunt from the room in front of him and he turned, hurrying into the study.

It was Cast. He lay on top of a struggling sister. He had a hand over her mouth, smothering her cries. Rush stood a few steps beyond. He wasn't paying any attention to the commotion on the floor. Instead, he stood before the closed door to the Oak Companion's sitting room, his hand raised in warning. Mica moved further into the room, his arms registering what Rush was rock sensing. There was someone in the room beyond, a woman, a sister. Mica recognised her signature. It was Bronda. If Bronda was in the manor, could Oria be here, too? Surely not. But it was possible. They had come in the back door and Bronda would have come in the front. With or without her mistress? Oria leaving the feast would be a break in tradition that made little sense. He stretched his senses, his arms feeling for the companion's signature, but she wasn't in the house. Good. They would have time to subdue Bronda.

From the corner of his eye, Mica saw Cast shift his position. The young Beran looked at Mica beseechingly, hoping for some instruction about what to do next. The woman beneath him must have sensed his drifting attention because she renewed her struggle.

'Is that you, Cecily?' Bronda called out from the next room, her voice muffled by the closed door. 'Have you fallen? I'm coming.' Then the door in front of them opened and lamplight filled the doorway.

Bronda gasped, dropped the lamp, turned and fled.

'Grab her!' Mica yelled at Rush. 'Hold her.'

Rush leapt after Bronda. In his wake, the rug under the broken lamp caught fire. It began with a quick low flame but leapt as the fuel accelerated everything. The speed of the flames was a greater threat to Mica's plans than the debacle with Bronda and Cecily. Mica ran past Cast and his captive and grabbed the rug, rolling it up and smothering the flames. The rooms filled with acrid smoke and the stink of lamp fuel. Behind Mica, Cast struggled to keep Cecily still. There was a sickening crack of breaking bone. Mica turned to see Cast rising off an unmoving form. Cast took a step back, staggered.

'It was an accident,' his voice was ragged. 'An accident.'

Mica stared. Then he heard a connecting door slam and then another and then running footsteps in the hall and on the landing. He raced back to the open study doorway and saw Bronda, panicked and running, with Rush in pursuit.

Bronda reached the head of the stairs, Rush a pace behind her. The man reached out and caught her, grabbing her long grey plait before she could take the first step.

Mica felt relief. Oria would be home any minute now, but they should still have time to secure the sisters in the basement and the capture of the Oak Companion would be calm and careful. He watched Rush, expecting the other man to cover Bronda's mouth with his hand before she could scream again. It never happened. Instead, she slumped to the floor with a knife in her side.

For a moment, everything seemed to pause, then Mica flew across the landing and took Rush by the throat. 'What have you done?' he hissed. 'I told you no violence! She was the companion's favourite. This waste of life does nothing but shame us.'

'Better dead and silent.' Rush's voice rasped under the pressure of Mica's hand on his throat, 'than causing us trouble.'

'We're not here to murder.' Mica leant forward, breathing into Rush's face. 'Get out of here. Wait outside in the kitchen garden. Better still. Wait in the greenhouse and *stay out of the way*. I don't want you in the house. I don't want Oria to lay eyes on you. Do it or so help me, I'll kill you.'

Mica released the other man and took a step back, keeping his eyes locked on Rush's. His rock skin pulsed with Rush's bitterness and resentment, and he let his own anger answer, arm to arm. The other man wavered and then backed down.

Rush turned away. He walked down the stairs and disappeared from sight.

Mica looked at poor Bronda's body and felt a wave of shame and horror at how badly things had turned out. The only violence he had intended was locking up the sorority for a few days and taking the companion into his custody. Not killing; never killing.

Mica couldn't afford to let his feelings rule his actions. Oria would return at any moment and she mustn't return to this: two dead bodies and a floor full of panicked sisters and edgy rebels. It wasn't just that he wanted to protect the companion from some sort of collapse at the sight of the disaster; he needed to ensure nothing else went wrong. That meant getting the plan back on track as best he could.

He put Rush from his mind and scanned the surrounding rooms. The situation was holding, just. The other rebels had felt the drama, but they were still in place. Anxious, fearful, deeply uneasy, but still following orders. The women they were guarding were oblivious to the deaths, but fearful enough. And furious. Like cats in a bag. Oria's sisters might be old, but their anger and outrage prickled Mica's arms, and their complaints were audible through the closed doors. He wished his rock skin was telepathic, that he could update his men with a thought. Instead, he had to go door to door, whispering amended instructions. They must wait. Keep the old women calm. Mica would be back.

Then he fetched Cast. The young man was silent and his hands trembled, but he followed Mica's directions and together they carried Bronda downstairs. They took her into the dining room and laid her on the long oak table. By the time they returned for Cecily's body, Cast was crying.

'We shouldn't have come,' he said. 'We should never have started this.'

'You're right,' Mica said. 'But we're here. The only choice we have now is to walk away or keep going, do our best to make sure nothing else goes wrong and no one else gets hurt.'

Cast stared at Cecily's body. 'I don't think I can. I don't...'

Mica put his hand on the young man's shoulder. 'I won't make you, but you need to help me carry Cecily downstairs to lie beside Bronda.'

Downstairs, they found tablecloths and covered the bodies. It didn't help, but leaving them exposed felt just as wrong. When they returned to the foyer, Cast moved to leave, to walk out the front door. Mica caught hold of the young man's arm, pulled him back. 'Not that way. Go out the back door. Go to your tent. Keep away from the festival. Don't talk to anyone. I need your word.'

'I promise, but I can't walk through the kitchen. The Berans. The cook and the other one. They'll see me.'

'They've already seen you.'

'But they'll be able to tell. They'll feel my shame.'

'We don't have time for this.' Mica glanced at the front door and then back at Cast. 'Oria will be back at any minute. Go, go! You need to go!' He gave Cast a push. 'Go. Leave through the kitchen.'

Cast took a small step in the right direction and then looked back at Mica. 'I wish I was dead. I wish I'd died.'

'You need to go.' When Cast failed to move, Mica grabbed his arm and began dragging him toward the kitchen, his voice low and angry, 'Is this what you want? Me, coming with you endangering everyone because you can't walk through a kitchen?' Mica felt sick at his own words but couldn't seem to stop himself, and he was at the kitchen door before he realised something was wrong. Absence is harder to rock sense, to take hold of, but he felt the emptiness of the kitchen before its meaning struck him. Even then, he didn't get it right. He imagined the cook and her assistant had escaped. Then he caught sight of them where they'd left them, still tied to one of the posts. They were dead. Even then, Mica misunderstood. He imagined they'd choked on their gags or that someone had tied them too tight. But it wasn't that.

When Mica caught up the lamp and carried it closer, it was the same story. Just like Bronda. Knifed. Rush had murdered them, stabbed them on his way out the door. Used a different kitchen knife for each of them. Two more people had died because of Mica, and this time it was two of their own.

8

The first thing Oria noticed was the sharpness in the surrounding sounds. Louder and brighter, so that it felt as though everything was close to hand. She heard a gust of wind and with it, a door swinging open. She was alive, then. Oria opened her eyes. The fall hadn't killed her. At least she assumed she'd fallen because she'd blacked out after opening the coffin. But she was alive. Alive! She knew she should be frightened about being on her own after a fall. At her age, broken bones spelt death, but the opposite feeling gripped her: that she'd escaped death. There was a physical warmth to it. And an oddness that Oria couldn't put her finger on.

The compacted earth floor was hard against her back. She wondered how much time had elapsed since she got the men to carry the coffin into the greenhouse. Pale light from a risen moon slanted through the glass panels. In the surrounding darkness, the plants cast inky fingered shadows.

By the Back, she'd been a fool to dismiss Bronda and now she was paying for it: alone and injured; help out of reach. What vanity to set out on her own at her age.

She looked around. Everything in the greenhouse had an edge, a crisp definition. And she was uncomfortable. The sleeves of her dress felt like tourniquets, and there was a similar feeling of constriction across her chest.

A footfall sounded beyond the bench near the door; then another.

'A hand here,' she called out. Her voice sounded odd.

The steps halted, but the person didn't speak.

'I think I'm hurt.' The strangeness of her voice confused her and it was a moment before she realised that whoever had entered was hesitating. She took a deep breath, and she felt some of her self-control returning. She rolled onto her side. There was no pain, but she moved slowly. Her head seemed clear of the rushing sensation that had plagued her all day and her stomach no longer burned. She put her hands to the floor and pushed herself upright. She must have pushed too hard because she shot upright, hit her head on the corner of the workbench. Oria reached up and felt blood on her scalp.

'I say... I need help here!' she called out.

There was no response, no footsteps, but she thought she could hear breathing.

'It's no use pretending you're not there,' Oria snapped, diplomacy deserting her as her habitual irritation returned. 'What's wrong with you? I don't care who you are or whether you're supposed to be here. Stop acting the coward. Get yourself out from behind that bench and bring a light— if you can find one.'

A man burst out of the shadow as though something in her words had released a fury within him. He didn't speak, just marched over to where she sat until he was standing over her, a look of hatred on his face. Oria didn't recognise him, but it was dark and there were so many young men in the camp these days. Impossible to know everyone. She framed her words, working out the best way to deal with the disturbed man.

Then he kicked her. Slammed his foot into her shoulder.

She fell back with a scream and tried to roll away. He threw himself on top of her. She screamed again, and he hit her.

'Think you can speak to me like that?' he said, his voice ragged. 'Scum. Traitorous scum.'

Oria had been called many things in her life, but traitor wasn't one of them. She forced herself to remain quiet, ignoring the fiery pain in her shoulder and arm. If she was younger, she might have struggled, but in her feeble state that wasn't an option.

He leant closer. 'That's shut you up, hasn't it? Do you know who I am?' he whispered, his breath hot against her skin.

She held still, but she knew that the danger he presented was mortal, that she would need to think of something.

'Rush Applauded,' the name slipped from his lips as a hiss. 'My grandfather was the keeper in Bass. They applauded at my birth. I got my second name the instant my people saw me. Then my province failed and now I'm here!' He shoved her hard against the floor. Pain reverberated through her left shoulder where he'd kicked her. 'And because I'm here,' he shoved her for a second time and she bit her lip to stop herself crying out, certain he must have broken several of her ancient brittle bones, 'this is as much my province as yours. No,' he seemed to reach for another, bigger thought, 'it's not yours at all. You don't deserve it. You're just some scum Beranish girl who's been selling herself to the enemy.'

Oria felt her horror growing. Then he put a hand over her mouth and pressed down hard, pushing her lips against her teeth. She tasted blood. She'd never survive this. She'd die here on the dirt floor.

'Look at you in that Companionari dress. It doesn't even fit you. They probably gave it to you and you thanked them for it.' A look of disgust passed over his face and he spat, a glob of saliva hitting her forehead. She tried to push him off, using her uninjured arm. She reached up and pushed her hand against his chest. Only it wasn't her hand. And it wasn't her arm either. Rock skin. Rock skin on a youthful arm.

The man took her face in his hands, smiled and hissed. She knew that if she didn't do something; he was going to rape her and kill her too. He let go for a moment, confident of his supremacy, and fumbled with his pants. She turned her head to her right. Beside her on the ground lay gardening tools: a hand shovel, a ball of twine, a rusted knife. She reached out and grabbed the knife. The handle was rough and pitted beneath her fingers. She thrust it into him and he slumped forward, pinning her to the ground.

Somehow, she thought he would come to life again and resume his assault. It seemed impossible that she'd killed a grown man. He should have been the killer; her, the victim.

It wasn't easy to extract herself. He was heavy, and she was in pain from where he'd kicked her. She persisted until she was free, crawling away, pulling herself upright with the aid of the leg of the potting bench. She staggered over to her attacker and felt for his pulse. Dead, thank the Back. She stood and then caught sight of the open coffin. The young Beranish woman was gone. Instead, her own body, an old woman's body, lay there. Empty of life. Her, but not her. Her corpse wore the beautiful hunting costume of the dead Beran. Too big and fine for those poor shrunken limbs.

Outside, the wind rustled in the trees, branches scraped against the panes of glass as though they wanted to reach inside. Oria felt as though she was living in a fourth story or a dream, only this was real.

She looked down and caught sight of her bloodied, tattered tunic and revulsion stirred her. She struggled out of it, ignoring the pain in her damaged shoulder. She stuffed the thing into a compost bin and then returned to the coffin. With some difficulty, she undressed her old body, salvaging the Beranish woman's hunting costume. Dressing herself was painful and she couldn't do up the leggings, but it felt better. She felt better. She slung the girl's belted leather pouch over her good shoulder and wondered what to do next. The pain was making it hard to think.

She wanted to go home but her household would see her as a stranger, some deranged Beranish girl. And if anyone found the body in the coffin, they'd think her a murderer. She needed time to work out what to do, but the pain was making her faint. She almost dropped within, used her meditative practice to ease the pain, but something held her back. What if this body was fundamentally different? What if she caused further damage? She needed somewhere safe to rest.

With a dangerous idea half formed in her mind, she took a last look at her old body in the coffin. She cried. No sound, just tears trickling down her face at the sight of her discarded form. Stupid grief, she chided herself. Self-indulgent. Worse: self-pitying. She was alive and should be rejoicing. She had to pull herself together, survive.

In an act of farewell, she laid a hessian sack over her ancient form and stroked her greying hair.

Outside of the greenhouse, she crept down the path toward the kitchen garden, doing her best to ignore the popping sound of oaks and corks germinating around her, without her willing them into existence. It was both reassuring and alarming to know this body had somehow kept a grip on her companionship. More than that, had intensified it because she was struggling to stop the acorns germinating around her. All the more reason to get to the twist tree grove where no corks or oaks could grow.

She hurried, passed the walled herb beds, and then ran. The moon was high; the summer night was bright. She reached the grove, steadied herself. Then, with a deep breath, she picked a tree.

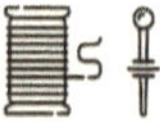

Oria awoke in a low-growing twist tree, the dawn sky wide above her, leafless branches hanging over her face. She turned her head to a horizon streaked a pale pinkish blue. Below her she could just make out the ground: a hand's span away. She felt good...

Good? She frowned. Then, in a rush, the shock of the events of

Harvest Night came back. The tree stiffened against her, the tips of the branches creeping across her body, searching for a better grip. She struggled to free herself and it intervened, dampening down her responses. It had seemed worth the risk last night. She'd needed a respite, and she'd remembered that the trees could be curative before they killed... She'd planned to take the cure for an hour and then leave. But she'd fallen asleep! How stupid! She just hoped the tree had done no permanent damage. Hopefully, it had only begun forging the link with her body. She tried to remember how long it took before the trees consumed their prey, but couldn't. It had something to do with the temperature.

She relaxed, loosened her muscles, and lay against the looped branches. Slowly, she shifted her head until she could see her left arm. Swollen, but nothing could hide the rock skin. So it *was* true. She was transformed.

She couldn't see the manor from where she lay, but it was odd that there were no sounds from its kitchen. It was dawn, but the silence felt wrong. Once again, the tree intervened, soothing her. Calm again, almost too calm. Time drifted by. Sometime later, when the dawn had turned to morning, she realised she'd done nothing, hadn't even tested the tree's embrace. How deceptive it was; how subtle.

Companionari telltales arose in her mind. Heads speaking from twist trees, asking their relatives for help, oblivious to their missing bodies. She would be different. She knew more about the province and its trees than anyone on the Stone Body so she would think of something. Oria had been given a second life. She wasn't about to lose it to a tree.

She closed her eyes and recalled all those childhood hours, sitting at the table in the companion's study, memorising the manor's agricultural texts. Oria hadn't needed to know the texts by heart, but rote learning was an exquisite Companionari task: slow and laborious. In her mind, she reached for the encyclopedia of flora, carried it to her desk. She remembered the feel of the wooden chair beneath her, the smell of her clothes mixed with the dusty scent of the book. Oria recalled the pages under her fingers. She remembered the listings for noxious flora, visualised leafing through the book. And there it was.

Twist tree, orig. *funeral tree*. Developed late Kareen period prior to settlement. Thought to have been among Dabid Harwood's botanic collection on arrival. Bioactive alternative to interment: tree's reproductive cycle dependent upon animal protein. Contemporary species, capable of utilizing live prey, emerged post-crossing. Propagation requires Department of Health permission. Emergency response to capture: mechanical assault to root system. Unaided escape: deep relaxation and careful movements. Medical responses to partial digestion: amputation.

And then there had been that addendum in ink, written by an ancestor, the advice that had driven her here last night:

I rescued a lass today. She'd been hobbling about on crutches after a fall from a horse. She must have tripped when navigating the grove. Got her out of the tree all right. It seems to have fixed her leg. Must want its live prey in good shape! Have written same to both Dept. Ag. and Dept. Hth. (Olivia Oak, June 523)

Above Oria's face, a twig probed the air, and she forced herself to ignore it. So... Project contentment and the tree might let her flee. She thought about it.

For ninety-four years, she'd had the sole responsibility for the province. She would use what she knew: calm certainty; authority; control.

There was a gap in the boughs beneath her bottom and another, larger gap in front of her. Up or down? Up, and she'd need to use her arms, and she didn't know whether the tree had cured her shoulder. Down then.

Oria closed her eyes and projected the rightness of her leave-taking. She drew up her knees. The tree responded with a wave of comfort and companionship that carried the illusion of love. She ignored it and intensified the rightness of leave-taking. This time, when she moved, she spoke.

'This is best for both of us. I'm the Oak Companion. Killing me would only bring awful retribution. I'll bring you a substitute. Not immediately, but as soon as I can. From now on, when anyone dies in the manor, the body will be yours.' She clasped her right leg and slipped her foot free, dropped her leg down, felt solid ground. She shifted her attention to her other leg, clasped it and got her foot free, and felt the tree's unease as sleepiness. It tightened its boughs; its twigs rattled.

'No,' she spoke firmly. 'I can't sleep. I must leave, but I'll also talk to cook and make sure she remembers to give you what we've finished with.' The boughs ceased their creeping movement, the twigs stilled.

The bottom half of her body was free, and she was kneeling on the ground, but her torso was still trapped. She began wriggling her way out. The movement brought a slight reaction from her captor, but she continued speaking, continued projecting her certainty until she was free.

The pain in her arm returned, but it wasn't the agony of the night before. Oria suspected broken bones had mended. She crawled away and stood up when she was clear of the branches. She was near the creek, so she continued toward it. There would be balm moss on its banks, a safe way to dull the pain.

Oria sat near the water, chewing. She kept chewing until the pain eased. Then she rested and contemplated her situation: twice she'd escaped death. A wanderer would tell her there was always a reason, a task that needed completing. Perhaps there was, if she could avoid being arrested for murder.

When she'd recovered a little of her strength, she eased the hunting cloak from her shoulders and spread it on the ground. Oria longed to explore this new body. She needed to examine the state of her arm and shoulder, but she felt vulnerable here, so close to the manor.

She would make a sling with the cloak, but first she wanted to see what was in Promise's belted pouch. Undoing the pouch was difficult with only one hand, but she did it. The first thing she found was a stone. A rock child. Presumably. Oria spoke a traditional welcome in a low whisper. She had never been certain the call of a rock child wasn't a phenomenon of faith, but she had always enjoyed the company of wanderers and spoke as much out of respect for the past as hope for the future.

Next, she found a folding knife, a simple tool with an oak handle, displaying none of the pearl or silver inlay that the Berans favoured. Instead, someone had burnt the rough outline of a dragon into the polished wood. She touched it with delight and brought it up to her nose, looking for some scent from the past. The aroma had disappeared, but the timber was silky to her touch. Likely, the knife was Promise's own work. Someone had loved her enough to include it with her grave goods.

She sat back on her heels for a moment and a wave of dizziness hit her. She picked a pinch of balm and chewed it until her head cleared a little.

The last two items included an oiled cloth parcel that contained seeds and a small piece of canvas covered in writing. The language looked like a dialect of Old Treaty. She could make out a few words. It read like a religious text or a fourth tale... She'd show it to the head librarian if she ever got back to Komey. Oria smiled, thinking about how much the library would relish the find. It almost made her feel guilty about holding the piece of canvas without wearing gloves.

She returned everything to its place in the pouch, except the knife. With some difficulty, she refastened the belt and then slipped the knife into her pocket. Using her good arm, she folded the cloak into a sling and lined it with balm. Then she used both hands to tie the corners of the cloak. The effort awoke the pain, and it was a relief when she eased her arm into the support. She plucked another handful of balm and chewed it as she began walking. She knew where she would go. The sand crater. It was about half an hour's walk if she skirted the camp. More often than not, there were children playing there. She would send one of them with a message. What she would say and who she would send it to were questions she'd yet to answer.

Oria felt better once she was moving. The pain in her shoulder was difficult, but the feeling of youth and vigour... well, it was enough to have her smiling despite her predicament. She headed for the point where the grove of twist trees met the oak forest. The trees would keep her hidden from the camp and the manor. Their sound reached her before she caught sight of them. Wood creaking, leaves rustling. Her trees, her oaks. She could feel their urge to surround her, like an itch beneath her skin.

The border between the last of the twist trees and the first oak was alive. Her trees leant into the twist tree grove like reeds under a gale, saplings erupting around them. She wasn't ready to try entering this new body, but that didn't mean she had no control at all. She slowed her breathing, steadied her emotions and the trees responded, righting themselves.

The forest fell silent and she walked on.

A little later, the ground dipped down, and she reached out a hand to steady herself, taking hold of the trunk of a young white oak. The touch jolted her hand in a way she'd never felt before: a sharp vibration against her palm, like the buzzing of bees. The ground hummed, trunks knocked and popped, leaves rattled. It only took her a moment to gain control, but in that moment, the forest had not only seen new life; it had thickened. She had never had the power to work on that scale. Her efforts had been piecemeal, lines and circles of trees, not entire forests.

When she left the shelter of the oaks for the rocky plain that surrounded the crater, she felt the forest longing to cling to her. If nothing else, Oak province would be safe now, assuming she survived. And that meant avoiding the soldiersisters Komey would send to find the companion's killer. She wouldn't be able to explain anything if she was full of arrows or locked in a cell, guarded by ignorant, brutish sisters.

The sand crater sank into the rock plain. Over time, its walls had weathered, producing cave-like overhangs that were perfect for children's games. Fresh water welled in the lowest point, surrounded by pale white sand. In summer, the children pretended it was the edge of the ocean. In winter, they built fires and cooked arnuts and chestnuts.

She was a few paces from the edge when she heard someone within. She peered over the lip and saw Mica's nephew. He was busy digging into the seepage with a vegetable knife. He paused, looked up and caught sight of her, then looked away again.

She spoke without thinking. 'Cook will miss that knife.' She eased herself into a sitting position and dangled her legs over the crater's lip. She couldn't remember the boy's name, but there was no forgetting the rest of him. He was wilful and disobedient. He'd stolen her horse. And this was the child she'd need to work with?

He glanced up at her again, licked his lips. 'Will you be telling her then, Huntress? Telling Cook?'

Oria paused, confused, and then remembered her clothing. A Beran dressed as a hunter was unusual, was notable. The boy wouldn't be able to resist telling everyone. 'I'm no huntress. I'm... I'm Promise.'

The boy stood up. 'I'm Doubt.' Then his eyes narrowed as he noticed her arm in its sling. 'How did you get hurt? Are you a refugee? I know lots of refugees. Where are you from? What are you doing here?'

She eased herself off the ledge and walked across the sand. She reminded herself that she too had once been that young, reminded herself of all the questions she'd peppered the sorority with. Perhaps Doubt's questions hinted at a chivalrous disposition. She recalled that he'd stolen the horse to embark on an adventure. A romantic, then. A boy with heart.

'The thing is, I need help,' she said.

There was something in his reaction to her words that told her she'd hit the right note. The boy wanted his life to matter. Of course he did. As did she. They shared that. And the boy's help *would* matter: it might save the province. She lowered her voice, 'I need someone clever, someone who knows their way around the manor. I have an important message for the companion's handmaid. Bronda. Do you know her?'

'A task?' His face lit up.

'Yes,' Oria nodded. 'A task, and it's a secret. I can't go myself because... I'm injured and I need to rest here. For a bit.'

He nodded, then looked down, scuffed his feet. 'I didn't steal the knife. I wouldn't keep it. Just borrowed it.'

'Of course. But you should have asked.'

They sat on the sand and she had him memorise a brief message, asking Bronda to meet her after sunset at the train station beyond the manor. She had scarcely finished speaking, but he was already moving, bursting with the importance of the task.

She caught his hand to slow him down and had him repeat the message. Then he scampered away, crossing the sand in a quick run, clambered up the slate wall and then paused.

'What if I can't find her? What if she's not there? She might be out walking or maybe she's gone to Komey.'

'Then you must speak to the Lady of Chambers.'

He repeated the title under his breath and then looked up. 'But Huntress, I don't know that sister. Is she old? How will I know her? I guess she would be old. What if I can't find her?'

'Just ask for her. Someone will find her for you.'

'What if they can't? What if they don't listen to me or she won't speak to me?'

Oria couldn't stop her irritation from showing. 'Obviously, you'll come back here.' She took a deep breath, reminded herself to be patient and kind, reminded herself of what it was like to be a child. 'Just make sure you don't tell anyone that I'm here. And after you deliver the message, come back. I need to know when it's done.'

He nodded and then disappeared.

Alone again, she bent and cupped a few handfuls of water, then washed her face and hands. She would have to go to Komey once she'd sorted out her household, never mind the danger. It was only in Komey that she'd be able to get the support of the broader Oak family to have this body recognised as the Oak Companion.

A breeze had picked up, warm with the promise of a hot summer's day. She looked around the crater for a secluded and comfortable position from which she could examine her condition and wait for the boy's return. The crater wasn't an exact circle. There was an indentation on one side. She went over to investigate and found it led to an alcove. She soon discovered this was the children's larder. The walls' slate layers protruded at odd heights, creating shelves that held pilfered items: a cache of Cook's tools; the rotten remains of some fruit; a pile of arnuts; and three stale travel biscuits. She ate a biscuit and then slipped the two others and the arnuts into her spare pocket.

She found a patch of smooth sand and sat, closed her eyes, and used her years of discipline to clear her mind. This was as good a time as any to investigate her new body. There was no sound in the alcove; there was no breeze. She let go of all thought and let Promise's body dominate, allowed herself to know the truth that she was always within, had always been within, would always be within. She was nothing more than the sum of her interior. Oria eased herself into the syncopated breathing that drummed out the world and helped her relinquish the illusion that she was outside: allowed her to let go of the effort of projection. And then she *was* within.

She found her pulse and rode it deep into Promise's body. At first, the novelty of her new form and the heat given off by her injuries overwhelmed her. She didn't fight any of the sensations. Fighting would only lift her back into her mind. She let the complexity swamp her, and for a while all she could sense was a tumble of youth, vitality and difference. But as she moved deeper into the body, the complexity dissipated. Beneath was the dark privacy of Promise. She examined her injuries and did her best to help them. She couldn't make everything right, but she encouraged the restoration that was already happening. Then she looked at Promise's rock skin. As she'd always expected, it was like bone, but unlike bone, it wouldn't admit her. Strange, but a puzzle for another day.

As she withdrew from Promise's body, she paused. There was something else that felt odd. Thinking that she'd missed some other Beranish difference, she dove deeper. But it was simpler than that. Promise was pregnant.

ikin leant down and ran his hand over the long orange grass that brushed the calves of his riding boots. The perfume wasn't really like a freshly cut orange; it was more intense than that, closer to key fruit. The scent was invigorating. He straightened up and felt a surge of excitement about his plans and, along with it, a compulsion to dismount and run through the grass. He chuckled, recognising the pull of grass fever. It wasn't hard to resist, not for someone whose intentions were firm. He sat solid astride his horse, closed his eyes for a moment, cleared his head.

Aikin expected Fox would find it a challenge to manage in the grass but didn't bother to look back and check on her. He'd hear her if she leapt off her horse. She hadn't been outside the city before. Well, not since he'd adopted her, but she'd had the benefit of his parenting, the example of his strength of purpose so he knew she'd be fine. Had to be fine. She'd pushed her way into this expedition. She'd embarrassed him into taking her on a field trip when he'd failed to free Wren from her medicated state. Demanded a revised birthday boon, a selfish one. She'd asked him in front of several senior Oak sisters, shamed him into agreeing. If she failed in the grass so be it. Aikin would just get Birch to tie his daughter to her horse and they'd keep going until they were clear of the grass.

And he'd determined a way to take advantage of her presence. Fox was going to be his witness. She, a Beranish-born woman, would talk of him in glowing terms as a defender of wanderers. And it would be the truth, which was the exquisite, elegant beauty of his plan. He had allowed for real danger, had opened the door to a kinetic rush.

Sergeant Glover brought her horse up beside Aikin's, scanning the valley, searching for some sign of the wanderer they'd ridden out to meet. 'I can't see him.'

Glover was Birch's idea. Another innocent to round out their party.

Birch drew even with them, frowning. 'Probably nervous about stepping into the grass. He'll be camped in the banewood, keeping his distance from our valleys if he knows what's good for him.'

'The banewood's almost as bad,' Glover said.

'But it doesn't drive a man mad,' Birch said. 'Any wanderer worth his title knows how to traverse a banewood forest without getting stung by its trees.'

Aikin slowed his horse to a standstill and lifted his glasses, searching for any sign of life. He lowered them a second later, as Fox's horse bumped into him. He turned to look at his daughter.

She was staring at the ground. The breeze fingered the strands of hair that had escaped her braids. For a moment she said nothing, then spoke in a rush, 'It's such a wonderful day. Why don't we take out the baskets and make our tea here? This place is perfect. Look at the grass!' Her last few words rang out like a command and then she fell silent, staring down.

Aikin did his best to tuck away his disappointment. It was a blow to see her succumb. 'It's the orange grass, Fox,' he spoke curtly. 'The grass is beguiling you. Keep your purpose in mind if you don't want to spend the rest of your life wallowing beneath the stalks.' He nudged his horse with his heels and the party moved forward again.

Fox's hands gripped her reins, but she didn't guide her horse. He moved of his own accord, beside Aikin's mount. Glover and Birch fell back, likely preparing themselves to jump to Fox's aid if she made any move to dismount. Fox gazed at the movement of the breeze on the heads of grain.

Aikin tapped her on the arm. 'Why don't you see if you can spot the wanderer.'

She felt for her glasses and blindly brought them up to her face without lifting her gaze from the ground. She examined the grass at her horse's feet.

'Lift your head up, Mistress,' Captain Birch said. 'You won't find him in the stalks.'

Fox dragged the glasses away from the grass until she was looking out at the horizon. As her gaze shifted, she sat up in the saddle and Aikin was pleased to see her normal expression had returned.

'Do you see anything?' he asked.

'Actually, I think I do.'

The party reined in their horses and lifted their glasses, following Fox's gaze. It was true. A man was cutting a diagonal path through the valley toward the ridge of banewood. He was short so the tall grass almost hid him, and he was unaffected by it. Aikin suspected the display was for their benefit. The man was showing off.

Birch was the first to speak, 'A wanderer with a strong purpose.'

'Let's join him. Let's walk the grass,' Fox said with an intensity that sounded fanatical.

'Keep your eyes up,' Aikin snapped.

She frowned but continued looking down.

'Up!' Aikin said.

She lifted her gaze, dragged her head up, and once again she was sitting higher in her saddle.

Aikin waved Birch forward, waited a few paces and then followed with Fox at his side. The sergeant brought up the rear, and they made their way to the wanderer. They were silent as they crossed the expanse. The only noise was the sound of the horses worrying their bits and snorting at the clouds of midges that swarmed through the grass, like puffs of black smoke.

When they had come within hearing distance, Birch called out a greeting. The wanderer paused and then responded with a wave.

Aikin watched as Fox craned her neck to catch her first glimpse of the man they'd been seeking. This was a significant moment for her: her first meeting with another Beran. You couldn't count Wren. The thought of that disastrous adoptee was unwelcome. Fox's sentimental attitude towards the woman had caused problems and Aikin wondered whether there was some way to separate the two now that Wren's baby was born and fostered. Wren had failed to conceive with Louis and the parley had decided there was little point in searching for another man, given her age. It meant there was no need for Wren to be kept at Oak house. Could he suggest retirement in the Mint Gazette? Could he pay some Companionari family to board her? He would write to Oria. The Oak Companion was ruthless when she needed to be. She wouldn't want Aikin to tolerate Fox's foolishness.

'It looks as though the wanderer is alone,' Fox said.

'It isn't surprising,' Glover said. 'They usually are.'

'Course,' Fox said, 'but I thought he might be with some refugees. From a failed province.'

'We would have heard,' Aikin said.

'I wonder whether he'll ask for our stories.'

'He might. He might ask for yours.' Aikin remembered his own excitement when he'd met a wanderer for the first time. Aikin had been nineteen years old, chaperoned by a senior sister on a visit to the province. The wanderer had been Quartz. Younger then, but already a respected storyteller. He'd asked Aikin for the story of his life. And Aikin had given it, short as it was. In return, Quartz invited Aikin to ask for some knowledge. He'd been studying Beranish keepers and the rules of succession so he'd asked about that.

The knowledge Quartz had passed onto him had been very long

and detailed and Quartz offered it in the traditional cycle format. Quartz had told Aikin about Virtue Remains, how various secret signs had appeared around the newborn Virtue's tent, which led to his ascension as the keeper in Oak. The contrary story had been all about the unorthodox succession practices in Kelp province. The fourth story had been a Companionari telltale, one Aikin had never heard before. It was about a woman creating havoc by rushing into things with good intentions. Somehow the fourth story had lingered in Aikin's mind. It was the beginning of Aikin's genuine respect for Beranish traditions. The story found its way into his life over the next few months, giving him flashes of insight into his own circumstances.

Aikin looked at the man in front of them. Now that they were close, Aikin could see that this wanderer was a stranger. A young man. He wore a cloak woven with patterns of curls that swept across his shoulders. Aikin hoped he wouldn't need to use force to get what he wanted. He glanced at Fox. She looked disappointed at the sight of the Beran, almost as though the wanderer wasn't who she'd expected him to be. Aikin wondered if she'd been hoping to come across someone she knew from her childhood. Better she didn't. That sort of thing unsettled adopted talents.

Birch dismounted when they were close enough, but she signalled to the others to remain on their horses. The wanderer smiled and then turned, executing a complete circle, holding out his right arm with his hand palm down, then turning it up again, welcoming them to the Stone Body.

'So we've found you, Wanderer,' Birch said when the man had completed the ritual. 'We left Komey hoping to speak with you but we didn't expect to find you here.'

The man looked puzzled. Then his brow cleared. 'Ah... your grass. Yes, I'm sorry. I know you don't encourage people to walk in it, but I like the scent. I hope you don't mind.'

Aikin noticed the strength in his voice: a timely reminder that the day's outcome was not predictable. There was always room for the unexpected. It was even possible that he could persuade the wanderer to part with his rocks.

Birch spoke again, 'This is Master Aikin Oak, Head of the Department of Beranish Affairs and his daughter Fox Oak. I am Captain Birch and that's Sergeant Glover.'

The wanderer focused on Aikin. 'Ah.' He nodded. 'A fellow collector of knowledge. I've heard about your department's library. Welcome Aikin. I am Malachite of Aries.'

Aikin moved his horse a few paces forward, glad that the formalities were over and delighted to be doing what he most enjoyed, speaking with Berans, 'I am pleased we have found you, Malachite. I am a fellow collector of knowledge. And I don't get out of Komey very often, but when I heard the patrols had seen a wanderer heading towards Orange Valley, I found an excuse to get away from my paperwork. If it would not take you too far from your path, if the stones would allow it, could we spend a little time together out of the grasslands? My daughter,' Aikin gestured to Fox, 'has a touch of grass fever and I don't want to tempt fate.'

'Of course.' Malachite agreed. 'I was heading for the trees, anyway. Let's travel together.'

They found a clearing within the banewood. Aikin, Fox and Malachite settled in for a lengthy conversation while the soldiers saw to tethering the horses, setting a fire, and boiling some water. After they were all seated, Aikin lifted a pouch on a leather thong from around his neck and opened it up, handing it to Malachite.

'What's this?' the wanderer asked, sniffing the contents. His cloak fell away as he lifted the pouch up to his nose. The rock formations on his arms were large and milky coloured, flecked with an intense coppery green. 'It looks like tea, but it smells like orange grass?' He sniffed it again to be sure. 'But surely it's not drinkable?'

Aikin laughed. He held out his hand for the pouch and then handed it to Fox.

'It does smell like orange grass!' she said.

'There's still a little work going on in plant breeding,' Aikin said.

'This is just cosmetic. It's black tea with the aroma of key fruit. I think it tastes better than the original, but I'm told that it's an expectation illusion.'

Aikin handed the tea to the sergeant who prepared the drink, before pouring it out into three palm cups decorated with oak motifs.

Malachite picked up his cup and examined it, noting the decorations. 'I see your name isn't a tribute. You're part of the Oak clan.' He took a sip.

'It's a big family,' Aikin said. 'There are hundreds of us. But yes, the Oak Companion and I are cousins. Sadly, no talent.' Aikin thumped his chest. 'Hence, the bureaucracy.'

'And Mistress Fox?' Malachite looked up, his golden eyes catching the sunlight, creating an even brighter shade of gold. 'What camp did you come from originally?'

Fox looked startled at being asked about her origins. It was something that a Companionari man would never have asked her. She answered correctly and Aikin felt an odd sensation of fatherly pride listening to her tell the wanderer that she was a daughter in the Oak family, that she had no other people.

Malachite looked down again, shifting his palm cup in his hand. A diplomat then: a man who could hold off insisting on knowing Fox's true origins or challenging her assertions. The thought that the wanderer's diplomacy might influence his reactions set Aikin's thoughts racing again. There was no telling what might happen, and the uncertainty was exquisite.

Malachite turned to Aikin, ignoring Fox's response. 'I hold some seventy stories of the Komey-based members of the current Oak family,' Malachite said, 'but I know little about the Oak family's day-to-day relationship to the Department of Beranish Affairs. Would you like to give me a story? I'll complete the circle if the opportunity arises and we may know something.'

'I'd be honoured to talk about my work with you,' Aikin nodded.

'Good.' Malachite smiled. 'But let's begin with a gift of knowledge on behalf of my people. Is there anything in particular that you would like to know about?'

'Beranish talents like my daughter, Fox.' Aikin leant forward, feigning enthusiasm for Fox's benefit. 'The talents are the subject of a current departmental committee, but I have a personal interest in the subject.' He looked at his adopted daughter and smiled before turning his attention back to the wanderer, who nodded. Aikin continued, 'And if you would permit me a second bit of knowledge?' He hesitated, watching the man in front of him.

Malachite smiled. 'By all means.'

'Rock children.' Aikin gave what he hoped was a self-deprecating laugh. 'You might not know that we Companionaris are romantics at heart, but we are... So this is a personal request. I'm compiling an annotated sketch book on rock children as a surprise gift for a young lady whose name I can't mention.' Aikin felt pleased to find he was, in fact, blushing at the thought of Whilomena.

In answer, Malachite moved his cloak, exposing a leather pouch. He untied it and opened it. Within were two rocks. One was small and irregular, a motley, pearly mix of fawns with golden highlights. The other was a larger piece of clean quartz.

'Children,' he addressed the rocks, 'meet Fox and with her are three Companionaris, a people who arrived on our shores only moments ago.'

'One thousand, one hundred and eighteen years ago,' Birch corrected him from where she sat at a little distance from the fire.

Malachite shrugged. 'The lives of rocks are measured in millions of years. It's different for them.' He lifted the rocks and held them out toward Fox, urging her to speak a word of welcome. Then he moved over to Aikin to repeat the process and finally stood up and walked over so that the soldiers could also welcome the stones.

Malachite returned to his place by the fire. 'Now let's enjoy ourselves. Let's share what we know and don't know. Let's ask and let's answer.'

Aikin began speaking, 'If I might begin with my question about rock children?' Malachite nodded and Aikin went on, 'I respect your belief in their sentience,' Aikin nodded toward the fetish stones, employing his most earnest tones, 'but why do you talk to them? I've heard no account of them changing or responding, so why?'

Malachite launched into a story cycle that covered a little of his own life and used a tale about a famous wanderer and his wild and demanding rock child as the second story. His third story was about a Beranish girl under the misapprehension that the receding god of the Companionaris was a mute rock child named Distant, who never answered. Fox clapped her hands as though Malachite had shown particular mastery, but Aikin felt disappointed. He'd hoped to hear something useful about rock children, a faith story or myth that might help him in his research. The only point to Malachite's stories was the advice to name one's rock child and treat it well. Hardly enlightening.

'That's so clever.' Fox smiled. 'The Companionaris always think talking to rock children is peculiar, but you're right, it's not so different to talking to a silent god.'

'And the fourth story?' Aikin said, eager now for the farce to finish.

The wanderer turned to Fox and asked her to recite the religious story of the Turning from the Companionari cannon.

Fox smiled at the wanderer and spoke, 'God turned his Back on Everyman; God turned her Back on Everywoman. Everyman saw God's Back in the Distance; Everywoman saw God's Back in the Distance. Everyman and Everywoman knew then, and we know now: we are not God and God is not us. The intimacy of childhood has passed. Instead, we cherish the memory of the Renunciation and its Gifts: the Love; the Turning Away; the Back; the Freedom.'

'What do you make of the story?' Malachite leant forward and touched Fox's hand. 'What does it add to knowledge and understanding?'

Fox withdrew her hand and Aikin was pleased she wasn't comfortable with the wanderer's physical attention. Aikin hadn't factored in the possibility the wanderer might find Fox attractive. But it wasn't surprising: the girl was clearly Beranish-born and was beautiful. He wondered whether the attraction would play for or against him.

Then Malachite launched into a discussion about what the Companionari story could tell them about the cycle. Aikin waited a while, long enough to avoid giving insult, and then he broke the intensity of the moment by refreshing the tea and sharing out the food. Malachite contributed some Beranish travel cakes; Aikin had brought fruit and cheese from the Komey markets. He moved the conversation on, gave Malachite some stories from Komey covering the day-to-day relationship between the Oak family and the department. He wanted to fulfil Malachite's request for knowledge. It pleased him to do the right thing. So Aikin gave a very full account of the workings within his department, despite the wasted effort it represented. In return, he asked Malachite about the relationship of stones to particular locations, whether there was a bond between individual rocks and particular plants and animals. Anything that might help him with his project to save the Stone Body and all its people.

'And these two?' Aikin indicated the stones on the open leather pouch. 'Do they have a home province?'

'Who knows?' The wanderer shrugged. 'Originally, they must have. But I don't know where they came from. All I can speak about is the corresponding natural rock. The quartz child reminds me of the hills on the western edge of Briar.'

'And the traditional plants near those hills?' Aikin opened a notebook and pulled a small pen from its spine.

'Many and varied.'

'Specifically?'

'Well, cork grass, lassitude, dust bush, stump trees...' Malachite shrugged.

'And the other stone?'

'It's schist. I don't know where it originated. And as for its corresponding plants, I'm not sure.'

'Malachite,' Aikin leant forward, his stomach tightening in anticipation. 'I have something to ask you. And I hope you will forgive me if my question causes offence.'

'A wanderer's ear is always open. Imperfect questions and imperfect answers are the purpose of a wanderer's life.'

Aikin looked at the man and held his breath. The uncertainty of the outcome was gorgeous.

'Would you give me your stones?'

Fox gasped.

'For study purposes,' Aikin offered. 'To allow me to render them in my book. I'd only use them for a noble end. I give you my word—'

Malachite placed his cup on the ground. The soldiers tensed, but the wanderer's next move wasn't aggressive. He rolled his pouch up and fastened the bundle around his waist. It seemed to Aikin that the rock markings on the wanderer's arms had swollen and taken on additional colour as he stood up. The man didn't look at either Aikin or Fox after that. He turned his back and walked away.

10

Fox rode through the banewood behind Aikin. Since Malachite had left, Aikin had looked flushed and most insistent that he needed to get back to the city. He was in such a hurry they'd left Birch and Glover behind to pack up the temporary campsite. Fox had a thousand questions, but she didn't ask any of them.

Coward. That's who she was. She wanted to accuse him of feigning admiration for Beranish culture, lecture him about the harm he'd just done. But she wouldn't. She'd stay silent and maybe tomorrow she'd sit at her desk and write a letter to him that would remain undelivered. Fox bit her cheek to stop her tears.

The path through the banewood was narrow, so Aikin led the way. Fox wished she could see his face. It would help her frame her questions about what he'd done and why. Because none of it made any sense. Aikin knew better than anyone that wanderers didn't just hand over their stones. The memory of Mica handing her his obsidian on the night they'd met had Fox double checking that thought. No, she was right. Wanderers didn't lend rock children. It was the stones that determined where they wanted to go and whom they wanted to travel with. The truth of that had been clear when

Mica's obsidian had abandoned her. But perhaps Aikin had found some historic account of something similar and had misunderstood. It didn't explain his story about needing them to create a sketchbook for a lover. Aikin didn't draw, and Fox didn't think he had a lover.

She watched him as he rode ahead of her. The tension of the incident hadn't left his body, and she felt unaccountably worried. She looked back at the campsite, caught a last glimpse of it. Birch was kicking dirt onto the fire. Glover was busy with the saddlebags.

At the sound of Aikin's voice she turned back again, 'You can't be a student of life without giving offence,' he gave her a quick smile. 'Still, I enjoyed meeting him. Didn't you?'

The path opened up, and Fox brought her horse up beside Aikin. 'Very much. He was interesting. I'm only sad he left with such a poor impression of us. Did you really think he'd lend you his rock children? I thought it was odd. You're usually so careful about our relations with Berans.'

'Odd? Not at all.' Aikin frowned. 'It was a matter of the heart. Perhaps that's why it seemed odd to you.' He nodded to himself as though he'd located the answer. 'Of course. You don't know that side of my nature. It's understandable that it would come as a bit of a surprise. It always surprises children that their parents have lives. I hope one day I will be able to introduce you to her, the woman I love. I'd like that.'

Fox was silent as they continued to pick their way along the path. 'I didn't know... that you had someone. But did you really think Malachite would lend you those rock children?' She broke off, unsure how to get at what worried her. Then she said it: 'He would never give them to you. You shouldn't have asked.'

For a moment Aikin didn't answer, and his expression gave nothing away. When he spoke again, his voice was light, belying the tension she could still sense in his body. 'We can take a different route home if you like. How about Ocean Valley? I've always loved it.'

'But you must have known he'd say no; so you knew you'd offend him...' Fox pressed, ignoring Aikin's question.

'On the contrary Fox. I never assume. Always leave room for the actions of the other. I was genuinely hoping he would say yes. I'm sorely disappointed.'

It rang true. That sort of notion was typical of Aikin. And lately he'd been talking about actions and reactions. Some theory, a book he'd read that he'd yet to pass on to her. A political treatise. 'If you'd told me you needed to borrow his rock children, I might have been able to help,' she said.

'Next time.' Aikin turned and smiled at her. 'Now that you're a junior, you're going to be busy, but we'll see if we can't find another field trip to take you on. They aren't all as exciting as today's, I'm afraid. Sometimes it's just a ride out to interview the refugees.'

From behind them, a cry for help sounded. Fox and Aikin reined in their horses, turning them back. Fox had to duck to avoid the slap of a leafy banewood branch. Bent low, she caught sight of Birch and Glover. They too were on the path, but had also turned back.

Aikin was the first to move. He took off at a gallop, heading in the cry's direction. As soon as she regained her balance, Fox followed. She realised that a part of her had been expecting this. Not the cry, but something. There had been, all along, an odd feeling in their encounter with the wanderer.

Birch and Glover were moving too, veering off the path, weapons drawn. Fox couldn't see any sign of a disturbance, an enemy, but her remnant rock skin prickled. The trouble must be deeper in the forest.

For a moment, there was only the sound of the four horses, then Malachite began yelling, again. The sound pierced Fox's uneasiness. It was all too real. Even so, she was slower than the others.

She followed them, tracking the sounds of their wild ride through the forest, one arm up to guard her face against the burning sap of the banewood leaves, the other holding the reins. Then she leant down over the pommel of her saddle, riding lower, trying to avoid the branches, letting her horse have its head. The sound of fighting grew louder.

The trees thinned out as the ground became rocky beneath her horse's feet. Boulders appeared in the surrounding landscape and then she was heading for a steep bank leading down to a dried creek bed. Malachite was on the opposite side, standing alone with his back to some rocks. Seven or eight ragged men surrounded him. Berans by their clothing and arms. Life must have become much more desperate than Fox had realised if Berans were attacking a wanderer. Then she spotted Aikin and the others. They were hurrying to Malachite's aid.

She started following, but her horse stumbled and slipped on the loose scree. By the time he found solid ground, and Fox looked up again, the battle had shifted. Now Malachite was halfway down the opposite bank and fighting hard. He was putting his rock skin to clever use, shielding himself and then tearing at the attackers. Aikin and the soldiersisters were fighting the outermost Berans. Then one of the ragged assailants lunged under Malachite's arm and slashed his hip. Blood flowed. Fox gasped. She urged her horse forward, frustrated that she was still too far away to help. And then she remembered her bow.

It was an ornament, really. Something the Companionaris wore when riding: an allusion to the early colonial days. She pulled her horse up short, grabbed her bow and nocked an arrow, wishing she'd been a better cadet during her novitiate. The first couple of arrows achieved nothing. Then she felled the man who'd been grieving the wanderer. Malachite glanced up and caught her eye, nodded his thanks. Taking advantage of the moment, another assailant lunged forward and cut across the wanderer's belly: a death slash. Malachite fell forward and disappeared from sight. The Berans turned on Aikin, Glover and Birch.

All three began backing away. Too late to save Malachite, not too late to save themselves. Fox hesitated, uncertain about what she should do. Then something cut short Aikin's retreat. An assailant had circled around and cut him across the shoulder, whooping aloud. Aikin fell to the ground and Fox kicked her horse forward. He jumped over a boulder almost unseating her and leapt up the opposite bank into the thick of the fight.

Fox used her long knife to dispatch the first assailant that tried to stop her. She pressed her horse forward until she was above Aikin. He'd fallen unconscious over a boulder. At least she hoped he was unconscious and not dead. She leant down, grabbed him by the collar and hauled him up, throwing his dead weight over the pommel of her saddle. She used her right hand to swing the knife at another attacker and backed her horse up, backed him away from the fight. Captain Birch seemed to have the same idea. She paired her horse with Fox's, closing their defences as their horses slipped down the slope toward the riverbed, backwards all the way. There was no sign of Glover.

Birch spoke under her breath. 'We have to flee. Can't win here. When I give the word.' For several moments, the two women swung their weapons and pushed hard against the enemy. Then Captain Birch gave the command, and they spun their mounts and spurred their horses away.

They raced through the forest, galloping past the trees and into the orange grass. Then Birch pulled up her horse.

'Keep going,' Fox called out. 'Malachite's dead. Glover's sure to be dead. Aikin's breathing, but he needs help.'

Birch shook her head. 'I have to go back. Those Beranish cowards will be gone now. Will have fleeced Glover's pockets and the wanderer's pockets too. Typical...' She began turning her horse toward the banewood.

Fox felt it, the slur. Like being called piss-eyed. She spoke without thinking, 'I'll go back. You will take Aikin.'

'Don't be stupid,' Birch snorted. 'This is soldiers' work. You're a daughter. You do your duty and I'll do mine.'

The words made sense, but they felt wrong, wrong in her arms and her heart. She had an urge to roll her shoulders, square up against Birch's insistence. The argument was clear and logical. Only it wasn't.

Birch was already moving, speaking over her shoulder, 'Master Aikin would want me to be the one.'

'Come back here right now,' Fox called out, certain she needed to be the one to check the dead. 'That's an order. Take Aikin into the city.'

Birch pulled up her horse and turned, not hiding the anger on her face, but she obeyed and together they shifted Aikin from Fox's horse to Birch's mount.

Fox approached the creek bed with caution. The attackers had vanished, but they'd left their dead behind. Malachite lay where he'd fallen. The poor man looked as though he was praying, slumped over his knees, forehead resting on the ground. Awful. She felt sick to think of the loss. Glover's legs stuck out from behind a boulder. Five of the assailants lay dead. She didn't remember so many dying.

There was no movement, so she dismounted, tied her horse to a dead branch, and stepped forward. There was little point in worrying now. If the assailants were still around, she'd be dead in moments.

Nothing happened. She forced back her urge to flee and stood at the edge of the scene, looking at all that remained.

Blood had soaked into the rocks and soil, leaving dark patches. There were weapons everywhere. The surviving Berans had run off without collecting them. That made little sense. Fox walked over to the first corpse. The man's arms were outstretched, his rock skin brown and streaked with dirt and blood. She bent down and then noticed a series of thin translucent straps tied around his arms. It wasn't rock skin at all. It was armour, made to look like rock skin. The killers weren't Berans. But why would Companionaris dress up to look like Berans? She wondered whether Aikin was involved. Surely not, not when he'd been injured. But it was strange. Aikin had felt odd. The entire field trip had felt odd, but she couldn't think of anything that would explain such a shocking attack. Perhaps some other house had done this, but violence between houses was almost unheard of.

She bent down and went through the dead man's clothing. There was nothing in his pockets, nothing at all. She looked at him more carefully. He was thin but not emaciated. It was strange that the killers were men: the Companionari military was largely sororities, not fraternities. Once again, she felt she was missing something.

She repeated her examination of the other dead killers. None of them had anything at all in their pockets and all were healthy, if a little thin. She even looked at their fingernails, which were short and clean. Next, she examined the weapons. They looked like the Beranish weapons that she'd seen in the department's museum and remembered from her childhood, but the decorations were rough, whereas those she remembered had been delicate and detailed. She moved over to where Sergeant Glover lay and rolled the woman's body over. She covered Glover's face with her shield. On a whim, she checked the woman's pockets, but there was little out of the ordinary.

Fox moved over to Malachite. She was uncertain about the rituals and death taboos of her own people, and her ignorance depressed her. She hoped that touching his corpse wouldn't cause offence. Fox rolled him backwards and winced as his head slapped the ground. Taking a deep breath, she pulled aside his cloak, untying the pouch that held the stones. They would call to another wanderer, but until then, she felt oddly responsible. They'd not wanted to be with Aikin, so she wouldn't be giving them to him. She'd give them to Mica when the wanderer next paid a clandestine visit.

Fox tied the pouch about her own waist and pulled her tunic over the top. She felt self-conscious, but she spoke to the rocks, explaining that she meant no harm. Next, she searched Malachite's pockets, but found nothing. She crossed his arms over his chest after removing his rings and adding them to the pouch.

She stood up. Somehow it was worse being here now that she'd seen that the attack was staged. And her arms hurt. She looked down. Welts from the banewood sap covered her skin. It would be a long ride home. She walked back to her horse and remounted.

Fox was close to Komey's outer wall when she spotted a group of mounted soldiersisters leaving the Wheat House gate. The lead sister raised her hand, beckoning Fox. Fox had the urge to turn and flee. Not a feeling she'd had before. She forced herself to sit up straight, dragged her hand away from where it had fallen over the pouch containing the rock children. She rode on, heading for the soldiers. As she neared, she saw they were wearing Wheat House colours on their epaulettes. She'd expected oak leaves despite the proximity of Wheat House. She'd expected her own house to send out its military.

'Mistress Fox,' the captain hailed her. 'We were just riding out to look for you. You're wanted in a parley. The Wheat Companion herself is calling for you.'

'I'm sorry, but I need to get back to Oak House and see how my father is.'

The soldier was nodding. 'That's why Mother Wheat wants you. Your father's with Mother Wheat.'

Fox's heart sank. If Aikin was awake, he would ask about the stones. He'd know she wouldn't leave them. She took a deep breath to steady herself and followed the soldiersisters as they turned back.

Soon, she was deep within the complex and treacherous heart of Wheat House, being ushered into one of the grand parley chambers on the first floor. The room was full of noisy conversation as people milled about, waiting for the parley to begin. She couldn't see her father, but she spotted the Wheat Companion sitting on the end of the parley bed, speaking with a footman, her elaborate hairstyle giving her the height she lacked. Fox moved towards a chair in the back of the room, near the door, but the Wheat Companion spotted her.

'Darling,' she cooed, her voice husky for such a young woman. 'I've been beside myself with worry for you. The entire city's been fretting since it heard you ran off into the banewood against Captain Birch's advice. Such a curious thing for a girl to do. Perhaps it's your background.'

The crowd turned and stared at Fox and Fox got a clear view of the parley bed. Aikin lay within: unconscious, face pale, a healing sister hovering beside him. She felt both relief and puzzlement. Evidently, he had some sort of connection with the Wheat Companion. He wouldn't be lying in her parley bed unless there was something substantial between them. But lovers? It seemed unlikely. She was the foremost companion, the most powerful woman in Komey; Aikin was powerful in Oak's hierarchy, but his reach was limited.

She made herself focus on answering the companion, 'Thank you for your concern Mother Wheat, but I'd best get back to Oak house, make sure everything is ready for my father's return.'

'Not just yet. Come sit beside your father.' The Wheat Companion waved a houseboy forward, and the boy carried a child's stool to the side of the bed.

Fox had no choice but to walk to the front of the room. In the back of her mind, she wondered whether the stool was an insult or whether the companion didn't know Fox was already suppressing and had reached adulthood.

The Wheat Mother clapped her hands, opening the parley. 'Welcome. Let the work of good government begin. This is a grave day and we must cleave together to find a way past the darkness.'

'Dark indeed, when a Companionari party is attacked in broad daylight,' someone called out.

Whilomena agreed. 'And I feel a certain responsibility as Wheat Companion, as the companion mother in the province that cradles our culture.'

'How could you blame yourself?' came a currying response from a sorority sister.

'Whilomena, darling,' a handsome young Aries man called out, 'what blame can attach to you?'

'But I am to blame.' The Wheat Mother rubbed her forehead. 'I'm the kind-hearted fool who's been feeding these refugees, letting them gather, letting them foment. And yes... I've been giving them my wheat and allowing them to camp in my province. I'm a fool. And now they're attacking us, picking us off—'

Fox couldn't help herself. 'They weren't Berans,' she said.

'Course you don't want them to be, dear.' The Wheat Companion gave Fox a patronising smile. 'We all sympathise. We understand your background.'

Fox bit her tongue, pushed down on her smouldering resentment. She couldn't afford to attract their attention. She needed to get away and hide Malachite's stones.

The Wheat Companion stood up, walked over to the window, stared out. The parley waited for her to speak. Silence filled the room. Whilomena turned and began pacing in front of the vast window, still silent, her head bowed in thought. She lingered. Several times she made to speak, then fell silent again. Even Fox leant forward, waiting to hear what the woman would say.

'I'm not just feeding refugees. I'm feeding most of the Companionaris whose provinces have failed. My wheat is going into all our impoverished houses. It's those houses where I want sentiment to count.' She looked up at the parley and Fox saw tears in her beautiful eyes. 'I want to help our dear brothers and sisters.'

Several of the guests wiped tears from their eyes and called out their gratitude and support.

'But with all these Beranish refugees...' she shrugged. 'I have to be practical to protect our people. And yet last month, a parley over at Bass House tried to gather the Bass Berans from where they've pitched their tents in Oak and bring them here! Set up yet another camp in my province. Then there's today's violence.' She waved her hand at Aikin and for the first time, there was the sound of genuine distress in her voice.

So it was true. They were lovers. But perhaps they'd not shared everything. The Wheat Companion seemed focused on maligning Berans and hadn't mentioned rock children at all. It didn't altogether surprise Fox. Aikin wasn't a man who shared his purposes. Perhaps he'd held back his interest from the companion.

The Wheat Mother shook her head. 'Much as it breaks my heart to do so, I've begun moving refugees down to the port.'

Fox frowned. Moving refugees? But why?

It was a young man from Olive House who asked: 'To New Lytalia? But the Pike Companion doesn't allow Berans in her port.'

'Yes, but they're in transit. I'm arranging work for the refugees in the motherland, in Galea.'

The young man stared at her. 'You're selling them?'

Fox felt sick. If Aikin was involved with this woman, this abomination, he was capable of anything. Fox needed to get out of the room and get news to Mica. A letter? Could she risk it? No. Even if she wanted to, no one would deliver it to the camp. But Fox could ask Oria to help.

Whilomena looked annoyed. 'And why shouldn't I recover my costs?'

'And which parley endorsed this?' the young man from Olive House persisted. 'By what right?'

Whilomena didn't answer him, turning instead to appeal to the room. 'Without change, genuine change, these companionship failures will continue to weaken us. Look at you,' she waved her arms at the assembled company, 'showing up for this parley, ready to make decisions when, at this very moment, over in Rice House and Prairie House and any number of other houses, parleys are busy making contrary decisions. Half the time the causes cancel each other out,' she laughed, and there was an unpleasant edge to the sound. 'And what no one seems to realise is that things won't stand still: the Berans will eat us up. What we need is one parley to deal with this crisis and one family to lead the way.'

There was an audible gasp. Several parley members half rose from their seats in protest, aghast at any suggestion of overturning the thousand year old system of government designed to decentralise power and slow down change.

The Wheat Companion lifted her chin, daring opposition. 'I've said it and I mean it!' She sat down on one of the cushioned chairs, leant back as if exhausted. 'So arrest me for sedition if it makes you happy, if you think it will solve our problems. I'll turn away over this. Look, I am turning away!' She shifted around so that her silk covered back faced the room. 'I'm ready to take the solitary path.'

Whilomena's handmaid began fussing around her mistress. The other members of the parley seemed uncertain about what to do. The Wheat Companion was openly suggesting disrupting the Companionari system of government and yet, in turning her back and aligning herself with the actions of the Companionaris' god, she was claiming a moral right to do so.

And then something unexpected happened. The Lacuna bell rang out and the room stirred as everyone reacted to the sound that signalled the news that a childless companion had died, that her body had arrived in Komey, and that all suppressing women should come and try their luck in the ensuing crossover. The parley's dramas were forgotten and the Wheat Companion leapt out of her chair and rushed over to the window. She opened the casement and leant out.

'What sort of flag?' asked the young man from Olive house, already on his feet and ready to run.

'Green,' Whilomena's voice was high with excitement, 'so it's a plant companion who's died. But I don't know who yet. Give me my glasses,' she held out her hand. Her handmaid hurried forward and handed her a pair of glasses. She leant back out the window again. Everyone in the room hesitated, wanting the news but wanting to leave. 'Oak! By the Back! The Oak Companion is dead and her body is on its way to the bell.'

11

Mica looked down at the dead bodies on the table in front of him. Four people. Cecily, the ancient sister Cast had killed, accidentally but no less dead. And the three murdered by Rush: the manor cook, her assistant, and Bronda. Mica was glad Rush was dead, but his death didn't undo the destruction he'd wrought.

Mica felt exhausted. He felt as though someone had beaten him, left him lying in the dirt. He pinched his thumb and index finger against the bridge of his nose. It didn't help. Not enough sleep and too much shame and regret. And then there was the death of the Oak Companion to contend with.

The rebels had waited until after midnight for her to come back from the celebrations, but she'd never appeared. In the end, Mica had sent out some of his men to see what had happened. They'd come back with the story of the Bass refugees unearthing a coffin and Oria going to sit with it in the greenhouse. Mica had imagined that she'd fallen asleep or was journeying within her body or had hurt herself somehow. But the old tyrant was neither asleep nor injured. She was dead in the unearthed coffin, covered with a hessian sack. And then there was the rest: Rush dead on the floor from a knife wound; the coffin's skeleton missing; and no sign of the person who had held the knife that killed Rush. He had no answer to any of it; no account to give Komey about who had killed whom or why. But he had his suspicions. Someone had stripped Oria's body and Mica couldn't help remembering that there were stories about Companionaris killing elderly companions and removing their clothing to induce crossovers. He wondered... Could Rush have blundered into a separate plot where a Companionari killer was trying to jump the crossover ahead of her Komey sisters? What were the chances? He sighed, finding it hard to believe his own conspiracy theory. And yet, Rush, a powerful Beran, was dead. Mica rubbed his neck, feeling the weariness of his failure. It made little sense.

He recalled himself to the present. The elderly sisters were the only hostages he had, so he would use them to negotiate with Komey to have the indenture lifted.

As far as the companion's death was concerned, he'd followed the rules. He'd prepared Oria for her last journey to Komey in the early hours of the morning. Prepared her properly. He'd found the casket. He'd put Oria in it, sealed it up and had sent her body to the city on the train. Two of his men with her. He'd told his men to insist on dealing with the head of the Department of Beranish Affairs, but whether that was the right thing to do, Mica wasn't sure. What a disaster!

He was facing the very thing he'd wanted to avoid, the whims and ignorance of an unborn companion's guardians, negotiating the camp's future in a mire of politics and foolishness. That's why he'd chosen Aikin. At least Aikin knew Berans, knew about them. The new birthmother wouldn't. Unless it was Fox... But Mica couldn't afford to indulge that hope.

Mica had promised to contact Fox when the next crossover took place. He would have to find a way. He would have gone on the train himself, only he owed it to the hostages to see they remained unharmed. His daughter's future would be safe if the crossover touched her. If not, he and Fox would have to plan how to get her away from Komey once she was born.

He rubbed his face again and glanced around the room. How long would it take Aikin to respond? Likely the man would reach out to Quartz, not Mica. And where the hell was Quartz? By now the camp must know there had been trouble in the manor, but Quartz hadn't appeared.

The dining-room door opened and Cast walked in carrying a plate. 'Brought you something.'

Mica looked at the food: bread, cold meats and olives, but his stomach turned. 'I don't want anything.'

Cast seemed to sag, whatever energy and purpose had driven him to bring the food, gone. He set the plate down on the sideboard, turned away, defeated.

Mica was mortified. He'd started all this. He had no right to ignore his men. That would change. He walked over to Cast and put his hand on the young man's shoulder. 'Thank you. You're right, we all need to eat.' Mica picked up the plate and held it out to Cast. 'Have some.'

Cast's gaze flicked to the bodies on the dining table. He shook his head.

Mica set the plate down again, but he picked up the bread, broke it into two portions, added some meat and olives. He pressed one serve onto Cast, kept the other for himself. 'The dead don't object to the living continuing with life. Eat. Denying life insults them.'

Cast didn't speak, but he nodded.

Mica led the way to two dining chairs on either side of the door and they sat and ate. Afterwards, Mica asked for a report on the sisters' welfare. 'They've eaten, I take it?'

'The same fare,' Cast said. 'And a little brandy. And extra blankets, just as you ordered.' Cast looked down at his hands.

'How are they?' Mica asked, tapping his own rock skin. 'How did they feel?'

'Furious.' Cast looked up. 'My rock skin practically blistered with their outrage.'

Mica shook his head. 'Frightened too, no doubt.'

Cast nodded.

'And the camp?'

The man shifted in his seat. 'It's getting awkward. People have been walking up to the manor, asking what's going on. We sent them away. Saury was up here too. She was asking for you. We sent her back to camp.'

'Good. And Doubt?'

'I haven't seen your nephew,' Cast said.

'Probably off playing some game,' Mica said. 'And what about Quartz? He's not around?'

'No.' Cast shook his head. 'Apparently, he took off last night. Told the camp's cook it was wanderer business. Left just after the feast.'

Mica didn't know whether he was relieved or disappointed. Then both men stiffened, rock sensing a wave of emotion approaching from the hall outside.

The door burst open, the force behind it so great it knocked Cast from his chair. Mica stood and Cast scrambled up off the floor, both ready to defend themselves. But the tension only lasted for a moment as their rock skin registered who it was. Cast's brother, Ramble, and with him was Mica's nephew. Ramble stood on the threshold with his back to the room. He was struggling with the child, trying to drag Doubt into the room.

'What's going on?' Mica said.

Ramble lifted his head to explain. Taking advantage, Doubt jammed his foot against the door frame and jerked away, almost breaking free, forcing Ramble back out into the hall.

Mica waved for Cast to remain in the dining room and followed the struggle into the hallway, careful to close the door behind him. He didn't want Doubt seeing the dead or Cast blurting out something he shouldn't. 'Let him go.'

Ramble took a firmer grip of Doubt's shirt. 'Your boy was

sneaking about. When I asked him what he was doing, he said he had a message for Bronda, but I rock sensed the half truth in that. I told him straight off Bronda wouldn't be taking any more messages in this lifetime and then he tried to run.'

'Stand still,' Mica snapped at Doubt.

His nephew stopped struggling and Ramble released him. Doubt stared at the floor, emanating waves of adrenalin that beat in time with his racing heart.

'What's going on?' Mica said. 'And why aren't you with Saury?'

'Because all she wants to do is talk to her rock child or go around the camp bothering everyone for stories...' he sniffed.

Mica came closer, stood in front of Doubt. 'What's this about a message for Bronda?'

The boy didn't look up, didn't answer, but the panic had left him.

'This is serious, Doubt,' Mica's voice was gentle, but he let the boy feel the power behind it. 'I need you to answer me.'

Doubt lifted his head. The boy's face was dirty, his shirt torn. 'I couldn't find you this morning.' He looked down again. 'So I went off on my own.' He shrugged. 'I was by myself. The whole day today. By myself. I didn't meet anyone. Can I go now?' Doubt addressed his question to the floorboards.

Mica turned to Ramble. 'Take him back to camp. Find someone to look after him? We should hear from Komey soon, but this business won't stay quiet for long and—'

'What won't stay quiet?' Doubt looked up, and Mica felt the flash of his curiosity.

'Never you mind.' Mica ruffled the boy's hair.

'Has it got something to do with Bronda? I'd like to see her, see if she's all right.' Doubt gave Ramble a dark look as though he would hold him responsible for any harm that had come to Oria's handmaid.

Mica eyed the boy. 'And why do you want to see Bronda?'

Doubt shrugged, and when he spoke, his voice was casual. 'Oh nothing. I just felt like seeing her... Chatting. You know...' Doubt shifted from foot to foot. 'If Bronda's busy, maybe the Lady of Chambers is around? I could see her instead.' He glanced at the staircase behind him as though he thought she might appear.

At that moment, Cast must have decided to see what was happening because the door opened behind Mica. Before Mica had time to act, Doubt had turned and was looking straight into the dining room. The boy's face stiffened. Mica turned and saw what Doubt was seeing: the dead bodies on the table. He rock sensed Doubt's panic. His nephew spun on his heel and ran. Ramble sprang to life and in moments he had Doubt in his hands again. He lifted him, carrying him back to Mica.

There was no point trying to hide anything now that Doubt had seen the bodies. Mica lifted him from Ramble's arms and carried him into the dining room, leaving the brothers behind in the hall. The wanderer held the boy as gently as he could. Doubt stared at the bodies and then buried his face in Mica's shoulder.

'I didn't want you to see this.'

'What happened?' the boy asked, his voice muffled.

'It's complicated.'

'You didn't kill them, did you? You wouldn't.'

'Of course not, but I need that message you've been trying to give to Bronda. You can see that something serious has happened here in the manor,' he nodded his head at the dead bodies, 'so that message is important.'

Doubt hoisted himself up so that his lips were close to Mica's ear. 'It was for Mistress Bronda,' he whispered, as though he could keep his secret by whispering. 'The message was for her.'

'But she can't receive it.'

'Then I have to talk to the Lady of Chambers.' Doubt wiggled with the effort of keeping his head up high enough to speak into Mica's ear.

'You can't,' Mica kept his voice gentle. 'I'm sorry.'

'Is she dead too?'

Mica stroked Doubt's hair. 'No, she's fine but you can't talk to her. I need you to remember who you are Doubt. You're not Companionari; you're one of us.'

'Then it's no good,' the boy spoke to himself.

'I need to know who sent you running into the manor,' Mica said. He didn't wait for Doubt's answer. Instead, he carried him back into the hall and closed the door behind them. He set Doubt onto the floor and crouched down in front of him so that they were face to face. 'Believe me, Doubt, this isn't what I wanted. I am responsible for this tragedy, but it's not what I wanted. I'm trying to fix things... We were trying to help the camp.' His words felt hollow in his chest, but he persisted, 'And now the Oak Companion is dead.'

The boy's eyes widened.

'We don't know who killed her,' Mica explained. 'The thing is, it's no time for secrets.'

Doubt bit his lip and Mica waited. 'I was to ask Mistress Bronda to bring fever powder,' the boy said.

Mica leant forward. 'For whom?'

'A woman. No one. Just a Beranish girl.'

'A Beran?' Mica sat back on his heels, puzzled. 'Not a Companionari woman?'

'No. A Beran,' Doubt said. 'But she's not one of us. I've never seen her before.'

Mica paused, struggling to make sense out of this new piece of information, struggling to find a pattern. Then he saw it, or thought he saw it. A desperate Beran would do anything to help her family. This girl was probably a refugee and someone had paid her to hurry the companion's death. But it still didn't make sense. How could a Beranish girl manage to kill Rush? He needed to talk to her. Mica stood up again. 'So where is this girl?'

The boy looked up at Mica and opened his mouth to speak, then seemed to hesitate.

'Don't lie. I'll be able to tell,' Mica said. 'We won't hurt her if that's what you're worried about.'

'I don't know where she is.'

Mica stared at Doubt. 'That's not true, is it?'

Doubt licked his lips. 'I mean, I don't know exactly,' he blurted. 'How could I? Exactly, I mean… I don't know. But I know where Mistress Bronda should meet her. I can tell you that. The train, just after sunset. Can I go now?'

Mica looked at the boy. He suspected that Doubt was hiding something still, and he was certain the boy would warn the stranger if he could. Mica wondered what to do with him.

'Can I go home now?' Doubt sounded pitiful.

Then Ramble spoke up, 'Why don't Cast and I wait for Quartz? We can take the boy with us.'

Mica looked at Doubt for a moment and then nodded. 'All right, but get him something to eat first and don't let him out of your sight.'

O ria woke to a clatter of stones and a thump. She hadn't meant to sleep, but she was better for it. She glanced up and saw that the day had passed her by as she'd slumbered, but there was no time to wonder because someone had arrived in the sand crater. Oria crawled forward and looked around the lip of the alcove and was relieved to see Doubt. The boy had returned. He looked worse than he had that morning. No tears this time, but his shirt was torn and grimy, and his hair was wet with sweat, sticking out from his head at all angles.

He caught sight of her and took a deep breath. She felt it, an answering in her body: preparedness. She felt it in her rock skin. Such a curious sensation. She felt him readying himself to talk. She was rock sensing him. Amazing. But there wasn't time to stop and appreciate her new sixth sense because it was clear from Doubt's demeanour that things hadn't gone as planned.

She scanned the lip of the crater, but there was no one. Just the long shadows of the sinking sun. He'd come alone. That was something.

She walked over to him and he looked up at her, his little face full of worry and fear. Yes, fear. Her arms felt his fear.

'What is it? What happened?'

He stumbled over a story of a coup, a kidnap gone wrong, but his rambling account didn't lessen the impact, or the stab of grief that hit her when she realised Bronda was dead, or her shock at all that had happened. 'Your uncle did this? Mica?'

Doubt shook his head as though he wanted to deny it, but his words confirmed what she'd understood, '... yes. Kind of. But not really, because he didn't kill any of them. That was someone else. Except for old Oria. Mica thinks you killed her and Cast and Ramble said you did. Did you?' He bit his lip and then continued before she could get a word in, 'I know you didn't mean to. Sometimes people make mistakes and there's an accident and—'

She clapped her hands. 'Enough.'

He stopped but his lip quivered, and it appalled her to see that he'd started crying. 'Don't cry...' She looked down at him, uncertain what to do. She lifted a hand, considered patting him, but he threw himself at her before she could decide. He flung his arms around her and sobbed into her tunic. She dropped her hand and stroked his head, ignoring the sticky feel of his hair.

This was understandable. Young boys were emotional, but it wouldn't do. Not today. She needed more information, more help. She eased him back, tilted up his chin and looked him in the eye. 'They just let you go? Surely they knew you'd come and find me?'

The question seemed to stir something in him because he smiled and a look of pride appeared on his face. 'Cast and Ramble were looking after me. We were on the far side of the camp because Mica wants to talk to Quartz straight away.'

She snorted. 'I bet he doesn't. But yes, I can see that. He'd want to be the one to break the news, frame it. Go on.'

'We waited, but Quartz didn't come, so I pretended,' he said. 'I pretended all I wanted to do was play jacks. Then I dug a hole...' he glanced up at her, 'with that knife. But I will give it back...'

'Yes. But go on. What happened then?'

'I climbed some trees. I did that for a while. Then I threw some acorns at Ramble.'

'Just Ramble?'

'I don't like him. He grabbed me at the manor and he wouldn't take me to see... Bronda.' Doubt sniffed, a jagged intake of breath.

'So you threw acorns at Ramble? Go on.'

The boy gathered himself, and she felt it as a tightening in her rock skin. Brave. He felt brave.

'They got up and moved further away from my tree. I guess they forgot to watch because when I climbed down they didn't notice and I walked away.' He smiled at the memory. 'I can walk without making a sound. It's not just my rock sense. I can be silent. Do you want to see? Close your eyes and see if you can hear me walking.'

He moved, ready to show off his prowess, but she caught his shoulder and held him back. 'Later.' For a moment, they stood together as she contemplated her next move. Then she felt a wriggling sensation in her rock skin: anticipation, shame, worry. Truly, rock skin was amazing. 'What?' she asked, looking down at him.

He shrugged but didn't answer.

'There's more. You're hiding something. Did you tell them where I am? Are they coming for me?' She looked at the rim of the crater. It was still empty, but the day had darkened.

Doubt shook his head. 'I didn't tell them about your being here because I didn't know for sure that you were still here.'

'I see,' she smiled. 'You protected me. But you told them about the message? You would have had to.'

He nodded.

She was silent for a while, thinking things through.

'What will you do?' Doubt asked.

She answered without thinking, 'Talk to Mica.'

He put a hand to her arm as though he might hold her back. 'You mustn't. He'll lock you up.'

'Not if I can help it. Not if you help me.'

Doubt shook his head. 'Mica won't listen to me. He's going to be cross that I ran away from Ramble and Cast. You can't talk to Mica. You should run away.'

'Running won't help,' Oria said. 'If Quartz isn't here, then I need to speak with Mica. And I'll need you to help me.' Doubt let go of her arm and began reiterating his advice for her to run, but she interrupted him. 'I know what I'm doing. Doubt Not. That should be your second name.'

'You're naming me?' he looked startled, pleased.

'And why not? You've an unerring sense of what's right. You're trusting of the people who deserve trust.' She looked up at the sky, at the emerging stars. 'It's nearly dark. We should be able to get to Mica's tent with no one seeing us. You can use those silent feet of yours. Show me your abilities because I need to speak to Mica alone. And not in the manor. There are too many men in the manor. It wouldn't be safe.'

'It won't be safe at the camp either,' he said. 'You should—'

She reached out and pulled him to her, hugged him. 'Doubt Not. I know what I'm doing. I have a plan.'

12

Fox let the crowd carry her forward, out of Whilomena's parley room. She let herself be rushed down the corridor and down the front stairs and found herself disgorged from Wheat House like a stop knocked from a barrel. Then she halted and let the crowd flow past. Someone elbowed her, another stood on her foot. Everyone was intent on their destination: to the bell; to their house; to some particular spot they remembered, the one that would command the most excellent view of the coffin's parade.

A stillness fell in their wake and with it came Fox's memories of Oria. The old woman testing Fox all those years ago in Kelp. Oria teaching her to journey within her body. Oria looking out for her interests. But Fox hadn't ever thanked her. Not for the testing and taking; thanked her for the small acts of kindness. All the stupid letters Fox had written, pleading for change, but Fox hadn't ever told the Mother she was grateful. Tears welled, but Fox was already moving.

If she kept going straight, she would reach the bell in minutes, reach the destiny the treaty had carved out for her and the fragile promise of a safe future for her daughter. But she was no longer leading a small life, alone with her concerns. She was carrying Malachite's rock children and the news of Whilomena's crimes.

She turned toward Oak House and ran, glad that the urgency of the crossover meant no one in Komey cared about moving slowly. As she ran, she sought a way to fulfil all her obligations. There was enough time to hide the rock children before she needed to get to the bell. And she would need to hide them. They would strip her naked before she entered a propagation room to test for the Oak talent. And yet, Whilomena's news meant that she couldn't afford the propagation night. Not if it cost Beranish freedoms. So she couldn't, wouldn't, go to the bell. But the way forward wasn't at all clear. She had no means of getting a message to Mica. One step at a time, she told herself. She would begin by hiding Malachite's stones.

She reached the avenue that fronted Oak House and stopped for a moment to catch her breath. The Lacuna bell sounded its second call. Two more and the crossover would begin. She lifted the hem of her tunic to dry her tears. They had welled up again and were trickling down the side of her nose. This time, it was selfish. She was mourning her future, the possibility of a kind of freedom, of returning to live in a province as a birthmother, of being near Mica. Red cotton foxes stared up at her from the hem. She wiped her eyes, remembering the lives in her hands. She had duties.

Fox started running again, turning off the avenue, making her way to Oak's kitchen gardens. The sisters lifted their heads at the sound of her feet, their hands never wavering from their work, stroking the plants that fed the house.

'Have you been to the bell?' one called out.

Fox shook her head, but didn't stop.

'What about the coffin?' another asked. 'Did you see the coffin being paraded?'

Fox shook her head again and kept moving. Then the third bell sounded and her stomach fluttered. She slowed and dropped her hands, touching the outline of Malachite's rock children. Where should she hide them? Her first thought had been the cupboard in the back of her quarters, but that wouldn't be wise. The cleaning staff usually ignored her suite, but she couldn't count on that continuing to be the case. She realised she'd been heading to the kitchen for a reason: it had extensive pantries. There were several places where no one ventured, well, only infrequently. Then the perfect spot came to mind. The kitchen had baked the Harvest Night pudding weeks ago. Willie wouldn't need the harvest spices for another twelve months. She fingered Malachite's pouch, felt the stones under her tunic. They felt prickly, uneasy beneath her touch. They didn't want to be left in the pantry. She had a notion that they wanted her to leave Komey, carry them out, and with that thought, the urge to flee the city was swift and sharp.

Fox frowned, feeling the desire to leave like a hunger in her hands and legs, as an ache in her arms. She couldn't leave without permission. It would mean her death. Worse, the Kelp Companion would withdraw her talent from Fox's home province for one generation. The cost to the people of Kelp was too high to contemplate.

She told the stones the same as she crossed to the kitchen door, making promises under her breath, glad there was no one nearby to see her talking to herself.

The kitchen was short staffed because of the impending crossover, but for the first time since Malachite had been attacked, Fox relaxed. The hands were used to seeing her. No one more than glanced at her as she made her way across the room. Except for Willie. The cook waved for her to stop the moment he caught sight of her.

'Whoa, whoa. Where are you off to? We can't have you missing the bell. We're counting on a win for Oak house.'

'I know, but I'm famished. I've been out with Aikin all day and the night will be long. I won't be a moment. There's enough time.'

Willie nodded and put down his spoon. 'Wait here. I'll get you something.'

'No. Please. Don't stop. I'll be faster on my own.' She hurried past. 'I'll take some bread and cheese from the pantry. I don't need help.'

He looked troubled, but picked up his spoon again and returned his attention to his pot. 'Be quick. And I didn't see you. You were never here.'

She was glad the kitchen was used to her independent ways. Even something as simple as a snack was subject to Oak House etiquette. She was supposed to ask her apartment manager when she wanted something to eat. The manager would speak to the viander of rooms, who would seek one of the cook's proxies, who would then order a light refreshment to be sent up to her private dining alcove. For a girl who still remembered cooking fresh-caught fish on the campfire , the slow rituals of Komey were hard to live with.

Fox hurried through the first two storage rooms and then slipped into the third to find something to eat before hiding the stones. She hadn't lied. She was famished.

The wanderer's pouch was uncomfortable against her skin. She halted for a moment, untied it and removed his rock children, before dropping the pouch into a bin. She put Malachite's quartz in her right pocket and the schist in her left, and then looked around the pantry. The room held cheese and bread and olive paste and jugs of water. The look of them was welcome and the pattern they made on the shelves was pleasing. She helped herself, without even bothering with a plate. Her arms had moved beyond itching. They stung. She glanced down. The banewood welts looked red, and some had blistered and burst. She'd do what she could to heal them from within when there was time, but she could see that she needed to visit the sanatorium. She reached for Malachite's schist with her free hand while she ate with the other. It felt cool and hard against her palm and almost seemed to draw the pain. Curious, she put down her bread roll and put her other hand into her right pocket, taking hold of the second child. Again, the pain eased. It was then she heard the whispering in the corridor.

'... big, like a fattened husband, but muscled,' said a male voice.

'With wings?' another asked.

'No, the Back love you. Berans don't have wings. That's just a myth. They're like us, only with rock skin and funny coloured yellow eyes.'

'But they brought her body loose. No coffin? No sisters with her?'

'That's what I heard. Not a single sister in sight. Just her and the Berans on the train. And her not even in a protective casket. Must have given the marshals a shocking fright.'

'Lucky marshals are beyond carrying children,' the second man spoke again. 'A shock like that can make a woman lose her grip on an embryo.'

Fox let go of the stones and stepped out into the corridor. 'You're talking about the Oak Companion, aren't you? What do you mean there were no sisters with her?'

The two young pantrymen, who'd been leaning against the wall, stood up when they saw her.

'It's only what I heard, Mistress Fox,' the shorter man explained.

'From whom?' Fox asked.

'I heard Mistress Sage speaking with her cousin about it. Is it true then? Have you heard the same?'

'No,' Fox answered. 'I've heard nothing.'

'Mistress Sage told her cousin that the marshals had to lock up the Berans who brought the late Mother Oak to Komey. Put them in the cells at the back of the station because of the ruckus they caused.' The man's face was avid with the news. 'Best thing to do with Berans, present company excluded,' he said, a slight blush creeping up his face as he eyed Fox. 'I mean, we've got those refugees camping outside the city's walls. And now they've started arriving by steam train, threatening people... I ask you, what next?' he appealed to both his colleague and to Fox.

'What do you mean, threatening people?' Fox asked, frowning.

'Making demands to see Master Aikin. Least, that's what I over-heard. Shouting that it was urgent: a matter of life and death,' he giggled. 'Always in such a hurry. Imagine it,' he turned to his colleague, 'saying something like that as though you didn't have any time? How embarrassing.'

'And the men weren't refugees...' Fox felt uneasy. 'Not if they were with Mother Oak's body. No, they must be Berans from Oak.'

The pantryman shrugged. 'But Mistress Sage told her cousin that it's a sure sign there's some sort of trouble in the province and the marshals did right by locking them up in the train station cells. Glad they didn't bring them into the city.' The man shivered at the thought. 'Keep them outside the walls.'

'But what sort of trouble could there be in Oak?' Fox asked.

'Who knows?' The short man blew out his cheeks and shook his head. 'Who knows what their wild ways are all about? They're different from us, aren't they?' He looked at Fox again. She felt his gaze on her eyes, knew he was thinking about their colour. Then his gaze slid down to her blistered and weeping arms. She wondered what he'd think if he knew about the rock children in her pockets and about her remnant rock skin, hidden away from the conversion process for all these years. She made herself refocus on the news of trouble in Oak. The men in the train station cells might be the solution she'd been seeking. They might take the stones and carry a message to Mica.

She smoothed down her tunic to give herself a moment to think. The train station was outside the city's walls. Normally, that would be a problem, but she had her birthday boon, her field trip pass.

Fox left the men to their gossip. As she was about to exit the pantry, she caught sight of the tea canisters, and the dust bush canister among them. She thought of Wren. Without giving it more than a moment's thought, she peeled the label from the dust bush tea and pressed it onto its neighbour, a canister of black tea. She put the dust bush canister under her tunic and left, hid it just beyond the wall. She would deal with the consequences when she returned. Perhaps when Wren returned to sanity, Fox would teach her to travel within. Perhaps the adopted woman could be like Fox: drink the tea with sanity but sequester a little slither of herself. If she did, if she could, Fox might have a friend, someone else who understand being a Beranish Companionari.

The station platform was home to the marshals and divided into three spaces. They reserved the end nearest her for passengers embarking and disembarking; the workshop took up the second area; and the marshals lived in the third. Fox glanced around and spotted the train sisters ahead, sitting around the cooking fire in their living quarters. Their home was open to the workshop and the platform, but there were weighted curtains screening it from the tracks. A sharp breeze emanated from the railway line, keeping the curtains in constant motion. The curtains sounded like an old loom as they slapped against the platform edge. It wasn't a home that Fox would have welcomed, but there was freedom beyond the walls. She doubted these sisters had to bother with vianders or cooks' proxies.

The three middle-aged marshals looked up and then stood at her approach. The senior sister wore a light blue padded jacket, and the others wore black.

'Madam Marshal.' Fox dipped her head at the woman in blue. 'Sisters. I'm Fox Oak, Master Aikin's adopted daughter and junior to the Department of Beranish Affairs.'

'Welcome, Mistress Fox,' the senior marshal's voice was light and warm.

'I'm sorry my father isn't here. He was injured today and what with the crossover...' Fox shrugged, already preparing to dissemble. 'The thing is, we heard that you're holding some Berans who brought the Mother's body in without a coffin, and that they've been asking for my father.'

'The men are here, all right,' the senior marshal nodded, 'but don't fret about the Oak Mother. She was in a protective casket. Nothing was amiss there, but all else was wrong.'

'Not wrapped in a curtain, then?' Fox asked.

'No, Back preserve us. They boxed old Oria right, but there were no sisters with her. Only the two Berans who brought her. Deborah here,' she inclined her head at the woman on her right, 'she called the guards out as soon as she saw them. Because the Berans didn't come with old Bronda who knows how to drive the train, as you'd expect in an emergency. No, they drove it themselves!' She shook her head. 'So down came our guards with their weapons out. We almost expected a fight, didn't we?' She turned to the other marshals, who nodded. 'But the Berans didn't struggle.'

'But they made demands?'

'My word, yes,' the senior marshal said. 'Demanded to speak to your father. Said it was urgent, said we had until an hour after sunset or we'd wear deaths on our souls. I was in two minds. I thought we should send for Master Aikin, never mind the hurry it involved, but the guardswomen said that nothing could take priority over the crossover, that the Berans had to wait until the last bell had rung, and then the guards would see who was available to listen to the message.'

'Did they say anything about Oak?' Fox felt an icy dread settling over her. 'Did anyone ask what's happened there and who it is who's under threat?'

'Don't you worry, Mistress Fox,' the youngest marshal said. 'A lot of Beranish drama isn't genuine drama. We see a lot of those folk, being out here beyond Komey's walls. Always in a hurry. They don't see the gift of time for what it is. Squander it without realizing.'

Fox could see the marshals didn't share her sense of foreboding. She needed to speak to the men from Oak. Find out what had happened. She turned to the senior marshal. 'Where are they now?'

'In the holding cells,' the woman answered.

'Take me there.'

'Ah mistress, are you sure? I mean no disrespect, but did someone say you could be out here?'

Fox pulled her papers from her pocket but didn't hand them over. 'I'm allowed, a birthday boon.'

The woman frowned but didn't reach out for the papers. Fox was Aikin's daughter. Aikin was a man, but a powerful one. These sisters would have dealt with him in the past. The marshal nodded and led Fox to the cells.

Soon Fox stood inside a small stone room, facing two large men: one with rust-coloured hair and rock skin; the other with dark hair and a sharp face. She hadn't realised how much she'd counted on Mica being there until she found he wasn't. But there was no time to waste if she wanted to get to the crossover, so, remembering her childhood manners, she signalled her heart and her head and spoke her name and credentials.

The men stared at her face and then stared at her bare, blistered and weeping arms.

'It is nothing,' her voice sounded apologetic. 'Just banewood sap burns.'

The man with rust-coloured hair looked up again. He motioned his heart and head and then spoke, 'I'm Skip. This is my cousin Wolf.'

The other man also moved a hand from heart to head, but he was already speaking, his voice rising in frustration. 'You'd better not be trying to tell us you're running Beranish Affairs, little girl. We haven't time for jokes.' He stepped forward. Filtered light from a tall window fell across his face. His rock skin looked as angry as his words.

Fox took a step back in surprise.

'Is this another insult?' He glared at her. 'Have they sent a camp-less girl to talk to us? Neither fish nor fowl, eh?' He shook his head. 'Look, if you've got any feeling at all for the people of your birth, get us out of this cell and take us into the city to see whoever is in charge. We're out of time as it is.'

Fox felt his insults burn inside her, but settled her emotions. 'You're not going into Komey and you should know that. You brought the Oak Companion so you know about the crossover, so you should also know that the gate mistress wouldn't let you in even if I tried to take you. And as for why I'm here and why you should speak to me... Well, the head of Beranish Affairs is ill, unconscious when I left him, but I'm his adopted daughter. You should be happy I'm Beranish-born. At least I've got enough sense to come here and ask you what's wrong.' Fox found she was breathless after her little speech and that her emotions had slipped away from her. She felt angry at the stupidity of the men in front of her, at her emotions getting away from her. Skip frowned, but Wolf continued to glare at her.

She glared back, daring him to insult her further. She didn't like these two, didn't feel any connection to them and it wasn't because she no longer had rock skin covering her arms: this went deeper. Fox had come here to help. She had wanted to give Malachite's stones to them, give her news to them. Well, she wouldn't. The rock children didn't want it. She didn't want it. She'd find another solution. And she didn't have time for their bad manners and ignorance. 'Give me your news of Oak or I'm leaving,' she said.

'If you're important, maybe you can treaty?' The first man, Skip, the one with the rust-coloured hair, looked at her. 'Because my cousin's right. There's no time left; no time to go sending messages.'

'Treaty?' Fox shook her head. The idea was absurd. They knew nothing of Komey. 'Forget that. Forget it. No one can. No one will. Not without a citywide parley and even then any agreement would have to go out to the provinces, to all the various manor sisters and mothers. Just tell me what's going on and I'll decide what to do.' She rubbed her forehead and the back of her hand stung as the movement disturbed her damaged skin.

Skip frowned. 'Have you got any sort of authority at all? Can you come back to Oak as an envoy? That might work.'

Fox felt it as a thrumming in her chest. Go to Oak. Leave the city. Malachite's rock children longed for it, she longed for it. But the risk to Kelp province was too great. She couldn't leave. Not without permission. She took a deep breath to control herself, dropped a slither of consciousness down into her body, tidied her feelings away like a good Companionari daughter.

Skip gave her a wary look and then turned his attention to his ugly cousin. When he spoke to Wolf, it was as though she no longer existed. 'We've got to get out of here and get back to Mica. This has been a disaster from the start—'

'You're working for Mica?' Fox found that she'd stepped forward and had reached out for the man's arm.

He stared at her in surprise, looking down at her blistered hand.

As soon as she'd uttered the words, she regretted them. Her daughter's life depended on keeping her relationship with Mica secret. And she didn't trust these two. 'I met him as a child before I was taken. Back and Path, tell me what's going on and I'll organise to get you out of here and send you back to Oak. Then I'll speak to Grevillea. With Oria dead, she is best placed—'

'Listen,' Wolf's voice was hard with dislike that felt personal to Fox. 'Mica took the manor last night and six people died. The Oak Companion was one of them.' He turned and spat into the straw that lined the cell. 'Curse her for living and curse her for dying because she was going to be our ticket to freedom from the indenture and—'

'What the Back?' Fox stammered. Death in old age was inevitable, but this? A killing? And Mica involved?

Now Wolf was speaking. 'Mica has the sorority locked up and he'll kill the sisters one by one until the indenture is lifted and the camp has a new deal about proper wages and decent conditions. That's the message; those are the terms. So he's expecting an envoy to come back with us. And to make sure it happens; he's going to execute a sister an hour after sunset if we don't return with some-one. We don't have time to wait for some best placed sister to follow us after you've passed on our message. If you want to save a life, you'd better come with us yourself and you can try to convince Mica to stay his hand. I'm not going to.'

Fox stared at the two men and felt the impossibility of it. Death if she didn't follow them; death if she did. Then she heard movement behind her and turned to find Acacia standing there, breathless, clutching a record book.

Fox spoke, explaining before the other woman could ask what was going on.

'Killing the sisters?' Acacia gasped. 'He must be stopped. But I can't go. I'm recording the crossover. I'm not even meant to be here, only I heard about this, these men being locked up, and—'

'Let me go,' Fox said. 'Give me permission. You're an associate. You've the right. I have a day pass, but it's just for the valleys.'

'You know this man, Mica?'

Fox nodded. 'From long ago, yes. From before. He's a wanderer.'

'He's our leader,' Skip's voice was full of pride. 'Mica's the only one who's even trying to help our people. Everyone else just sits back and watches the suffering, makes it into stories.' He spat into the straw.

Fox found she was frowning as she listened. Mica couldn't have changed that much in such a short period, could he? It was just months since they'd seen each other, created their daughter. How had he become a man who could kill? It was impossible?

Acacia was speaking again, 'Yes, I suppose... It's not ideal but I could give you permission. I have my record book with me. I'll record it and the marshals can witness it.'

Fox touched the other woman's arm. 'Thank you. But you must make sure that everyone knows I didn't run away. Kelp's fate depends upon it.'

Acacia nodded. 'Just don't let me down. Return as soon as you can.'

'I will.'

After that, it was a simple matter. Acacia secured the release of the Berans and they boarded the train with Fox. As the train eased forward, Fox heard the muffled sound of the last bell. She had to hold her breath to stop herself from releasing her daughter embryo. She had imagined the crossover so many times: its freedom; its promise.

Touching the incision in the dead companion's palm, in Oria's palm. Fox being the one to receive the gift. It had been a dream she and Mica had shared. Instead, she was here on a train bound for Oak with all her hopes dashed, with most of her relationships in tatters.

Fox closed her eyes, gripped the seat, and swallowed her sorrow as the thought of the crossover washed through her. She tried to stop thinking of it and failed. Each pregnant woman would do it, touch the ritual cut on Oria's palm. Then they would walk to the propagation rooms with a single pot of soil containing an acorn for company. The new birthmother would wake the next morning, not to a room open to the sky, but to a canopy... If the matrimony was strong. She'd always been sure that her daughter embryo would be the one to attract the Oak gravity. She'd never doubted it. Hadn't Oria said all those years ago in the testing tent, she'd never felt a stronger talent? And to have had the Oak companionship so close to her womb... The Oak companionship. The key to the province where Mica lived. But Mica wasn't the man she'd thought he was and this journey to Oak was not the journey she'd been wishing for.

It was only then that Fox remembered she didn't have any dust bush tea with her. When she'd hidden it, she thought she'd be returning in a matter of hours. She wondered how long it would take for her body to revert to its original form, whether the pieces of rock skin she'd hidden beneath her arms as an eleven-year-old would awaken and what state she would be in if she didn't get back to Komey in a hurry. What irony. This was the first time she'd felt more allegiance to the Companionaris than to her birth people; and this was the first time she'd been without the narcotic that kept her from resuming her Beranish identity.

The back of her hands and arms were numb now. She wondered how much damage the banewood sap had done, but perhaps it was a good thing that her skin had blistered. If her rock skin re-emerged, the sap burns might disguise it. It might buy her a little more time to return to Komey and resume taking the dust bush tea and living her obedient, Companionari life.

13

Mica rounded the corner of the manor and entered the kitchen gardens. He'd insisted on doing the routine inspection himself. He knew he was avoiding thinking about fulfilling his awful promise to kill a sister an hour after sunset. At the very least, he should be directing the fruitless search for Doubt's mystery woman. And where was the boy? Doubt had slipped away from Cast and Ramble and hadn't been seen since. Another distressing worry.

He caught sight of the stables, and his heart sank. He'd forgotten about the horses. He had little doubt they'd be in their stalls, locked in since the night before. His men would have turned the stable hands away when they tried to walk up from the camp and the stable sister was locked in the basement. The animals were probably unfed, untended.

He hesitated, uncertain whether he should call for help, but it was quicker to go feed them and water them himself. He didn't let himself think about the fact that he was glad of the delay. Killing a sister, an old woman... The idea was abhorrent.

He was crossing the lawn when he caught sight of a light in the tack room. There was no reason for anyone to be in there. No stock feed in there. Nothing in there for anyone at this time of night unless they were fetching a saddle and bridle. He started running. He couldn't afford to have anyone racing off to Komey to share information about the position here.

Mica pulled up short at the stable's forecourt, glad to see the stable doors were closed. Whoever was inside wasn't ready to leave. He stretched his rock sense and was surprised at the emotional signature that greeted him. Saury. Alone. What was she doing here, and how had his men let his apprentice slip through the cordon around the manor? He opened the stable door and stepped inside. As he walked down the central aisle, the horses snuffled and whickered.

Saury spoke from the doorway to the tack room, 'I fed them. I gave them some water.'

Her emotional signature was ripe with a sharp, pained loneliness. Another person he had failed. And this one mattered. Fox's sister deserved better.

He came forward, joined her at the threshold of the tack room. 'It was good of you to look after the horses.'

She looked pleased at the praise. 'They were hungry. I know how to feed them and fill their troughs. I come here a lot. I'm friends with Canción and a little bit with El Embaucador, but he bites when he's annoyed, so you have to be careful.'

Mica smiled at her. 'It was lucky you were here. I won't ask how you slipped into the stables with none of the men noticing. There are some things going on at the moment. Nothing you need to worry about.'

'Doubt says I'm good at sneaking about. He doesn't like me.'

Mica made a mental note to talk to the children. They were siblings now, siblings of a sort. They needed to be kind to each other. 'Let's walk back to camp together, then I'll have to come back to the manor. Doubt should be home soon. Quartz too.'

'I don't mind being alone.'

Her signature said otherwise, but Mica didn't contradict her. Instead, he stepped into the tack room and extinguished the light.

They left the stables and headed for the camp. As they walked the path through the twist trees, Mica asked her about the homework he'd set her, collecting stories in the camp.

'People only tell me fourth stories. I think it's because I'm a child.'

'Which ones did you hear today?'

'Lots about the Stone Body. I got those from the old people. The other grown-ups didn't give me anything. They said they were busy. ... and the children don't want to talk to me, even though I told them they had to give me their stories.'

Mica smiled. He kept his voice neutral, 'That might be why. People don't enjoy being told.'

He felt her pause as she absorbed his words, could feel her accepting them. She reached up for his hand and he gave hers a squeeze. He would have to make sure she didn't spend so much time alone. He wished he could tell her about her sister Fox and the baby, but Saury had enough to deal with adjusting to a new camp without the burden of an adult's secret. Perhaps later, when she was older, he'd bring them together. He realised he'd stopped listening, that she'd begun describing a Stone Body story he'd never heard.

'... and it turned into a wild thing. Not an ordinary man or an ordinary woman, a statue that moved, a mirror monster that killed things. Statues can't move, can they?'

He gave her hand another squeeze. 'No. But fourth stories don't tell us about what's real. They suggest meanings. It's our job as wanderers to think about the Stone Body turning into a statue that moved—'

She interrupted, 'It wasn't the Stone Body that changed. It was a rock child, a lonely one that hurt people. An old man from Bass province told me about it.'

Mica would have asked more but someone called out his name and the wanderer felt hurried footsteps approaching. He turned and saw one of his men on the path behind him.

'You need to come back. An envoy has arrived from Komey. She's waiting for you in the manor.'

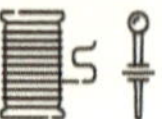

There was no one to receive Fox when she arrived at the station in Oak. The platform was in darkness except for the light the train carried into the station.

The driving sister was the first off the train. She jumped down from her seat beside the wood-fuelled steam engine and walked across the platform into the shadows. Moments later, a spark flared, which was followed by the soft glow of lamplight. Fox climbed down. Skip and Wolf emerged from the next carriage. They hadn't wanted to ride with her, nor she with them.

The sister hung the lamp from a hook on the station wall and then lit a second. She looked at Fox, as though she would accompany her if Fox insisted, but Fox shook her head.

The marshal placed the second lamp on another hook, lighting the way to the station's exit. Then she turned and headed into the platform's living quarters without a backward glance.

Fox headed toward the exit. Skip and Wolf were ahead, waiting for her to follow. As soon as they saw she was coming, they were in motion. She followed, still struggling to manage her feelings. Mica killing people, his actions robbing their daughter of a future; it was inconceivable. There must be some other explanation and she would find it. Had to.

Outside, the night sky was high and bright with stars and the sight of it lifted her spirits. She was on the Stone Body. She was in a province. That at least was a balm to her worries, and she savoured it as she followed the men to the manor. She caught sight of a faint glow to the side of their path, recognised it. Firelight. Camp light. She'd know it anywhere, even if it was the first camp she'd seen since being uprooted from home. She had to drag her eyes away as she followed Skip and Wolf into the manor and all the duties, constraints, and sorrows her arrival represented.

The men left her alone in the entrance hall. At first it seemed odd, leaving her unguarded, but the more she thought about it, the more disrespectful it seemed. They didn't rank her. She wasn't a threat. She was a placeholder, brought here because they could find no one better. Her first thought was to find the sisters and free them, but she dismissed the idea. Someone might get hurt, and the old women would have a dozen different ideas about negotiating with Mica. She was in a better position to convince him to surrender than anyone else on the Stone Body. But she wouldn't stand waiting in the entrance hall. She'd use the time to gather information.

Fox tried the door to her left and found herself in a sewing room. She lit a lamp to confirm her suspicions, but it was indeed empty. She left, carrying the lamp, and tried the next door. It led to a passage to the kitchen, which was also empty. She retraced her steps, crossed the entrance hall and opened another door. The dining room. Horribly filled. Not with the living; with the dead.

She started at the sound of Mica's voice at her back, 'Fox? Come away. Please.'

She turned and saw him: exhausted, worn. He stood in the doorway and then turned away. She followed, closing the door behind her. A honey-eyed girl, a child, stood alone in the foyer. Incongruous to see someone so young in a place of violence. Somehow Fox's hands found her pockets, found Malachite's stones. As though they had the power to heighten the little rock skin that remained to her, Fox felt the two people in front of her, felt them properly, rock sensed them. Mica was full of shame and regret. But the girl... She was something else. On the surface she felt like curiosity and fatigue, but Fox rock sensed the depth of her, and it was familiar. The child felt something like a memory, Fox's memory of her mother, her grandmother, and her father. Only here, in the girl, it had been reworked into someone new. This had to be Saury. Had to be.

Fox could feel the child's own recognition of their kinship. She stared at Fox and her signature was a bundle of longing and hoping, uncertainty and certainty.

Fox let go of the stones as the girl broke free of Mica's hand and ran toward her. Fox braced for contact, but when the child got closer, she slowed, shyness overtaking her. Then the tight sorrow that had bound Fox since leaving Komey, loosened, and she smiled. 'I think we are family. I think I am your sister.' She looked up at Mica for confirmation, and he nodded. Then she frowned as she realised her home province might have failed. 'What's happened? Has Kelp been abandoned?'

Mica held up his hand. 'Kelp's fine.'

Saury came closer, looked up at Fox. 'I'm here on my own. It's because I'm a wanderer.'

'Not yet,' Mica said. 'It will take you a few years yet.'

The child was even closer now, their toes almost touching. She glanced back at Mica and then turned back to explain to Fox, 'I am Mica's apprentice, so I am like a wanderer. Did you know about me being born after you left?'

Fox nodded. 'Our mother was pregnant when the Oak Companion took me. I knew you were coming.' Fox put a hand on her sister's shoulder. Warmth radiated from the girl and Fox felt the comfort and depth of their kinship. For the first time in what had been a very long and difficult day, and a long and lonely life in Komey, Fox felt glad. Deeply glad.

But it didn't undo all that had been done. When she looked up from the girl and saw Mica, her happiness dissipated. She recalled the bodies in the dining room and the coup and her heart hardened.

Mica took a step back and his hand reached for his chest as though she'd wounded him. But he didn't offer an excuse or apology or even an explanation. When he spoke it felt more like a complaint,

'I'm surprised they sent you Fox. Did they think it would help to send a Beranish talent?'

'Don't call me that.'

'I never meant—'

'And they didn't send me. I came to save a life. That's why I'm here. Am I too late? Have you done it yet? It's more than an hour after sunset, so I guess you've killed some poor old sister?' Fox heard Saury gasp, but kept talking, 'I can't believe you would do something so vile.'

'What's she talking about, Mica?' Saury asked. 'You didn't kill anyone, did you?'

A look of pain passed over his face, but he shook his head. 'No. I haven't. I hope I never have to. Perhaps I won't have to.' He looked up at Fox. 'I held off, waiting for the Oak envoy and now you are here.'

Fox took a step toward him. 'Six people, that's what your men said. That's why I am here. And to save the seventh.'

Mica met her gaze. 'Believe me, I hope you can. I want nothing more.'

'I saw the dining room. If you didn't kill anyone, you need to explain how they died. Komey will need to know.'

Mica shook his head, but he began his account of Harvest Night as though Saury wasn't there. Listening was hard. Fox still couldn't reconcile the man she knew with someone who would kidnap the Oak Companion to force a new agreement.

'But my men and I are not responsible for Oria's or Rush's death. We're on the trail of their killer. But I think she's flown. And I'm sorry I offended you, but I just wish they had sent you instead of you volunteering. I just hope the Stone Body has brought you here for a reason.'

'I'm here because you've created chaos.'

'I had no choice, Fox. Our people have been dying because of Oria's wilfulness and entitlement. I had to act, force her to give us a fairer deal.'

Fox gestured at the closed door to the dining room. 'And this is that better deal?'

'Do you think I wanted this?' He was pale now and his rock skin looked equally pallid. 'I had no choice.'

She glanced at Saury, saw the fear in her face. Fox knew she should stop arguing with Mica or wait until they were alone, but she didn't seem able to hold off. The images and memories flooded back: the loss of the future she'd coveted for their child, the bodies in the dining room, the events of Malachite's death. It was all too much. It spilt over, driving her words on and on, 'Whatever your grievance, you should have talked with Aunt Oria—'

'My grievance? Are you mad? Have you forgotten about the indenture?'

'Of course not. How could I?' She came toward him, aware that Saury had stepped back, was edging away. 'But the indenture was an economic necessity. The companion didn't enjoy imposing it.'

He didn't respond, just stared at her, a look of genuine astonishment on his face. Then he started speaking again, 'An economic necessity? And you talk about Aunt Oria as though she was a kind old woman I could reason with...' He shook his head. 'I know it's not your fault that you're in Komey, that you're embedded, but you've got no idea what's been going on out here and I suspect you've got very little idea of what Oria was really like. She could be kind, could be benevolent. I know that. I'm not stupid. But she was unbending when she thought she was doing right. The indenture was wrong, but she wouldn't listen to reason. We tried. We all tried.'

Fox thought about the recent events in Oak. The problem with the timber. Had she missed something else? There had been more suicides. She knew that, but she didn't see how that was Oria's fault. 'The suicides?'

He shook his head as though he couldn't quite grasp the depth of her ignorance. 'Look Fox, talking about the indenture as an economic necessity... Well, it shows that you don't understand what an indenture means. An indenture is slavery.'

He paused, seemed to wait for something. Maybe an acknowledgement that he was right.

Fox held her breath. The Berans as slaves... She shivered. She needed to tell him about Whilomena's plan to sell Berans to the Companionari motherland... But how could she when the sisters' lives were in his hands? When his answer to problems was violence?

She glanced at Saury. The girl had closed the distance to the manor's front door and looked as though she was ready to run.

Fox inclined her head at Saury. 'We should stop. This isn't good.'

Mica looked around and then turned back to Fox. 'You're right. We mustn't do this. You think I don't want your judgement, but you'd be wrong. I welcome it, but not until you've looked at Oria's actions with the same hard certainty that you've used to judge mine. Judge her: not based on the memories of her kindness in your childhood. No, judge her on what she did to us.'

Fox looked into Mica's eyes and saw the man she'd always known: the passionate, good man.

'I'll tell you what,' his voice lifted. 'I'll trade you a sister's freedom for your judgement on the companion. And then you can judge me all you want because I'll know that you're reacting to facts and not some moonlight memory of your adopted aunt. Then I'll find some sort of deal to offer the new birthmother: something you can carry back to Komey to help us out of this mess.'

Fox was nervous about a life depending on her judgement, but she understood that this was a way out, a way for Mica to avoid the execution. She nodded. 'All right, but I can't judge unless you tell me about the indenture.'

He looked relieved at her words. 'And I need to show you the greenhouse, but first I'll find someone to take Saury back to camp.' He turned to the girl and held out his hand. Despite the worry that was still clear on her face, she put her hand in his. Fox found she had once again reached for Malachite's rock children.

Mica watched Fox as they made their way toward the greenhouse. She looked up, caught his gaze, and the lamp he carried illuminated her eyes, giving the gold an emerald tint. Beautiful. He couldn't help feeling glad to be walking beside her, even though she was still angry, still upset. He began speaking, giving her his account of the rebellion. As he spoke her anger and dismay increased and he couldn't help admiring her for it, for the strength of her feelings, but he needed her to understand that life had become impossible in Oak.

'I want to give you the story cycle of the indenture, so you can make your judgement on the companion and on me.'

'Go on then.'

He took a deep breath and began, 'The first story scarcely needs telling because you know me already. The only thing you don't know about me is that I've been carrying this notion that our world is dying.' There was a flash of surprise and alarm and then he felt her tuck it away just like a true Companionari, just like Oria used to do. He pressed on, even though the cycle he was creating seemed bleak and inadequate. 'I felt it everywhere: in Oak, in Eden, in Aries... wherever I went, it was the same. I wondered why. There's an old story that the rock children fuel the Stone Body's circulatory system, keep it in health. I wondered if the stones were failing. This is my first story.'

He lifted a low hanging oak branch out of their way before continuing, 'The second story is the camp's perspective on the indenture. We knew Oria. We knew her as a decent woman. She leant the camp money in return for our time. She didn't entrap us, but we were trapped; Oria didn't abuse us, but we were abused.'

He felt, more than saw, Fox frown.

'Look at it like this. The Companionaris revere time. Perhaps they are right because time is freedom. And while Oria might not have intended us harm, she bound our time so tight that we couldn't escape her. Our harvest bounty payments weren't sufficient to free us. And then I invited in the refugees from Bass and they had to be fed and our debt grew, mine particularly.'

'So there's fault on both sides,' she said.

'Fault? I don't know. I'm not sure that's the right way to think about it. We tried to negotiate. She wouldn't negotiate, so we had to act. The indenture was killing us, literally. That's the second story.'

He could tell that she had listened, had given his account her full attention, so he moved onto the third story, the dissenting account. 'Oria told me Charity beggars the soul. I don't think it was the story of her heart, but it's the only third story I have.'

'That's it?' Fox asked.

Mica halted outside the greenhouse and turned to Fox. He needed to finish the story cycle before they entered the building. 'I'm afraid so,' he sighed. 'I wish I knew more.' He reached for Fox's hand in the dark and held it. 'This is the fourth story.'

'Once upon a time, the people wandered into the slate plains and couldn't find their way home. At first no one was worried: they had their tents and their supplies and at night they sat under the stars and offered wanderer stories about their adventure. But soon, their food ran out and their pile of firewood shrank. Hunter found no game at all. There was nothing nourishing for Cook's pot. The people became frightened. The days passed slowly. Wanderer ran from tent to tent, collecting stories about hungry bellies and cold toes. Cook baked flat bread and spread it with the sap that bubbled out of the burning logs. Finally, a dawn broke when Cook had nothing to put in the pot but a piece of dough that was smaller than her hand and nothing to build a fire with but a couple of twigs. Cook looked down at her fireplace and felt so dismayed that she promptly returned to bed.'

'Later that morning, when Cook awoke, a great fire was roaring between the campfire stones and seventeen loaves lay rising on the warming tray, ready for baking. The camp ate well that day and as the magic recurred, they ate well in the days that followed. At first, Cook gratefully accepted the praise the camp heaped upon her head for being so careful in husbanding their meagre stores, but eventually, Cook worried about what had happened and confided in Hunter. The next morning, while Cook slept, Hunter sat atop the highest boulder on the plains and waited. In the hour before dawn, when the sky lightened, a giant shadow appeared in the south. It rose higher and higher until it split the sky between shadow dark and dawn. When the sun rose and lit up the world, Hunter saw that the Stone Body no longer lay down, forming the ground. It sat up, looking down on him. Then the Stone Body reached up a hand and plucked some hair from its head, delicately placing it in Cook's hearth. Where the hair had been, logs burnt merrily. The Stone Body reached back up and plucked at its chest, right above its heart, delicately placing its flesh in Cook's baking tins. Where flesh had been, dough rose near the warmth of the dancing fire. Hunter looked back at the Stone Body. Blood flowed from the wound, winding a path to the campfire like a map on canvas. When Hunter came down to eat his breakfast, he knew that the trail of blood showed the way home.'

Fox cleared her throat. 'I'm not sure what that means, why you chose that story.'

'The fourth story chooses itself. Tonight I need a judgement, not your insights.'

'Then I would say that the fourth story makes me think that charity doesn't beggar the soul. But I'm not judging you or Oria based on a mystery story. I have to base my judgement on all four stories and on what I know. I'm sorry...' she broke off, pulled her hand away from his. 'I said I would give you my judgement and I will, but I don't yet have it. I wish I could have spoken with the companion. Her account is incomplete. You must give me a little longer. Perhaps this should wait until the morning, unless you are planning to kill a helpless, defenceless, elderly woman tonight if I don't come up with this judgement?'

He shook his head. 'No. It's late and I too need time to think. But you should know that I mean our people to be freed of the indenture. We will not tolerate it any longer.'

'We're bound to the Companionaris,' she said, 'and they to us. That's the point of the treaty.'

Mica opened the greenhouse door, holding his lamp aloft to light the way. He stepped aside to let her pass, holding the door for her. She walked around the potting bench and caught sight of Rush's body. Mica felt her shock as an icy sensation beneath his rock skin. He hadn't prepared her for what she'd see. It had seemed better not to when he needed her honest judgement.

'This is Rush?' She asked. 'This is the one who did most of the killing?'

'Apart from the accidental death of the old sister called Cecily, yes.' He walked past Rush, made his way over to the coffin. She followed him. He held up his lamp, shining its light into the empty casket.

Fox leant forward, examining the coffin. She bent down to look at the silver inlay. 'This is strange,' she whispered. 'There's a name here. Promise.'

Mica found that he was also whispering. 'An old name. There are stories...'

'Of course. Where there are Berans, there are always lots of stories.' Fox moved away from the coffin and walked over to where Rush lay on the ground. 'So someone else was here? Someone killed Oria and this man?'

Mica followed her with the lamp and held it high while she examined the dirt floor around the body. 'We think so,' he said. 'A woman. A Beran.'

She pointed to a series of marks on the ground. 'These crescent-shaped indentations look like heel marks. Someone lying on her back could have made them, trying to gain purchase. What do you think?' she asked him.

He frowned. 'I suppose it could have been self-defence. Rush was violent.'

She nodded. 'And Oria's death might be coincidental. Perhaps she died of shock. The missing girl probably took pity on her and laid her out in the coffin.' Fox looked up at him. 'Did you check Oria's body for injuries?'

He shook his head. 'The treaty forbids doing anything more than placing a companion's body in its protective casket and sending it to Komey: with sorority members if they are available, with us if they're not. And the sorority was not available.'

'Perhaps the coffin was empty when Oria opened it,' Fox said.

Mica wondered whether he had the energy to give her the knowledge of the fabled Beran named Promise, whose coffin this undoubtedly was. He had eaten little today, and he hadn't slept the night before. And the argument in the manor's entrance hall had been distressing. He wondered if Quartz would arrive soon. He didn't relish giving his former master the story of the kidnapping, but he needed to, needed Quartz's help. Mica rubbed his eyes.

'You're tired,' Fox spoke.

There was kindness in her words and he realised how much it hurt to think they were lost to each other: enemies by circumstance. 'The coffin wasn't empty,' he said. 'I had one of my men check with the refugees who dug it up. They felt something shifting inside it when they carried it. Promise was a real person. She died not long after the treaty was signed, but the story is long. Perhaps I'll give it to you in the morning after you give me your judgement?'

'That sounds wise.' She nodded and rubbed her temples as though the day had been long for her, too.

He almost said something about it being the first wise thing he'd done in the past few days, but intimacy and friendship were behind them. Instead, he ushered her from the greenhouse and led her down the path to the camp.

14

The trees surrounding Oria strained and creaked, leant in despite her steady efforts to settle them. Doubt glanced back at her, worried by the unnatural movement. For most of the walk to the camp, Oria had kept them in check; somewhat. But they reacted whenever she got upset or lost concentration and this body seemed fretful. She gathered its fears and tucked them away. The forest settled again. She waved Doubt on.

She had told the boy that everything would be fine. She hadn't been lying, but Mica was a dangerous man. She'd underestimated his anger in the past. Another blunder and she might really end up dead. Dead again. Before she'd had a chance at life in this curious new body. She needed to convince him she was who she said she was, that they could be allies of necessity.

The leaves started their rustling again, the trunks creaking. She sent a slither of consciousness into her body, soothed it. The trouble was, Promise's body teemed with feelings. Too many to manage. She fell back on the method she hadn't needed to call on since she was an adolescent, still learning to manage her emotional life. Positive thoughts.

She picked up her pace, caught up with Doubt.

He looked up at her, brow furrowed. 'You make a lot of noise. You should step more carefully. If my uncle's men are in the forest, they'll hear you.'

She spoke over the top of him, 'Everything is going to be fine.'

He didn't look convinced, but he kept walking. 'They'll look for you, Huntress. They think you killed people. Maybe they're here, searching, hearing all your thumping.'

'If they're looking for me, they'll be at the station or checking the road to Komey,' she kept her voice low, matching his. 'They won't be here. There's no reason for anyone to be here. There's nothing here except trees.'

'And you,' he said. 'And me. But Huntress, some of my uncle's men, will definitely be searching the tents.'

She clicked her tongue. 'That's why we're going to assess the situation before we walk into the camp.'

He thought about it for a moment and when he spoke his voice was even lower and his footsteps slowed to a halt, 'But if we get close enough to rock sense them, they'll rock sense us. What are we going to do?'

She waved for him to keep going. 'We'll use our eyes. We'll climb a tree before we get too close. We'll see what's happening, whether tents are being searched.'

He didn't look convinced, but he stopped talking, and she used the silence to tell herself a positive story: Everything would be fine. Everything would be all right. Her companionship gifts were stronger than ever. Her body was pregnant with a daughter. The province would be safe for generations. She might even be strong enough to fell trees and strip cork bark from trunks. And wouldn't that be something?

She kept herself and the trees calm as she followed the boy. When the smell of smouldering campfires reached them, Doubt halted in front of a large oak and looked back. The tree was taller than its neighbours but still climbable. They'd have an excellent view once they were up in its branches. She nodded her approval.

This was the bit she'd been nervous about: climbing. The habits of old age were with her. She hesitated under the boughs. She could grow the branches in just the right places, but if she did so, she'd frighten the boy. Oria looked at the trunk, uncertain. Doubt stepped in like a miniature older brother, telling her where to put her hands and how to use her feet to shimmy up the trunk to reach the first branch. Demonstrating, his thin legs embraced the rough oak bark, before he dropped down and told her to try. She hesitated. He told her to use her rock sense. Rock sensing had felt automatic when she'd come upon him in the crater and she'd felt his distress and loneliness. That ability was still with her. She could feel his impatience, but beyond that, she didn't know what he meant. Oria recalled Berans talking about being able to feel the Stone Body and everything on it, but couldn't recollect how they said they did it. She stood there feeling foolish, her rock skin silent and unhelpful.

Doubt shook his head and laced his hands. 'Here, I'll boost you up to the first branch. It's easy after that.'

She looked from his laced hands to the lowest branch. It had been a long time, but she remembered this from childhood. She was careful not to rest her weight in Doubt's palms for more than the moment it took to project herself into the tree, but it worked and for a second she felt herself flying into the tree's arms like a girl. Like a girl!

Quickly and carefully, before Doubt had time to look up, Oria worked the boughs above them. She grew their branches, tangled them, made a sturdy platform. A few seconds later, Doubt was beside her.

He pointed at the natural-looking platform she'd created. 'We can sit there, Huntress. It's perfect.'

She nodded and followed him up. It felt wonderful to be so high and so young and so clever. That made her laugh, that feeling of brilliance. It was a bit of her younger self she'd almost forgotten.

'Shush,' Doubt said.

'There's no one to hear me.'

'You should be more careful,' he said. 'You're older than me. You're meant to be more sensible.'

She leant forward, peering at the camp beyond the edge of the trees. It was as though every Beran in Oak was not only awake but standing around and talking. Oria couldn't hear words, but she could see the shadows of people. Some sat around fires. Most stood in small clusters between tents, heads bent in conversation. That didn't seem normal. She wondered how long they would have to wait in the tree before everyone went to bed.

The bough beneath Oria creaked, and the tree's leaves fluttered. She needed to remain calm. 'Everything will be fine,' she said, as much for her own benefit as Doubt's. 'We just need to wait until they go to bed.'

He looked sceptical. 'That will be ages.'

'Then you should tell me stories to pass the time.'

'You sound like a baby,' he complained. 'You should be the one telling me stories. Besides, I'm not a wanderer.'

'But you've been places,' she pointed out. 'You went to Kelp.'

She felt him react, turning to her in surprise. 'How did you know about that?'

Stupid. A stranger wouldn't know. Oria knew, but not the stranger she was pretending to be. She lied, even though she knew that he'd sense her unease. 'I overheard it when I was walking to the crater. I passed someone. Is it true? Have you been to Kelp?'

She hadn't convinced him. She didn't need rock skin to know that, but he began telling her about Kelp. As his account of his journey progressed, he relaxed. The night deepened, but there were still people about, so she took her turn. She told him stories about other provinces as though she'd heard the accounts of Aries and Eden and Briar from others, not lived them.

When the camp finally appeared asleep, they climbed down from the tree.

Doubt led the way through the trees, and now the number of corks outstripped the oaks. Oria felt her arms tingle each time she passed one. They seemed to affect her more than their hardwood cousins. The cork bark thickened in her wake even when she was careful to school her thoughts.

They slowed at the edge of the camp, crept forward, and when they entered it, they were cautious. The embers of camp fires gave off a deep red glow, but their light was too low to penetrate the shadows and Oria felt relatively safe. As they moved through the camp, the painted figures on the tent walls shifted with the occasional breeze.

She had told the boy to take her to Mica's tent. And if the wanderer wasn't in his home, they'd have to walk up to the manor. No choice. But Doubt had been sure that Mica wouldn't stay in the manor and she felt the boy was probably right. From what she knew of Mica, he'd make a point of scorning a Companionari dwelling. If he was up at the manor, Oria was certain they'd find him in a tent pitched in the gardens, his bullies surrounding him. But it would be harder to reach him unseen if he were in the manor gardens.

Doubt touched Oria's hand and pointed. Some young men were emerging from a nearby tent. There was laughter and pushing and shoving as they slipped out from under the canvas door flap. She doubted these were Mica's followers. These were boys, intoxicated by the sudden change in the camp's atmosphere. She and Doubt moved back into the shadows. A couple more youngsters joined the group. She debated retreating, but they'd already waited for hours. Then the group moved away, splaying and re-forming as it rolled toward the central fire outside cook's tent. It was a stroke of luck. Anyone watching would focus on the young men. She and Doubt could move without attracting attention.

Doubt looked back at her, worry on his face. She nodded for him to keep moving. He shrugged and once again took the lead. They crept forward, tent by tent, inching closer to the centre of the camp. Canvas paintings caught Oria's eye: a woman with golden hands, framing a pale blue lake over her heart; a figure of a man with crimson feet, running across the crests of waves. Doubt pulled her sleeve, halting her progress, recalling her to the present.

They were still in the shadows, but had drawn closer to the group of young men. One young man was laughing, stepping from rock to rock on the stones defining the coals of the central fire. He clowned around, pretending to fall toward the embers, and his friends laughed uproariously. There was no anger in the air, just bravado. These boys saw themselves in what had happened: it was a triumph of youth over age; idiocy over prudence.

'Which tent is your uncle's?' she whispered, her head close to Doubt's ear.

He turned his head and looked at her, bit his lip, frowned. When he spoke, his voice was less than a whisper, 'I think we should see if Quartz is back, Huntress. Uncle Mica already thinks you killed the companion.'

Oria shook her head. 'No. I need to see Mica.'

Doubt met her gaze, didn't back down, and she could feel his determined defiance in her arms. She wished she'd done more than sit in her chair when she'd last visited the camp. She didn't know whose tent was whose and wasn't sure how she could have lost track of what was going on in her own backyard.

Doubt was whispering again, 'Why don't you stay in Quartz's tent? No one will look for you in there. You'll be safer.'

She willed him to move, but she could feel his unwavering determination. He held her gaze as though he dared her to break his resolve. She felt an unaccountable liking for him. He was a pleasant child. His kindness almost weakened her resolve, but she couldn't afford to waste any more time.

When he spoke again, his voice had edged up a notch, 'You can't make me take you to Mica.'

Oria put a finger to her lips, and they both stilled, rock sensing a slight stirring in the surrounding tents.

Doubt stepped even closer, put his lips to her ear, 'My uncle wouldn't hurt you, but you can't go to his tent because some others might.'

She'd never find Mica without Doubt. There had to be some way to persuade him, but where they stood now, between tents full of restless sleepers, conversation was too risky. Then she caught sight of a lone cork tree and it gave her an idea.

She took Doubt's hand and led him to it, calling on her companionship powers to thicken the bark. She faced the tree, moved deeper into its shadow, motioned for Doubt to do the same. The bark would capture the sound of their conversation, give her a chance to use her persuasive powers.

'You've been a good friend to me,' she said, still keeping her voice to a whisper. 'You're a good friend to this province and to the camp.' In her old life, she would have bullied him into obeying her, but already this new life tasted rich with other considerations.

It surprised her to find that she'd decided to tell Doubt who she was. It was a risk, but it might give her some insights into how Mica would react, how he might receive the news of her identity change. And that would be useful. But it was more than that. She found she had an urge to share her life. She remembered similar feelings from her own adolescence and early adulthood. It made her wonder whether Promise's body was having an influence on her mind. But the awareness changed nothing. She still wanted Doubt to know. Perhaps he deserved the truth in return for his loyalty and kindness. 'If I tell you why I need to see Mica, can you keep the reason secret, at least until I've met with him?'

'Of course, Huntress,' he murmured, but she could feel his pride at being asked. 'Doubt Not. That's what you named me.'

She leant forward and spoke close to the tree, willing him to believe her, 'This is going to sound strange,' she began. 'I'm actually the companion.'

She felt him still. He didn't say anything.

She continued, feeling awkward and unconvincing, her voice low and hot as she stood with her face near the bark in the heat of the summer night. The situation felt ridiculous, but she pressed on, 'Something happened to me and I ended up in this body. I'm the only one who can treaty with Mica and sort out what he's done.'

Doubt didn't react. Then he stepped back: a tiny movement. He looked at her and smiled. Then his smile slipped, as though he realised it wasn't appropriate. 'Still best to wait in Quartz's tent, Huntress.' There was no mistaking the disbelief in his voice.

'I'm telling the truth,' she insisted. 'I am Oria. I'm the twenty-third Oak Companion.'

Another half-smile flickered across the boy's face, but then he was frowning again. 'Quartz will know what to do,' he spoke soothingly, a foretaste of adulthood in his voice.

'You're not listening,' she said, struggling to keep her voice under control. 'You heard about the coffin they found yesterday?'

The boy nodded.

'This body was inside it.' Oria touched her chest. 'I was there: old me; me in my body; the Oak Companion. We were in the greenhouse. I was. I opened the coffin and saw her: this body. It was dead, but perfectly formed, like it was sleeping. I touched it, and then found myself alive, living in this.' She put her hand to her chest again. 'What they found was my old body, an empty shell. I'm here. I'm alive.'

Oria glanced back, looked over her shoulder, scanning the surrounding camp. All was as it had been. She could hear the boys still clowning around the fire, but the rest of the camp was asleep and she and Doubt were still alone beside the tree. She looked down at Doubt. 'I can treaty with Mica and save the sisters. I can restore order. If I'm mad, as you so clearly think,' she stared at him, challenging him to hold her gaze, 'then you can remind him of the Beranish law of compassion. That's how you can protect me.'

Doubt shifted from foot to foot, looking as though he was uncertain now about what to do in the face of Oria's insistence on her sanity.

She could see that he needed another nudge. 'You were surprised I knew about your trip to Kelp. I was the one who lent you a pony.'

Doubt looked startled and took an involuntary step backwards.

Oria smiled. 'Exactly. And I guess a stranger wouldn't know that Quartz once had a wife, but she died in the winter camp in the hills about fifteen years ago.'

Doubt's eyes widened.

'Now, let's get on with it,' she said, still careful to keep her voice low. 'We're going to Mica's tent.' She took him by the shoulders and turned him around so that he faced the camp. 'It's time to sort out this mess.'

Fox woke to a scuffling sound and a muffled whisper, followed by silence. She lay still, listening. Had Saury woken or had Mica changed his mind and returned to the tent? She waited. The night was still. She could hear Saury's gentle breathing from the curtained sleeping nook. Then it came again: another whisper, and a mumbled reply. Fox sat up, heart pounding.

There was a shadow in the ruddy glow beyond the tent, signalling movement. She saw them, two figures outlined at the canvas door. The smaller of the two bent down and began struggling with the door ties, trying to get in. Fox didn't need Malachite's stones to know she and Saury were in danger.

She pulled on her tunic and looked at the painted curtain hiding Saury's bed. Wake her sister? Run? Was there enough time? The would-be intruders were at the door, blocking the only exit. Fox felt for the small knife in her pocket, took it out, opened it. She stood up and moved closer to get a better look. She was half dressed and only just woken; they were ready and alert but she would protect Saury. She'd been an idiot to accept Mica's offer of his tent when there'd been so much violence in the province. Her place was in the manor. She should have kept Saury with her in the manor. She frowned, realising that she was thinking like a Companionari, not a Beran.

The scrabbling at the tent door ceased, and the figures moved away. Fox waited: every part of her tense and alive, but nothing happened. Tension faded and in its place she felt a momentary exhaustion. She moved slowly, folded her knife, put it back into her pocket. She made her way back to her bed, sat on the edge. She wouldn't sleep, but she could rest.

She was still on the edge of the bed when she heard the noise again: soft like an animal. This time it came from the rear of the tent. Slowly, carefully, Fox stood. She would wake Saury and they could probably slip out the tent door. Fox turned and walked toward Saury's sleeping nook then the surrounding canvas shivered and shuddered. She turned, already knowing what it meant, but needing to look. Someone had pulled the back wall from its moorings. Someone was crawling through the gap between the dirt floor and the loosened canvas wall. And a second person wasn't far behind. Change of plan. No time left to wake Saury. No choice left, beyond using her words. She would persuade them to leave.

'Don't,' she said, her voice low but firm. 'Don't try it. Back out while you can. Mica will be back at any moment. He won't be happy to find you here.'

Already standing, the first figure stopped moving. The other scrambled upright. It was too dark to make out faces, but their body language spoke of surprise. And then she realised she was looking at a woman and a child. Relief swept through her.

But when the woman spoke, her voice wasn't friendly, 'And who are you?'

Fox lowered her knife, hesitated, uncertain now. Her hesitation seemed to inflame the other woman.

'I said: Who are you?' the woman had kept her voice down, but it was still hostile.

Fox gripped her knife, didn't put it away. She doubted she would need it, but she would protect Saury. Behind her, from the nook, she heard movement. Saury was awake. Fox willed her to stay hidden.

'I'm a guest here,' Fox spoke quickly, hoping some of her Companionari training remained clear in her tone, 'This is my accommodation. You need to leave.'

The boy bent forward, peered at Fox. When he spoke, he sounded confused more than anything, 'But I live here. With Mica and Saury. And I don't know you.'

'Then why didn't you come in the front door like a normal person?'

'Someone tied the knots the wrong way. I could have undone them, but I was worried someone would notice me. See the Huntress—'

A soft thud, the sound of Saury jumping down from her nook, interrupted his garbled tale. Saury came forward and then halted. 'Doubt? But who's that with you? You woke me up. What's going on?'

The woman put a hand on the boy's shoulder before he could answer. 'We need to go,' she said to him. 'We haven't got time for this. Go back to bed. We'll leave you in peace.' It looked as though she gave Doubt's shoulder a tug. 'Come along.' But Doubt didn't move and this time she gave the boy's shoulder a shake. 'Come on. I told you; we haven't got time for this.'

The boy slipped out from under her hand. He walked over to Fox. 'Sorry about scaring you but the Huntress—' he broke off, peering at Fox's arms where the ruddy light from the cook's fire penetrated the canvas, falling across her torso. 'You're a sister?'

'She's not a sister,' Saury said. 'She's my sister. My lost sister.'

The comment seemed to set off something in the strange woman. She swore under her breath, looked from Saury to Fox, and then crossed the tent. She caught up Fox's hands, scanned her face. 'Back and Path. Fox Oak!' she spat out the name.

Fox peered at the woman but still couldn't place her.

The stranger continued talking, her voice low but no longer a whisper, 'What are you doing in my province? You need the companion's authorization to visit Oak and you don't have it. And with your sister who was meant to spend her life in Kelp? You know how dangerous that is, what the cost is... By the Back, you've grown since I last saw you,' the last bit spoken as an afterthought. 'I didn't recognise you at first. I suppose it's been some years. But you don't know how delicately things are balanced here.'

Fox shook off her grip, took a step backwards.

Then the boy who was clearly Mica's nephew, spoke to Fox and Saury. He sounded embarrassed, almost ashamed, 'The Huntress thinks she's the Oak Companion, magicked into some telltale body. I'm trying to help her. She wants to talk to Mica.'

The woman turned on him. 'You believed me. And now, just a few minutes later, you don't believe me. I thought you had more sense, but I forgot I was dealing with a child. It's not your fault.'

'I'm eight,' he said.

'You're seven,' Saury said.

'But I'm nearly eight. That's not a child.'

The woman ignored them, turning back to Fox. 'And you? Almost as childish as those two. No doubt you need intimate stories to convince you of the truth that's standing in front of you. Well, let's be quick about it because there isn't any time to waste,' she sniffed, her voice louder now as though she'd forgotten whatever had caused her to creep around the camp and whisper. 'We walked to Komey, you and I, when you were a child. I tested you for talent.'

Fox stared at her, but was almost certain she'd never seen the woman before, never mind her bizarre insistence that she was Oria. Perhaps Fox had met this Beran in the trading halls in Komey. Unlikely. Beranish women needed chaperones when they had business in the city and many just avoided the place.

Fox walked across to Mica's desk and picked up the wooden candle holder. She lit the stub and held the candle up, examined the woman. No, she didn't know her. The strange, dishevelled Beranish woman stood in the candlelight with her head held high, meeting

Fox's gaze. Fox turned to Doubt. He shrugged his shoulders. Saury did too as though Fox had also been asking her opinion.

'You knew my name,' Fox turned her attention back to the woman. 'But a name is just a name. Yes, I walked from Kelp to Komey with Aunt Oria when I was a child, but that's common knowledge.' Fox almost spoke again, a few more words... a few kind words to soothe a confused soul, but as she examined the woman's clothing in the candlelight, she realised something that stopped the words in her mouth.

In Aikin's sitting room there was a long display case filled with antique Beranish clothing, part of his personal collection of Beranish artefacts. And this woman was wearing what looked almost identical to the classic treaty period male hunting costume in that cabinet in Komey. Fox frowned and an image of the coffin in the greenhouse flitted through her head. The missing skeleton could have worn something very like this.

Fox licked her lips, wondering if she was dealing with the tragedy of a sexual assault and a traumatised woman or some magical event. Her grandmother had told her that the Stone Body could throw up anything it wanted to. Mostly, it didn't want to. Fox shivered. Probably just the victim of Rush's assault, lucky to escape with her life. And the experience must have unhinged her. Probably one of Mother Oak's Beranish servants dressed in the corpse's costume. Someone who had heard Fox mentioned in casual sorority gossip and recognised her from her description: golden eyes and wild hair, but bare arms, a Beranish talent, posing as a real Companionari woman.

'Why don't we sit down for a moment?' Fox said, gestured the cushioned wooden bench across from Mica's bed.

Saury and Doubt began moving. The woman was slower to accept the invitation but after a moment she sat next to the boy, her eyes fixed on Fox. Fox lit another candle and carried both to the table in front of the bench. Doubt was pale with exhaustion and now that the night air had cooled there were goose bumps on his bare arms and legs. The woman looked even worse with bruises on one arm and an angry scratch on her forehead. A quick search of Mica's larder revealed bread and water. Fox brought both over to the table. Doubt helped himself, Saury too, but the woman ignored the food. Fox picked up the blankets from Mica's bed. She gave the first to Saury and Doubt, who wrapped it around themselves after a quick tussle about who was in control. She held out the second to the woman, but she remained unmoving, her demanding gaze still fixed on Fox. The boy leant over, took the blanket and spread it over the woman's legs.

'Eat Huntress.'

'I told you not to call me that.' The woman broke her stare to frown at the child, then she stretched out her hand and took a piece of bread and then picked up her glass of water. Took a sip. Fox took a seat and waited.

The woman returned her glass to the table with a sharp sound. When she spoke, her voice was even more confident. 'I can't imagine what you're doing out here on your own, Fox. Don't tell me an Oak parley has been silly enough to send a junior to quell a rebellion...' Then she shook her head as though it wouldn't be a surprise. 'And what's happened to Aikin? I assume he must be in trouble or he'd be here himself under chaperone. He wouldn't send you.'

Fox had been about to launch into her own speech, voice her own speculations about the woman's presence in the greenhouse, but the words died on her tongue. For a moment, the tent fell silent.

'You want more proof?' The Beranish woman smiled, and Fox saw how pretty and young she was. 'Of course you do. You were to have Sven to make a daughter embryo, but we ran into some financial problems and you had to take Louis...' She looked at Fox, expectantly.

Fox said nothing. It was information that anyone could have learnt.

'Not good enough?' The woman smiled again. 'Very well. Something older, something more personal. There was a little girl I tested in Kelp. She was ill. Do you remember that? I found an illness in one of the camp children?'

Fox nodded, a chill ran down her spine.

'And then I tested you. Cut my palm to feel your talent and the Kelp Mother tried to claim you and your father disowned you and cursed your mother—'

'You really are Oria?' Fox said, astonished to find that against all sensible judgement, she believed.

15

Fox listened as the woman... No, not *the woman*. She listened as *Oria* gave her version of the events of Harvest Night and the subsequent day, '... so evidently, the body's name is Promise.'

Doubt looked up at Oria. 'I thought someone named you *after* Promise. Are you saying you're the real Promise?'

The companion inclined her head. 'I'm Oria. And this body? It belonged to a real person whose name was Promise. That's all I'm claiming.'

Fox noticed that Doubt had shifted. He'd put a bit of space between himself and Oria. She reached for Malachite's stones, wondering why she hadn't thought of using them when Oria had made her outlandish claims. Emotions buffeted her: Doubt, struggling against his fear; Saury, full of tired excitement that was focused on Fox; Oria, wound like a spring.

Doubt was talking again, telling Oria about Promise, '... she died a long time ago, hundreds of years. Maybe even a thousand years ago.' He was still fighting his fear. Then Fox felt his signature change as love won out. He shifted on the cushioned bench, moved back to his original position, his leg once again touching Oria's.

'Huntress, you need to talk to a wanderer about this. This is serious.'

The Oak Companion waved her hand, dismissing the idea. 'We don't have one here, not yet, and there are decisions to be made. Just finish telling me what you know about this woman, Promise, and I'll decide if it's relevant.'

'But he's not allowed to build a cycle,' Saury said. 'He's only a boy.'

Doubt gave Saury a scathing look. 'I never said I was going to.'

Oria held up a hand. 'No one's building any cycles. I'm only asking Doubt to finish telling me what he's heard about Promise. The boy is as free as anyone to share what he's heard.'

Saury's signature dipped, awash with embarrassment and shame. Doubt shrugged, but his feelings were triumphant. Fox let go of Malachite's stones as though they'd burned her fingers. She didn't remember rock sensing being like this, knowing what you didn't want to know. Maybe she'd lost the skills to live with emotions, or maybe Malachite's stones were amplifying the children's signatures.

The boy started speaking again, 'People say that Promise was the keeper in Oak. But it was called The Heart Lies Here back then because this is where the heart is on the Stone Body. All the provinces had different names and—'

'Yes, fine,' Oria interrupted, 'but concentrate on Promise.'

He gave the companion a disapproving look, but continued with the story, 'Promise got stolen by the Companionaris. I think they didn't have a manor or an Oak Companion back then... I'm not sure. But there was fighting about plants...' He frowned. 'I think it was about plants. Maybe it was boats...'

'In Oak?' Saury scoffed. 'It wouldn't be boats.'

'Those details are not important,' Oria said.

'There was fighting,' Doubt gave Saury a withering look, 'and Promise got stolen. The Companionaris threatened to kill her if we didn't give them the land, but that didn't work because land isn't something you can give away.' He shook his head. 'I mean, you can't give away land. That's like trying to trade a breeze or some sunlight. Besides, killing Promise would have been sad, but a new keeper would have been born in her place. Maybe a boy.' He shrugged. 'Or another girl.'

'But what happened to Promise? It's obvious she survived for a few more years. This is a woman's body, not a girl's.'

'The Companionaris adopted her and because she was the keeper, they got her to let them use the land. Everyone says she was a slave.'

Fox felt the weight of the word. Slavery. She had to do something about Whilomena's schemes. Perhaps Oria would help, only Oria in her new body wouldn't have any power in Komey.

Doubt was still speaking, '… then Promise killed herself so another keeper would be born in her place.' He looked at Oria. 'I don't know if the Companionaris have a story about Promise. If they've got one, Mica could use it as the third story.'

'There's a fragment. Not about Promise but someone who could be her,' Oria said. 'She was called Troth, and she was a keeper from Oak. She fell in love with a Companionari man. They were travelling to Komey when some Berans attacked and they killed her.'

Doubt looked impressed. 'You should tell that story to Mica.'

'If he comes to his senses, I might.'

Recalling her sister's feelings of humiliation, Fox turned to Saury, keen to offer her a chance to take part. 'You're the closest person we have to a wanderer. It might be helpful to hear a fourth story.'

Oria spoke before Saury responded, 'I have all the stories I need for now.' The companion looked at Fox but inclined her head toward the children. 'You should put them to bed. You and I have important work to do. We need a plan for Oak and a folktale won't help us with that.'

Fox shook her head. 'I think you're wrong. I think you should listen to Saury.'

The girl looked uneasy. 'Only if Oria wants to. I'm just an apprentice. I have some fourth stories. The old people give them to me, but I've never had to choose one for a cycle.'

Oria rolled her eyes and Doubt began objecting to Saury using the word *cycle*.

'Wait, wait.' Fox held up a hand. 'Let Saury tell us a tale. Oria's new body is magical. A fourth story might help her work out what to do next.'

The girl bit her lip, but she nodded. 'Mica said that I'm allowed to share stories, so long as I don't pretend I'm sharing knowledge.'

'Very well,' Oria said, sounding resigned.

Saury blushed but her voice was steady enough when she began speaking, 'It's not a cheerful story but Mica says you have to choose the one that wants to be told. So I can't help that it's awful. This is it, this is how it goes. There was a time when Wife was married to a violent man who wouldn't let her leave her tent. She called out through the canvas, asking Keeper for help. Keeper said he couldn't do anything because he had to look after the land. She called on Wanderer for help, but he said his job was collecting stories. She opened the door flap and asked Cook for help, but Cook said her job was feeding the camp. One night, Wife cut Husband's throat while he slept through a terrible fever. His blood ran under the flap of the tent and dripped into Cook's pot. Cook didn't notice, just stirred the stew and fed it to the camp. Everyone died except Wife because Wife felt too sad to eat. That's it.' Saury bit her lip. 'It won't help, will it?'

Fox regretted asking for the story. It was an awful tale: as though the only path to freedom was violence, and violence invited more violence, more suffering. She couldn't help thinking of the bodies in the manor dining room. She doubted that she'd ever be able to listen to stories about murders and killings without that image reappearing.

'Well, thank you for that cautionary tale,' Oria said, rolling her shoulders. 'Now you two can take yourselves off to bed.'

Doubt yawned and started moving, preparing to get up from the bench.

Saury followed him, but it seemed she hadn't quite finished, because she turned to Oria. 'Mica says stories are like siblings in a family. You're meant to find all the threads that make them a family.'

The children left, each one disappearing into their own nook. After the painted curtains stilled, Fox and Oria sat silent. If Fox had been holding Malachite's stones, she might have understood what Oria was feeling, but her hands were empty. Her own longing was for a pattern in the family of stories. She couldn't see one beyond the violence.

It felt as though they had wasted the night, but Oria didn't seem at all defeated. She questioned Fox about events in Komey and Fox told the companion everything that had happened, only holding back the truth about Malachite's rock children. Fox trusted Oria, but each time she went to speak about the stones, she found her hands had drifted to clutch the quartz and the schist.

Oria sat forward as she listened, candlelight playing on her youthful features. Fox finished by outlining her agreement to judge Oria in return for one sister's freedom.

Then Oria spoke, 'You won't be popular when you return to Komey. But I appreciate you did what you did for me and for Oak. I'll do all I can for you. I don't imagine you'll ever make a dutiful sister, too strong willed, still too Beranish at heart, but there are already too many obedient little sisters.'

Fox smiled. It was the first time in many years that she'd heard someone describe being Beranish at heart as a good thing. Her aunt's words made her bold. 'About the indenture...'

Oria frowned.

'I need to understand why you imposed it...' Fox continued. 'Because of my agreement with Mica.'

Oria's frown deepened.

'Apart from the Wheat Companion's slavery venture, this is the only province to use bonded labour—'

'My reasoning isn't any of your business,' Oria's tone cut through Fox's blossoming confidence. 'And the evil that the Wheat

Companion proposes doing with those poor refugees? You can't compare it to what I brokered with Oak's keeper before he died.' Oria glared at Fox. All the earlier hauteur returned. 'There is no need for your judgement. I will negotiate with Mica directly. Your job is done. I'll see what I can do for your cause in Komey, but your work here is finished.'

'But Aunt Oria, it is you I would bargain for. Your position will be much stronger if I compel Mica to honour your freedom. Don't you see? I must judge you. And it must be my judgement. Yours won't do.'

Oria sat still. Fox didn't need to touch Malachite's rock children to know the companion resented being called to account by anyone, let alone an adopted family member. Fox watched as Oria struggled with her options, her dark hair framing a youthful face that was creased with another soul's concerns. It was strange: an old, new face. Fox wondered whether Promise's youth would fade quickly now that it clothed such an aged entity.

'Yes,' Oria spoke slowly. 'You are clever, Fox, and that's part of the reason I fought for you to be adopted by the Oaks. Very well, you may judge me. I will use my freedom to broker a deal with Mica. That may take some time, for I won't just forgive the camp's debt, but—'

'But you don't have time.' Fox interrupted. 'If you don't go to Komey and have your companionship recognised, the parleys will think the crossover has failed and they'll act on that. And the way things are in Komey...' She shrugged. 'Well, our future will be in Whilomena's hands. She has half of Komey in her pocket and her province lies border to border with Oak. She'll probably claim this land and put her minor expression sisters in the manor to see if they can grow a bit of grain. I think you should get to Komey as quickly as you can.'

Oria frowned.

'And even then...' Fox hesitated. 'Well, it won't be simple. Think about it. What will Komey do to you when the Companionaris see the Oak companionship inside a Beran? Not a child whose body they could realign with dust bush tea, but a full grown woman? Think about me, about my life. I'm bare-armed and powerless and I'm still distrusted outside Oak House. And you? Well, just look at your rock skin, Aunt Oria. It's rampant. I don't think they'll be content with a daily dose of dust bush tea in your case.'

Oria stared down at her russet rock skin. A silence fell between them.

Fox followed the path of her thoughts to its logical conclusion. Likely, Oria wouldn't be allowed to continue to live. The Companionaris wouldn't tolerate a companionship going so awry. It was one thing to have an adopted Beranish girl as birthmother. It was quite another to have a Beran turn up to claim one of the important companionships. And that's how they would see it. Aunt Oria's current situation made a mockery of generations of careful breeding; of the adoption program; of the restrictions on Companionari men travelling unaccompanied in the provinces. A spontaneous companionship in a Beranish body would break the monopoly the Companionaris had over agriculture and they wouldn't tolerate such a future. No, Oria wouldn't live out a single day. She would die accidentally, and her death would open the way for a proper crossover.

'They will kill me,' Oria spoke up, surprising Fox with her tandem realisation. Sadness filled the Oak Mother's voice. 'I can't go back, can I?'

Fox shook her head. 'No. Not like this, no.'

'Then I'll have to take the province and break away from Komey,' Oria paused, thinking, 'but that won't work either.' She slapped her thigh in irritation. 'If I don't claim the Oak companionship, they'll send soldiersisters to process the remaining bounty and disperse the camp. Even if the Berans helped, I don't think we could stop them.'

She looked up at Fox and, for the first time, Fox saw defeat in the other woman's eyes.

Fox took a deep breath. 'I have an idea. I will give Mica my judgement and secure your freedom, release my embryo, go to Komey, and claim the Oak companionship for my child.' Fox held up her hand to stop Oria's objection. 'In name only. You will always be the companion, but you will have to pose as my handmaid while we're in the city, claiming my daughter embryo's inheritance. Then, when we return here, you can rule. But you'll need Mica's help, and Quartz's too. They'll need the truth.'

'It might work.' Oria thought for a moment. Then she gave a short laugh. 'And there's an odd symmetry here, Fox, because this body is pregnant with a daughter.' She touched her hand against her youthful belly. 'Yes,' she looked pleased, 'we can swap the children. Promise's child is likely to inherit my gravity at my next death, at least I imagine it will. So the world should fall back into alignment. And we'll present my daughter as yours and carry on the charade. We'll give her dust bush tea and bring her up as a Companionari girl. And your girl can express the rock skin she's likely to inherit from you. It will work and no one will know the difference.'

Fox thought of her lonely upbringing, of losing her rock skin, and wondered about the fate they were choosing for Promise's baby. But who was Fox to judge Oria's plans when Fox and Mica had planned the same fate for their child? A lifetime of dust bush tea and a Companionari identity... What had to be done had to be done. Promise's baby's loss was Fox's daughter's gain. She looked up at her adopted aunt. 'So how will we prove me birthmother when I'm not?'

'I'm not sure. Somehow, we'll need to work out a way to smuggle me into the propagation room. If it was an ordinary room, I could sleep halfway across Komey and the acorn would germinate, but it's warded.'

'Yes.' Fox thought about it. 'Yes. But it must be possible. I'm sure we can find a way.'

'And a lifetime in Oak Province? Are you willing?'

Fox looked down at her hands to hide the emotion she felt. Had her adopted aunt so little idea how she longed to live near a camp, to be in a province near other Berans? She only wished it were Kelp, or that Mica was the man she'd believed him to be when they conceived their child. She stepped within her own body for a moment and settled her feelings, then looked up at Oria and spoke. 'I'm willing.'

Oria nodded. 'Then release your embryo.'

'Now?' The plan felt rash. 'Right now?'

Oria nodded.

Fox closed her eyes for a moment and felt for her daughter embryo. Slowly, she released it, giving it room. Immediately, she felt it change. 'It's done.' She opened her eyes. 'And your child?' she asked.

'Promise's child wasn't bound. It grows already and the age will probably match within a week or two. If not, I can bind her.'

Fox looked relieved. 'Now all you need to do is to tell me about the indenture and then we can send for Mica.'

'Really Fox, the indenture is none of your business,' Oria's voice was hard again. 'You are an Oak daughter with a duty to the province of your name. You will tell Mica I acted fairly.'

'Are you ashamed of the indenture?'

'By the Back!' Oria glared at her. 'What a ridiculous suggestion.'

'So you had a reason for imposing it?'

'Of course I did.' Oria paused again. 'If you must know, I wanted to treat Oak's people with dignity.' Fox opened her mouth to comment, but Oria held up her hand. 'You asked and now you'd better listen. My family has had this companionship, we've been here,' Oria pointed at the ground where they sat, 'from the time when the great parley used the companionships we'd brought with us from our homelands to help both our peoples.' She shrugged. 'I've got a right to make decisions that are hard: decisions like the indenture. I know what I'm doing.'

'But I still don't understand why it had to be an indenture: why not just support the camp until the next productive season? Loan the money?'

'A loan needs surety. All they had to trade with was their time. The indenture was a fair exchange. We traded what we had: my money; their time.'

Fox nodded. 'Thank you. That helps.' For a moment, there was silence between them. Then Fox spoke again, 'I think we're ready. I'll give Mica my judgement in the morning.'

Oria shook her head. 'No, it has to be tonight.'

Fox felt tempted to argue, but she saw the sense in it. They needed an agreement between the camp and the manor, and there was no time to waste. 'But he mustn't sense you before I've given my judgement. He'll be suspicious of any strangers.'

'I'll wait outside the tent. I'll shutter my emotions. He'll focus on you. I know what I'm doing. He won't sense me.'

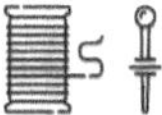

Mica stood in front of the door to his tent and called out Fox's name, doing his best not to wake the camp. He'd imagined they wouldn't be speaking again before morning and he'd been hoping to receive Fox's judgement on his own, but the moon was still high and he had Quartz standing beside him.

He felt a wave of Fox's nervousness as she opened the tent door. For a moment, it was strong enough to mask the signatures of the sleeping children. It didn't bode well for her judgement on the Oak Companion. And if she supported Oria's actions, she wouldn't be supportive of Mica's. Well, she wouldn't be the only one who had judged him harshly. Quartz stood heavy and disapproving at his side. The senior wanderer had returned to camp with a grim story of a wanderer's death at the edge of one of the Companionari valleys. It matched Fox's account of the strange skirmish that had injured Aikin. But it was Mica's calamitous news that had been the focus of his and Quartz's conversations.

'Come in.' Fox stood aside.

Mica followed Quartz inside and introduced him to Fox. The

interior of the tent looked oddly unfamiliar, as though a few hours of Fox's presence could change everything.

She gestured to the cushioned bench. 'Please. Have a seat.'

It was strange seeing her in his tent, behaving as though it were her own. He walked over to the bench seat and dropped into the cross-legged seating position of a wanderer, ready to listen. Quartz followed suit, a slight frown on his face. Mica could feel it, too. There was someone outside, nearby. A woman, awake but strangely empty of anything other than attention. He wondered if she was Doubt's stranger, but she didn't feel ill or injured and Doubt's woman had asked for fever powders. Perhaps Fox had an associate, someone who had travelled with her to Oak. The hidden nature of the woman's emotions suggested the stranger was Companionari. The thought that Fox could be duplicitous hurt, and he had a feeling that she'd brought him here with more than her judgement in mind. He'd do well to tread carefully, but he couldn't seem to find caution in his heart. Not with Fox sitting in front of him in his tent, something he'd longed for.

He considered the problem of the mystery woman outside the tent. She was waiting for something, fixated on his tent. But it also meant she wasn't running. He didn't need to give chase. Mica could wait. He would find out who she was after Fox had given him her judgement. Quartz must have come to the same conclusion because his signature was as easy as it could be under the circumstances.

Fox sat down opposite them. She did that Companionari trick and shut down her emotional signature so that he could no longer read her. He caught sight of her arms as she poured out three glasses of water. When he'd seen them earlier in the evening, they'd look blistered, which had made sense when she'd told him about the ambush. But her skin looked drier now. At first he thought it was just scabs forming over the burns, but when she passed him his water, it seemed to him her rock skin had regrown. He wondered whether she'd stopped taking her dust bush tea. Surely not. Not when doing so would risk severe censure. Perhaps it was just a physical reaction to her injuries.

Quartz spoke first, 'You wanted to see Mica?'

She nodded. 'But it's good that you're here too. It's about my judgement on the Oak Companion. Mica told you about our agreement?'

'Yes.' The senior wanderer nodded.

'And you accept it too? You'll honour it?'

'Yes.'

'Very well,' she began, turning back to Mica. 'This is my judgement: the Mother is old...'

'Was old,' Mica corrected.

'Yes.' Fox nodded, gave a short laugh. 'Yes, she was old. That's the truth. The thing about the old is that they know a great deal,' she spoke deliberately, as though each word needed to be chosen with care. 'Aunt Oria lived through lots of seasons. She saw a lot of provinces and she knew a great deal about a great deal. But she made the mistake of behaving like a mother: she calculated every option and decided what was best.'

'By making us choose between starvation and slavery?' Mica felt his anger rising. Fox still didn't get it. Mica thought he felt some seepage of powerful emotions from the woman outside the tent.

Quartz stretched out a hand and touched Mica's arm. 'Listen to Fox. Just listen.'

Then Fox was speaking again, 'You said that the Mother spoke of beggaring the soul?'

Mica rubbed the stubble on his chin and then nodded.

'But she was trying to save you.'

'By enslaving us?' Mica shook his head, disappointed that Fox would try to wrest virtue from sin.

'The Mother was wrong,' Fox continued. 'She broke the rules of hospitality by forgetting the Companionaris had enjoyed your hospitality when they first arrived on the Stone Body. And she should have offered you hers. It wouldn't have beggared you. It would have been returning the favour. And if that wasn't reason enough, she should have remembered the lesson of her own God's Turning… If the Turning is to be believed then all of us are part of the same generation under God: brothers and sisters on the path to adulthood. When we squabble, when we don't listen to each other, it's as though we haven't realised that our parent has gone: left us to grow into our own collective divinity. We must work together as brothers and sisters. The companion chose for you, harming the province and harming herself by playing mother. She should have asked for your opinion and, together, there might have been another solution.'

Fox looked at him, held his eye. 'You asked for my judgement on the companion and I've given it. You also invited me to judge you. I heard a story recently… about one person's decision spiralling out and harming others. A story about a woman who acted alone, without counsel or comfort. The harm kept growing. You had more choices than she did. You weren't in immediate danger. You could have taken counsel and gained comfort.' She turned to Quartz. 'He could have spoken with you and the others in the camp. You could have acted together.' Quartz nodded, and she turned back to Mica, continued speaking, 'You didn't, so the harm kept growing. You were wrong.'

Mica felt the censure. It was lighter than he'd expected, or maybe it was just that he was ready for it or felt the fairness within it. 'I accept your judgement. All of it. Take a sister with you in the morning when you go back to Komey.'

'And I can take any of the manor's sisters, regardless of her current condition?'

Mica felt Quartz's emotions sharpen. He looked at the other wanderer, but Quartz didn't voice any objection, just shrugged his shoulders with a slight frown on his face.

Fox's phrasing was odd, but Mica couldn't see the harm. Perhaps the woman outside was a sister they'd overlooked. The possibility that a sister had escaped their net had long been one of his worries. 'I can't see why not.' Mica nodded. 'Yes, you may choose any one of the manor's sisters, regardless of her condition.' Then he turned his head and called out to the stranger, his voice loud in the night air. 'Hey you! You outside. Quartz and I can feel you. We know you're there. You can come in now.'

He felt Fox's tension return, but the stranger responded to his words with relief. Her steps were quick as she headed for the canvas door. She pushed the door flap aside and, defying all his expectations, he wasn't looking at a Companionari sister. A beautiful young Beranish woman stood before him. This person had to be Doubt's friend, somehow cured of her injuries. It had to be. And even though Mica didn't know her, the woman had an emotional signature that was both foreign and familiar. But above everything, above his curiosity, was the sinking feeling that Fox had betrayed him.

And then the girl spoke, confusing everything, her voice loud and demanding, 'I am Oria,' she said, 'twenty-third Oak Companion and head of the House of Oak. I am alive.'

Mica found that he was standing, and that Quartz had also risen. In their sleeping nooks, Mica felt Doubt and Saury reacting to the increased volume in the tent, rousing them from their sleep.

The woman continued speaking, 'I know this must seem strange,' she waved a hand at herself, 'but I assure you I am who I claim to be. And I am prepared to negotiate. Not here, but tomorrow with fresh heads. And then, when we've settled with the camp, Fox and I will leave for Komey to reclaim my rights. In the morning, I will sit with you, Mica, and with you, Quartz,' she spoke to each in turn, 'and we will reopen the question of the indenture, with good will, just as Fox has suggested in her scandalously harsh judgement of me.' She turned to Fox and gave her a long, hard, disapproving look before turning back to the two wanderers. 'But I will sit with you, neither threatened nor encumbered, a free woman.' She looked at Mica then. 'Because you gave Fox your word, Mica, one sister's freedom regardless of her condition, and I am the sister that she has chosen.'

'Are you all right, Huntress?' Doubt's voice sounded from his sleeping nook.

The woman... Oria... spun around, surprised to hear his voice. And it was that, more than anything, that convinced Mica that despite all appearances, the Beranish woman in front of him might be telling the truth. She hadn't felt Doubt awaken. She'd been preoccupied, hadn't known to keep her rock sense open. And her emotional signature, which had seemed so familiar, resolved into something that resembled the old woman's: fresher, stronger and more vital, but still true to the woman he'd known as the Oak Companion.

16

Mica parted company with Quartz at the senior wanderer's tent before beginning the lonely walk back to the manor to resume his post. Quartz had offered him a bed and when Mica had turned it down, had offered to come with him, but Mica was too tired for anyone's company. He knew he'd get more sleep if he was alone in the tent he'd pitched in the manor garden. The morning would come soon enough and he'd need Quartz then: they'd share the challenge of facing this strange version of the Oak Companion.

Mica started up the darkened path, hoping the fresh night air would clear his head. And it helped. It was peaceful out. The walk was doing him good and there was still enough time for a few hours of sleep before the negotiations began in the morning.

Thinking about the Oak Companion, he shook his head. Oria, in a Beranish body: in the body of the fabled girl keeper named Promise! What a dreadful thing. He wondered whether she knew that the body gave her a legitimate claim to Virtue's tent and title. Surely Oria couldn't claim the keeper's role and yet the Oak camp had been without a keeper since Virtue's death. Was Oria the Stone Body's choice, then? Mica tried to shrug off the thought that his enemy might be Virtue's replacement. Surely the Stone Body wouldn't give the care of his beloved province into the old woman's hands?

He found he'd rested a hand on his pouch as he walked and that he was rubbing his finger over the bump in the leather formed by his dearest rock child: his snowflake obsidian. The wanderer halted, frowning, feeling the first stirrings of a demand. He didn't want it, didn't want any of the rock children to send him wandering tonight. He needed to keep walking up the track to the manor, needed to lie down and sleep, needed to wake fresh. He took a few more determined steps in the manor's direction, but the unconscious urge he had obeyed when he'd felt for his pouch resolved itself into the distinct voice of the obsidian. He paused. Against his better judgement, he let the demand sound to him. Perhaps it was just some whim he could listen to and then dismiss. Some simple thing. But as soon as he opened his senses, the stone pressed forward, pushing him hard, calling him to turn off the path, to turn off now! He reached under his shirt and removed the obsidian from his pouch, frowned, let it rest in his hand. It felt hot and burning against his palm, alive and hungry to move him like a pawn on a chessboard.

Mica was puzzled. The stone hadn't spoken in months since it refused to remain with Fox after they had created their daughter embryo. So why now? He'd always thought the stone had some strange and singular interest in his relationship with Fox, but tonight, that didn't seem to be the case. The rock child wasn't calling him to return to his tent in the camp, didn't want him to return to Fox. No, it wanted something else and the call was strong and insistent. It wanted him to leave the track and beyond that simple imperative there lay a desire that was thick and messy, almost unreadable in its desperate, ropey excitement. The stone felt like a dog that had just caught a sent. The call quivered and pointed, pointed off the path.

Mica stood his ground. He needed to know more to judge what to do. He opened his shirt and brought the obsidian up to his heart, pressing it against his chest. The stone's voice settled into his lungs.

It was hard to breathe. He coughed. He used his rock sense to listen, enduring the discomfort, just as Quartz had taught him as a teenager. The separateness of the stone disappeared as their various needs and desires settled into the familiar hierarchy that placed the stone's imperatives in front of his own. And so it was tonight: above all else, a commanding and insistent wash of emotion and desire that he should leave the path. The stone was desperate, famished with longing and excitement. It wanted him to carry it somewhere. Somewhere close. His mouth watered with the stone's need. He turned his head, seeking the source of the sudden excitement. To his right lay the diggings that had dislodged Promise's coffin and, with a sudden dreadful comprehension, he understood what the stone wanted.

He felt his rock skin blanch at it, but he couldn't deny the meaning of this call. The obsidian wanted to go to the diggings. The obsidian wanted him to break the sacred taboo: to climb down into the excavation, to lie down on the exposed soil. He shuddered and found he had taken an involuntary step backwards, but the stone's only response was to renew its urgency, pressing him to move forward.

Mica pushed back, holding the stone's desire at bay, giving himself space to think. The call was bizarre; the desire was wrong. Now he regretted refusing Quartz's offer to walk up to the manor and share the discomfort of Mica's travelling tent. He needed the older wanderer's advice. Should he deny the call since he knew it was wrong to enter the gash in the earth?

He opened his fist and looked down at the obsidian. The white flecks in the stone reflected the moonlight, giving the rock child an unfamiliar luminosity. He'd trusted the call of the rock children all his life. Shouldn't he continue to trust it? But lying in the grave... Just the thought was abhorrent. He felt tears on his face, but couldn't distinguish whether it was the extraordinary intensity of the child's longing for the earth or his own desperate longing to flee the call and run to Quartz for help as though he was still a child. Mica hesitated, but already knew he would obey, that he couldn't deny the obsidian what it wanted.

He took a step forward, gripping the rock in his right fist. He took another step. And then another. And then another. He forced himself to walk over to the diggings. He stared down into the hole. The shadows within seemed to beckon. Velvety. Dark. He could smell the earth's pungent breath. He felt himself blush as though he were a voyeur, doing this for his own selfish pleasure. No wonder this was forbidden. The obsidian burned hot in his hand, hurting him. He didn't need to touch it to his chest. The stone's intense desire was clear and compelling as it welled up inside him. He must climb down into the hole and touch his mouth to the dark earth. He must, even if it killed him.

Asking the Stone Body's forgiveness, he jumped down into the pit. The earth walls felt close and cool and fragrant against the heat from the rock child, which had spread from his hand, up along his arm and into his torso. Swallowing his shame at his increasing, and undeniably physical desire, he lay down along the length of the grave. He closed his eyes and pressed his face and mouth against the dirt. He clasped the rock child in his hand. A sound escaped him, a sigh that was his own, and the stone's utter relief and pleasure. He closed his eyes and gave up his fate into the mystery of the Stone Body.

For a moment, he felt as though he was on the edge of drugged sleep and he almost resisted the pull of the earth. But the obsidian burned and pressed and he allowed himself to surrender. He felt the thread of a pulse of the Stone Body shuddering beneath him, then the world faded as he let the process sweep him away.

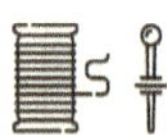

Oria felt wonderful. The morning was fresh and the path to the manor was full of sunshine. Despite only having had a few hours' sleep, she felt rested. She'd forgotten what it was like to be young, to feel restored after a hint of sleep. Everything was so easy in this new body. Everything moved quickly: her step, her thoughts, her recovery from her injuries. And her mood! She glanced at Quartz. The old man was ahead of her on the path. She'd already forgiven him when minutes earlier he'd exasperated her. He'd invited the children to walk up to the manor on a day when there was serious business to conduct, when the poor old sisters were locked in the basement. It was neither the time nor the place for children. And Oria hadn't yet talked to Fox about Saury. Because Fox needed to keep her feelings in check. There was no future where Fox could maintain a relationship with anyone from her birth family. Quartz's thoughtlessness had made everyone's life more difficult.

But then, just moments after they'd left the tent, Oria's mood had lifted at the scent of oak in the air. She'd had a moment or two when she'd needed all her focus to suppress the bubbling life in the surrounding acorns, but she'd settled them.

She'd felt so exuberant, so full of life, that she'd had to stop herself behaving like a child. She'd jumped over the small eruption of stones across their path outside Mica's tent. Poor Quartz had stumbled over them, stopped to peer at them as though they were to blame for his clumsiness. Oria had felt sorry for him, then reminded herself that it was Quartz's age and inattention that had allowed Mica to get out of hand. A province's senior wanderer was supposed to keep track of the younger wanderers. And look at the mess they were in: sorority members killed; the kitchen staff dead; Whilomena with an excuse to move against the province. And Whilomena selling Berans. That, at least, wasn't Quartz's or Mica's fault. No, that was Komey's shame. Oria would find a way to call Whilomena to account.

They were halfway to the manor when Quartz stopped. He turned and stared at the foundation grove, looking toward the diggings where they'd unearthed the coffin. At first, Oria thought he was being polite and giving her an opportunity to stop and recall the significance of the site. But he did nothing, didn't turn to acknowledge her, didn't nod or shift his shoulders or sigh. He just stared at the piles of dirt. She frowned and felt her new rock skin bristle like a cat arching its back. She could feel Quartz wanted to move and yet didn't want to move. And she could sense something of the same from Fox and from Saury. Only Doubt seemed to be himself. He grinned at her, shrugged, palms up.

She turned to Quartz. 'What is it?'

He held up his hand, unmoving. Then the spell broke, and he leapt from the path. He ran, hurtling through the oaks toward the diggings, calling out over his shoulder, 'It's Mica's stones. They need help.'

Fox and Saury were already in motion, rushing after him. Doubt only hesitated for a moment before taking off, too. Oria left the path, her rock skin electric with the emotion in the air.

Quartz halted at the edge of the hole where they'd found the coffin. He gasped and then cried out Mica's name.

The children and Fox reached Quartz's side. Fox looked down and then fell to her knees. 'No! No, please no. Mica.'

Oria arrived at the edge of the diggings and saw the body. It lay prone where the coffin had rested. Several oak leaves had settled into a fold on the back of Mica's cloak. He was unmoving, without even a hint of breath. Dead.

But he couldn't be... He couldn't be because he'd been with them only hours before. She felt her own disbelief and shock blending with the sudden grief of those around her. The surrounding trees creaked and rocked and she had to force herself to calm them.

Mica had started all this. He'd caused the killing; he was meant to help restore the peace. And she'd spent the morning preparing to debate the province's future with him: to weaken his position and build her own. And, more than all of that combined, he couldn't be dead because she couldn't stand another death, another young man closed to life. It was too much.

Quartz spoke first. 'Stone Body forgive me.' And with that, he clambered into the grave and squatted beside Mica, rolled him over. Dirt clung to the young wanderer's face. One cheek carried the livid mark of an hours-old corpse. Quartz groaned, leant back against the earth wall and covered his eyes. The colour had drained from his rock skin. Fox was sobbing aloud now, and the children were crying. The sound of their distress left Oria feeling unsteady at the lip of the pit, the swirl of everyone's emotions buffeting her. Fox's feelings were strongest. The young woman's grief was ripe and hot; full of anger and longing. So this was Beranish life, this intensity of shared feeling?

Oria frowned. It was odd that Fox was distressed. Doubt's grief was understandable, but Fox had only just met the wanderer. Oria would need to think more on it later, but right now she was uncertain in a way that was unfamiliar to her. She thought she should climb down and help Quartz, but was too frightened to move. A fear of losing Promise's body if she climbed down into the coffin's resting place overwhelmed her. Oria sent her consciousness within and settled her emotions. It helped. The feeling of sinking beneath the needs of others faded. She was herself again.

'Something must have happened,' she made herself speak. 'Some violence. Why else would he be here?' her voice had risen again. 'It doesn't make sense. He can't be dead.' A wave of emotion swept through and she felt the now familiar sensation of acorns unfurling. She reached for her pragmatic self, her old woman self and the world fell back into place. 'He wouldn't be here of his own accord,' she said, her voice calm again. 'I mean, here of all places. There'd have to be some reason for him to climb into this... grave. See if you can find any signs of an attack,' she instructed Quartz. 'There's got to be some explanation.'

The wanderer ignored her, but dropped his hands from his grief-stricken face.

'See if there's an injury,' she insisted.

Out of the corner of her eye, she saw Fox struggle back onto her feet. The young woman reached out and pulled Doubt to her, holding him tight. She held out her other hand for Saury and the girl leant against her older sister. Everything felt wrong and out of kilter and Oria couldn't tell whether it was because of her newly found rock sense or because there were currents here that she'd missed.

'His... Mica's...' Saury's voice faltered and then she tried again, 'I can feel his stones calling.' The girl gripped Fox's tunic as she leant forward, peering into the hole. 'I think they want to leave.'

Fox spoke softly, 'They do. They want to get out of here.'

Quartz looked up at Fox in surprise. 'You can feel them?'

Fox didn't answer, but she let go of the children, moved closer to the edge of the hole, looked as though she was about to climb down.

'It's not safe,' Oria said.

Quartz seemed to agree because he held up his hand to stop Fox. 'It's enough that I've broken the taboo. No one else needs to. I'll pass up the rock children.' He leant forward and unfastened Mica's leather pouch, opening it up to reveal five stones. He spoke soothingly to the stones, picking up two and passing them to Saury, then taking two for himself and slipping them into his own pouch. One stone, a bluestone chip, remained. Quartz looked from the stone up to Fox. Oria followed his gaze. Tears were running down the young woman's cheeks as she stared at the rock child.

'It's calling to you, isn't it?' Quartz said.

Fox didn't answer, but she held out her hand for the stone and Quartz passed it to her. She clutched it to her breast as though it offered some comfort.

'We should leave,' Oria interrupted. 'I don't think it's safe here. We should fill in this place. There's something going on here. Anything could happen.'

Quartz shook his head. 'No. Mica needs to lie here a little longer.' The old wanderer brushed the dirt from Mica's face. 'And as for this place, we won't be filling it in. Dangerous it might be, but the Stone

Body's speaking and I need more stories to make sense of the words. Mother Oak, you'll give me the account of your transformation?' He looked up at Oria and she could see that there was no question in his mind that she would obey.

'Well, yes,' she agreed, 'but there are other matters we have to deal with today. The deaths of the sisters and the future of the province.'

Quartz nodded, 'But not now.' He turned away again and began feeling the earth beneath Mica's body. 'The land's voice is more important. It's never spoken like this before: giving a second life to someone like you who has had their fair share; killing another who deserved more.' He reached right under Mica, feeling along the length of the dead man's torso. 'I don't know what it means, whether it's punishment or promise. I don't understand anything.'

'What are you doing?' Doubt asked.

'Mica's obsidian wasn't in his pouch.' Quartz moved down and began checking under Mica's legs. 'I didn't hear its voice, but I don't like to leave it behind if it's here.'

'It must be there,' Fox said.

Again Oria felt the heat of Fox's grief, but she kept her attention on Quartz. 'Come away, old man,' she couldn't help the sense of panic that was creeping into her voice. 'If it doesn't call, it doesn't call. Come away. It's dangerous here.'

Quartz withdrew his hand and glared at her. 'Why don't you go up to the manor?' He turned to Fox. 'And you should go too and take the children with you. Doubt,' he looked at the boy, 'I want you to speak to Mica's men, tell them your uncle's dead and that I want them to present themselves here to witness what's happened.'

'That's too much to ask,' Oria said. 'The poor child's just lost his uncle.'

Quartz shook his head. 'Doubt has duties, family duties.' He turned his attention back to the boy. 'Tell Mica's men they must leave someone behind to guard the manor and the sisters, but the rest should come here. I'm trusting you to see to that. Leave nothing to the Oak Companion. She isn't our friend in this matter.'

Doubt wiped his tears and then looked over at Oria for confirmation. She felt his divided loyalties. She smiled, nodded, hoped he understood she didn't need his protection.

'And what should I do?' Saury sounded hesitant.

'Go back to camp,' Oria said.

'No, I want her with me.' Fox held out her hand to the girl. 'We'll walk together. All of us.'

The manor was quiet when they entered the front door. They found the rebels in the kitchen and Oria listened while Doubt did a credible job delivering the news about Mica's death and arranging for someone to remain in the manor to guard the basement. It felt strange to Oria to stand by and listen to others giving the orders, to accept the guise of the less important person, the person without a role. She had to force herself to remember that the ground had shifted. She might still be the Oak Companion and, no doubt, the camp would know all about her soon enough, but she could no longer play the autocrat. It would no longer serve her or her family, or the province.

The men left and Doubt, taking his new role seriously, left too, accompanying the remaining rebel down to his post in the basement. Fox, Saury, and Oria were alone in the kitchen. Fox sat down on one of the abandoned kitchen chairs and rested her head in her hands. Saury sat beside her. Oria found she had to rub her arms to ease the burden of Fox's excessive pain. Oria glanced around the kitchen. This was her place, her home. It was time she resumed control. 'I want to be ready when Quartz arrives. Would you mind waiting here and then bringing him to the upstairs sewing room when he arrives?'

Fox nodded, her grief still heavy.

'And when you bring him up, please stay with us. I need you in the room. You're a clever strategist. The Oak sorority will be stronger with you in the province. The children can keep each other company, but you need to be part of the negotiations.'

Fox nodded, but looked surprised at the unexpected praise.

Oria turned to Saury. 'And I'd like you to take care of Doubt for me. He and I seem to have grown fond of one another and when he's finished his task for Quartz, he's going to feel alone. Mica's death is hard for both of you, but he's younger and will need more help.' Oria felt Saury's spirit lift. 'Take him out to the stables to visit the horses. He's very fond of them. It will bring him some comfort.'

Upstairs, the house was quiet and unpleasantly still. They would meet in the sewing room, but first Oria wanted a moment alone. She opened the door to her study. The room smelt of burning oil, charred timber, and burnt wool. She stood still and closed her eyes, allowing her imagination to roam through the rebellion, throwing up images. She didn't want them erupting when Quartz was with her and she was trying to negotiate the settlement. Better that they came now. When they slowed, she opened her eyes and focused on the burn mark on the floor. It would stay. She would have it cleaned and waxed. The mark of what had happened was important. History was important and the companion's study was an apt place for it. Perhaps those who came after her would learn from it and choose better courses than she had. For she was beginning to admit that the camp's grievances had some legitimacy, and that Fox's judgement could very well be right.

She walked over to her desk and sat down. It was a delicate secretaire, crafted from oak. This had always been a favourite place for her to sit and think. No one disturbed her when she was working at her desk. Oria leant forward and opened up one of the small drawers and felt a jolt of renewed surprise at her youthful rock-covered hand. She pulled out the letter from her father.

Dearest,

Now that I am dying, I find I can't let go of the notion that I haven't spoken to you about the things that matter. Your mother was always so concerned about bringing you up to take her place in Oak. I hesitated in case those small things I have knowledge about might seem too slight in the face of the importance of that life.

They are slight, but you may find some of the following quite useful…

Oria's eyes ran over her father's advice, detailing various methods of dealing with difficult family members, all of whom were long dead, and his recommendations about staff appointments, which were over fifty years out of date. Her frustration rose. She had remembered the letter as more significant. All she could find on the page was a hint of her father's sweetness. She turned the page over, hungry for even that small comfort.

… and so my pet, remember to give cook a week off after Harvest Night because she has a cousin in Aries whom she loves to visit. The delicious dinners you'll receive in the months following are well worth the discomfort of her absence.

And don't forget that knowing best isn't the most important thing in life. Remember that God Turned to give each of us a chance to act as adults and that those around you should be as free as you to exercise their destinies: even the Berans who will be in your power for all that they imagined that the return of their land would give them back their freedom. So whenever you feel the urge to decide what's best for others, be cautious.

Oria, I'd have you remember this: a world that doesn't change isn't alive. Don't place tradition above good sense and don't place Companionaris above Berans. Both people thread together here: our years on the Stone Body have changed us more than we'd like to admit.

But Dearest Oria, I'm probably wasting this paper with my cautions. I know you will do well for Oak. How could a girl with her own heart so full of love not do a wonderful job as the Oak Companion?

Your loving father,

James

P.S. It is never too late to undo wrongs. You will have a second chance, an opportunity to reverse decisions. Don't let your pride blind you to what is good and right.

Oria's hands shook as she refolded the letter. She hadn't remembered the bit about getting a second chance. He couldn't have known. It was little more than an awkward phrase, but it felt like more.

17

Fox brought Quartz upstairs. They didn't speak as they made their way toward the sewing room, and she was glad. She wasn't ready to talk about Mica, and Mica was the only subject that would have come to her lips. Her beloved, her only genuine friend. How she wished their last hours together had been different. She'd have been by his side. They'd have spent every minute together. He was gone now, and she was more alone than she'd ever been. It was all she could do to corral her emotions, but she would. The business of the Stone Body demanded her attention.

Oria was seated in the sewing room when they opened the door. Fox thought her adopted aunt looked older already, as though the force of her long life had changed Promise's youthful body.

Quartz sat down in the chair beside Oria, then leant back to open one of the casement windows, ignoring Oria's raised eyebrow at the liberty he was taking. Fox sat down near the door. Her hold on her emotions had slipped. She'd been thinking about the fantasy she and Mica had shared: her living in Oak, Mica beside her. It felt like dust in her mouth. Without thinking, she reached out mentally and touched her embryo, felt the steady pressure of its growth. How she wished Mica was alive!

She stopped herself, alarmed that she'd indulged her grief yet again. Fox drew a stronger line around her feelings: bound them up. She reached for a pile of lace patterns on the table beside her, distracted herself by rearranging them by age and complexity.

Quartz was the first to speak, 'I've arranged for someone to come up from the camp to fix lunch.' The wanderer crossed his legs, exposing a surprisingly muscular calf for a man of his age.

Oria glanced at him. 'Yes. You've made your point. Clumsy. But yes, you're in control of my home.' She paused while she examined the pieces of lace in her basket, picking up one and beginning to knot. 'Well, here's a story for your collection.' She rested back in her chair and crossed her legs, unconsciously aligning herself with Quartz. 'Whilomena, young Mother Wheat, you remember her from the Harvest Ball I held here four years ago?'

'Ah, yes,' Quartz nodded. 'Scared all the men you invited by propositioning them.'

'That's her.' Oria began a series of complex knots that Fox would never have attempted, let alone tried, during a crucial meeting. 'Fox tells me she's engaged in some sort of seditious business in Komey, attempting to get control over all the other parleys.'

Quartz shrugged. 'So? All that means is that the Companionaris re-order themselves. What do we care?'

'No, that is not what it means.' Oria laid down her lace making. 'I don't understand everything, but Whilomena is dangerous.' Then she turned to Fox. 'Tell Quartz about what happened to Aikin and about Whilomena's grab for power. He needs to know about this.' She picked up her lace again.

Fox told the story of the orange grass, of the tea she took with Malachite and Aikin, of the wanderer's death. She omitted the enslavement of the refugees. She would tell Quartz later. She worried his reaction would make today's negotiation impossible. And she didn't mention taking Malachite's rock children. Fox still couldn't bring herself to admit to possessing them. But she'd forgotten how silent and attentive a wanderer could be. Mica had been similar, but somehow it had been easier with him than it was with Quartz. The old wanderer stirred. He cleared his throat and she faltered. For a moment, the room was silent.

'Do you want me to go on?' Fox said.

The old man's gaze bore into her, and she shifted in her seat. She wondered if he was waiting for her to admit she'd taken the rock children, but she was worried he'd take the stones away from her.

'I just wanted to give you a moment to recollect your story,' he said.

Oria looked up from her lace work and stared at Quartz.

Fox scratched at her injured arms and hesitated.

'It's just that it's important, when speaking to a wanderer, to give him a full account,' Quartz's voice was calm, but there was no mistaking the underlying disapproval.

Fox sat mute, not trusting herself to speak.

Oria looked up at Fox. 'What's going on?'

'That's what I'd like to know.' Quartz watched Fox.

'I kept Malachite's stones,' Fox admitted in a rush, and felt sudden tears well up in her eyes as her grip on her emotions faltered. She dampened them down again and looked over at Oria. 'I'm sorry I kept that bit from you, Aunt Oria. It was... Somehow I didn't feel like talking about them.' She looked across to Quartz.

The wanderer nodded.

'You have the murdered wanderer's stones?' Oria sounded shocked. 'Here?'

'In my pocket.' Fox felt for the stones: Malachite's two and now, Mica's little bluestone chip.

'Yes,' Quartz almost hummed to himself as he spoke. 'Of course.'

Oria turned to him. 'I knew something was odd when she reached out for Mica's last rock child.'

'She's a wanderer,' Quartz said.

'A wanderer?' Fox looked from Quartz to Oria, then drew her hands from her pockets. She turned them over and stared at her blistered arms. Crystalline lumps had formed in place of her burns. 'It's rock skin, isn't it? I thought it was just blisters from the banewood sap.' She ran one finger over the lumps on her hand. The touch sent a tingle down her spine and her new rock skin flushed an iridescent blue before fading back to her ordinary skin tones. She was growing rock skin again and she couldn't help the soaring sensation that the knowledge provoked. And the guilt. It had to be because of the remnant rock skin she'd hidden and the events of the past two days. She looked up at Oria. 'I didn't take my tea last night. My code must have fallen out of alignment. I didn't realise it would happen so quickly. And also—'

'I don't think that's what's happened,' Oria said.

'I agree,' Quartz said.

Oria spoke again, 'Your rock skin didn't develop after one night without dust bush tea. Think about it.' She stood up and walked over to the window, moving aside the curtain. 'You hid those stones before you missed drinking your tea. There's something else going on in the world, some other force.' She turned around to face Quartz. 'You sense it, don't you?'

'I think so.' The wanderer frowned.

Oria dropped the curtain back and returned to her chair. She looked at the wanderer. 'You suspect something new at play?'

Quartz shrugged. 'I don't have all the stories.'

'Bah,' Oria sat back in her chair. 'It's not enough that you have my house and my sisters. You're hoarding your knowledge as well.'

Quartz began speaking but Fox interrupted him, 'You think I'm a wanderer?'

He nodded. 'I don't know in any absolute sense, but yes. Rock children sometimes call ordinary people if they're in danger, but you've been called twice: once to Malachite's stones and now to Mica's. It's almost as though the tea couldn't compete. Your destiny was too strong. I think—'

'No.' Oria interrupted. 'That's taking things too far. Fox's destiny is bound to me: for the sake of the province and for the sake of the

Companionaris and the province's Berans. She can't wander. She needs to stay here in my new sorority.'

Quartz raised an eyebrow.

'I need her to resume taking her tea. It's the only way I can protect the province.'

Fox listened with half an ear as Oria revealed to Quartz their plan to retain the Oak companionship by having Fox claim the crossover and then swapping their children. The other part of her mind focused on the idea of being a wanderer.

'So,' the chill in Quartz's voice penetrated Fox's thoughts, 'Fox is giving up her life, and her vocation, to benefit you and the culture that stole her from her parents.'

Oria glared at him, but nodded. 'If you want to put it like that, yes. But that isn't the entire story and you know it.'

Quartz continued speaking, 'And yet, we should accommodate your changed circumstances, no questions asked?'

'Have you gone soft in the head, man?' Oria snapped. 'We won't survive without this charade. And I resent your choice of words! We didn't steal her, as you very well know. The treaty took her to benefit everyone. To feed everyone.'

Quartz shook his head. 'None of that is relevant now. You're in Promise's body. You can companion the oaks as you are. Leave Fox alone. You don't need the manor house or Komey's recognition to do the job. It's only vanity that's making you want to fight for your old life. I'll find a place for you in the camp and the province will flourish—'

'No,' Fox interrupted. 'That won't work. It's not that easy. Komey wouldn't stand for it. The Companionaris will kill Aunt Oria and induce a crossover. They wouldn't allow a companionship to remain within a Beran. And even if, by some miracle, the Companionaris accepted Oria, we'd still have a problem because there is something else,' she hesitated, but now seemed the right time to explain about the enslavement. 'We need Oak House to stop Whilomena. She's sending refugee Berans to Galea. She's planning to sell them.'

Quartz's rock skin darkened and he turned to Oria. 'You knew about this?'

'Not until last night, no.'

He nodded. 'That's some comfort, but we have to stop her. This is intolerable. I won't stand for it. So, we must sort out our grievances. Then we must work out what we can do.' He paused and then seemed to gather himself. 'You asked me earlier if I was hoarding knowledge. Not knowledge, no, but there are some stories that I need to tell you before we discuss the indenture.'

Oria picked up the piece of lace again and began knotting, focusing her attention on her hands. To an outsider, it could almost have seemed that the companion had lost interest in what Quartz was about to say, but Fox knew the opposite was true. Oria was using the handwork as a focus. She was preparing to listen to Quartz with all of her faculties. Fox watched as Oria's fingers flicked across the threads that hung from the lace. Her movements were swift and rhythmic. Clearly she wanted to know what Quartz had to say, but it was more than that. Oria must think there was something extra to be learnt from what Quartz would reveal, possibly something subtle. Fox placed both her hands in her lap and closed her eyes, focusing her thoughts, and dropped into her body. For a moment, the sensation of the growing embryo and her grief for Mica distracted her, but she recalled her purpose and the gravity of the situation. She needed to move beyond her personal anguish. She spread her attention throughout her body until she was in alignment, waiting with still and peaceable attention for what Quartz had to say.

'There's a set of fourth stories: the backwards stories,' he began. 'We don't know what they mean or where they came from, but they're concerned with the world upside down: people being born into the wrong body; the laws of nature being broken; roles being reversed.'

Fox felt something stirring in her memory.

'I'm not saying that they've got anything to do with what's been going on,' Quartz continued, 'but a companion mother being reborn in Promise's body and girl wanderers appearing like weeds reminds me of those stories. I'll give you an example.' Quartz cleared his throat and then began. 'Wife and Husband lived together under a rock eave about a day's walk from where we are now, in what used to be called The Heart Lies Here. Theirs had begun as a happy marriage: children; grandchildren; hunting; cooking; laughing and loving. And they'd been content: Husband hunted boar; Wife cooked boar. Wife's boar pot seemed generous and full; Husband's spears seemed sharp and swift...'

Fox stiffened. She recognised this. This was the story that Mica had told her! This was the story that had soothed her fears after she and Mica created their daughter embryo. Had Mica told Quartz? She strained forward, urging her new rock skin to function. She took hold of the rock children, Malachite's and Mica's, and it felt as though the room responded, deepened. This story had messages for her. This story had some particular meaning she'd yet to grasp.

'But as the years passed,' Quartz continued, 'Husband and Wife felt burdened by this life. First-born Daughter died in childbirth; A hog gored first-born Son; Second-born Grandson was frail and weak; Third-born Granddaughter fell from a cliff. Husband and Wife lingered over their losses and longed for comfort, longed for something better. They begged the Stone Body to bring about change: free them from the grinding sorrows in their life.'

The story seemed darker than Mica's and Fox felt uneasy.

'Husband complained that the sun burnt his eyes when it rose in the east; Wife couldn't help crying when she saw the river flowing downstream. After a while, neither of them could bear to live another day under the eave in The Heart Lies Here and so they determined to end their lives. They buried the hilts of their knives in the ground, boar knife for Husband and boning knife for Wife, and prepared to throw themselves onto the tips to bring an end to their suffering—'

'This isn't right!' Fox interrupted.

Quartz stopped speaking. He and Oria stared at Fox.

'I know this story. And that's not how it goes. Husband and Wife don't try to kill themselves. Why would they do that when everyone knows that hardship is life's shadow? No,' she shook her head, tightening her grip on the rock children, 'in the real story they're just bored and they go wandering around the Stone Body and then the Stone Body takes pity on them and turns the world upside down to please them.'

'That's the children's story,' Quartz said. 'That's the version you must have heard. This is a story for adults, for people who know pain, who have suffered, who understand that some of us might choose to die rather than go on living when there's no joy.'

Fox found her heart was racing and her hands were sweating from the heat of the rock children in her palms.

Quartz continued telling the story. 'But just before Husband could act, Wife put a hand to his arm. She wondered if they should test their certainty that all life is sorrow before choosing death. So they travelled for a year and a day, visiting every part of the Stone Body, but everywhere they went they found the same story: tears when rain fell from the sky; grief when the sun set in the west; wind carrying stories of lost lives; rocks covering graves. When at last they arrived back home, they sat down in despair and wept. Husband lay flat on the ground and let his tears fall into the river; Wife lifted her face to the sky and wailed. Husband's tears flowed into the river. The river swelled until its banks broke and the pressure of the water was so great, it flowed backwards. Wife wailed. The sound was so loud that the ground rumbled, sending rocks dancing into the air. When Husband and Wife saw what they had done, they felt strangely comforted by the Stone Body's reaction to their sorrow. They fell asleep then and when they awoke the next morning, they discovered the Stone Body had held onto their pain. The sun that woke them rose in the west and didn't snap at Husband's weary eyes and the river wound its way upstream, bringing a new smile to Wife's leathery old face.'

Quartz was silent as the words settled. Fox let her body absorb the last few moments of the story. She was uncomfortable with this version, but she wrapped herself in it and felt it touch her through and through. She felt its tone; probed its gaps and surprises; tasted Wife and Husband, and tasted the Stone Body's mercy. It made her wonder about the lack of mercy for Mica, and for her. Was her grief not strong enough to change the world?

'It's not a good fourth story,' Quartz was speaking again. 'Husband and Wife are too dependent on the Stone Body's compassion. They're not made to come to terms with their grief and the world doesn't fall back into place as it should. And what about Husband and Wife as people? What about them walking away from their families and their duties? They changed the laws of nature when every listener knows they should have changed themselves. That's what the backwards stories are like. I wouldn't have brought it up if it were the only one. But there are hundreds of them. There's a story about Husband and Wife swapping their clothing and opening their eyes to find themselves in different worlds. Or the rock child that loved its elderly wanderer so much it turned back time and created a world of infants. And there's the one about Cook breaking the earth taboo and digging a huge, deep pit for her fire, then falling into the hole she'd made and waking up to find herself on the other side of the Stone Body with a full-grown twin beside her. Crazy stories.'

Fox opened her eyes and saw that Oria was frowning and had put down her lace. Fox stretched her rock sense, feeling Oria's surprise at the story. The companion had taken it personally, as some sort of challenge.

'Backwards stories indeed,' her adopted aunt said. 'And that story of Cook is too bitter on the day that we have found Mica dead in the depths of the Stone Body.'

Quartz nodded. 'Perhaps it will be the fourth story of his death.'

'How do you read this tale?' Oria looked across at Fox.

Fox was uncertain about whether she could speak. She felt the story was telling her that the Stone Body would change things for her. But the only thing she wanted changed was Mica's death.

Instead, she said something bland about the Stone Body loving Husband and Wife.

Oria clicked her tongue in irritation. 'There's something deeper. I thought you felt it too. This is a story that challenges us to expect change: demands we take part in creating the conditions that generate it, to the point of doing wrong by others.'

Fox shivered. 'So the world could be like that?' she spoke haltingly. 'Upside down?'

'Not literally.' Oria picked up her lace making again. 'But different, yes. The story says the world must evolve if we're to continue living in it.' She shrugged.

For a while no one spoke, then Quartz cleared his throat. 'A good reading, Oria. And an opportune moment to make a start on change as we consider the indenture.'

Oria bit off a piece of thread. 'We are different people: Berans and Companionaris, but bound and threaded together. We won't always see things the same way or put the same value on a particular outcome. But, I agree with you Quartz. It's a good story for the negotiation. So the indenture must go?' Oria looked up, her face youthful in its readiness to be flexible. 'In its place, I will accept your word as surety on the camp's debt.'

Quartz nodded. 'And I will free the sisters on Mica's behalf.'

'That's settled then.' Oria put down her lace and began to get up.

'No.' Quartz shook his head. 'It's far from settled. We want a transformation, not a simple return to stasis. We want rocks in the air and water flowing backwards and our reasons are written across the Stone Body in the suicides and the degradation of our people. The story casts a shadow and sends an obvious message.'

Oria lowered herself back into her chair. 'And the message is...?'

'An end to the treaty in this province,' Quartz continued.

'What?' Oria gasped.

'As the first step toward a new treaty for the whole of the Stone Body. I want an agreement between your family and the Berans of Oak...' Quartz stood up and paced. 'One,' he counted off against his index finger, 'we will share our land and accept you, your family, and your sorority into our camp as equals and you'll give up your residence in the manor. Living in the camp will give you substance. It will give you some right to be here, some position on the Stone Body. Two, the companionship monopoly ends and our people inter-marry with the Oaks if they so desire. Three, we want an end to forced adoptions in this province and to the use of dust bush tea. Fox here,' Quartz pointed in her direction, 'is entitled to live in the body she was born with.'

'The body we find ourselves in is not always our own.' Oria glared at Quartz.

He returned her stare. 'But our destiny should be. Why don't you ask Fox what she thinks?'

Fox felt their attention shift in her direction.

'Do you want to live out your life in a Companionari body with your actual nature hidden beneath your skin?' the wanderer asked.

Fox looked down at her arms. She ran her fingers over her resurgent rock skin. It glowed blue and with the change in colour; she felt a hint of Oria's fear; a taste of Quartz's weary anger; and a glimpse of something else in the air. When she answered, she spoke the truth. 'The only way I could ever know what my body means to me is if I am allowed to feel it in its true state. It's the same for you,' she looked up at Oria. 'Living in that body... Well, you might find something of Promise inside you. But you won't know what it is until you stop forcing your will on everything. I think we should agree to all of Quartz's suggestions. Otherwise, we're like a blind version of Husband and Wife. Everything is different, only we can't see what's changed. My first life was the life of a Beran. My second was as an adopted Companionari. I don't know who I will be in my third.'

Oria sighed and then looked at Fox. 'Very well. Forgo dust bush tea and return to your original body. Technically, you'll be breaking the treaty and putting Kelp's Berans at dreadful risk. But I have ordered the change and that could give you some protection if you're found out, my difficult status notwithstanding. Some protection until we see these changes in our lives and discover whether there'll be an answering change in the Stone Body.' She turned to Quartz. 'I hope that your fourth story bodes well and true because our lives and this province are lost if we misstep.' Quartz met her gaze and then Oria turned back to Fox.

'We'll have to hide your arms while we're in Komey claiming you as the birthmother, but I suppose we'll manage. All right then, Quartz,' she looked back to the wanderer and this time her gaze was more forgiving, 'we have a deal, but Fox and I must leave for Komey and I need to think on our strategy. It might be best if we walk, at least part of the way.' She put the lace back in the basket and stood up. 'Confidence goes a long way in Komey and travelling slowly speaks volumes about confidence.'

'Just a minute,' Quartz interrupted. 'I want no doubt about this. You're conceding, Oria? To the end of the indenture, shared land, inter-marriage, and the end to the adoptions?'

Oria looked around the sewing room, stared at the painted images of daisies that covered the walls, and then turned back to Quartz and nodded. 'How can I refuse? The companionships are dying. Provinces are failing. Your people are killing themselves.' She looked at Quartz. 'Yes, I agree and my child can take her talent where she will, deeper into the camp if that's her inclination.'

'And Wren?' Fox asked. '*The end of the adoptions…* Does that apply to her too?'

Oria paled at the question. 'Ah, poor Wren. Yes. I don't know how, but we'll find a way for her too.'

Then they began working out the details of the next few days. The sorority would remain confined for the moment. It would give Quartz and Oria time to speak to the camp and ratify the new agreement without worrying about the sisters' reactions. In the meantime, Fox would write out a message for Oak House and for Aikin, telling them she was well, that the province was in safe hands again, that she would walk back to Komey with some of the sorority and that she was carrying good news. Oria had advised against staking

Fox's birthmother claim on paper. There would be time enough to prevent the breakup of the province. Even with Whilomena's political ambitions, it would take days for the parleys to agree to either abandoning Oak and dispersing its population or handing the leases over to its neighbours.

But in all their arrangements, one thing was missing: they had no answer to Whilomena's plans to enslave the Beranish diaspora. Fox would always be powerless as a Beranish birthmother and Oria must keep herself hidden and keep secret the province's new treaty, at least for now. Neither one could act to save the Berans from the Galean ships or bring back those who'd already been taken. Fox just hoped that they'd come up with a plan during the journey to Komey.

In the afternoon, before Quartz took the new treaty to the camp, they gave Mica's body to a twist tree. Fox thought that her heart would break with the vision of it: the body in the tree's arms, the pattern of the branches against the sky.

18

'How nice is this?' Whilomena smiled at Aikin. 'Being together on the Cava River, leaving Komey's troubles behind us.'

Aikin smiled, but he felt uneasy. He needed this trip. It was his best chance to acquire more rock children, but he hadn't liked the timing. Komey was still reeling from the news of his aunt's death and the crossover's failure. Perhaps it was lucky that Whilomena had insisted. He might not have come otherwise. His head still ached from the incident with Malachite and he was worried about what Fox was doing. She'd run off to meddle in the troubles in Oak, hadn't thought to do anything more than leave notice with that associate, Acacia, the woman from house records. She should have waited to speak with him, her own father. But he'd promised himself to enjoy this trip with Whilomena, not dwell on the troubles facing Oak House. And Whilomena looked wonderful. So wonderful she almost had him forgetting his lingering pain and his worries about the future. She stood beside him at the prow of the barge, near the figurehead that reared up extravagantly above the flat vessel. The barges that travelled between Komey and New Lytalia didn't have figureheads, but Whilomena had wrested some sort of concession from the proud and independent riverhood. This barge had been renamed the *Grassy Splendour* in Whilomena's honour, and they'd fitted it with Galean engines that made a mockery of time, and a figurehead that memorialised the Wheat Companion.

She reached up and tapped the carving's head and giggled. 'And this is lovely. I think they really captured my hair, don't you?'

Aikin took a step back to compare the wooden woman to the live one. There was no doubt about the likeness, and the figurehead's face was well done, but it didn't catch Whilomena's essence. But the hair was right. The wooden locks curled delicately like shavings falling from a plane. It was hard to fault the craftsmanship, but the real woman was infinitely lovelier. He wanted to reach out and touch her.

'No artist born could ever capture you,' he murmured.

She laughed. 'That's lovely, Aikin, but do stop staring at me.' She made a face. 'They can't hear us, but they can see us and you're staring at me like a lover.'

Aikin stiffened, glancing back at the riverhood crew and at Whilomena's entourage. There were too many people about. The crew wasn't interested in them, but Whilomena's sorority members and the small complement of soldiersisters who had accompanied them on the trip were watching. Scrutinising every movement. He frowned, hating the situation, hating the enforced secrecy.

'Oh, come on Aikin. Don't be touchy,' she chided. 'We slept through the boring part of the trip—'

'In separate cabins.'

'But now we have a glorious day ahead of us. Get over this silliness about wanting all of Komey to know about us. I told you, we can announce ourselves after Komey's accepted my leading parley idea. I can't afford criticism and gossip at the moment. And don't sulk about it either, because what has to be, has to be.'

'I'm not sulking.' Aikin watched the dark riverbanks and the empty landscape sliding by. The Pike Companion's province would be nothing without the port. Her land was uncultivated and unproductive, but the port controlled and levied every single trade between the Stone Body and Galea.

'You are so sulking, but you won't be for long. We're going to have great fun.'

'Watching your slaves being loaded onto a ship?' He turned to face her, still consumed with resentment about the illicit nature of their affair.

'No, because they're already on the ship.' She pouted. 'And they're not slaves, Aikin. They're not! They can return to the Stone Body once they've worked off their food debt—'

'And paid for their passage back across the Komic Sea,' he pointed out.

'Well, of course.' She shook her head. 'You can't expect the traders to carry the Berans for nothing and I'm certainly not paying for their passage back from the motherland. Anyway...' She frowned. 'Stop being so nasty Aikin. We won't be looking at any of my *labourers* either on ship or off ship. We're just checking that everything is in order and collecting my payment for factoring their debts.' She smiled, pleased with her sophistry. 'And then we can go shopping.' She clapped her hands and laughed. 'And you know how much you and I both love shopping.'

'And the wanderers you promised me?'

'Are yours, just as promised.' This time, her smile was warm and genuine because she loved giving him gifts. 'I've sent for them to be taken off the ship and they're waiting for you in the trader's warehouse. But your word, Aikin,' she held up a finger, 'you won't let them go running around telling everyone on the Stone Body about my arrangement to factor refugee debts? You can't just let them go when you've finished with them. I don't want them telling fireside stories to other wanderers about the deal I've made.' A worried expression crossed her pretty face.

'No, darling.' He smiled. 'I'd never hurt you. Those wanderers will come back on the barge with us and they won't be talking to anyone.

I'm taking them to Komey and they'll stay in our cells at Oak House until all this blows over and prosperity returns.'

'You might be better off killing them when you've finished with them.' She didn't look at him, just ran her fingers along the handrail. 'What is it you want them for, again? You didn't say.'

Aikin held his breath for a moment. Could she be joking about killing them, or did she mean it? Nothing in her demeanour suggested humour. 'About that, about getting rid of them after...' he said. 'I wouldn't have suggested it, but that was my intention. I was loath to burden you with the thought.'

She looked up at him and smiled. 'Oh, but I'm not as weak as I look, Aikin. You should know that by now.'

He nodded. Her small, elegant frame had never deceived him. But he hadn't realised that her pragmatic mind stretched as far as his own. It would make their futures easier, but it wasn't just that. It would mean that they could share the burdens and pain of power. He remembered Lester Adamite's famous words lauding his wife in *The Age of Intent* and realised that he felt about Whilomena, the way Adamite felt about his wife: *Oh, the sweetness of my dear and loyal companion. How I flourish; how I bloom in your presence.* Now more than ever, Aikin wished he could marry Whilomena: that she would marry him. But he didn't say so. He couldn't. Not yet. He just looked at her with gratitude. 'I'm glad you spoke up, Whilomena,' he said. 'It brings us closer.'

'So, tell me why you want those wanderers. I want the truth. What are you going to do with them before you kill them?'

He decided to tell her part of it. 'I want their rock children,' he whispered, leaning forward, but not too close, nothing to make tongues wag.

She nodded. 'More taboo artefacts? Are they important? Is this some special project?'

'You could say that, yes.' He grinned at her. 'There's more I could add, but it would spoil the surprise.'

'A surprise?' She looked delighted at the thought. 'For me?'

'For you and me and Komey, although the city won't understand the half of it. And if I'm right, it's going to be no end of help with this first parley you're trying to create.'

She turned to face him, solemn now. 'I know you think I'm frivolous.'

'You are.' He nodded.

'Yes, and spoilt.' She held his gaze. 'But I love Komey and us, the Companionari people. And I'm no fool. I can see the trouble we're in: the provinces failing; the refugees.'

'The Oak crossover failing,' he said.

'Yes,' she agreed. 'We won't be able to survive this crisis with our existing system of government. This parley of mine can carry us through the dark times. And there'll be side benefits too,' she smiled again and pulled herself up to sit on the handrail, her arm wrapped around the figurehead for balance so that she was closer to where Aikin stood. 'I'll be able to make our relationship public; I'll be able to rewrite the social rules.'

Aikin almost told her then, but didn't. What was the point in promising her a dowry that would give them the exclusive power to answer the provincial failures when he still couldn't do it? But if these wanderers she'd found for him had stones, he'd try out his new idea on his childless cousins, Glory Bass and Talia Oak. Neither was pregnant, and both were ready to risk their lives for a chance at companionship powers.

But Aikin was worried. Treating his cousins was an immense responsibility. What if he killed them like he'd killed the others? He wouldn't be able to keep his experiments secret much longer. He'd already involved far too many Companionari women in his trials. And his continued interest in locating wanderers couldn't go unmarked indefinitely. But this new idea of his would create new companions. It must! The ledger in *The Book of Kinesis* listed marriages, not failed engagements, and there was only one route left: through the skin. And if he was right? Well, his marriage to Whilomena would be the least of it. They'd save Oak and the fortunes of the Oak family. Why, he'd be able to transform the Stone Body, forge a new treaty with the Berans that was more favourable to the Companionaris and let Whilomena re-order the body politic to suit her fancy.

He smiled, and Whilomena smiled back. She was right. They had the day together, and the trip back, and he would get his wanderers and there was no reason they wouldn't be carrying stones. So he and Whilomena should enjoy themselves. The shadowy pain in his head, the stiffness in his shoulders, his worry about Fox, and the enforced secrecy of his relationship with Whilomena? Well, they were nothing on a day when he and Whilomena had shared a decision over the wanderers, had renewed their bond. Trust was a sweet thing.

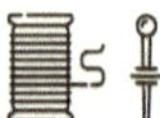

The deck rocked beneath Aikin's feet as the crew opened the final lock and the barge moved downriver toward the port. Whilomena suggested it was time to return to the captain's cabin, but he said no. Couldn't bear to be indoors. Besides, he wanted to watch the port, get a feel for the place before they disembarked.

New Lytalia. The town had grown up around the mouth of the Cava. It was the site of the first settlement, but most of the Galean settlers had moved upriver to establish Komey within six months of their arrival. That was before the settlers renamed themselves Companionaris, before they found and then hid the secret to creating companions.

The land around the Cava's mouth was marshy and beyond that it was steep and flinty and the port was windy in all seasons. Unsuitable for farming. Aikin didn't mind the wind. It was full of salt and promise blowing in from the Komic Sea. The port had not only survived; it had thrived. The steady traffic of Galean and Lytalian traders moving produce across the Komic Sea ensured a stable Companionari population that built tall weathered houses and provincial embassies on the steep and narrow streets.

Aikin counted seven ships at anchor and wondered which one carried Whilomena's Beranish refugees. Impossible to tell. He squinted. There seemed to be a crowd of people standing on the quay, watching *The Grassy Splendour's* progress. Evidently, the locals had come out to greet Whilomena. There had been a time in Komey when her youth and beauty had attracted an obsessive cult following. He peered at the crowd. The furthest section seemed to be filled with men. That was odd. With Whilomena, it was usually mothers pushing their daughters forward, hoping the girls would find favour and maybe, one day, they'd see their treasures serving in the Wheat sorority.

He frowned. It looked as though there were two distinct crowds. The furthest one seemed clustered and full of men with just a couple of people walking its perimeter. The other was looser and stood closer to the *Splendour's* berth. He looked at the distant group a little more closely. The people walking the perimeter were wearing uniforms. Military sisters circling a group of men.

Aikin turned, keen to see whether Whilomena had noticed the crowds, but he couldn't see her or her entourage. They must have gone below deck. The riverhood crew was busy checking the ropes and stowing the barge poles. The deck vibrated with the movement and noise of the Galean engine that hurried the barge toward the quay. He turned back to the wharf. The view was clearer now. The soldiersisters were guarding a group of Beranish men. Odd. But he'd been right about the other crowd. It was a welcoming party.

The welcoming party was a nuisance, but the Berans and the Pike militia were infinitely more troubling. It was obvious to Aikin these were some of Whilomena's refugee slaves. And why on earth were they gathered on the quay instead of being tucked away on the ship? Whilomena wouldn't be happy about it. It was the sort of thing that stimulated local parleys. Like as not, one of the port parleys would make some sort of decision against transporting any Berans to Galea, then Whilomena would have no end of irritation lobbying everyone involved to turn that about.

By the time the Wheat party had disembarked, the crowd of local worthies had surged forward, blocking the view of the refugees. Whilomena was the first off: a sister in front and a sister behind, helping her make her way over the gangway as though she might slip and fall. Aikin smiled, knowing how robust she was. He followed close behind, not wanting to be separated when they had work to do and shopping to enjoy.

Whilomena smiled and shook hands with people in the crowd who'd gathered to welcome her. There were gifts of flowers, hand-woven fabrics and elaborate pieces of lace. All handed over with assurances from older relatives that their daughter... niece... grand-daughter... had done the work herself: woven it, knotted it, grown it. It made him wonder what the Pike Companion would say. Her people and her port fawning on the Wheat Companion.

Whilomena kissed the cheeks of little girls and touched the hands of mothers, and passed the presents back along the sorority line, the end of which reached all the way to the skipper's cabin.

Then a Lytalian trader pressed forward through the crowd and bowed to Whilomena. 'Mother Wheat,' he boomed, his phlegmy voice carrying a slight whistle. 'Charmed to see you here in town; charmed to have my ship under your contract. Now ma'am,' he paused, frowned and half turned toward the rest of the wharf, waving a hand at the just visible Beranish men beyond the welcoming crowd, 'I've separated out all your wanderers, just as you asked. Couldn't put them in our warehouse, far too many of them and I've got precious cargo inside that might get damaged. But ma'am...' he turned back to look at Whilomena, pushing back his hat, exposing his sweat dampened hair, 'by the numbers, it's going to dent our agreement. There's just so many of them.'

Aikin's stomach knotted. After all the care he'd taken to ensure that his interest in wanderers went unnoticed; after all Whilomena's efforts to see that they swept her *labourers* off the Stone Body without comment, this fool was trumpeting their business.

Whilomena frowned at the trader. 'I think they have deceived you, Sir. There are not so many wanderers in the whole of the Stone Body as you have men standing on the quay.'

The local crowd, which had wandered away, seemed to gather itself again as people listened to what was being said and eyed the men.

An elderly woman called out a question, 'And what are these men *for,* Mother? We rarely see Berans in New Lytalia. And their men don't have any business being here, surely?'

'Are you settling them hereabouts?' a middle-aged man asked. 'Because we're not really set up for them. There'd be nowhere for them to camp. And their women would come after our young men. Which would be a tragedy because we've always had the freedom of the town down here. Not had to put up with walls like the men in Komey do.'

Aikin stepped up to Whilomena's side and started speaking before she answered. 'Mother Wheat's doing a favour for the Department of Beranish Affairs. Nothing to worry about. The refugees won't be staying here. We're doing an exchange with the motherland. The motherland will help feed them during the crisis.'

Several people looked relieved.

Whilomena gave one of her dazzling smiles to the crowd. 'So good of you to come and greet me. But I'm here to work.' She turned to the trader. 'Perhaps we should retire to your office?'

The crowd dispersed, walking in small groups over the uneven planks and eyeing the men, no doubt talking about all they'd seen and heard. Whilomena's party made its way toward one of the green wooden warehouses built on the quay. She sent most of her sorority back onto the barge and then stationed the rest in the trader's front office where they sat about on the uncomfortable spindly legged chairs so loved in Galea. By the time the trader ushered them into his inner sanctum, it was just the three of them.

'Back and Path, man!' Whilomena glared at the trader across his zinc-covered desk. 'What were you thinking, letting all those men stand about on the wharf for anyone to see? This is a delicate business. Affairs in Komey are tricky.'

'But you told me to separate off the wanderers.'

Aikin spoke, 'And what, exactly, did you tell the Berans on the ship when you called for the wanderers?'

'Just what Mother Wheat's note said.' He sat behind his grand desk, his hat beside him, his hair plastered with sweat. 'That the wanderers would stay on the Stone Body...' He shrugged. 'Asked them to come forward. Don't know what else you expected.'

Whilomena stood up, leant over the desk. 'Fool. And who wouldn't then claim he was a wanderer? We'll have to sort them out. Send most of them back to the ship. And we'll have to do it under the eye of every window facing the port. It won't do. Not at all!'

'But I've got china stored in the warehouse,' the man complained, 'and silks, too. I can't have all those men in there.'

Whilomena sat back down, but she held the man's eye and her voice was icy when she spoke, 'Leave us alone.'

Aikin watched the trader leave, then glanced around the room, checking that they were alone, that there weren't any unnoticed openings. There was nothing but bare white walls, a series of upright wooden chairs and the zinc-covered desk in front of them.

Whilomena walked over to the door and checked the corridor. She closed it again and came back to sit beside Aikin. She pulled her chair close. 'Too many ears in this place,' she complained. 'Aikin darling. I'm sorry, but I need to get them out of public sight, load them back on the ship, send them off. We can't be fussing around trying to work out who is who and searching them for silly stones. Next time I'll get the wanderers out before I send them all downriver and we won't have this problem.'

He shook his head. 'No, you mustn't. I need their rock children.'

'Can't you just get some other wanderers from a nearby camp? There's no shortage on the Stone Body.'

'When you end up having to kill them, there is.' He looked up and met her eye. 'The men you've got are perfect. No one will miss them. They're already displaced.'

'What are you *really* up to, Aikin?'

'I told you: I'm doing something for you and me, for the Companionaris and the Berans—'

'Then you need to explain.'

Aikin thought about it for a moment and then nodded, drawing his chair even closer. He told her about becoming convinced that all the companionships were facing imminent failure.

'Don't be stupid,' her laugh was breathless, awkward, and her hand fluttered as though she could push the idea away. 'A couple of weak companions doesn't mean we're all failing.'

Aikin thought her reaction was strange, flighty and fearful. 'Have you noticed any changes in your abilities?'

'Me?' she cleared her throat. 'Me?' she laughed. 'Oh, no.' She shook her head. 'No. Of course not. Everyone knows how powerful I am.'

Her denial didn't sound right, but the trader's office wasn't the place and this wasn't the time, so he let it pass. Instead, he laid out his thinking about the failed companionships and she listened. She looked as though she wanted to argue, but she listened. '... catastrophic agricultural collapse is already on top of us.'

'And you've found a solution? Something to do with wanderers' stones?'

He nodded, told her about *The Book of Kinesis* and its curious ledger and his efforts to date, '... so I've wasted most of the stones and lost more than a few lives and I've nothing solid to show for it. There's only one stone left, and I suspect it isn't the real thing. That's why I need these rock children. I'm going to try subcutaneous application. I can't think of any other way because there has to be some sort of joining of rock to woman, and woman to rock.'

She looked disgusted, but just shrugged her shoulders. 'If that's what's necessary, that's what's necessary. Komey's current efforts won't fix things. Did you hear the parleys are calling for the Oak candidates to spend another week in the propagation rooms? Stupid. Oak House is finished. A week, a month in the propagation rooms. It won't make any difference. They're just going through the motions because they can't bear to admit the province has failed. And most people know it too. I also heard there are five different wakes planned.' She shook her head. 'I'm glad we're not in the city. I don't want to drink to the memory of your family's bounty.' She looked up.

'That's the thing, Whilomena. It's my family we're talking about. Never mind helping Glory Bass, even though she is a cousin. She can wait. But I've got to try with Talia. And these wanderers are my best chance.'

Whilomena licked her lips. 'It might be messy. The wanderers won't just pass their stones over. I wish you'd told me earlier. I could have made different arrangements. That stupid, ignorant trader. Probably never laid eyes on a Beran before, let alone a wanderer.'

'If there weren't so many witnesses,' Aikin sat back, 'if there was no one about, I'd have all those men out on the wharf killed and then I'd search the bodies.'

She shook her head. 'I know. But even if you could do it without being seen, who'd kill them for you?'

'That's doable,' he said. 'Three of the soldiersisters who accompanied us work for me.'

She didn't look pleased.

It was his turn to shrug. 'Captain Birch and Privates Scott and Fable.'

'Well, that's something. But we don't have the numbers. Not for open confrontation. But...?' She hesitated.

'Go on.' He held her gaze.

'Well, there's always poison, isn't there? We could feed those men. We could gather them in the trader's warehouse and feed them.'

'Then carry all those bodies to the ship...?' He shook his head. 'No, but I think you're onto something. Let's load them all back onto the ship under guard. Then we poison them: all of them. Women and children too. We don't want any Beranish witnesses. Then the trader can throw the bodies overboard once he's out to sea. But you'll lose all your money, Whilomena. And we could be stuck here for days.'

'Never mind the money.' She waved her hand. 'This is vital. And we don't have to be stuck here for days. I'll have them loaded up right now. They'll be thirsty and we can poison the water. I have a source in port. Not that I'm in the habit—'

'No,' he agreed. 'I never thought you were.'

'But there are people in New Lytalia who deal in many things, and I inherited some of those contacts from my mother and I've made some of my own. And we can use your Birch and the others to see to it. Afterwards, they can search the bodies. I assume they know what they're looking for?'

Aikin nodded.

'And you and I will go shopping,' she said. 'We'll act as naturally as can be, and we can be out of here before night with the rock children in our hands.'

'And the sailors?'

'Well, yes. That's an issue, but I'll pay off the trader and he can keep the crew on board till it's done and they've weighed anchor. No one goes into port. And I'll pay to ensure that none of those men cross the Komic Sea again. They'll talk in Galea, but...' She shrugged. 'Hopefully, you'll have succeeded by the time the news sails back. That or I'll have gained my leading parley and no one will dare touch me.'

'You'd do all that?'

She nodded and smiled, slipping her arms around his neck and leaning forward to kiss him on the mouth. 'For Komey; for the Companionaris; for you, darling.'

In the end, it all went smoothly. The trader was persuaded, and the men were swept from the quay and loaded onto the ship. Captain Birch visited a certain woman in town, who hurried a parcel of spices to the ship: a gift for a distant friend. Aikin and Whilomena went shopping. And just before nightfall, after the Komey party returned to the barge and the crew prepared to leave New Lytalia, Birch, Fable and Scott arrived with a small bundle. Aikin opened it on his own, in the skipper's cabin. It contained two rock children and an extra sachet of poison.

19

ica woke up in a body that was whole, healthy and familiar, unaware of how much time had passed. He found himself on a floor in a strange room, feeling confused. The last thing he remembered was going into the diggings, but he wasn't in the diggings now because he could feel wooden boards beneath him. He felt as though he'd slept rather than passed out. Slept for weeks perhaps, but somehow he suspected it was days.

Everything had cleared: the pressure in his head; the stone's call; his own drowsiness, his physical desire for the Stone Body, for the heady perfume of the soil. He waited a moment before opening his eyes or moving, but there was nothing to show what had happened and no memory returned to help him. The call of his obsidian rock child had vanished and with it, the urge to remain lying down. Feeling both alarmed and foolish, Mica opened his eyes.

He seemed to be in a vast formal room, a Companionari room, an enormous parley chamber. He was on a thin rug and there were low burning, fixed lamps on the wall. Mica sat up and then realised there was someone beside him.

He turned around, alarmed that he'd not sensed anyone. The person mirrored him, turning toward Mica. Mica was shocked to find he was looking at himself: at a young man whose clothes were Mica's and whose face and body resembled Mica's in every respect. For a moment, as they stared at each other, there was a buzzing in the air, a feeling that something was about to happen, that something would indeed happen. Then the other man's expression shifted as he appeared to recognise Mica, and the buzzing faded.

'Who are you?' Mica whispered. 'Where am I? What happened?'

The man didn't speak, just mirrored the look of alarm on Mica's face. The buzzing returned, and that feeling of imminence, that anything, anything at all, could and would happen.

Mica's rock skin prickled with the other man's fear and the feeling increased like fire licking up the side of a log. Then something about the circular nature of the experience alerted the wanderer to the possibility that the stranger wasn't just copying his movements, he was mirroring Mica's inner life. The wanderer calmed himself, reminded himself that he was alive and whole, that he'd find his way home, that all would be well. He smiled at the stranger, and his smile elicited a grin. The stranger's smile grew, shifting his features, making his face look foreign and individual even though his face was Mica's own.

For a moment it occurred to Mica that he was dreaming but the feel of the room, the smells in the air, the ascending light of dawn: all that was solid and normal.

Then he glanced down. Both of his hands were empty. The obsidian rock child was missing, and he'd been gripping it when he lost consciousness. Mica fell to his hands and knees and began patting the floor, but couldn't find it. He felt for his pouch, but it had gone. He looked up at the strange version of himself. His twin reached out a hand and touched Mica's shoulder. There was a tickling sensation in Mica's head that felt like need and want and something else that was amorphous but compelling. It was as though there was something on the tip of Mica's tongue, but he didn't have the right language to speak it.

'Are you the obsidian?' he asked his strange double.

The man in front of Mica remained still. His hand hadn't moved from Mica's shoulder, but something swept through Mica's mind: black like dark water; white like chalk dust; a thought, but not a thought. Mica had felt nothing like it before. But within his arms, he felt something more familiar, the pull of a rock child calling. Not words but a sentiment that felt akin to a shout of: *Here!* He looked at his twin and wondered. Had the grave transformed his obsidian rock child into a man?

The stranger dropped his hand from Mica's shoulder, waited as though expecting something, as though he wanted something.

The young wanderer's heart pounded, and he found he had tears in his eyes and his face almost hurt with the spread of his grin. His twin mimicked him, expectation building where fear had reigned just moments earlier.

Another stone image flowed through Mica, vast but focused: a complex net of colours and sensations, full of dancing need and quick pull. Mica did his best to hold on to the feeling, sift it for some sort of meaning or change, for some sort of language, but it was useless. He couldn't read the mental experience even though he felt certain that it was meaningful, that it possessed a grammar.

The stranger stood up, and Mica followed his example. Mica felt conscious that this was the moment all wanderers had longed for: a rock child unfolding, becoming something else. Some wanderers thought rock children might blossom into new entities and free the Berans from the Companionaris. Others had thought the children would become new elements in the Stone Body, would mature into sentient cliffs; fresh peninsulas; new tors; and whole new provinces: more awake than the rest of the Stone Body, but part of that whole. Mica had always imagined rock children returning to their point of origin and merging back into the Stone Body, their purpose remaining a mystery. But this? This man-twin had only everbeen mentioned in some of the crazier backwards stories of dancers dancing new life. No one had taken the idea seriously.

Mica stared into eyes that mirrored his own but spoke of the profundity of their difference.

Without thinking, he touched his hand to his heart and his head and began introducing himself. 'I am Mica, wanderer, servant of the Stone Body, guardian of rock children.' The stranger clapped his hands, watching Mica's gestures with intense focus, as though he were waiting for something to begin. Mica hesitated, uncertain what to do next.

The familiar feeling of calling returned, like an echo of a friend's escalating need for attention.

Then he had it. A twin would have a name: would be welcomed into a family and a home. 'Welcome,' he spoke to his twin as a father to a new son. 'Welcome to this life on the Stone Body...' He sought some inspiration for what to say next and found the twin's name in his head as naturally as he found his own. 'Obsidian! I name you Obsidian for who you were when I first knew you and who you are now. We'll look for the second part of your name as we come to know you. You will know it when it's spoken. For now, you are Obsidian. Welcome to your body; welcome to your life. We have longed for you; waited for you.' Mica smiled at the exquisite truth in the ritual words. 'Your existence is precious.' Mica reached out and touched the rock man's chest and felt the warmth of a brother bond. Then he noticed the rock skin on his outstretched arm had changed from its usual opal hues to a deep black with chalky white flecks. Even the faint scars on his hand were gone, as though he'd grown younger.

Mica dropped his hand from his twin's chest, a little nervous at the changes. Then he made himself relax, reminded himself to remain positive and welcoming. He focused on his happy memories of life with the rock child, hoping it would ease the rock man's path into this new life. He recalled his feelings of gratitude when the obsidian had stayed with Fox, and his joy when the rock child had returned to his pouch.

As if in response to that return to love, Obsidian reached forward and clasped Mica in a tight embrace. Mica felt a flash of stone thought that was electric. A brother bond to a stone twin: something unimagined.

'But I wonder why we're here?' Mica spoke as much to himself as to his twin. He didn't know what Obsidian understood about their temporal circumstances or the current nature of the world. So he began explaining. 'I think we are in a room. In a Companionari building. I don't think it's our manor in Oak. It's too big. But why aren't we in the diggings? Perhaps your birth moved us through the Stone Body...' Mica walked toward a shuttered window to orientate himself. 'No, of course we moved. It makes sense. I don't know why I'm surprised. We are all birthed through a body. And a birth takes time and moves you from one place to another. I wonder what day it is. I wonder what's been going on.'

Mica opened the shutter and looked out on the dawn, breaking across a familiar landscape, but it didn't belong to Oak province. A title sprang to mind: *View of the Lacuna bell from Wheat House*. He knew this landscape from the tapestry that had hung in the kitchen at the manor. As a boy he'd made a habit of examining it whenever he visited, wondering about the Oak Companion's city. So he was in Wheat House in Komey and obviously some time had indeed passed since he entered the diggings. How much time? And why was he in Wheat House at all? Not even Oak House. How strange.

One of Obsidian's stone thoughts washed through him, uncomfortable this time. Mica shivered and looked around. Obsidian was watching the door, frowning. People were coming, and they didn't feel like friends.

Mica moved away from the window, searching for somewhere to hide. Chairs... A large bed... and then he had it. Screens. Several stood at the back of the room. And Obsidian saw them too, because Mica's desire to hide escalated to a compulsion. He looked over at his twin. Desires like this were part of the language he understood. He stepped behind a screen; Obsidian mirrored his movements, stepping behind another.

Voices became audible outside the door: laughter and conversation. Mica watched the room through the hinged slit between the sections. The door opened and people streamed in. Someone touched a dial and the low-burning lamps brightened. Another stepped over to the second window and opened the shutter. The lamp light faded again as more of the white light of early morning filled the room.

A beautiful woman in wheat-themed clothing held an unsteady hand to the elbow of a young man who, by his clothes, looked to be a member of the Aries family. She drew the young man to one side, brought him close to the screen where Mica was hiding. Mica thought she might be the Wheat Companion and the boy's first whispered words confirmed it.

'... of course, Whilomena. I said I'd support your parley idea,' he nodded, 'and I will.'

'Good boy,' she patted his arm, her voice slurred with alcohol. 'And I've kept my word. You'll be pleased to know that those costly Rice refugees have left Aries for good.' She slipped a purse into his hands. 'Call this an advance on the arrangements I've made.'

Mica frowned. What was she up to? What business did the Wheat Companion have with the Berans from that failed province?

'I must say, Whilomena,' the young man smiled and pocketed the purse, 'I admire your good sense. I'd have supported your parley idea even without this, but it helps. Life in Komey is expensive.'

'So it is.' She winked.

They drifted away then. The boy to a parley seat and Whilomena to the parley bed.

Mica was worried by what he'd heard but made himself set his worry aside as he became aware that he was upsetting Obsidian. The shimmering sensation emanating from his twin, faded. Calm again. Mica thought about what he'd heard and felt from the Wheat Companion. Her signature had been full of the bravado of alcohol, but beneath that was a complex excitement, hunger even. And when she'd spoken of the Rice refugees, he'd felt her greed. He wondered what she was up to. He'd have to get back to Oak to discuss this with Quartz, and the sooner the better. But what could she be planning? There wouldn't be many Rice people in Aries: not more than forty. Most had settled in Kelp.

Soon the parley room was full of people: exquisitely dressed young men and women who looked dishevelled. Most were in their teens, with only a handful in their twenties. Lamp light bounced off jewelled hands and picked up the gold and silver thread that decorated clothing. Mica recognised the Oak motif on the dress of one girl and on the pants and dress coats of several of the young men. Other designs included fish, horses, rice and wheat.

The Wheat Mother sat down on the foot of the bed, gave a little laugh, and kicked off her shoes. 'What is it about parleys when you haven't slept?' The secretiveness had disappeared from her emotional signature, but Mica could still feel suppressed hunger and excitement beneath the alcohol.

'Well, late night parleys always increase the number of Companionaris in the world,' one of the teenage boys spoke, looking thoughtful in an affected, theatrical manner. 'We know that. So morning-after parleys are full of regret or triumph. Depending on whom you ask.' He laughed, and the room laughed with him.

'But this isn't just any old morning-after parley,' the boy standing beside him said. 'It isn't every week that we admit a crossover failed. Yet one has. We all saw the Oak sorority's missive. The extra days in the propagation rooms didn't help and now the Oaks are in mourning for more than just their Mother. Their house and their province are finished.'

The Wheat Companion nodded, but Mica could feel it was counterfeit, a ruse. There was no sorrow within her, only the suppressed excitement of a secret held.

She began speaking, 'It's not every dawn that ushers in the reality that one of our greatest provinces has failed. Propagation rooms with empty pots of dirt, with no sign of germinating oak trees. I think we have a responsibility to face the truth that we're in real trouble and the old ways of managing our affairs no longer serve us well. So…' She clapped her hands, rocking with the movement. 'This parley is open! Let's look to the future. I'm asking you, begging you, for the sake of Komey and all the Companionaris: give me my leading parley.' She leant forward, conspiratorially, drunkenly. 'I can help us,' she lowered her voice. 'I've got something amazing that can change our fortunes, but I need people like you… this generation.'

'You have my support!' the Aries boy spoke up, with no hint of complicity in his voice. 'And why?' He turned to face the other parley members. 'Because we can't deal with these unfolding provincial disasters without strong leadership. So I say yes, by all means, yes. And if any family should lead us, it should be the Wheats!'

A cheer went up. Some parley members stamped their feet unsettling Obsidian; others stood up and raised their glasses. Behind the screen, Mica recalled the last events he could remember: Oria in camp, in his tent, claiming to be alive within Promise's body, claiming she was still just as capable of companioning the oaks and corks as she'd ever been. He wondered why Oria and Fox hadn't moved to secure the province, why Komey seemed ignorant of events in Oak. Mica wondered whether the Stone Body had brought him here to speak out or to listen. At the thought, his twin sent a flood of images: a kaleidoscope that could have meant nothing or everything. Mica couldn't read it. But he could understand the thread of anxiety that stung the underside of his rock skin. Obsidian was afraid, so they would wait, they would listen.

The crowd fell silent again. All eyes seemed to rest on the Wheat Companion.

'Let everyone know,' the Wheat Companion spoke again, standing up and lifting her glass up high, 'that we are not in retreat. I meant it when I said I was doing something about our problems. I have plans that will see the dawn of a prosperity beyond your wildest dreams.'

A few people cheered, and many stood up to join in the toast.

The Wheat Companion sat back down and waved a hand for the parley members to take their chairs. 'Sit, sit.'

An older man in clothing embroidered with oak leaves remained standing. 'I've something to say.'

Mica looked at Whilomena and saw her frown with displeasure, but she nodded for him to continue.

'Let's be honest here. Yes, there's some sense in political change, but Whilomena all of your promises of prosperity... Well, they're dishonest. The reality is we're facing the end of our time on the Stone Body.' He looked around, staring down the room, daring anyone to argue the point. 'Provinces winking out, year after year? I say we use this leading parley, which I don't object to, to open talks with Galea about a return. We'll not last here without our companionships.' He turned back until he was looking at the Wheat Companion again. 'What do you say, Whilomena? Would you be willing to initiate something?'

Mica felt himself relax. The Stone Body must want him to understand the Companionari position. Their withdrawal would have shocking consequences, more and worse famines, but the Berans would be better off. Better off living a hard life, managing with their traditional plants and animals, than being subservient in the companionship prosperity.

'No,' the Wheat Companion spoke loudly, cutting off the murmurs about a return, 'and I'll tell you why I'm saying no...' She lowered her voice again, 'I have something to say that changes everything.' She leant forward as though inviting everyone in the room into her confidence. Mica felt excitement rippling through her. 'A return *would be* sensible if we had no alternative; if we were just going to sit back and let the great families die out.' She nodded her head, looking at the older Oak man who'd suggested it. 'If we were prepared to let Komey fall to pieces, let the barbarians take over amid the ensuing famine.'

Mica stiffened at the insult. Calling them barbarians!

'But I'm not prepared to lie down and accept our fate—'

'Grand sentiments,' the older Oak man interrupted her in his dry, even voice. 'But pointless. There is no alternative but a return to Galea.'

'But that's where you're wrong.' Whilomena smiled. 'A friend of mine and I have been looking for answers,' she lowered her voice, conspiratorially. 'We've experimented...' the crowd shifted in their seats and several people looked around to see who else might be involved. 'Yes,' Whilomena smiled, 'we've experimented and we believe we've found the answer to our problems. There were difficulties, yes. Certain items were needed,' she paused over the word *items*, 'and there were certain conditions that had to be met.'

'Back and Path Whilomena,' the Aries boy called out. 'What are you talking about?'

'Making companions,' she whispered loudly. 'All natural. Quite natural. It's got to do with rock children. We can transform ourselves and replenish the companionships, but we need rock children.'

Stone thoughts hit Mica with full force as Obsidian reacted to Whilomena's suggestion. The young wanderer fell against the wall behind him, barely keeping his feet under the assault of the rock man's reaction.

Whilomena waved her hand, forestalling any interruption. 'I can't tell you what we've discovered. It's a new part of the Wheat bounty and it's going to stay that way, but I'm going to send out our soldiers. They're going to take every single rock child from Beranish hands and bring them into the careful husbanding hands of the Companionaris, where we will care for them properly and permanently.'

Whilomena's voice sounded loud in Mica's ears. Obsidian's rock thought flooded his head, pressing him forward. Suddenly, he burned with a desire to show himself. He put his hand out to the screen. It crashed to the floor, turning heads. A young man screamed. Several people got to their feet. Mica moved toward Whilomena, who stared at him with her mouth open. He felt fury mounting within him: his own, hot and hard, but Obsidian's too, misted with confusion and grief. He had to stop the Wheat Companion.

'How dare you?' He strode across the distance between them. He grabbed her by the hair and pinned one arm behind her back. Obsidian had stepped out from behind his screen as well, but he seemed disorientated.

Mica spoke to the parley members, doing his best to ignore the rushing sensation in his head. 'Touch our beloved rock children and we will make war with you. We'll throw you off the Stone Body. You can swim back across the Komic Sea to the place you came from. You'd better start those talks with Galea, and soon.' He looked around the room, catching startled faces, fearful glances. 'And you,' he turned back to the Wheat Companion. 'Send out those soldiers and we'll kill you.'

Obsidian's movement caught Mica's attention. The stone man walked into the crowd. He knocked over a chair, stumbled and the air seemed to shiver. A second boy screamed. The sound seemed to confuse the rock man. He crept forward as though he could no longer be certain of his destination. Mica pulled Whilomena toward the door and prayed Obsidian would follow. The rock man looked up, his face a picture of misery. He found Mica's eye and that seemed to steady him. His steps became more deliberate, and he moved over to the door. The pressure in Mica's head eased.

Whilomena struggled. 'Help me!' She reached out a hand to the Aries boy, but the boy evaded her, a look of terror on his face.

Mica reached the door. Whilomena kicked him. He tightened his grip, but didn't have a free hand to open the door.

'Help me!' Whilomena shouted. The crowd didn't move.

'Obsidian,' Mica said, 'open the door.'

Obsidian looked up and Mica saw his intense distress, but the rock man obeyed, reaching out and opening the door. 'Walk through,' Mica instructed. The rock man obeyed again, and Mica followed, throwing Whilomena to the floor and slamming the door behind him. He would have liked to have locked it, but didn't have a key. Instead, he caught the rock man's hand in his and they ran.

20

Mica gripped Obsidian's hand as they ran through the Wheat House gardens and into the busy main street of the Mint Gazette, their pursuers close behind. The outraged parley members should have been easy to outrun, but they'd been joined by the Wheat House guards and worse, Whilomena's soldiersisters. Mica didn't need to look back to feel how close they were. He rock sensed them, heard their shouts. Soon enough they were right behind him, one of them reaching forward to grab his cloak. Then the outstretched hand disappeared in a tumble of arms and legs as the leading soldiersister tripped over a cobble and brought down those around her.

Mica seized the opportunity to pull Obsidian through a hedge, across a lawn, through another hedge, and into the chaotic side streets of the gazette. It worked. The sensation of pursuit faded, and Mica turned towards the city's wall and, beyond it, Mint Valley and the promise of freedom.

Then Obsidian stopped.

The rock man pulled up short, wrenching Mica's shoulder. Mica turned, urged his twin to move but couldn't budge him. Obsidian dug in his heels and the intensity of his rock thought made the air shimmer or so it felt to Mica because Mica's head hurt and he felt weak and exhausted. It was all he could do to stay on his feet. He didn't let go of his twin's hand, but he stopped trying to move him and the pain and fatigue receded. Obsidian patted Mica, tried to embrace him, planted a sloppy kiss on his cheek.

Mica extricated himself, took a step back. He wasn't sure how they could remain safe, but he'd start by assessing the immediate danger. He stood tall, stretched his rock sense, feeling for their pursuers and was relieved to find they were still running in the wrong direction, chasing nothing. It wouldn't be so easy to evade a Beran, but he wasn't being chased by Berans.

Mica looked at his twin. 'So? Where to now? What are we going to do now?'

He didn't expect an answer and Obsidian's demeanour suggested the words meant little or nothing to him, but the man shivered, frowned, looked up and down the narrow laneway. Then he seemed to catch a scent or something like one because he lifted his head, sniffed the air, turning about as though trying to catch hold of something. When he looked back at Mica, there was an expression of delight on his face. In one fluid motion, he grabbed hold of the young wanderer's arm and started running.

Obsidian dragged Mica down the street, twisting and turning all the way to the hedged garden, then across the gazette's main street and in and out of other gardens and laneways. He led them uphill, deep into the fringes of the eastern side of the gazette and then halted at another hedge. This one, tall, raggedy and ill kept.

Obsidian didn't hesitate. He bent down and pushed his way through the woody vegetation, pulling Mica with him. The garden and house within looked derelict. Mica just hoped it was. They could hide in an abandoned house. They could stay there until Obsidian was ready to leave the city.

But it wasn't abandoned. Obsidian had led them to the home of their one remaining friend in the city: Louis Oak.

Just days later, as the sun was setting, Mica used the gate to enter that same garden. This time, his twin was behind him and both of them were dressed as Louis' footmen.

Louis had found a use for them and running the birthfather's errands in the elaborate outfits of footmen gave Mica a disguise that allowed him to listen and learn. Obsidian had been right to keep the two of them in Komey. Mica needed to know more about Whilomena and her sudden interest in rock children, why she thought the stones held the key to creating new companions. That was something he couldn't learn in the province, and it was something the Berans needed to understand if they were going to protect themselves.

Obsidian fitted his feet into Mica's footprints. The young wanderer had told his twin to follow him closely, and it had become apparent that while the rock man understood some language, he was literal in his responses to requests.

Louis had turned out to be much as Mica had remembered him. While it was true that he was living in impoverished circumstances in the back reaches of Companionari society, Mica soon learned that Louis had remained connected to some of the most influential people in the city. The old birthfather had explained to Mica his most recent method of earning his keep: embarrassing former lovers into loosening their purse strings. He conducted his business affairs by letter as he no longer left his house, but he employed his neighbours as his envoys. Now he had Mica and Obsidian as his footmen, they had taken over delivering his missives to his old associates and paramours. With their arms covered, hats pulled low and their golden eyes cast down, the twins moved in and out of the great houses running Louis' errands and listening for any hint of news about what the Wheat Mother was up to. Mica just wished the results had been better.

He knew little more than he had at the start.

The young wanderer sighed as he and Obsidian walked up Louis' path. In the garden surrounding them, wheat and other less edible grasses grew through rusted tools. Empty and bent crippet cages hung from the eaves and an old yellow-coloured dog lay flat in a dust bowl in front of the back step.

Louis had given Mica a brief history of the Mint Gazette when they'd first arrived. Helping the poor had been all the rage in Komey some two hundred years before. Parleys vying with each other to donate land to house the city's destitute and then gazetting the same in florid and self-congratulatory language. The settlements took up various pockets of land in the lee of the city's walls, becoming known as the gazettes. The Mint Gazette was named after the nearest valley. It was home to about two hundred individuals: retired bureaucrats, domestic staff, and distant relatives of the Oak and Wheat families. The bureaucrats lived on small annuities and the domestic staff had modest wages. The rest, the poor relatives, survived on family and house charity, only tolerated because no one knew when their weak code might produce a random crossover success.

Louis' dog caught sight of Mica and Obsidian's approach and thumped its tail. Obsidian clapped his hands and laughed out loud, patting Mica's shoulder to make sure that Mica had seen. The wanderer felt the familiar wave of rock images inside his head. Though he still could not understand the rock man's language, he was now used to the odd sensation of having rock thoughts slide around his mind.

'Yes,' Mica agreed, 'he is a good dog.' He reached up to touch Obsidian's hand, but the rock man had already moved. He'd abandoned his work of following in Mica's footprints and had hurried forward, crouching down and wrapping his arms around the dog, smothering Louis' pet in kisses. The dog licked Obsidian's face and the rock thought in Mica's mind fluttered in response.

'Stop. Stop.' Mica crouched down beside the rock man and dog, and separated them. 'It tickles. My head tickles.' Then he took hold of Obsidian's hand and drew his twin toward a back door that was hanging from a single hinge. The dog righted himself and ambled after them.

Inside, the house was full of shadows from the growing twilight. Obsidian sniffed the air and then hurried past Mica, the dog close on his heels. The rock man made a series of clicking and kissing noises as he moved into the hallway. It sounded as though he was calling a small and shy little animal rather than a fully grown human being like Louis.

'All right, all right!' a gravelly male voice called out from the room ahead. 'I can hear you. You make that much bloody racket, anyone could hear you.' Their host waddled into view and Mica felt a wash of hot rock thought as Obsidian cried out in delight. His twin rushed forward and embraced Louis, then picked up one of the man's enormous hands and rubbed it against his face, like a cat marking a much loved human.

Louis laughed and freed his fingers from the rock man's embrace. 'Recognises quality, he does.' The old man held up his hands and gave Mica a knowing look. 'They've felt up the best tabby in Komey. Died for me, they did. Couldn't get enough of my code. Hot property. If I wasn't so exhausted, I'd be bumping those soft, white, thighs and arses in the best parley chambers in our city, as you and your young lady well know, you having done the bumping for me on one occasion.'

Mica blushed and held up his hands to halt the flow. 'You shouldn't talk about Fox that way, or what happened between us.'

Obsidian put his arm around Louis' shoulders and smiled at Mica, mirroring Louis' leer.

Louis reached over and turned on the wall lamp. The hall brightened with soft yellow light. 'Prudish lot, you Berans. By the Back, I need to sit down. My legs are killing me.' He looked around the wide hallway and spotted a chair. He tottered over to it and sat down. The chair's legs strained beneath him. Obsidian and the dog sat down beside him on the floor, oblivious to the odd picture they made. After a moment the dog stretched out on the ground and Obsidian moved to imitate him.

'Don't, Obsidian,' Mica said. 'He'll only lick you and I won't be able to concentrate.'

The rock man sat back up and leant his head against the plaster wall, still smiling. His dark curly hair was awry and a childish expression of delight and excitement lit up his golden eyes. Mica wondered whether all rock men were like this: mute, innocent and almost infantile. And yet, Obsidian had skills, could look after himself. He'd been the one to insist they hide behind the screens in Wheat House before the parley had begun; he'd found Louis. The rock man smiled at Mica, aware of the young wanderer's scrutiny. Mica wondered if he looked as youthful as his twin did, because Obsidian appeared younger than when they'd first arrived in Komey. He suspected that if he had a mirror, he'd see that Obsidian's strange nature had pared back both their years.

'So, what have you brought me this time?' Louis rubbed his hands together. 'Apart from information, that is.'

Mica cleared his throat and began speaking as though he was Louis' footman. 'Carmel, Mother to the Aries Companion, sends you this small gift.' Mica leant forward and passed over an exquisitely wrapped box. 'She wishes you an increasingly brief life.'

'She said that?' Louis paused in his rush to unwrap his present. 'And what did you tell her?'

'That you were struggling with the temptation to visit her.'

'And?' Louis leant forward in his chair and leered at Mica.

'And she snatched her handmaid's purse and gave me this.' Mica pulled a fistful of coins from his coat and handed them over.

'Lovely!' Louis grunted.

Obsidian looked up at the sound of the grunt and then repeated it several times, making Louis smile and the dog cock his head.

Louis lifted the lid of the box. Inside was a wheel of goat's cheese and a parcel of dried fruit. He shook his head. 'You see this?' his voice was hurt. 'She expects me to live on this. Now you know why I have to press them harder. If I didn't push them I'd be stick and bone.' He shook his head and then turned to Obsidian. 'Fetch that small table in the kitchen, will you?' He patted the stone man's head and then mimed his request.

Obsidian stood up, but the rock thought in Mica's head was dark. The rock man didn't like working. He preferred to play or eat. But he stepped past Mica into the kitchen, picked up a small table, carried it back to the hallway on his head. Mica followed, fetching two stools to complete the unorthodox dining arrangement. There was hardly any room in the hall, but Louis lived out his domestic life in whichever space he fancied.

'Good lad, good lad!' Louis said to Obsidian and then set the gift box down on the table. 'Now if you'll just be so kind as to fetch the bread and that jug of milk.' The old man mimed pouring a drink and then waved for Obsidian to return to the kitchen.

'Don't.' Mica held up his hand. The rock thought Obsidian was sending was becoming uncomfortable. 'I don't want him having a tantrum. You know how much noise he can make and we can't afford to attract any negative attention.'

'Don't you worry about that.' Louis began ripping apart the cheese with his bare hands. 'You're my men now. No one will bother you while you're working for me: twin footmen in the employ of Louis Oak's renowned courting services.'

'I'll get a knife.' Mica returned to the kitchen and gathered up what they needed, including some more food and drink. He returned to the table and took the cheese from Louis's hands. 'You'll enjoy it more on a plate.'

Louis licked his fingers and then ruffled Obsidian's hair, leaving a smear of goat's cheese behind. Mica tried not to look. He had spent his own life in the kind of modesty and moderation that was traditional for wanderers. Perhaps it would have been different if he was married to Fox. His life on the road would have been the same: solitary and simple. But his tent would have been richer. He thought of Fox carrying their baby. A sister for Doubt and Saury.

The impossibility of that joyful happy ending hit him with force. Even if Oria really was who she claimed to be, even if that meant

Fox could come and live in Oak, Fox was unlikely to favour Mica. Her dismay at the deaths his actions had set in motion had been palpable. If not outright enemies now, then they certainly found themselves on opposite sides, given her perplexing allegiance to Oria.

Mica felt a touch on his arm and looked up. Obsidian was standing beside him. The rock man leant down and kissed him on the head, ruffling his hair in the same manner that Louis had ruffled his twin's. Mica smiled and waved Obsidian back to his stool. 'I'm okay. Sit down and eat.'

The young wanderer turned his attention back to the meal, cutting the cheese into pieces. He gave Louis a portion that was about four times larger than his own and Obsidian's, and the dog's.

'What did you learn?' Louis eased his buttocks in the small chair, trying to find a more comfortable position. The chair squeaked beneath him. 'Any more answers on this business of yours?'

'Aries has solved its refugee problem.'

Louis nodded. 'But you knew that, yes? That's the gist of what you'd already overheard?'

'Aries is full of the news that the refugees were marched to New Lytalia.'

Louis frowned. 'And?'

'Nothing more than that. I don't know what's planned for them, but I fear for them.'

Louis chewed then spoke with his mouth still full. 'What else?'

'No one knows anything about this business with the rock children and some new way of creating companions. Nothing. People are talking about it mind you, there's even a rumour of some miracle that the Bass family have regained their bounty, but no one knows anything. The kitchen staff I spoke with in Aries House was divided: some people thought it had to do with rock children and the Wheat Companion's plans; some believed it was a sign that your god was returning; others were convinced that the rumours of a new Bass companion are just gossip.'

Louis grunted and Obsidian imitated him, breaking into a chorus of grunts that made the dog lift his head and bark.

Mica continued speaking, 'I should go over to Bass House and try to find out what's going on.'

Louis shook his head. 'I'm afraid I don't have any contacts there. Only competitors.'

'We could offer your services,' Mica said.

'The less said about my services the better.' The old man shook his head again. 'Everyone knows that I can't get it up anymore, that Fox was my last triumph, and you and I know that I can't even claim her.' Louis wiped a small tear away with his food covered fingers. 'It's too hard Mica. It's too painful. Argh... you should have seen me in my youth!'

Mica ignored Louis' self pity. He remembered it well from the days they'd spent together with Fox. The man could talk for hours about his pitiful plight. The young wanderer interrupted him, 'Do you think the Wheat Companion's claim that she can make companions could be true? Could she have stumbled on some old Companionari lore? Have you ever heard any rumours that the companion mothers were made and not brought across the Komic Sea?'

Louis winked. 'My reputation relies on it.'

Mica didn't smile at the joke. 'No, I'm serious Louis. I want to know about the first companions because if there's a connection to rock children... Well, that would be the place to find it.'

Obsidian tried to lick a piece of cheese from his chin, his tongue struggling to reach the food.

Mica continued speaking, 'I need to know everything you've ever heard about the origins of the companionships. I've got a feeling that this is the reason Obsidian wanted us to stay. But we won't find the answers in house gossip. I need to know more about the history of the companionships. About the early years. And I want to know what the Companionaris saw when they arrived here after their journey across the Komic Sea. Did they see rock men? Did they see plenty or poverty?'

'That's ancient stuff, that.' Louis waved a dismissive hand. 'Me, I studied code and breeding and sex and courting when I was a boy. I was always a pretty lad and I have glorious code. Glorious.' He smiled in recollection, for a moment forgetting about the food on his plate. 'And later I learned about gossip and trading goods and favours, but not history.' He shook his head.

Mica moved his chair closer to the table. 'Yes, and I appreciate everything you've told me, especially the news that Whilomena and Aikin Oak might be a couple, but I have to know more about the past, about where the companionships came from.'

Louis shook his head again. 'Don't we all? But that's the point, isn't it? It's a mystery. A gift from God before the Turning.' Louis shrugged. 'At least that's what most people say.'

Mica frowned. 'But what does that mean and when was it supposed to have happened? There must be myths about it. Because something happened. Maybe it was just before the journey, maybe it was en route, maybe it was after you arrived. All we know is that there aren't any companion mothers in Galea. They're all on the Stone Body. So it's got to be connected to this life: the Companionaris' life here on the Stone Body. There must be accounts, speculations...'

Louis picked up his knife and spread goat's cheese onto his bread then added a slice of tomato. 'Fables and that sort of thing?' He frowned. 'That's what you mean?'

'Yes.' Mica nodded. 'Yes, that would be an excellent start.'

Louis put the bread and cheese into his mouth. 'I could get you into a library,' he spoke with his mouth full, then put the last tomato on his plate and cut it in half. 'The Department of Culture's the place where they keep that sort of thing.'

'Can Obsidian and I get inside it?'

Louis sighed and shook his head. 'It's in Wheat house. Whilomena's domain.'

'Too risky, then.'

Louis rested an elbow on the table with his chin in his hand, ignoring the tomato on his plate while he thought over the problem. Obsidian copied him, resting an elbow on the table and lowering his chin into his hand. With his other hand, the rock man continued to feed himself small pieces of bread.

Louis looked up again, brighter now. 'Wait on. There's another place you could try. Now you won't get much Companionari history from this, but you'll get early accounts of rock children and rock men, if there were any about when my people landed here. And, well, perhaps, there might be some mention of the early companions interacting with them,' he began sounding uncertain. 'A bit of a long shot, I guess.'

'No. That's a good idea,' Mica said, feeling more enthusiasm than his host. If there was a connection between rock children and creating the first companionships and if he found accounts of first contact, then he might work out what the Wheat Companion was up to. 'Where is this place?'

'The Department of Beranish Affairs. The library is in Oak house. And I've got connections in the kitchen there. Willie, the cook, is a friend and... Well... Oak House is my family home. We'll tell Willie I'm researching Beranish sexual practices... We'll tell him you need to check a few references for me. It will make sense. He'll love it! We've still got most of that bunch of tomatoes, haven't we?'

Mica nodded. 'In the kitchen.'

'Good. They're scarce this year and he loves them. I'll ask him to get one of the pantry boys to run you up to the library in return for the fruit. And then, afterwards, you can do some more errands for me. Collect some more tokens of appreciation.' He rattled the coins in his pockets.

Mica nodded. He felt happy for the first time since the meal began. A warm burst of rock thought slid into his head. 'It's a good plan and Obsidian likes it too.' The wanderer stood up, ready to go. 'So let's get started.'

Louis held up his hand, shaking his head. 'Have to wait until tomorrow. All the great houses are busy in the evenings, bursting with people. The Oak House kitchen will have too much to do to be worrying about our little research project. No, you'll have to go in the morning.'

Mica nodded, sitting back down again. As much as he hated to delay, it made sense. There was no point in drawing attention to themselves and risking being recognised. He and Obsidian would be better off waiting for a quieter moment.

21

Aikin washed his hands three times and then dried them on a freshly laundered piece of linen. He felt good. He'd already had one spectacular success using a small rock child on Glory Bass, and he was certain Talia's results would be the same. Aikin wanted to keep the companion-making process as secret as possible, but he couldn't help the pride he felt on hearing the rumours about a miraculous re-emergence of the Bass bounty.

There was only one regret: that the first new companion wasn't an Oak House woman. He'd treated Glory Bass before working on Talia Oak. Better to risk the life of someone outside Oak House and better to use the smaller stone to reduce that risk. Course it meant that Talia needed to absorb the larger rock child, which meant two days of pain instead of one. Not for the first time, he wondered whether he should have given Talia the small talc chip that had been with the first rock children Birch had collected. But Aikin was worried it wasn't a real rock child. No, he'd made the right decision.

He paused for a moment before turning to face Talia. It was worth remembering the words of that great pioneer, Astoria Caballo. It must have been even harder for her when she set up the first Companionari province, with hostile Berans in every direction.

Patience and prudence carry when you're thinking for the next millennium.

He nodded to himself. She was right and he should listen to that advice because he, too, had to think for the next millennium. What did the pain of one woman matter in that time frame? If Talia's treatment failed, he would source more rock children and try again. If she died, he'd find another member of the Oak family to work with. He frowned. While he could get another girl without too much trouble now that he was confident of his method, he hoped this one wouldn't die. She was a pleasant young woman; he was fond of her. Well, the young were supposed to be strong, weren't they? She'd probably survive; Glory had.

He turned and looked at her and felt reassured. She didn't look as though she was about to die. Her face was flushed, but she seemed well. He walked over and sat down beside her, pulled back the covers to examine her wounds. There were dozens of cuts on her torso that looked as though they had been painted with a chalky preparation, tinged a nasty reddish-brown. It was the residual from yesterday's treatment, blood and something else. He bent down, inspecting the wounds. They looked clean and almost healed. He moved closer still and sniffed the air above the cuts, but there was no hint of corruption.

'Today is the last dose,' he said. 'Then we can let them heal over, but I'm afraid I have to cut all of them open again because the incisions have almost closed.'

He waited a moment, but she didn't respond beyond a slight nod.

'If you think positively, it might help,' he spoke encouragingly. 'I always find it does. Remember that you've got a good chance at genuine companionship level talent. I'll plant a couple of acorns when we've finished this morning, and you'll be able to see the saplings when you wake tomorrow. Maybe sooner. It just depends on how quickly your body assimilates the powder.'

Talia nodded again and smiled. 'I know. I don't mind the pain,' her voice was strained. 'I mean, I do, but I don't care about it and nor should you. Keep going.'

Aikin stood up and moved over to the dresser where he'd placed a bowl full of water in which sachets of antiseptic and analgesic herbs were soaking. He fished out the sachets and carried everything over to Talia: the bowl, a scalpel, a fresh linen cloth, and the box that contained the last bit of powder that carried both their hopes. He set them down and washed yesterday's residual from her skin. Even though the first treatment had only been given the night before, it was miraculous to witness the way the cuts had already begun moving from scab to new skin. The powder seemed to speed healing and ward off infection as well as potentially conferring companion-ship powers. Who could have imagined it? All those rock children sitting idle in the hands of wanderers... He washed the mess away and then picked up a scalpel and began to re-open the wounds, tipping a little rock child powder into each and rubbing it in with his index finger.

Talia gasped each time he cut her and moaned when he rubbed in the powder. He looked up now and again, checking his young cousin's face. She was perspiring and he could see her suffering in her clenched jaw and the tears that slipped from the corners of her eyes, but she didn't complain. Aikin found himself distressed, but focused his thoughts on what her pain could achieve: a renewal for the Oaks and beyond that, the possibility of salvaging the entire Companionari culture. It was worth it, no doubt.

He finished Talia's front and rolled her over onto her stomach, repeating the process. She shivered, biting a corner of the sheet to steady herself. He touched her skin to see whether her fever had worsened, but there was only a slight warming from the strain of coping with the pain. He went back to work, keeping his mind focused on finishing efficiently and quickly.

And then it was done. Aikin rolled her over again, onto her back. He picked up the soiled cloth, the bowl, the shielding box, and removed them.

He felt elated despite the unpleasant nature of the treatments he'd had to inflict. He'd see Whilomena, let her know how Talia was doing and then luxuriate in the gossip she'd have about Glory's sudden companionship powers. And he'd have to remind Whilomena to be discreet. He sighed. A little late for that. If he knew Whilomena, she'd already have slipped, wouldn't have been able to resist gloating. Ah well... Never mind.

When you love, love what's in front of you, not some phantasm of perfection.

The famous thoughts of Gideon Aries on life as a Companionari husband. It was good advice. And Aikin had taken it. After reading Gideon's autobiography, he'd adjusted his thoughts on what to expect from his future wife. But he still hoped Whilomena was being careful about how much of their secret she'd given away.

'That's it,' he said to Talia. 'It's over.'

'Good,' she sounded relieved.

He washed his hands in a fresh bowl of water. Then he went about the business of changing the bed linen beneath his cousin and coaxing her to drink several glasses of herb infused water. Finally, he cleaned her face with a damp towel and covered her with a clean sheet. He tipped the waste water into the water closet and bundled the soiled linen into a bag. He'd go down to the furnace and dispose of it before taking his lunch. Then he'd visit Whilomena before returning to sit with his patient. Before leaving and locking the room, he pressed acorns into three pots of soil that he'd positioned in front of the window.

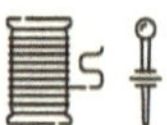

Mica and Obsidian made their way from the Mint Gazette toward Oak house. They were once again in the garb of footmen with Obsidian looking ridiculous because he kept running ahead like a child, hurtling down the gravel path and then waiting impatiently for Mica to catch up. Mica walked at an even pace, keeping a wary eye on their surrounds. He touched his left pocket and felt reassured by the feel of their employment papers. Even though Louis had assured him again that there was little risk for them in Oak house, Mica was nervous about today. After all, he and the rock man would venture into a part of the house that they had no genuine right to enter. It had been different with the audiences Louis had him seeking in the past. Those had been legitimate and the people they'd spoken with had been more worried about minimising their association with a man like Louis than about questioning the origins of his new footmen.

Mica glanced down at the basket he was carrying. Louis had filled it with tomatoes. The fruit lay on a scented bed of basil leaves that the birthfather had insisted Mica steal from a neighbour's garden. Louis had then arranged the fruit as a four-sided pyramid, holding the tomatoes in place with a frame that he fashioned out of wire and green silk ribbon. The effect was mouth-watering and elegant. The man's skill had surprised Mica. Louis had retired to his study before returning with a letter.

He'd recited the opening lines of the note from memory:

'*To the dearest and most talented of chefs in all of Komey, I'm requesting your help in a private research project that promises to recover several lost, Beranish lovemaking arts...*'

Then he'd waved the wax-sealed letter under Mica's nose. 'I've promised Willie an advance copy of the research and I've told him I suspect the Oak library contains the missing texts. He'll see you're not disturbed. I've asked him to keep a pantry boy on watch at the door.'

The young wanderer just wished he shared his host's confidence. Mica glanced up to where Obsidian waited at the crest of a small rise that looked down on Oak house. And then, when he'd caught up with the rock man, they started down the path together. This time, when Obsidian moved to run ahead, Mica put out a restraining hand. 'Stay beside me. And when we get to the kitchen, keep close and keep quiet. Act as I act, but don't mimic me. I don't want you to stand out.' Mica didn't know how much his twin understood, but Obsidian's comprehension was improving by the day.

The rock thought in Mica's mind was cool, but it didn't have the chill that he associated with the buzzing imminence of trouble. Obsidian would do what he'd asked, but it wasn't in his nature to accept constraint.

They walked the rest of the way to Oak House in silence. Mica steadied his thoughts and prepared himself for the clandestine operation. Even assuming the cook sent a pantry boy to act as a lookout, it would be hard to find useful information in the short time they had. They might need to return over several days. It wasn't a comfortable prospect.

Their introduction to the kitchen was smooth and Willie's face broke into a broad smile at the sight of the gift. The man held up the basket to admire Louis' work and then inhaled the smell of basil. Mica handed over the letter and the cook had one of his assistants serve them each a slice of cake while he prepared to read Louis' note: washing his hands and finding his glasses. Obsidian beamed at the cake and then, heedless of Mica's warnings to keep his eyes lowered, the rock man beamed at Willie. The cook returned the rock man's gratitude with a warm wink. But then he took a step nearer to Mica and leant forward, whispering 'Companionari footmen you aren't,' he nodded to himself. 'Your eyes might pass for a honey brown for those who don't know better, but I've travelled a bit in my time. I know Berans when I see them.'

Mica stiffened; his heart raced.

'No, don't you worry,' Willie patted the wanderer's shoulder his voice still low. 'You're not so easy to pick and your secret's safe with me.' He gave Mica's shoulder a squeeze. 'Dressed like that, with those long sleeves... Most wouldn't realise.' Then he turned his attention to the letter and Mica felt his heartbeat returning to normal again.

Reading the letter taxed the cook's abilities, and he poured over the words with a thick index finger. What he read seemed to meet with his approval because he called for a pantry boy and sent the lad upstairs to check that the library was empty. When the boy returned, and Mica and Obsidian had finished their cake, Willie sent the research party into the house, careful in his instructions to each of them to watch themselves and to make sure their behaviour reflected well on the kitchen.

With the pantry boy keeping watch in the corridor outside, Mica and Obsidian found themselves alone in the library. It was a large room that was furnished with comfortable seats and reading tables and lined with bookshelves. Mica noticed some tables had papers spread across them. For a moment, he feared that this signalled the likely return of their owners, but when he looked closely, he noticed the open books and sheets of writing paper were dusty. He was glad to see that research happened slowly in Komey.

'Obsidian,' Mica said, resisting the urge to whisper, 'there are lots of books here. I'm going to concentrate on seeing what I can find. You can do whatever you want, but no whooping or running. And no leaving the room without me.' Mica put a finger to his lips and in response a cool rock thought slid into his head, and he felt suddenly fearful, uncertain whether the rock man would obey. 'Remember that we aren't among friends, despite the cook's kindness. So we must be careful.'

Obsidian stepped closer to Mica and took him into a tender embrace. He stroked Mica's hair like a mother reassuring a child. Mica felt comforted, his confidence in the wisdom of his rock twin renewed.

The young wanderer moved over to the shelves and picked out books at random. Within a few minutes, he understood that there was a system in the room that was based on the subject. In the beginning he found himself in a section dealing with hand skills: Beranish weaving and sewing; Beranish woodwork and glory boxes. The next section seemed to deal in advice. He found a book for young bureaucrats about dealing with Beranish disputes over rents and labour costs. He would have loved to have had time to look at that book more closely, but now wasn't the moment. Mica moved on. Across the room he encountered an Old Treaty dictionary. He figured that Beranish history couldn't be too far away. A jittery rock thought jumped into Mica's mind and he looked up.

The rock man was pacing up and down in front of some archive shelves that Mica had eliminated early on as dealing with traditional Beranish animal husbandry practices. A strange shiver passed over the rock man's frame and he stopped for a moment and tapped his fingers against the spine of several books before drawing back his hand and shaking his head. He looked up at Mica and it shocked the wanderer to see that the rock man was crying.

Mica walked over and put his hand on his twin's arm, but Obsidian kept moving: shaking his head, touching the books and then recoiling. It was the same set of books each time: eight crimson-bound volumes entitled *Discourses on Generation & the Art of Agrarian Management of Beranish Peoples*. Mica reached up to have a look. Obsidian sent a shard of rock thought across the young wanderer's consciousness. Mica paused. He withdrew his hand and looked at the volumes more closely. There didn't seem to be anything wrong with the books, at least not from the outside, and Obsidian himself had touched them repeatedly. The young wanderer reached up for the first volume and grasped it. Instead of feeling a single book move under his hand, he felt the volumes move as a block. He lifted his other hand for balance and carefully lowered the block of books down from the shelf. As soon as he had it in his hands, he realised he was holding a box disguised as books. He laid the box down on the nearest table, its fake book spines facing away from him, and then he saw the clasp.

Obsidian danced around him. The rock man had become more

distressed. Mica opened the catch and lifted the lid. Inside the box lay a slim volume bound in blue leather. A title was embossed on the cover.

'The Book of Kinesis,' Mica read the name aloud and picked up the book.

Obsidian chattered with a mixture of clicks and groans and the rock thoughts in Mica's mind jumped about with the same rhythm, but the rock man did nothing to prevent Mica from slipping the volume into one of his pockets and returning the box to the shelf.

'Shush,' Mica crooned, stroking his brother's hair. 'If this is what we need to read, then we'll read it. But we must look at it somewhere else.'

Obsidian seemed to sigh. His nervous movement settled down again.

Mica led the way across the room and opened the library door. The passageway was empty except for the pantry boy. The wanderer slipped out of the library with his twin beside him.

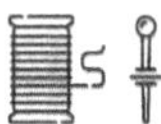

Fox stood beside Oria in the dress room on the top floor of Oak Manor. In front of her were hunting costumes, receiving robes, travelling clothes, dresses, and other outfits. Each garment stood on its own on a dress-maker's dummy so that its folds fell correctly. The room stretched the length and width of the manor, punctuated by oak posts that supported the roof. Fox couldn't count the number of manikins, but there had to be over a hundred.

Oria said she wanted their arrival in Komey to be noticed and gossiped about in all the gate houses to build a groundswell of support for the candidature of Fox's unborn child. Fox must dress beautifully, in the finest handmade garments and she would ride the best of the manor's horses. She would be fresh, rested and ready to seize any opportunity that would allow her and Oria to manipulate the testing process.

Oria frowned and dusted a piece of lint from the shoulder of a parley jacket. Fox couldn't help noticing how out of place the companion looked in Promise's body. But she had to admit that Oria had done well adapting to her changed circumstances. She'd dealt openly with the camp during the days of discussion; hadn't allowed her usual hauteur to emerge. The result had been the endorsement of the arrangements that Quartz, Fox, and Oria had made.

Oria moved over to a green velvet parley jacket and brushed off the shoulders. 'Dust! Make sure you tell the dress sister to clean up here once you free the sorority.'

'I'm nervous about releasing them,' Fox said. 'They've been captive for too long. I'm worried it will be like entering a wasps' nest.'

Oria nodded. 'It will be. They might be old, but they're strong. And I can feel how nervous you are. Settle your emotions and show them you know what you're doing.' Oria held out the jacket's sleeve. It was fluted and covered in delicate ribbon work. 'I haven't worn this in about fifty years. I think it would fit you and the green will look wonderful with your eyes. And the sleeves will reach to the tip of your fingers. If you avoid moving your hands about, no one will notice your rock skin.'

Fox scratched the back of her hands. There was no hint now of the welts that she'd thought were burns. New crystalline formations covered her knuckles. The sight sent a shiver through her that was part fear of being discovered in Komey, part hope of a return to Beranish life. But that and the chance to live in Oak province no longer meant what it once had. Mica was dead. The thought made the discussion of dresses feel obscene. 'I should let the sisters out. I can come up here later and get the clothes I need.'

'No.' Oria turned to face her. 'You need to know which things to choose in advance. And you need to be unhesitating. That's what will convince them you're a worthy birthmother and that your child is the legitimate crossover heir. We don't want them to talk about your baby needing a regent.'

'Are you sure we shouldn't trust them with the truth?'

Oria spoke, 'We've been over this. They're good women, but most of them are old and some are foolish. And some of them are quite conservative. Besides, it's good practice. If we can convince them you're carrying the next companion, we won't have any problems in Komey.' She moved on to look at another outfit.

Fox followed Oria's gaze and found she had been touching her rock skin. She dropped her hands.

'And don't fiddle like that. Don't scratch at your hands. It's unattractive, and it makes you look childish and it will draw attention where we don't want it.' Oria moved on to a flowing summer jacket that was embroidered with daisies. She stepped back to admire the garment from a distance. 'I think you should tell the dress sister to pack this one, too. You can wear it in Komey. Some will recognise it as a good omen. My grandmother used to wear it and her gravity was prodigious. Oh, and this too.' Oria moved over to a manikin dressed in a set of light silk travelling clothes. 'They'll be good for the road and they're not so precious that I'll regret lending them to you. And see how long the sleeves are. One rolls them up, but you can wear them down.'

'What will you wear?' Fox followed Oria as she moved deeper into the room.

Oria paused and looked back at her. There was a deep frown on the companion's face. 'Why should I change my clothes?' She pulled her hunting cloak closer about her shoulders. 'These are fine.'

'But you don't look like a Beranish maid. And you're supposed to be my handmaid.'

'Just tell everyone that I served you when you spent the night in the camp and that you've chosen me for my kindness. They can't argue with that. The selection of a handmaid is a decision that's always made for personal reasons and, with Bronda dead, the position is vacant. They won't like me being a Beran, but there are precedents. But be careful to make sure they know I'm pregnant. That way, they won't insist on me being chaperoned in Komey. And call me Promise. *Oria* is out of the question. And you'd better start now so that you get used to doing it. *The companion's Beranish handmaid,*' Oria laughed at the thought. 'Tell them you chose me because you liked me and I'm pretty.' She smiled.

Fox didn't find the idea amusing. She was too worried now that the first test of their charade was upon them. She fell silent as they continued through the dress room. Her hands fingered the stones in her pockets, and their touch offered some comfort. The idea of arriving in Komey as an impostor was disturbing, as was the prospect of lying to the Oak household and to Aikin.

When they'd settled on her wardrobe, Oria withdrew to the sewing room and left Fox to go down to the sisters on her own. In her imagination, the cellar had been more like a dungeon, but she walked down a flight of broad and shallow, lime-washed steps leading to a beautiful ornate green door. Everything was clean and well maintained and she realised the cellar was simply another part of the manor's kitchen: a larger, deeper, subterranean pantry. The last of Mica's men had left, leaving the door unguarded.

Fox checked her sleeves were pulled down, covering her rock skin. She slipped the key into the lock and turned it, opening the door. Thirteen elderly women crowded forward, blinking in the sudden light. The youngest looked to be in her sixties, the majority in their seventies. Their clothes were rumpled and their hair awry, but there wasn't the remotest sign of fear in any of their faces.

'Who are you?' one asked. 'It's clear you're Beranish,' she frowned, stepping closer, peering at Fox. 'Beranish eyes... But not dressed like one.'

Another old woman pushed forward. 'What's going on? Have you any idea how long we've spent in this insufferable place? Days! No, a week or even more. I gather, by the look of you, Komey has abandoned us and the camp has helped itself to our wardrobes? Typical.'

'I think you're wrong there, dear,' an ancient turned to the speaker. 'Don't you recognise our unexpected redeemer?' She pointed a gnarled finger at Fox. 'It's young Fox Oak, grown up. Good to see you, young woman. I trust you've become someone important?'

Fox had rehearsed this scene several times, and she was glad that she had. 'Sister, you're right. I am Fox Oak, adopted daughter of Aikin Oak. I carry in my body the new Oak Companion.'

The sisters fell silent at the news and a moment later, several cried out in grief at the sudden realisation that Oria must be dead.

A lean old woman with close cropped hair spoke up, 'Those rebels did it, didn't they? Murder, was it? Or was it the shock that killed poor old Oria?' She shook her head, speaking again before Fox could answer. 'Course we wondered. What with no word from her.'

'It was shock,' Fox spoke again. 'At least we think so. The rebels sent her body to Komey. I came to attempt your release because my father was delayed... ill. And then... Well, the crossover reached out to me en route.'

'En route? All the way from the bell?' The lean old woman looked astounded. 'You didn't even touch old Oria's body?'

Fox nodded.

'But why were you on the train in the first place?' another woman asked. 'Why not call on a more senior family member? And you must have been here for days. Why did you leave it so long to let us out?'

'Enough!' Fox turned and began walking up the stairs. 'We leave for Komey in the morning with Quartz and a few others from camp. And I want you with me. We haven't horses for everyone so we'll take the train and then walk in so the distance is manageable.'

'Taking Berans?' one elderly woman complained. 'Oria wouldn't have done that. She wouldn't have taken them at a time like this—'

'That's quite enough!' Fox stopped and turned back, looking down at their wrinkled faces. 'You don't know the difficulty involved in securing your release or the complexity of the situation in Komey.

As for my travelling companions, I require several Beranish witnesses when I reach Oak house, including Quartz.'

'Yes, birthmother,' one woman demurred, 'but what about the manor? Who will look after it while we're away?'

Fox realised she'd let the discussion go on long enough. Oria had insisted that Fox must gain control of the sorority from the very beginning. So she turned and continued up the stairs. 'That's not your concern, but one of you will need to organise our provisions—'

'Cook can do that,' one sister grumbled.

'Cook is dead. We have no staff.' Fox kept walking. 'From now on, you're cook.' She glanced over her shoulder at the woman.

'Yes, birthmother,' the woman bobbed, half curtseying.

Fox walked on, past the kitchen and down the hall, feeling the women following like lambs. 'We'll need enough food for a day's walk,' she said. 'And get your sisters to help. Oh, and I've taken a Beran as my handmaid, so she'll be sleeping in a guest room tonight.' Fox halted in the hallway just before the stairs, catching the new cook's eye. 'Send refreshments to the sewing room.' The new cook nodded and the rest of the sorority stood in the hallway, expectantly. Fox looked over the group as though searching for someone. 'I want to plan my wardrobe. Perhaps the late mother's dress sister is here?'

'That's me, birthmother,' the dress sister spoke up.

'Good.' Fox nodded. 'I'm ready to select my wardrobe.'

'Very good, birthmother,' the sister nodded.

'And the rest of you can make ready for the departure.' With that, Fox turned her back on the old women and climbed the stairs. She wished she could enjoy the momentary success. It augured well for the future of Oak province. Only... Only, underneath everything, was the dreadful loss of Mica.

22

The Berans of Caballo and their entire herd of three thousand horses lifted clouds of dust as they travelled toward Komey, so that the city's inhabitants were aware of their approach as soon as they woke and looked outside. But not Aikin. He woke before dawn and dressed with great care, showing little outward sign of the excitement he felt about the prospect of checking on Talia to see whether the treatment had succeeded. As soon as his houseboy had finished attending to his needs, Aikin made his way to his cousin's room. He checked the hallway to see that it was empty and then unlocked and opened Talia's door. It was dark inside her room, but not so dark that he couldn't see the oak trees. Trunks, branches, and leaves obscuring the window and then bending to sweep across the ceiling. It was all he could do not to dance on the spot. He'd done it! Not once, but twice. Revived two companionships: Bass and now Oak. He'd saved his family's fortunes. He stepped inside, careful to close the door behind him, lit a lamp and carried it to Talia's bedside. She was awake and waiting for him, a huge smile on her face.

'I've been lying here, smelling the new oaks.' She grinned. 'The leaves move toward me when I inhale. Look.' She sucked in a big breath of air. Aikin swivelled around and watched as the leaves in the young trees fluttered. She laughed, and the leaves shivered in response. 'I have to concentrate to stop them growing. They'll break the ceiling if I let go. It's a strain holding them back. I can get up, can't I? We've finished, haven't we? I think I need to get out of here, get away from them.'

He smiled. 'I need to check your wounds, but yes.' He looked down at his watch, checking the time, and then found a chair, drew it to her bedside and sat down. 'We've got the Wheat Companion's new prime parley in twenty minutes. So that's your first duty.'

'Who else is coming?'

'A select group.' He smiled. 'People who can help us, people we can trust. You'll be able to share the complete story with them, but not with anyone else.'

Talia returned his smile and he couldn't help his renewed sense of delight. What a triumph! Talia had turned out to be just like Glory, only in Glory's case he'd opened her bedroom door to find bass spawning, hatching, growing and spawning again in the tank beside the bed: spilling over onto the carpet in their multitude. Glory had left the room with a hidden legacy of silver-blue scars under her dress and Aikin had taken the fish to the furnace in the boiler room. He'd wanted to be discreet. Overly prudent, really. Shouldn't have bothered, because there was no need to hide Glory's new bounty. He could have taken the fish to the kitchen and revelled in the cook's stunned expression. Certainly, Whilomena hadn't been prudent. She'd told him about her loose parley talk and about the two crazed Berans who'd attacked her after overhearing her interest in collecting rock children. He sighed. The Wheat House soldiers still hadn't found those two, which meant the Stone Body's wanderers would get wind of Whilomena's plans. All the more reason to send out the militia for the rock children today, make a clean sweep.

Talia spoke, interrupting his thoughts, 'And I feel better. Completely better. It's amazing.'

He nodded and drew his chair closer. She was dressed except for her shirt, which she'd undone so that he could examine her. He ran a finger over one of her rapidly healing cuts. The skin was new and the same silver-blue colour as Glory's. He rested a hand on her stomach. Her skin was cool and healthy to touch. He looked up and saw that she was blushing.

'I'm sorry,' he apologised. 'I just wanted to be sure you were well.'

'No, don't be sorry.' Her blush deepened. 'I'm grateful. I never dreamed I'd inherit a companionship, but you've given me one. I can grow trees.' She stared past him to the oaks. 'I'm not even sure I can stop them growing.'

Aikin turned to admire her work. 'You'll get the hang of it, I'm sure.'

Filtered dawn light crept into the room between the leaves. There was a sudden snapping sound as one pot broke in two. They both laughed.

Talia was the first to sober. 'I just hope I can manage the province's people and bring things back into harmony.'

He turned back to face her. 'I'll be frank with you. Glory will have an easier time than you will. There's no one left in Bass, so she can rebuild it in peace. You've got the legacy of a rebellion to deal with.'

She took a deep breath, a look of worry on her face. 'But I thought things had calmed down. I mean, they're not fighting right now and the old sisters have survived?'

He shrugged, picked a piece of lint from his lace cuff. 'It seems so. At least so Fox wrote in her note. But she hasn't shown up yet. If she's all right, she's moving ostentatiously slowly and I can't think why. I wish she'd just ride the train and get herself back here.'

He hesitated, wondering how best to advise the seventeen-year-old in front of him, how to turn Talia's need for support to his advantage. 'The point is, you've got a delicate political situation, so the new sorority you select will need to be strong.' He paused for a moment, on the brink of an idea. And then he had it. He'd advise Talia to appoint Fox as her handmaid. It was a risk. He wasn't sure of his adopted daughter, especially after her foray to Oak province. He wasn't certain he could control her, but he knew her weakness. Wren. He would leverage her feelings for Wren. And if he could persuade Fox to manage Talia to her adopted father's advantage... then Aikin would have Oak in his pocket, along with Komey.

He suggested it and was pleased to see Talia was listening. 'Fox is Beranish born, but I wouldn't hold that against her,' he said. 'She'd make a wonderful handmaid. She's clever, but kind, and she's had an excellent education.'

Talia continued studying him, a small frown on her face. 'You'd recommend I do that? You think it would help?'

'Oh yes,' he straightened his waistcoat. 'I think it would be enormously helpful to you in your dealings with the local Berans to have someone like her on board. Appointing Fox as your handmaid would signal the camp that you are a companion mother of some sensibility. Course, it's completely unconventional, but these are new times.'

Talia nodded. 'I've spoken with her a couple of times, but I don't really know her. She's a few years older than me.'

'Everyone you choose will necessarily be older than you,' he pointed out gently. 'Now that you are the Oak Mother, you must mix with all sorts, be friends with all sorts and all ages. And I'm sure I could make one or two other suggestions about who you could appoint.'

Talia looked relieved. 'Thank you, Aikin. I never thought I'd have this sort of responsibility. My family didn't educate me for it.'

He had to resist the urge to rub his hands together with glee. This was working out well. 'Nothing like a fresh approach under the guiding hand of a staunch friend. Now, Talia,' he gave her a stern look, 'the details of this, exactly how I created your companionship gravity, how it's actually done, that has to be kept secret until we have all the existing rock children in our care. We're only allowing a select few in Komey to know the full story.'

Talia looked down at her hands as though she'd found a sudden interest in the quality of her bedding.

Aikin wondered whether he'd overplayed the avuncular man, but Talia began speaking, 'There's something else I wanted to ask you.' She blushed.

'Go on,' he urged.

'It's just that... I wondered whether you would like to join me? I mean, as my husband in Oak. I know it's dreary for a man out there, what with the need to be chaperoned, but...' she trailed off.

Aikin smiled at the naivety of her approach, but couldn't help being flattered by the invitation. How wrong his own mother had been all those years ago when she'd told him he was a fool to think of marriage. Not only could he marry, he could marry anyone at all! Soon he'd be fending off offers. 'You wouldn't be asking me if you'd seen my code,' he said, feigning modesty.

'I don't need to look for code, do I? I've got enough and you're the one who gave it to me. I can choose from the heart.'

'We don't know for sure that your child will inherit. Code could still be important.'

'I'm willing to take the risk.' Talia pulled her shirt closer about her body but didn't re-button it. She was no longer blushing, and she looked up at Aikin, meeting his gaze. 'You're not like the other men in Komey. I've never met anyone like you before. I want your code. You're the only person who's been able to work this out. That means something. That makes your code special. You helped me, looked after me. You gave me good advice. I'd like to take you with me to Oak. I think it would be a good life.'

Aikin took a deep breath, finding himself touched by her offer. Touched and tempted by the simplicity of what that life offered. But it was not to be. He loved Whilomena, and he loved his ambitions. 'There's someone else.'

'Oh,' Talia sounded young and vulnerable again.

'It's a matter of the heart, of my heart,' he explained. 'And of the future of Komey.'

'Oh.' Talia frowned. 'I see.'

For a moment, she was silent. Aikin knew that she probably didn't see and wondered whether she was angry or just hurt.

Then she spoke again. 'But perhaps we could still make a child... I want... I mean, would you join me while I'm here? I'm not due to ovulate for another day, but you know what they say... You should always try before and after if you can afford the fee. Not that you need my fee.' She blushed, embarrassed at the idea of money changing hands in place of a marriage. And, no doubt, she'd realised that the Head of the Department of Beranish Affairs, the man who'd created her companionship, hardly needed any fee she could offer. He didn't answer straight away. He should have expected this, had a contingency plan. 'I can't,' he said.

'Can't?' She looked confused.

'It's not in my nature to be with more than one person. I'm sorry.' He shook his head. 'But I'm honoured that you asked...' his voice trailed off.

Talia sat up and buttoned her shirt. Aikin stood up. For a moment, there was an awkward silence between them.

'I've given my life over to the future of the Companionari people,' Aikin spoke honestly, wanting to give her a better explanation. 'You can't please yourself, either physically or emotionally, when you've made a choice like that. You're no longer free.' He smiled at Talia, trying to give her something: some meaningful part of him. 'I suggest we both consider for a moment the words of Dabid Harwood: *When you serve knowledge, you serve knowledge alone.*'

'I'm that man. At least, I try to be. And now you must excuse me. I've got something to do before we meet at the Mill House for Whilomena's first prime parley. You'll be there, won't you? This, between us,' he waved his hand, feeling awkward, 'it hasn't changed anything, has it?'

She shook her head.

'Good, because this parley is vital. And you're ready? You're prepared?'

'To do my circus trick with the oaks in front of the parley guests?' She nodded. 'Of course.'

'It's important,' he said. 'We need the soldiersisters this parley can call upon. And if I might suggest something?'

She nodded.

'It's best if you go straight to the mill house from here. Glory's powers continued to grow after she woke. If you're the same, you'll have trees erupting before you've learnt to control them. We want a spectacle but only for a select audience. I'll join you there as soon as I can. There's just one little errand I have to run first.'

Aikin left Talia sitting on the edge of her bed, the oak trees leaning toward her, still constrained by their soil despite their broken pots. He'd have to get the dust boy up here in the next day or so to clean. And the gardeners? Have the trees planted? Some sort of ceremony. Three new foundation oaks...? It was a nice thought. Perhaps they should send one to the province when Talia left with her new sorority? He nodded to himself and hurried down the hall. Yes, indeed. It was a good idea.

Aikin had little time to spare, but he headed to the library. He wanted *The Book of Kinesis* in his pocket. He'd dreamt about it being damaged, being taken, being read by someone else. Irrational, but the book needed a new home. Better to have it in his coat pocket until he found one. Besides, it could be useful in Whilomena's prime parley. He might read a couple of passages after Glory and Talia revealed their scars and showed off their talents. Not that he needed the book in his hands, not when he'd committed so many sweet phrases to memory. Pity the work was anonymous. He would have liked the man or woman who wrote it elevated to their rightful place in Companionari history.

Which section should he quote from? Something weighty from part one? Something representative of the book's political philosophy? Certainly, it was that section and not the ledger at the end that had touched his soul, never mind that it was the ledger that had given him the power to create companions. He recalled his favourite philosophical passage:

Social change is a kinetic rush, a waterfall of energy. Think of the state of the world at the moment before change. Potential energy is ripe. Think of the world the hour before change; the week before change; the month before change; the year before change. In each case, the cross-section shows a level of investment. Work, in the form of agitation, has created kinetic capital, which is then spent in change.

Social agitation can be measured and understood in the same manner in which physical agitation is measured and understood. The ratios and formulae that empower the physicist and her sister the economist have finally found their place in the social sciences.

With these tools, wrung from history, the student of physical sociology becomes the mistress of kinetic investment, the mistress of the pace of change and the Author of the Future.

When Aikin had first read those sentences, he'd felt as though a clear bell had sounded inside him. The way the book spoke of cause and effect as a dressmaker might speak of fabric and pattern... Aikin shivered and hurried his steps, turning right, away from the stained glass window of Cook and Hunter, away from the stairs down to the atrium. He was glad the house was still at breakfast and the office doors were yet to open.

He sighed. He doubted many at today's parley would be interested in political philosophy, never mind that the anonymous author's intellect and curiosity had saved them from the humiliation of an eventual return to Galea as beggars. Well, perhaps he could quote something from the second half? The personal advice section was easier to understand, but it wasn't electrifying like the political stuff. He hurried up a flight of stairs to the level of the library. In the end, he wondered whether it wouldn't be best to just read the ledger, just read it and let them hear the words that had changed all their lives.

Aikin opened the library door, looked in, and was relieved to see no one was in the room. He hurried over to the shelf, reached up and lifted down the box, but it was weightless in his hands. He pulled the lid open.

Empty. It was empty.

He spun around and looked at the reading desks, but they were as he'd last seen them. He began rushing, conducting a crazed search that a part of him knew would be pointless because he knew where he'd hidden the book. Still, he did it. He searched. He swept his hands over the shelves, scanning titles. The book wasn't there. He jogged around the library, now bending down to look under the desks, now searching the floor. There was nothing there. Nothing anywhere. He threw the cushions from the seats. He checked the windowsills and behind the curtains, his thoughts racing. Nothing.

But who would have it? Whilomena? Surely not. She hated reading. And what about Fox? She used the library: what about her? But no, he knew he'd last looked at the book *after* she'd left for Oak, so it couldn't be her either.

He ran back to the original shelf and recommenced his search: frantically working his way through the library section by section in case he'd missed it the first time, in case the housekeeping staff had re-shelved it in the wrong place. But surely not... because they knew they weren't allowed to clean in here. For a moment he thought he'd found it among the cookery books, but the book in his hands turned out to be a text on Beranish herbs. He cast it aside and kept moving. Kept searching. He lifted all the dusty papers from the desks. Nothing. He ran his hands along the very top of the bookcases, but they were bare. He got up onto a chair to make absolutely sure, but they really were bare.

The book was gone.

Gone.

Aikin stood in the middle of the room, panting. He felt a deadening sensation settle into his chest.

Be vigilant. If another follows your path, either knowingly or blindly, you will no longer control the nature or pace of change. Be ready; be flexible; be ruthless; be fast.

Was he ready? Could he handle the increasing complications? The attack on Oak Manor. The death of the Oak Companion. The recent attack on Whilomena. The disappearance of *The Book of Kinesis*... He pushed against his growing panic, trying to regain the sense of certainty and triumph he'd had when he left Talia's room. He *was* ready and he *could* handle anything and everything that arose. Aikin reminded himself that he didn't need the book; he already knew what he needed to know. The book was just a sentimental thing, an object. The book had promised change and change was happening. From now on, it was Whilomena's parley that mattered.

Aikin left the library and, oblivious to the spectacle he was making, raced downstairs and out of the house. He turned onto the servants' path toward Whilomena's mill house folly. Calling it a path was an exaggeration. It had changed since he'd walked it the day before. Today it was more like a track in a forest. Clearly, Talia had walked here, flourishing cork oaks and white oaks in her wake. Could she have the book? But no, she'd been locked in the room. It couldn't be her.

Whilomena, then? Was it conceivable?

He decided to see whether he could catch Whilomena before she reached the folly, but first he needed to get past Talia's trees. He left the path, ran through the new grown forest and emerged on the Wheat House lawns.

And there she was.

The Wheat Companion was alone, strolling in the landscape, dressed in gold. She glittered against her surroundings. It was the sight of her that made him notice the air for the first time. Though the morning was warm, the sky was tinged black. Thundercloud black, but without a hint of storm. She looked spectacular. He walked across the lawn, his legs aching from his panicked run. He called out her name, and she stood, waited for him. He started running and then reminded himself to be calm, to avoid any unwanted attention. But he couldn't seem to contain himself. After a couple of paces he was running again.

$$23$$

ikin pulled up beside Whilomena, almost slipping on the grass.

'You're sweating,' Whilomena said. 'And I saw you running like you haven't got a penny in your pocket. Silly boy! You didn't have to run.'

He bent over, resting his hands on his thighs. 'Did you take *The Book of Kinesis* from the library?' he looked up at her as he asked.

'Stand up,' she hissed. 'You look ridiculous.'

'Did you take it?'

'Of course not. Why would I take your stupid book?'

'Well, it's gone.' He stood up straight, faced her. 'We have to assume it's in the wrong hands.'

She didn't answer, just turned away, continued walking across the lawn. 'This isn't like you,' she said. 'You rarely worry so much. And you haven't even told me about Talia. I assume it worked? I mean these trees...' she waved a hand at Talia's forest. 'I'm going to speak to her about keeping them out of my gardens. This is my grass, after all.'

He nodded, keeping pace, still out of breath. 'She's struggling to manage them.' They stepped off the lawn and onto another one of

Komey's gravel paths. 'So you haven't seen my book?' he said, unable to keep his mind off his loss.

'You need to stop worrying,' she said. 'Hold your nerve. If my new parley members give me their soldiersisters, I'll send them across the Stone Body like a new broom, gather up all the Beranish fetish stones. And while that's happening, I'll work on tightening my control over the city. I'll be ready for any Berans who come running after their pebbles.' She laughed, 'Watch me, Aikin. I'll catch those wanderers and sell them off to the traders and no one will know what we've done or how we've done it until it's too late.'

Aikin smiled at her audacity, but, despite her reassurances, he felt consumed by the thought of his missing book. 'Perhaps I left it on a desk and someone's taken it. It's the thought of it being stolen that worries me.'

'Don't talk to me about thieves!' she clicked her tongue. 'Have you seen the sky?'

Aikin glanced up and, for the first time, registered the thought that the darkness must have some sort of explanation.

Whilomena kept talking, 'Caballo province has failed and that idiot Sousette has brought the entire Beranish population *and* their horses to our doorstep. Three thousand beasts! They've kicked up half the countryside along the way. I'll kill her if she let those horses trample my wheat. I bet this is *my* dirt from *my* fields.' Whilomena looked back up at the sky. 'I bet this earth is mine. She could have sent an envoy like a normal person, but no... Well, at least we're in a position to send her horses and Berans home with a new and more sensible companion.'

Aikin glanced at her and couldn't help pointing out that they didn't yet have the rock children.

She patted his arm. 'Exactly, but we will. In the meantime, those Caballo Berans are expecting to be fed. I don't care about your book going missing, but we're going to do something about the Caballo companionship as a priority.'

Ahead of them, Aikin spotted the parley guests, surrounded by more oak trees, waiting beside the small red door that led to the folly. He was relieved to see Talia in their midst, and Glory too.

The Wheat Companion waved. She spoke to Aikin out of the side of her mouth, 'Smile Aikin, smile.'

He took a breath and found he could mimic her.

There were several large and well-maintained mills just beyond the city's walls, but Whilomena's great grandmother had built the ornamental mill within the grounds of Wheat House for holidays and parties and private parleys. The building counter-levered over the Fraise River and when you were inside, it felt as though you were floating on the water. An ornamental wheel turned in front of a large picture window, offering views of wheat through sunlit sprays and sparkling droplets of cascading water.

Aikin surveyed the people who waited ahead of him. Gaitaz, the twenty-two-year-old Aries Companion who had wealth, influence, and an iron grip on the Department of Agriculture. Most of the younger women in Komey mouthed Gaitaz's opinions. Standing beside her was Marcelle, the twenty-three-year-old heir to the Mallow companionship, who was also notorious for her money, but had less power than she'd like. Neither woman followed convention, and both were ambitious. On the other side of the door stood Jane Paperwood, the only known carrier of the pine companionship gene, a bitter woman who'd never been able to germinate a seed. With her stood two other women that Aikin hadn't met, but knew to be the descendants of two long-lost companionships. All were living beyond their means, but had deep connections in various military sororities.

Talia and Glory stood in front of the door. Talia looked exhausted. No doubt it was the effort of trying to manage the trees. Glory's life was easier, but Aikin suspected the Fraise River would shortly begin to stink, overstocked with fish. With them were four men. Aikin had selected them. They shared with Aikin the curse of ugly code and good brains, but unlike Aikin, all were sons of military women and all had debts.

Each person was there because they were already careless of tradition and hungered for greater power; or because they had vulnerabilities and could be manipulated.

'Welcome,' Whilomena smiled. 'Welcome. Let's hurry and get inside.'

A couple of the parley visitors eyed the trees and the darkening sky, but others just giggled at Whilomena's suggestion they hurry.

'Laugh all you like,' Whilomena pretended to pout, 'but blame Sousette for the rush. She's the one who's brought all this dust down on us. I swear my hair is turning black in front of my eyes.' She pulled a large key from her chain, fitted it into the lock on the red door, and thrust it open. She hurried within and the parley guests followed. They moved down the hall into the large parley room.

The guests seated themselves in the comfortable chairs, which were all within reach of occasional tables overflowing with food and drink. Whilomena sat on the foot of the bed and called out to Aikin, patting the space beside her. Everyone in the room caught sight of the movement; everyone in the room, including Talia, stared. A companion mother only ever called a man to sit beside her on the parley bed when she was announcing an engagement.

'Congratulations, Master Oak,' Marcelle gave him a lingering look, 'I didn't know you were so good otherwise I'd have asked you to recite your code in Mallow House.'

'He has something better than code,' Whilomena said.

'Better than code?' Marcelle frowned. 'What on earth is better than code?'

'He's about to change Komey's flagging fortunes to our mutual benefit.' Whilomena winked at the other woman.

Marcelle fanned herself and then turned to her friend Gaitaz. 'The excitement! Clandestine parleys, inexplicable engagements. I'm not sure my childish heart can take it.'

The rest of the parley laughed, eyeing Whilomena, trying to assess her prospects. No doubt hoping they hadn't made a social and tactical error in accepting the Wheat Companion's invitation to join the new prime parley.

Whilomena clapped her hands to open the parley and then spoke to Marcelle and Gaitaz, acknowledging them as the most powerful guests in the room. She told them she knew they were familiar with her plans to create a prime parley. Then Whilomena flattered them by including them in her outraged complaints about Komey's most important citizens having so little say in the affairs of the Stone Body, when their produce was expected to support an increasing number of beggars. For a moment, Aikin was glad that Sousette had arrived with her three thousand horses and hundreds of hungry Berans to feed. It leant weight to Whilomena's words. By the time the Wheat Companion had finished speaking, both Gaitaz and Marcelle were nodding as though the idea for the prime parley was as much their own as it was Whilomena's.

'So, this is the core of our new parley.' Whilomena waved a hand, encompassing everyone in the room.

'These people?' Gaitaz frowned at the low code men and the talentless women. 'You can't be serious. I thought you invited them as witnesses. Surely?'

'I can understand your hesitation,' Aikin spoke now, 'but we have chosen each of you for a reason. This parley will be the cornerstone of a Companionari revival and good code isn't the only asset we're after.'

'What's he talking about?' Gaitaz asked Whilomena. 'Most of this lot wouldn't get an invitation to any of the Aries' sewing rooms, let alone my own. Except for you, Glory.' She smiled at the new Bass Mother. 'Wonderful thing, your spontaneous gravity. Congratulations.'

'Hold on a moment,' Whilomena held up her hand, speaking gently. 'If you could just listen to what Aikin's got to say, I think you'll agree our parley invitations were exactly right.'

Gaitaz looked affronted, but she fell silent. It was Aikin's turn now. He stood up and began pacing in front of the picture window. 'I'm afraid I have to begin by uncovering a lie. This view,' he gestured at the wheat gardens beyond the Fraise River, 'is a lie. We've been living a life that's based on deception.'

A young man from the Rice clan moved to object, but Aikin held up his hand to ward him off.

'If you could just indulge me for a moment longer…?'

The boy settled back into his chair, still frowning, but willing to wait.

Aikin gave him a thoughtful look. 'Have you ever thought about where the companionships came from? Originally?'

The boy cleared his throat. 'Some say they were a parting gift at the Turning, but history tells us we created them in the days before we crossed the Komic Sea. They're our property, the fruit of Galea, but ours. They're what we brought to the treaty, carried in *our* bodies.' He thumped his chest, proud despite his own poor code and his family's failed province.

'We didn't make the companionships in Galea. We stole them from the Berans after we arrived,' Aikin said.

This time, all the parley members protested. Both Marcelle and Gaitaz rose from their seats. Only Talia and Glory failed to react.

Aikin looked more relaxed in the face of their affront than he did at the start of the parley when they were still on-side. He moved back and sat on the windowsill, waited until their protests died down before he spoke again. 'Our ancestors were refugees, not pioneers. They were fleeing poverty and failure in Galea. We were riff raff with no means of support. We were clever and manipulative, but we contributed nothing to this place. We had nothing to offer in treaty and nothing that was needed by the Berans.'

Jane Paperwood protested, 'But everyone knows the companionships existed. The Berans were starving when we arrived, eking out an existence, and we brought them an alternative path: a path that offered harmony between plant, animal and person—'

Aikin cut across her, 'We created the hunger with our presence. Then we created the companionships, which resulted in the Berans losing their natural advantage and becoming dependent on us. It all happened *after* we arrived here.'

'Who cares when the companionships were created or how?' the handsome young Rice boy looked irritated. He glanced around at the rest of the parley for support and the others nodded. 'The point is, now that we've got them, the companionships belong to us.'

'I agree, but we *did* steal them,' Aikin spoke matter-of-factly. 'Have you ever wondered about the generation of wanderers who were killed soon after our arrival?'

Marcelle spoke up, 'We compensated the Berans as part of the treaty. We're reconciled now so there's no need to feel guilty about the skirmishes that took place when we first arrived.'

'But have you ever asked yourself why it was mainly wanderers who died?' Aikin stood up again and resumed pacing.

'Clash of cultures,' Jane Paperwood spoke. 'The leaders of the weaker people always get killed. Yes, we were poor when we came. And yes, there was some theft and destructive behaviour. We were taking their land, disrupting their habits. The wanderers tried to stop us and we fought back. It was inevitable: sad, but inevitable. But we have a right to be here. We play our part through our bounties and, frankly, I don't know what you're talking about when you keep insisting we stole them.'

Aikin answered confidently. 'What really happened is that we killed every single wanderer because we needed their rock children. And we blinded the Berans to the stolen origin of the companionships with those killings because the wanderers had kept the lore of fetish stones secret. The Berans didn't even know what we took from them in that wave of slaughter. I don't know how the rock children helped the Berans husband their plants and animals because they aren't helping them now, but we created the companionships with the stones.'

'The rock children?' The young man from the Rice clan frowned.

A man who'd remained silent until now addressed Whilomena. 'You spoke about rock children at the other parley. You said we needed them. What did you mean? Has this got something to do with Glory's new companionship? And what's with all the oak trees? Is there a new Oak Companion?'

The Wheat Mother nodded. 'Yes and yes. One stone equals one new companionship.'

Aikin continued the explanation, 'That's how our ancestors created the first lot. We stole the stones and used them to alter our code. I suspect that we've come to the end of their potency. That's why the companionships are failing.'

'My companionship isn't failing,' Gaitaz protested.

'Nor is my mother's,' Marcelle agreed. 'There's no problem with our cotton.'

Aikin nodded. 'For now, yes. But I don't think your family's gravity will last long enough for you to inherit it. And yours is likely to fail too.' He looked at Gaitaz. 'As will the Wheat Companion's.'

Gaitaz frowned, but she didn't reject the proposition. She looked over at Whilomena. 'Do you agree with him?'

The Wheat Mother looked as though she wanted to shake her head and deny Aikin's words about her own precious companionship, but she didn't. 'My grandchildren. Maybe. Probably, yes. Eventually everyone. All the companions.'

The room fell silent for a moment and then Gaitaz spoke again, 'You've worked out how to exploit Beranish stones?'

This was the moment that Aikin had waited for. He left his perch on the windowsill and came over to sit beside Whilomena again. She would answer. She had the authority that he lacked and the awful nature of what she needed to propose couldn't come from him: couldn't come from a codeless bureaucrat.

Whilomena sighed and ran her fingers through her hair. 'I asked you to come here today because we need each of you. Aikin and I combed through the entire population and you have the qualities that we need. This is what we face.' she leant forward and braced her hands on the edge of the bed. 'A choice between the end of our people and our way of life or a renaissance. Sometimes I think we forget what the Turning meant.' She pressed the heel of one hand against her forehead and closed her eyes momentarily. 'We're alone. We can't look to God for the hard questions.' She opened her eyes again and rested her hand back onto the bed. 'We have to face our future as adults and accept the hard consequences of understanding and action.'

She waited a moment and let the thought sink in. 'What Aikin has discovered is that rubbing fetish stone dust into cuts on the body, changes a woman into a companion. Gruesome, but simple. There it is: the greatest and deepest secret of our culture.'

'I find that hard to believe,' Jane Paperwood spoke, her mouth pinched in disapproval. 'Frankly, this is feeling too ridiculous.'

Whilomena sighed and shook her head. 'You didn't see the trees outside?'

The other woman shrugged. 'A delayed crossover. It's not unheard of.'

Whilomena turned to Talia and Glory. 'Show them.'

The two women stood up and untied their dresses to reveal their scars. They turned to face each person in the room before re-fastening their clothes and returning to their seats.

'No doubt Glory's new talent isn't news to you,' Whilomena said, and several heads nodded. 'But Talia's isn't public knowledge. She only completed her treatment last night and her companionship powers are still emerging.' The Wheat Mother turned to Aikin. 'Show them what Talia can do.'

Aikin pulled two acorns from his coat pocket and held them up between each index finger and thumb. Then he walked over to the window, where two pots stood ready. He planted one acorn in each. Then he lifted a carafe of water from Jane Paperwood's table. Before he could return to water the pots, there was movement beneath the soil and two green shoots appeared. As he crossed the room, they elongated and differentiated as they transformed into seedlings. In moments, seedlings became saplings and then formed into small trees.

Aikin put the useless watering can down. 'Come,' he said, waving Talia forward.

As his cousin walked across the room, the young trees strained to follow her movement.

The parley was silent.

'Show them what you showed me this morning,' he said. 'Inhale.'

Talia breathed in and the leaves fluttered.

'So there it is,' Whilomena spoke. 'Thank you, Talia.'

Talia moved back to her place, her brow creased with concentration, but the trees continued growing, a little slower now, but still perceptible. Aikin carried the pots outside, threw them into the Fraise River and then returned.

'Thank you,' Talia looked relieved. 'It's a struggle to keep them in check.'

He looked at the others in the room, spoke quietly, 'Talia's new code will last a thousand years if the past is any measure of what we can expect.'

'If knowledge of this process got out...' Marcelle paused.

'Exactly,' Whilomena nodded. 'It would be a disaster. Every Companionari with any ambition would be out hunting for rock children and we'd be at war with the Berans. At the very least, we'd lose our monopoly. That's why this parley is so small.'

The Rice boy frowned. 'But how does this process make a particular companionship? Rice, say, and not cotton?'

Aikin shrugged. 'I don't know, but I suspect it's proximity. In Glory's case, I had some bass I'd imported from Galea and they were right beside her. And with Talia, I planted acorns. But I don't know for certain. All I know is that it works and it will save us.' He looked around the room and held the eye of each guest.

Whilomena stirred and then spoke. 'If this parley commits to helping us gain control over the rock children, then for the foresee-able future, it will be you and your direct descendants who will decide who is to be treated and when. We won't be able to hide all this, not all of it. We won't be able to hide behind the pioneering veil, but we can retain control over the supply of rock children if we're swift. It's the exact process that must be kept secret. We may want to honour the past by only treating those who have a legitimate claim to a companionship. Such as you, Jane.' she looked across the room to where Jane sat with a look of avid attention on her face. 'But not necessarily and not gratuitously. And we'll treat our men too to improve their code. Good, intelligent men who deserve a better chance in life.' She looked at the men in the room. 'So that the children produced, the companions' offspring, will have an even greater chance of inheriting. But first, all the fetish stones carried by wanderers must be gathered, and those wanderers will have to go.'

'Go?' Talia frowned.

Whilomena didn't answer, just waited for Talia to follow the thought through.

'You're talking about killing them?' Talia spoke again, softly this time.

'Yes.' Whilomena turned to her. 'When Aikin asked you whether you'd suffer for your family, he wasn't just speaking about physical pain. Being brave is easy when you don't have to face hard choices. We can save everyone on the Stone Body from starvation, Companionaris *and* Berans, but don't think for a moment that we can move into that future without paying a price. The wanderers would never let us crush their stones. They would rather see us all dead: their own people included. There is no other choice.'

Aikin nodded. 'There *is* no other choice. Each stone I've taken during my experiments could have been given without loss of life. I offered each wanderer that chance.' He leant forward, anxious now that they understood he hadn't acted unthinkingly. 'None took it and none ever will.'

Talia said nothing.

The Wheat Mother spoke, commandingly now, 'I ask you, this leading parley, to endorse the gathering of every rock child.'

'Aye,' the voices in the room sounded.

Aikin looked up at Talia. She wouldn't meet his eye.

Whilomena continued, 'And I ask that each of you give over to my authority every single loyal soldier you can command so that today I can send them out to gather the stones on our behalf...'

'Certainly,' someone called out.

'Have them... you're welcome to them,' another agreed.

Talia still hadn't spoken.

'And you, Talia?' Whilomena asked. 'It must be hard for someone who's so young. You've little experience with the burden of companionship. It can be a frightening responsibility. I suppose if you're not yet up to this level of maturity... Well, I suppose a regent—'

Talia blushed. 'I'm not afraid of responsibility. I'll be eighteen in a few more months. Lots of the pioneer mothers were even younger.'

'That's true.' The Wheat Mother nodded. 'Yes, you're very much in that courageous tradition. So, you're ready to endorse this course of action? Brutal and abhorrent as it is to each one of us?'

'There is no other way?' Talia asked, looking over at Aikin, her face stricken. 'Maybe we could work with the Berans, share what we know. Talk to their wanderers. Explain.'

'No.' He shook his head. 'If there was another way, believe me, I would have used it. I've already explored every other option.'

'The companion's Path, is the lonely Path,' Whilomena said. 'I need your answer, Talia. You can't leave this to a god who has turned. We must each take responsibility. Do you choose life for the majority at the cost of the deaths of the wanderers? Do you choose life? What's your answer?'

'Yes,' Talia whispered. 'Life.'

'And do you have soldiersisters loyal to you?'

Talia hesitated. 'Only one. My cousin. She's older than me. She's in a military sorority. She'll help if I ask her to.'

'Good,' Whilomena's voice was warm.

Aikin turned to the others in the room. 'I'll ask each of you to call out the number of soldiersisters you can command.'

As the parley members took turns calling out their contribution, Aikin felt his tension ease. It would work. It would take some hours to arrange, but it would work.

24

Oria looked out the carriage window and watched the train slow to a halt. The breathy huffing of its steam engine fell silent. The marshal rang the bell announcing their arrival as though the wheat fields were awaiting them, as though the bobbing seed heads were eager to greet them. They were half a day's walk from Komey, still a little short of the banewood and the valleys, but they would disembark here. Fox was following Oria's plan to the letter, at least in the matter of their arrival in the city, so they would walk the last little distance into Komey.

What hadn't been part of the plan was making the Berans travel in a separate carriage and making them wait while the Companionaris disembarked. It felt personal, even though it wasn't. It had been a senior sister's idea, not Fox's fault entirely, but it was humiliating. Oria found it difficult to meet Quartz's eye, knowing this was the way Berans were treated.

Things would be different in the future. She had little idea of what would eventuate when they returned to the province, but she had little doubt that a great deal would change.

She stood up and joined Quartz at the carriage door, then followed him down the steps into the wheat. The children were already on the ground, standing a small distance away from Fox and the sorority. Quartz had spoken to Saury about keeping away from Fox during the journey to Komey. Things were complicated enough without the child attracting too much attention. But Oria could see it, could feel it: the longing in the girl, the hunger to join her older sister.

The painted train looked garish against the pale yellow background of the wheat. Oria watched as the marshal hung the steps on the side of the train and then made her way to the wagon to unload the horses. Four of them. One for Fox; the other three were for the frailest sisters. The marshal led the animals down the wooden ramp and over to where the Companionaris waited.

Quartz's voice was loud in the emptiness, recalling Oria to her role in the charade, 'Help your mistress,' he said. 'She needs her handmaid.'

Oria noted the amusement on the wanderer's face, but there was nothing for it. She had a part to play and she would play it well. She hurried forward and took her place at Fox's side, helping Fox mount, ignoring the slight headache that was building behind her eyes.

The first hour of the trek was uneventful. On Oria's advice, Fox had insisted that the sisters walk ahead while she followed with her handmaid at her side. Quartz and the children formed a small separate party, travelling about five minutes behind. The arrangement gave Fox some relief from the sorority and kept Saury from Fox.

Oria walked at Fox's stirrup. She was glad that they'd decided she shouldn't speak to Fox beyond what was necessary. Her head hurt with the effort she was making not to germinate oaks. It wasn't like being in Oak province. Here, the renewed potency of her companionship powers was more difficult to manage. She could feel acorns around her. There were a surprising number of them scattered across the landscape. Acorns with scaly cupules that promised oak trees. Others with wavy cupules longing to become cork trees. All of them pushing at her, hungry to burst from the soil. It was all she could do to stop them germinating, stop the trees from popping up and forming more acorns, acorns that would drop to the ground to repeat. Repeat and repeat until they replaced the wheat with their forests. The existing forests in Oak had had a calming effect. Here, she needed her lifetime of experience to halt the potential tsunami of growth. Hard to imagine what would happen if she'd had less control over her abilities.

Over the long hours of the walk, Oria became more adept at managing her body's hunger to produce trees, and her headache eased.

Every now and again, one or other of the sisters would drop back for a confidential word of advice with the new birthmother. Oria listened to various unflattering accounts of her own companionship and character, as well as recommendations to the young birthmother to make improvements. Oria's domestic routine was criticised. They put forward absurd suggestions for the better management of the province. Fox listened to each idea with great care and always thanked the speaker. Oria spent the first part of the walk planning the best and quickest method for pensioning off the entire sorority. But like it or not, she had spent most of her adult life with them. They were family: family in all its messy, disloyal, jostling glory.

As the sun moved higher in the sky, the heat increased. The smell of the horse beside her filled Oria's senses, bothering her, and her feet hurt. She reached up and rested her hand on the back of Fox's saddle to take some of the weight off her legs. She had done little walking in the past few years and it appeared Promise wasn't used to it either. Her feet blistered, and the touch of her leather sandals against her skin was sharp and painful. And her leg muscles ached. She stared at the view in front of her, framed on one side by Fox's leg against the honey-coloured belly of her horse and on the other by the white-cloaked form of a sister, dawdling for yet another chat with the new birthmother. The woman must have sensed Oria's gaze because she glanced back, taking in the sight of Oria's hand on the back of Fox's saddle.

The sister glared at Oria, staring at her hand, before speaking to Fox, 'Birthmother, that Beranish woman of yours has got no manners at all. You should send her back to walk with her own people. It's not too late to appoint someone more suitable as your handmaid. There'll be any number of well-educated young Komey girls who'll jump at the chance.'

Oria knew she should let go of the saddle, and lower her eyes. But she felt irritated and something old and stubborn within her refused to do the sensible thing. Instead, she maintained her position and gazed ahead at the wheat grass that smudged the plains. A couple of sisters turned to see what was happening. Oria realised too late that she'd made a mistake. She had an audience now, and she'd placed Fox in a difficult position.

Fox cleared her throat and then spoke, 'I know you're new to service Promise, and that's why I've kept you near. Even though we're walking through fields, this is a formal occasion. Anyone might see us. We are Oak's face out here in the Wheat Companion's province. I can't ride to Komey with my handmaid resting against my saddle. When we're at home, we may do as we please, but not here.'

Even though Oria agreed with every word Fox had spoken, even though she admired the young woman's gentle but firm manner, Oria felt as though someone had slapped her. She pulled her hand away and a wave of anger swept through her, making her blush, flushing her rock skin. The bells on Fox's saddle blanket tinkled with the sudden movement. Oria realised, too late, that she was glaring at the younger woman.

Fox's frown deepened, and it appeared every sister in the travelling party was watching, ready to judge the strength of Fox's grip on her new household.

'Go and join Quartz and the children.' Fox's voice was icy.

Oria obeyed, let Fox and the sorority walk on, used the moment to busy herself. She examined her sore feet. She lifted them one by one, pulled her sandals away from her soles. Blisters had formed and burst. The raw skin beneath was worn and dirty. The sores burned in the dry air. She heard footsteps hurrying behind her and looked up. Quartz and Saury were still a distance behind, but Doubt was sprinting toward her, a look of delight on his thin little face.

'Your feet are too soft, Huntress,' he announced as he halted beside her.

'Promise,' she corrected him. 'You've got to get used to calling me Promise.'

He looked at her feet and then whistled under his breath. 'They look awful. You should step more carefully.'

She shook her foot, trying to dislodge the small grains of dirt that had caused so much pain. 'You look after your feet and I'll look after mine.' She resumed walking, doing her best to ignore him.

He followed, undaunted, untroubled by her tone. 'Quartz is telling Saury stuff about rock children that I already know, so it's boring for me to walk with them. Saury hardly knows anything.' He shook his head and sighed. 'Mica was going to teach her. I guess Quartz doesn't have much choice.'

Oria glanced at the boy. His complicated feelings about Saury and his grief for Mica would have been clear even without rock skin. She tried to project some kindness into her voice, 'It's good that Quartz has got you to help him with Saury.'

The boy shrugged, but she felt a slight lift in his spirits.

They walked on in silence. Oria watched Fox. The girl rode well. She looked regal on her horse, on Oria's horse. 'I've done this journey many times,' Oria told Doubt, 'but never on my feet. I'm usually the one on the horse.'

'Feet are best because you can feel when the ground changes. It makes it easier to tell where you are.'

'What do you mean?'

Doubt looked up and then frowned at her, uncertain about whether her question was serious.

'I'm not sure what you mean,' she repeated.

He gave her a pitying look. 'Real Berans can feel the Stone Body through their feet. We always know where we are. I guess it will be the same for you, eventually. I guess you don't know what you're doing because you're in a new body.' Oria frowned, and he took it as an invitation to continue explaining, 'Getting lost would be like... not knowing where your fingers are,' he laughed at the absurdity of the idea and his nose wrinkled. He held up a hand, wiggling his fingers to make the point. Then something new seemed to occur to him, 'Huntress, why did you change bodies?'

'I don't know.'

'If they'd dug up a man's body, do you think you'd have woken up a man?'

'I don't know.'

'If you dig up another body, do you think you'll change again?'

'Enough!'

He fell silent, but it didn't last long. Soon he was explaining more about knowing where you were on the Stone Body. '... you can feel it here.' He touched his left clavicle.

Once again, Oria realised how little she understood about Beranish life. Well, that would change, beginning now. 'What else can you feel?'

'Everything.' He pointed at some boulders jutting above the wheat. 'Try feeling those. They're easy. They're so round.'

Oria looked at the rocks in front of them. They were wonderfully round: round like rocks in a painting.

'Stop looking with your eyes,' Doubt said. 'No wonder you can't feel anything. Here,' he held out his hand, 'I'll lead you and you can shut your eyes. It might help you sense things properly.'

Oria put her hand into his smaller one and closed her eyes, allowing herself to be led. For a while all she could sense was sound: their feet on the earth and the more distant sounds of the sisters in front of them and Quartz and Saury behind. Then her rock sense began picking up the thready heat of the mixed emotions of the party. But Doubt had said she could rock sense the Stone Body like a person and that part seemed to be missing. She tried to forget about being led among people so she could focus on the land. But it didn't seem to work. 'I can't feel anything special,' she complained.

'Keep trying,' he said, pulling her to the right as their route shifted.

She kept her eyes closed. Her feet still hurt, but not as much as they had before. The ground felt softer beneath her, almost as though she were walking on pillows. She halted, pulling Doubt to a stop.

'The ground feels better, gentler.'

He squeezed her hand. 'Walking is like this, like holding hands. You and the Stone Body are touching, so you've got to be careful not to pinch each other. Why don't you take off your sandals? It's even better without them.'

Oria opened her eyes and let go of Doubt's hand. She slipped off her sandals, tucking them into the bag she carried on her back. Her first few steps were cautious, and a small rock dug into her left foot. 'Ouch!'

'You're using your eyes again. Close them and I'll lead you.'

Once again, Oria put her hand into Doubt's, closed her eyes and began walking, bracing herself against what she might encounter.

'Relax,' he instructed. 'You can't feel anything when you're all stiff like that.'

Oria dropped her consciousness into her body and made herself relax. She felt the ground soften and the pain in her feet eased. A wonderful embracing warmth suffused her rock skin with a feeling akin to the feeling you have when you are truly at home and at one with the place you're in. Doubt was right. She opened her eyes, but as soon as she did, the sensation in her arms disappeared and the ground felt hard and sharp again. She closed her eyes. 'I can't do it with my eyes open.'

'I'll lead you. I don't mind.'

'I think I can feel which way the path is going,' Oria said. She followed Doubt's lead, enjoying the relief of stepping on welcoming ground. 'I think I can feel your footsteps, too.'

'You're getting better. If you practice, you'll feel the shrubs, the trees, the other animals.'

Oria opened her eyes, met his gaze. 'I know what that's like. I've always been able to feel oak trees.'

'Not just oak trees, Huntress. You'll feel everything.'

Oria wished they had more time on the road. She wished they had walked the entire way to Komey. She would have liked a month or more to get used to this, but they'd reached the ridge of a rocky outcrop and ahead of her was the banewood ring that surrounded Komey's valleys. They were here. Already. So close. The sky was dark. 'If the weather was clear, we'd be able to see the outline of some of the city's buildings over there.' She pointed at Komey.

Quartz spoke from behind her, 'I can feel people,' he said. 'Lots of them.'

Oria turned around and realised that she and Doubt must have been moving slowly because the others had caught up with them.

Then Oria felt it too. Ahead of her, beyond where Fox and the sisters continued walking through the wheat, she felt signatures. People and something... Something living. Horses. She could feel them moving through the banewood and she could feel the riders' emotions: tangles of pain; ribbons of hurt. 'Berans. Riders,' she said. 'But what's wrong with them?'

Four riders emerged from the trees.

Fox and the sorority had caught sight of them now. Fox continued riding forward, but the old women dropped back, flanking Fox, respectful and protective. Oria felt renewed respect for her ancient sisters.

Quartz spoke, his tone worried, 'That's odd. The horse people rarely leave their province.'

'It's not a good sign,' Oria agreed.

'No,' Quartz said.

Together they looked out into the distance and watched as more riders emerged from the banewood.

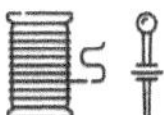

Mica sat at a small desk in one of Louis' front rooms and stared at his notes in frustration. He'd made very little headway with the book he and Obsidian had found in the Oak House library and he'd a growing sense of urgency about the situation in Komey. At first, he'd felt that he and Obsidian could afford to stay for a while, disguised as Louis' employees, but the number of soldiers in the landscape seemed to increase and the city felt hostile. Mica had to suppress his urge to flee, even as he sat in the relative safety of Louis' house.

He bent his head and tried another passage. The language was much more difficult than he'd expected, full of technical terms and obscure notions that were hard for an outsider to understand, all written in a dead language that he hadn't studied since childhood. Initially, he wasn't worried. Obsidian's reaction to the book was a motivation to persist, and Louis had lent him an Old Treaty dictionary to supplement Mica's sketchy knowledge of the ancient language. Mica had thought he would find something quickly. Certainly, Obsidian's every effort seemed bent toward making Mica attend to the book. But disappointment had set in.

The text was alien and its notion of a mathematical analysis of history and culture seemed misguided to Mica. He picked up his notes. They represented a sleepless night's work. He re-read the last paragraph he'd translated.

Divide your culture into seven segments and assign a letter of the alphabet to each segment as follows. Let T be the segment concerned with education of young; let U describe the nature of government; let V cover all that relates to religion; let W be the nature of exchange; let X be the area of culture that deals with the science of feeding the population; let Y be the nature of relations between individuals based on age, gender and position; and let Z be the relations between differing groups. Now you are ready to calculate the values for each segment. First, then, to T. If the young of your culture are fostered in learning, being paired with adults as to nature or to inclination or to the advantage of their parents, begin the equation as follows T=1. Where fostering is but one element in a scheme, but still the dominant, subtract 0.2...

Mica sighed. What ridiculous drivel! He should commandeer a train and head home. He should warn wanderers that their rock children were in danger from the Wheat Companion. Mica wondered about Fox. Was she all right? Was she still angry with him? What would she and the others make of his sudden disappearance? And what had Quartz negotiated for all of them in his absence? He wished he could leave for home. He had a duty to leave... But Obsidian wanted him to stay, to understand this stupid book. Why? Did it hold some sort of key to what was going on in Komey?

And then there was that odd piece of gossip that Louis had heard from his neighbour just this morning: another miracle, another companionship re-emerging, but no one knew which one. It sounded like a fourth story to Mica but, even if it wasn't, surely that was all the more reason for them to leave and seek wiser counsel?

Yes, that's what he should do: leave. He couldn't stay here translating ancient texts to please his twin when rock children were at risk. Mica closed *The Book of Kinesis*, placed the dictionary on top of it, and pushed back his chair. He looked up and found Obsidian standing beside him.

'It's time we left,' he spoke firmly to the rock man, accompanying the statement with a gesture of walking fingers.

Obsidian reacted immediately, sending agitated rock images at the wanderer, making the air thrum.

Mica felt exasperated. 'There's nothing useful in here and the city's teaming with soldiers. There are stories here, Obsidian, but I can't make sense of them. And I can feel danger in my arms. We should get out while we can. We should leave this morning.'

Mica moved to rise from his chair, but a wave of pain hit him as his twin let loose an overwhelming burst of rock thought. Mica gasped and sat back down, his vision so blurred his hands seemed like someone else's hands: aged, frail, skeletal. Then the pain and sickness subsided and his eyesight returned. 'That was you?' He glared at Obsidian. 'That hurt!'

Obsidian poked the book with his index finger, as though its touch could burn, then snatched back his hand, making a whistling sound between his teeth. This time, the rock thought that assailed Mica was gentle and the desire the young wanderer rock sensed was pleading.

Mica rubbed his temples as he spoke, 'All right. All right. But we can't stay here much longer. We can't. There's too much danger here.'

Obsidian reached out again with an index finger and pushed the book toward Mica. Then the rock man rubbed his finger on his shirt as though he wanted to wipe away the memory of the contact with the text.

Mica pulled the book toward him. 'I'll work for another half hour. The morning is still young, but that's it. Then we say our good-byes to Louis.'

Obsidian backed away, sat down against the wall.

Mica opened the book again. He began flicking through the pages, looking for some sign that they contained information he and the rock man needed to know, something that he'd missed during his first examination. He returned to the table of contents and ran his eyes down the page. He'd translated the title of the last section of the book as *Marriage Ledger*. The word *ledger* hadn't been familiar to him. But he knew the Old Treaty word for *marriage,* so he hadn't bothered double-checking that. But thinking about it now, he realised he might have made a mistake. The word might have other meanings. He picked up the dictionary and looked it up.

The entry was long. The first meaning did indeed deal with marriage, but the second gave the word gravity as an alternative. He re-read the last item in *The Book of Kinesis'* contents list with the new translation: *Gravity Ledger*. He looked up at Obsidian. The rock man was quiet and seemed to wait. No rock images touched Mica's mind. 'Okay, not there yet, but close.' Mica looked at the phrase again. He now felt certain that *gravity*, which was an old-fashioned word for companionship power, was correct. Perhaps *ledger* no longer fitted properly? He reviewed the alternatives. *Registry? Account? Register? Archive? Record?* He looked up at his twin.

'Companionship Records,' he whispered. The young wanderer felt a deep chill, almost a precognition that he'd found the key to understanding everything that was happening in Komey. 'This is it, isn't it?'

Obsidian was silent.

Mica turned the pages and began reading the list of women's names in the first column. Perhaps they were candidates for companionships? The second column dealt with money. The third listed what he translated as *gifts received*. Beneath the heading was the notation: *Wndr. Stns. d.w.* All the gifts were stones and the first two notations made the awful truth obvious. The gifts were wanderers' stones. But he frowned at *d.w.* and called out to Louis, 'What does *d.w.* stand for?'

There was the sound of shuffling feet, and then Louis appeared in the doorway. 'Dahlia Winter, the Brassica Companion.'

Mica shook his head. 'No. Something else. Something you'd find in a table. In accounts or on a receipt.'

'Like a receipt for goods?' Louis asked.

'Yes. Just like that.'

'Then it's probably dry weight.'

All sound in the room seemed to fade. Obsidian was still. Louis waited in the doorway. Mica put down the dictionary he'd been holding. Slowly, the broader implications of the ancient text hit him. A generation of wanderers had died after the Companionaris arrived on the Stone Body, their rock children disappearing with them. It had taken more than a hundred years for the descendants of those wanderers to hear calls again.

'They killed the rock children and the wanderers, too. That's what this is all about,' he spoke to himself. 'But why?'

The rock man remained where he was, watching Mica, his eyes wide and frightened. Mica felt Louis' silence deepen.

Mica thought back to all he knew about the Companionaris' arrival: the food shortages that were ascribed to the rudimentary state of Beranish agriculture, the death of an entire generation of wanderers. *The death of an entire generation of wanderers and their rock children.* The enormity of the crime was hard to grasp. 'But why?' He spoke aloud as though Obsidian could provide him with the answer. 'Perhaps they imagined the stones would boost the chances of crossover candidates?' Mica shook his head. He knew he still wasn't quite getting it. He was missing something.

The rock image that Obsidian sent was subtle. It didn't hurt this time, but was strong enough to let Mica know that he was right in thinking he hadn't found the answer, that he hadn't quite understood the full implication of what he'd read.

The young wanderer continued speaking aloud, running through the various elements. 'They killed all the wanderers; they took all their rock children. And Obsidian doesn't think it was anything to do with the crossover?' he paused, looking from the rock man to Louis. 'And if not that, why did they do it?' Mica was silent for a moment, letting the elements fall into place. '... Because gravity, companionship power, was not something they had when they first came here. *They were acquiring it!*' The enormity of his insight was stunning. 'Killing our wanderers and murdering our rock children to steal from us... Because we *had* what they wanted? Because *we already had* the power to companion.' He looked back at Obsidian who was standing, now. 'They stole something we already had.' He stared at his twin. 'What is it you can do?'

Obsidian smiled and tilted his head to one side. He danced a little jig, a quick pattern of steps.

Mica stood up and slipped the book into his pocket. 'Let's see what you can do. Come on!'

Mica caught up Obsidian's warm hand and led him down the hall, with Louis following. They passed through the kitchen and out into the yard. Mica looked around the tangled mess that was his host's garden. Well, the wheat didn't need any companioning, any encouragement to grow. Even the compost pile was thick with it. But there'd be other seeds in there. Seeds that had no companion to call them forth unless Obsidian had that power.

The dog stood up and ambled over to watch them. Obsidian bent down and gave the animal a generous hug.

'You can make things grow, can't you?' Mica spoke to his twin.

Obsidian looked up and smiled.

'Please,' Mica gestured towards the compost pile.

The rock man let go of the dog and climbed up onto the damp, wheat covered mound. The dog bounded up beside him, sniffing the ground. The rock man cocked his head as though listening, then reached out and took Mica's hand, pulling Mica forward until the wanderer stood before him. Then the rock man began making a series of kissing and clicking noises: the same he used to call Louis when they arrived home from errands. Mica watched the ground beneath their feet. There was a shiver of movement. For a few moments nothing was visible and then the mound came to life as hundreds of tiny green shoots appeared between the wheat stalks, growing taller and taller until they emerged as a bright and varied crown over the dread monoculture of Whilomena's bounty. The dog barked, and Obsidian sat back on his bottom and clapped his hands with delight.

25

Aikin looked across at the Caballo Companion. Hard to believe the woman in front of him was Companionari, let alone mother to the wealthy horse province. *Formerly wealthy*, he corrected himself. With the news that Caballo had failed, Sousette and the rest of her family would slide down to the bottom of Komey society, turning her Berans into refugees. Unless Aikin helped Sousette, and somehow he didn't think so.

It was odd, but the woman already looked poverty-stricken and he doubted it was because of the recent change in her circumstances. Sousette was dirty, but the dirt was old and ingrained. She would have been at home in a ramshackle gazette house. She was out of place in the grand Caballo travelling tent. The woman's hair was long, and she wore it pulled back into a single, ill-formed plait. Her face was lined from a life spent outdoors. She wore scruffy leather pants and a blanket-weave cloak over her shoulders. There was horsehair, dirt and animal grease on her shirt, in her hair, on the cushions they sat on, and even on his own laundered clothes. And the tent stank of horses.

Sousette leant forward and handed him a glass of kumis, the fermented mare's milk drink that was a famous part of the province's bounty. There was a dark crescent of dirt beneath her finger-nails. He forced himself to smile, doing his utmost to project a warm and compassionate demeanour. She merely glanced at him and then turned to pour a glass for Whilomena, holding it up for the Wheat Companion who accepted it, took a tentative sip, not quite managing to hide her pained reaction to the taste.

'You're right to savour it,' Sousette sighed, mistaking the expression for grief. A tear slid down her weathered cheek. 'Without new foals, there'll be no more milk. We have to enjoy our kumis while we can.' She wiped the tear away, forced a smile back onto her face and continued talking, rambling.

Aikin was glad that Whilomena and Sousette didn't expect him to join their discussion. It gave him time to concentrate on what he and Whilomena were about to do: lead Sousette's wanderers into Komey, poison them and take their stones. And all the while, back within the city's walls, their allies were working on assembling soldiersisters to begin the general sweep for rock children. Unbidden, words from *The Book of Kinesis* slipped into his head:

Violence, calculated or random; personal or impersonal, has played a role in every instance of social change. For the Author of the Future violence is a catalyst. The Author may step down and join humanity: playing the role of the good person or playing the role of the bad person, as to taste.

Aikin decided he could taste the bad man, but didn't care because he knew his companionship revival would save lives. Perhaps he was the good, bad man.

'Sousette darling,' Whilomena's voice was full of warmth Aikin knew to be insincere. 'I am moved and concerned. No one in Komey could help being moved and concerned. But all these people...? To travel with so many. What made you decide to bring all of your Berans with you? The wanderers and the keeper I can understand, but...?' The Wheat Mother looked at Sousette and spread her hands. '*All* of Caballo's Berans?'

Aikin glanced up at the Caballo Mother. Sousette held her glass in mid-air and blinked. 'I thought you understood...'

Whilomena remained silent. Her immaculate and beautiful face was a picture of sympathy and patience, but it was clear that she expected an explanation. He looked back at the Caballo Companion and saw that the woman was crying again.

'Foals stillborn...' Sousette put down her glass and wiped her tears with the corner of her dirty cloak. 'I never thought I'd live to see the day. You understand the love of provincia?' her tongue rolled over the Old Treaty word. 'Sometimes it's stronger than the love you feel for your own children and for Komey. At first we thought it was an illness. Then I stopped being able to bring the mares into season.'

'How dreadful,' Aikin said, wishing they could hurry this up and get the wanderers into the city.

'I'm still hoping.' Sousette turned her grief-stricken face toward him. 'Part of me wanted to stay in Caballo, believing it would all be all right. But I couldn't. And I know I should have left the Berans behind, just brought the horses. I can hear the Turning speaking to me, but I won't listen.' She stared at him with uncomfortable intensity, her watery eyes fixing on his. '*God turned his Back on Everyman; her Back on Everywoman. Everyman saw God's Back in the Distance; Everywoman saw God's Back in the Distance. Everyman and Everywoman knew then, and we know now: we are not God and God is not us. The intimacy of childhood has passed. Instead, we cherish the memory of the Renunciation and its Gifts: the Love; the Turning Away; the Back,*' she quoted the familiar phrase without a hint of irony. 'I couldn't turn away. I'm here like a spoilt child-god with all these lives in my hands, unable to save them, unable to leave them to the dignity of their adulthood.'

'No doubt about it, love is your weakness,' the Wheat Companion sighed and nodded, a look of sympathy on her pretty face.

Sousette shook her head. 'I'm not looking for your pity, Whilomena, just compassion for my people. I beg you: don't blame them for *my* failings. I should have turned away. Instead, I've burdened you. I've come as a refugee to Wheat; I've come to rest my head and the heads of my beloved Berans on your generous bosom.'

Aikin glanced at Whilomena, curious to see how she would react to an account that couldn't be more carefully designed to repel any tender feelings she might have had for the Caballo Companion and her Berans.

Whilomena set her glass down on the table and looked up at the other mother. 'That's why the sorority isn't with you? They didn't approve?'

He wondered how Sousette would account for her missing sisters. Their absence had to be damning. But the Caballo Mother didn't get to answer. The sound of horses and voices outside the tent interrupted the meeting. And in the sudden intrusion, Aikin caught a hint of the unexpected and felt a familiar surge of adrenalin. How he loved the rush of change. The world rolling forward.

Sousette looked up, a puzzled expression on her face. 'That's odd. I gave orders for the horses to be tethered, rested... Unless...' her expression brightened. She stood up and the sweep of her cloak sent a waft of stale horse stink in Aikin's direction. 'The sisters must have changed their minds and followed us,' her voice carried the joy the thought brought her. 'Excuse me for a moment.' She smiled at Aikin and Whilomena and then hurried to the door of the tent. She stepped outside, and the flap fell closed behind her.

Aikin glanced at Whilomena. 'Do you think it's her sorority?'

The Wheat Companion snorted, looking amused. 'Not likely. She's mad, you know. Did you see what she was wearing? And the state of her! It wouldn't surprise me to hear she's completely unacquainted with bathing.'

'The smell is evidence of that,' he said.

'I know it,' the Wheat Companion said. 'And that outfit! She looks as though she's wearing someone's discarded carpet.' Then the Wheat Mother fell silent as the noises outside grew louder.

Aikin listened too. The air was full of women's voices, and

between them the jangling of bits and the ring of saddle bells. He wondered whether he'd been wrong. Perhaps the Caballo sorority had changed its mind and Sousette's sisters had come looking for her. 'Let's go out and see who it is.'

'But let's tip out this ghastly drink first.' Whilomena poured the contents of her glass onto the ground behind her seat. Aikin followed her example, then led the way through the tent doorway, pushing the canvas flap aside. As he did so, he reminded himself to embrace change. The thought lightened everything and gave him a surge of confidence.

Outside, he looked at the scene in front of him and couldn't help smiling. Not the Caballo sisterhood, no. It was his errant daughter, Fox, leading a horse, surrounded by a gaggle of ancient Oak sisters. He spied the old Oak wanderer, Quartz, and with him a pretty young Beranish woman who was holding hands with a boy and a girl. It was an extraordinary sight. Unexpected and fortuitous. Another wanderer for his collection and his daughter returned when he needed her to help with Talia! It was hard to stop from laughing out loud at the sheer happenstance of events.

Fox looked up. Saw him. A complex expression of worry and guilt slid across her face, only to be replaced with a smile. A rather forced smile. He wondered why. Then she caught sight of Whilomena and the smile disappeared, replaced with scarcely concealed dislike. It was then that he noticed his adopted daughter was dressed far too formally for her age and station, and that the ancient sisters were fawning all over her: that the sisters had scarcely glanced at Whilomena, who normally attracted the bulk of all sycophantic attention. What was Fox up to? Something was going on.

He spoke before Whilomena could get a word in, 'Dearest daughter, I'm *so* glad to see you.' He moved forward and embraced her.

'Likewise, Father,' she said. 'How gratifying to see that you're well.'

He let her go, stepped back, didn't question her about why she seemed so tense. There would be time for that later.

The Wheat Companion stepped over a pile of manure and came forward, giving Fox her hands. Fox dipped her head, but with less deference than Aikin would have expected.

'How worried we've been about you,' the Wheat Companion's voice was warm and welcoming, but didn't cover the bite of disapproval. 'Heading off to Oak on your own... What an extraordinary thing to do.' She let go of Fox's hands.

'I was just telling Mother Caballo that we are also on our way to Komey,' Fox explained.

Aikin looked around at the Oak sorority and the rest of Fox's party, then turned back to his daughter. 'I've been expecting you for a while now,' he said to her, 'but not the entire Oak sorority. But what a delight.' He nodded and smiled at the elderly faces around him and then turned back to Fox. 'I got your note that all was well, that you'd be returning. I'm looking forward to a full account of the rebellion.'

'It's a long story, Father, but I have restored order.'

Her tone surprised Aikin. Evidently the experience in Oak had matured her because she seemed to have assumed a level of authority in her dealings with the province. He supposed it might be useful. Provided Talia didn't take offence and continued to be malleable. But he'd have to get Fox on her own and tell her to proceed with a touch more humility. He didn't want the new Oak Companion to take umbrage and reject the idea of taking on Fox as her handmaid. Still, he could sort that out when they got to Komey, after he and Whilomena had dealt with the Caballo wanderers and Quartz.

'I should present everyone.' Fox turned her attention to Sousette and Whilomena, ignoring Aikin. 'Mother Caballo, I'm not sure you know roveryone in the Oak sorority, and neither you nor the Wheat Mother will have met our Beranish guests.'

He frowned, wondering what Fox was playing at.

Fox looked back at her party and then began the introductions. She worked her way down from the oldest member of the Oak sorority to Quartz, to the pretty young Beranish woman, and finally to the children.

Aikin felt uneasy. Why was Fox directing the conversation to the two companions and not to him? And why had Fox brought such a strange collection of Berans with her? And why had she dragged the whole sorority across the Stone Body? He could almost understand her bringing the Berans with her, given her background, but she shouldn't have brought the old women and she should defer to her father, not take on airs.

'No room for everyone in my tent, I'm afraid,' Sousette interrupted his thoughts. 'We'll need to sit down out here on the ground. But don't worry, the hospitality of Caballo is legendary. As we always say, where there's mare's milk, there's kumis; and where there's kumis, there's home,' she faltered at the last few words, a fresh lot of tears sliding down her grubby face.

'You're too kind, dear Sousette,' Whilomena turned to her, 'but perhaps we should walk straight into Komey? The city will be eager to see you and the Oak sorority.' She turned to the elderly women near Fox. 'It will only take an hour and we can talk as we travel. Do you feel you could manage?'

'Of course,' one old girl answered.

'So long as there's no hurry,' another agreed.

Several sisters nodded, smiling at the Wheat Companion.

Sousette looked relieved, too. 'You're right, of course, dear Whilomena. What a good, kind companion you are. And what better way to walk than through fodder, and what better way to talk than among horses?'

Aikin looked at the Caballo Mother and spoke as casually as he could manage. 'And bring your keeper, Sousette. A wanderer, isn't he? How unusual. I am looking forward to meeting him.'

Sousette nodded, confirming what Aikin already knew. 'Dear Patience, yes. Doubly blessed. He's off organising some of the younger men, but I'll fetch him. He'll want to come.'

'And you know what?' The Wheat Mother looked thoughtful.

'You should bring your other wanderers, too. Why not? We can certainly do with hearing their stories before we parley.'

Aikin buttoned up his coat, making ready to move, doing his best to disguise his interest in Sousette's response.

Whilomena continued speaking, her voice full of concern. 'Plans need to be made, provisions organised. We'd appreciate having the benefit of the Caballo camp's knowledge.'

Sousette gave the Wheat Companion an ardent glance, reaching out a hand and touching Whilomena's arm. 'I see you understand the Beranish way. So many Companionaris are ignorant of the beauty of camp culture.'

'How true,' Whilomena agreed, patting the other woman's hand.

'Quartz?' Fox turned to the Oak wanderer. 'Would it suit you to walk in now or do you and your people want to camp out here?'

Aikin frowned. Fox was behaving oddly. He turned and spoke to Quartz, eager to counter Fox's disruptive suggestion that Quartz might want to stay behind, beyond Aikin's reach. 'Please come into the city with us, Quartz. We could use your account of events in Oak.'

'Yes, the children and I will walk in with you. Thank you.'

The Caballo Companion began calling out instructions to several Beranish horsemen to fetch Patience and the other wanderers. Then she turned back to Aikin and the others, smiling. 'No need to wait. Let's make a start. The Caballo wanderers are all on horseback, so they'll be with us before we reach the city's gate.'

Whilomena smiled and held out her arm to the other mother and they moved away, arm in arm; Aikin went to follow, then noticed the Oak sorority, standing stock still, staring at Fox as though they expected something from her. He hesitated, frowning.

Suddenly Fox was speaking, her voice loud in the banewood clearing. 'I am the new birthmother.'

Her words created a sudden silence. He stared at his adopted daughter.

Sousette and Whilomena turned back, frowning. The horse people stopped what they were doing to listen.

'An unexpected joy,' Fox sounded nervous. 'As you know from my note,' she glanced at Aikin, 'I felt I had no choice but to give up on the idea of attending the Oak crossover once I heard the sisters were in danger and the province needed help. I couldn't speak to you.' She stared at him now, as though seeking his understanding. 'I didn't know what to do. I felt I had to sacrifice my chance at the bell...' She hesitated, watching him.

He nodded, but didn't smile.

She took a deep breath and continued. 'Well... then, I was on the train,' she turned her attention back to the rest of the group. 'The train was about to leave. The Lacuna bell sounded, and I let go of my daughter embryo by accident. It must have been a powerful marriage because the gravity reached out and found me even though I was on the train and didn't get to touch Oria's body. I didn't know until after I'd reached Oak and the trees responded to me. And then it seemed right that I should stay and deal with the situation... as birthmother.'

Aikin realised he'd been listening to Fox with his head tilted as you do when something makes little sense. He was used to thinking of the Oak companionship being settled with his treatment of Talia. It took him a moment to comprehend what the girl was saying. He must have frowned because Fox reacted with another explanation.

'I'm nervous. Isn't that silly?' She smiled and there was an uneasy edge in her voice. 'I guess the old Mother was right when she found me as a child and said that I had a powerful talent.'

An elderly sister beside Fox offered her hand to Fox, but his adopted daughter ignored the offer, instead putting her hands in her pockets, fiddling with something.

She began speaking again, 'I sound as though I'm telling the four stories, telling you I'm nervous,' she laughed. 'It's such big news. Maybe it deserves four stories. But you'll have to tell me what happened in Komey after I left, when everyone thought the crossover had failed.'

Aikin caught sight of Whilomena and realised she was about to speak, so he spoke first, uncertain of his beloved fiancée's diplomatic skills. 'You're right to call on the tradition of the four stories,' he infused his voice with warmth and respect, forcing out his dismay at this additional complication. *Embrace change*, he reminded himself. 'The four stories offer a wonderful method for approaching the unknown and discussing the unexpected.' He caught sight of Whilomena and was pleased to see that she was content to let him go on speaking.

'And you're right, there was dismay at the apparent failure of the crossover,' he continued. 'The city was in mourning. We held more than quite a few wakes. Most of the Oaks wore black, and no one could speak of anything else. One hardly knew where to turn for hope. But this is an odd time. Maybe it's a time that calls for a fourth story because something unusual took place here too. Talia Oak, our dear, dear cousin,' he looked at Fox, nodded, including her as family, 'a young woman with only the slightest hint of talent, experienced a spontaneous and inexplicable surge in her companionship powers.'

There was a sound, a splutter, that came from the young Beranish woman Fox had introduced as Promise. Then Fox stepped toward him, away from the sisters who'd been hovering since she'd begun her speech. 'Talia?' She looked at him questioningly. 'Are you sure?'

'Our province is blessed.' He shrugged. 'That's the only sense I can make of it — now that I hear your news.'

The Wheat Companion nodded, agreeing. 'That's the sense I make of it, too. What joy for the Oaks! What a prodigious family you are.'

'And all the more reason to hurry to Komey,' Aikin urged. 'Talia is about to leave for Oak. You'll need to speak with her.'

His adopted daughter still seemed shocked by the news. 'Yes.' She nodded. 'Yes. I need to see her. She doesn't understand about the situation and the arrangements I've made for peace.'

'Or that you are the birthmother,' the girl called Promise spoke up. 'The rightful claimant on behalf of your unborn daughter.'

'I say!' one of the ancient sisters spoke, glaring at the young woman. 'This is none of your business, girl.'

'She's impossible, Mother Wheat,' another complained, addressing Whilomena. 'The birthmother took her on as her new handmaid, but the impertinence! For Back's sake, Mistress,' she turned her appeal back to Fox, 'let's leave Promise here with the horse people. She's quite impossible and she'll be an embarrassment in Komey.'

'Be quiet!' Fox spoke with surprising authority. 'Until Talia and I speak, nothing changes. We must hurry to Komey.'

26

Mica's discoveries about *The Book of Kinesis*, about Obsidian's talents, meant they needed to escape Komey. He had to get news to the camps, give the Stone Body's Berans the information they needed. He didn't let himself think about the future. His only task was saving wanderer and rock child lives.

He and Obsidian couldn't go anywhere near the city's gates. There were too many guardswomen and soldiers about, but he'd left Louis' house imagining he and his twin could climb the wall where it dipped down behind the Mint Gazette. Once again that plan fell to pieces, only this time it wasn't Obsidian's fault. There were soldiers walking the wall, bright against the darkened morning sky. He and Obsidian turned away before they were seen.

They returned to Louis' house, and it was the old man himself who came up with the idea to ask Willie, the Oak House cook, to help them slip through the house gate. Like all the great houses, Oak House backed onto its own bit of valley, its rear wall making up part of the city's wall. The trading hall's back gate opened onto the grass to ease the movement of timber and cork. With only one external gate and one mistress to manage it, Louis was certain that the twins could escape that way and that Willie would find the means.

Mica and Obsidian dressed in their footmen's livery, and Louis handed Obsidian a basket of produce, dark-skinned courgettes with golden flowers still attached. He gave a letter to Mica to carry, begging for Willie's help. It was frank. There was no deception, just a plea for help. Mica hoped that Willie's fondness for Berans was strong enough to protect them.

Mica didn't share his fears with Louis, and he was careful to shield them from Obsidian. To an observer, their farewell could have been the daily parting of employees going about their domestic business. Except for Louis' fussing. He was too fastidious about pulling down sleeves, tying down hats, pushing up cravats, reminding his footmen that demure Companionari men always keep their eyes lowered. Obsidian seemed to understand the need for caution because he was quiet with the worry over his wardrobe and uncharacteristically careful as Mica led him through Komey's paths and gardens.

The care was called for. The landscape was bristling with militia. More soldiers than on any other occasion Mica and his twin had ventured outside. Most of the soldiers seemed preoccupied, hurrying toward the northern part of the city without giving the twins a second glance, but some were still intent upon looking for Mica and Obsidian: searching the landscape with emotional signatures that left Mica in no doubt they were hunting particular quarry. But the pair passed by without incident, using their rock sense to avoid trouble, marching down the city's paths when trouble couldn't be avoided.

Mica was sweating by the time they reached the kitchen and was just thankful the room was almost empty in the lull between breakfast and the preparations for lunch. Thankful for that and for the welcoming smile Willie gave them. Mica handed over the letter, nervous in case Louis had misjudged his friend, in case the open admission of their clandestine presence was more than Willie would be prepared to overlook for the sake of a basket full of courgettes and Louis' gratitude. The cook read the letter and then slipped it into his pocket, frowning.

He spoke quietly, 'Didn't I say you were Berans the first time I saw you?' He nodded. 'That's what I said. Picked you right away. But I didn't realise the whole of it... Wanderers collecting stories. That's what you're about, isn't it? Not that Louis gives much away in here.' He tapped his pocket where the letter rested. 'But I know enough about you lot to know you wouldn't be here if your stones weren't insisting that you had to be. I'm right, aren't I? You're a wanderer?' He looked at Mica, an odd sort of eagerness on his face.

Mica nodded.

'And your brother... well, I can see he's not a wanderer like you. Anyone can see that he's different. Your secret's safe with me.' He tapped his nose. 'But I'm going to say a few words to my staff. Can't help that. Second time they've seen you and they've got eyes and ears. Still, my authority counts in this room. You've got nothing to fret about in here.'

Mica let out a sigh of relief and nodded his assent. Obsidian mimicked him, nodding rapidly and rhythmically and sighing, noisily.

Willie turned to his staff, raised his voice, 'Now you lot... Listen carefully. I know you've seen our visitors. Well, you're not to go tattling about them. Not everyone in Komey understands Beranish life. I'll not have any of our Oak camp people bothered by soldiers. Not in my kitchen! And these two are our people. Family. Oaks.' One by one, the assistants and pantry boys nodded.

Mica had doubts about the wisdom of drawing attention to them. He'd hoped that their disguise had made them unnoteworthy. Now Willie had spoken something of the truth, their presence wouldn't remain secret for long. He just hoped the staff would be silent for long enough for them to pass through the house gate.

The cook turned his attention back to a pot that was bubbling on the stove in front of him. He dipped a spoon into the broth and then lifted it to his lips. He sipped some of the aromatic liquid and nodded, pleased.

Mica was finding it difficult to keep still. He wanted to press the cook to find a way for them to get out, but he knew he needed to give Willie a chance to think. He only wished he could help, but he didn't know the layout of the house well enough to make any suggestions and didn't know how to get through the trading room to the house gate, let alone how to distract the gate mistress. Mica just hoped that Willie understood the urgency. He doubted the cook knew the level of scrutiny the twins were facing.

Unlike Mica, Obsidian seemed untroubled now they were among friends. He sat down on the slate floor of the kitchen like a child and pulled five acorns from his pocket, using them to play jacks. Mica watched the rock man scowl in concentration and then grunt as he tossed the acorns into the air. His twin tried to catch them on the back of his big hand, but the throw had been way too extravagant. The acorns scattered across the kitchen floor and the rock man raced after them on all fours, growling and barking at them as though he would muster them.

'Shush...' Mica said.

His twin swivelled around and looked at him, frowning, setting the air buzzing, but he stopped barking. Mica watched him gather the acorns and then drop them back into his pocket.

The cook set the spoon down and turned to Mica. 'Probably slip you out while lunch is being served.' He nodded to himself. 'The traders don't sit with the house for lunch, but if I send them a platter or two and say it's in celebration of the news about Talia, well...' He shrugged. 'That will make perfect sense and they'll swarm all over the food and won't think twice about it. Then you can slip past. Which leaves us with the gate mistress.' He shook his head.

Mica frowned, wondering who Talia was.

Willie continued talking, 'I guess the gate mistress would fall for the same ruse. But she'll need to be offered better quality food or she'll take offence. Wouldn't enjoy being treated like a trader.' He squinted, thinking. 'A delicacy. Something tender and expensive that will draw her away from her post. Likely we'll have to set up a table for her round the corner from the gate and I'll put a boy—'

'Kitchen!' a man's voice interrupted.

Mica glimpsed a housekeeper entering the room in a great flurry of movement.

'Kitchen!' the man called out. 'We have visitors.'

Mica turned away, shielding his face, and Obsidian bowed his head so that his hat became more pronounced.

The housekeeper was a tall man and his coat tails flew behind him as he strode deeper into the room, creating a great dash of colour. Three houseboys followed him, their cheeks flushed with excitement. None seemed to notice the strangers in the kitchen. Too preoccupied.

'... from the province!' the man spoke breathlessly and sat down on one of the kitchen chairs without so much as glancing at the twins. His houseboys lined up beside him like soldiers, eyes straight ahead, arms rigid at their sides.

The cook wore a puzzled expression on his face. 'But surely the province can't have heard about young Talia, not yet.' He frowned. 'Did we send out a train with the news? Has the sorority returned?'

The housekeeper half nodded, half shook his head. 'Sort of. As far as the sorority is concerned, yes. But this isn't about Talia. It's a different business, this.'

Mica wondered again who Talia was, but he was far more concerned with the news that there were visitors from Oak. He glanced at Obsidian. A warm rock thought touched him and he suspected his twin understood he was thinking of Fox. Likely, Fox and Oria had brokered that agreement with Quartz in Mica's absence and were now in Komey for Oria to claim her continued companionship. Mica was glad that their escape route over the wall had been blocked. He might see Fox before they left.

The housekeeper continued speaking, 'The sorority, all of it, walked in. Barbarians with them too, quite a number,' he spoke in gushes of sound, still catching his breath. 'We'll need something for all of them to eat. Something quick and refreshing. But best to give them something light because the Wheat Companion has got plans for later. She and Aikin are with them. And there's more… The Caballo Companion's there too, with some of her barbarians. Came in together. But our sorority looks exhausted.' The housekeeper shook his head. 'It's a vanity that, walking in when you're too old for it. Never mind about the time being savoured and house wealth. There's a right time to show off and a wrong time.'

Mica felt his pulse race as he listened to the housekeeper's confusing account. The Oak sorority… *barbarians* with them and the Caballo Companion and her *barbarians* with her…? Then the realisation hit him that, amid everything, the housekeeper had mentioned the Wheat Companion. If Whilomena was involved, every wanderer and rock child would be in danger. He needed to get to Quartz and quickly.

'They're eating upstairs then, the Berans?' Willie asked the housekeeper. 'Or will Mother Talia want them fed in the kitchen?'

Mica started, frowning. *Mother Talia?* A rock thought hit him, so filled with dismay that it almost flattened him. He turned to Obsidian. Could this be the second spontaneous companionship that Louis' neighbour had spoken about? If it was, Mica dreaded its origins. He looked across at his twin. The rock man stared back, heedless of the housekeeper. So it was true: the Wheat Companion had already begun murdering rock children to make new companions, and this woman, Talia, was one of them! Mica wondered who else was involved and how widespread was the knowledge in the horrific ledger. He used his rock sense to feel for the emotion emanating from the people in the kitchen. The talk of Talia failed to upset anyone. In fact, the only reaction he could detect from Willie and the housekeeper was pride. Evidently Talia's claim to the Oak companionship was uncontroversial, which meant that none here knew the ledger's secret.

'Eating upstairs, they are,' the housekeeper continued. 'Grand company. Even those barbarians look grand types. They're to eat something reviving with us here at Oak House. The Wheat Companion's taking them off after that. On a tour to see that little mill house of hers, where she'll give them lunch.'

Obsidian moaned.

The housekeeper started and stared down at the rock man sitting on the floor. 'Who's this then?'

'A friend.' The cook rinsed his hands and wiped them down on his apron. 'Never mind that. Let's sort out what's needed for our guests.'

'Something wrong with him?' The housekeeper leant forward in his chair to stare at Obsidian. 'Barbarian too, or mixed blood maybe, but what's he doing here?' Then the man noticed Mica and sat back, staring at them. 'Two of them? Twins? They're not those two everyone's been looking for, are they? I tell you what Willie, you'd better get them out of here right smart. We've got enough trouble with the people we're supposed to be looking after without sheltering barbarians who disrupt parleys, attack companions.'

'Not these two.' The cook shook his head. 'No, no, no, no. These two have been around for years. They're Louis Oak's footmen, descendants of an adopted talent from Briar. Nothing special about them.' The cook waved a hand at Mica and Obsidian dismissively. 'Don't you be bothering about them. They're just about to leave.'

Mica moved over to where Obsidian sat and rested his hand on his twin's shoulder and the rock man quietened.

'Always had a taste for something fancy, that Louis. Funny fellow.' The housekeeper stood up again and his boys looked lively beside him. 'But mind you send them on their way. I don't want them wandering about my house.'

Willie didn't answer, just busied himself pulling down several cutting boards and laying them out on the bench. 'How many for refreshments, then?'

The housekeeper began counting the numbers off on his fingers.

'There's all the old companion's sorority... Then there's the Wheat Companion and our Master Aikin Oak.'

The cook pursed his lips and blew out a long whistle at the mounting numbers.

'Then there's the Caballo Mother and maybe four of her barbarians. And our adopted girl, Aikin's daughter, she's there too.'

Mica's heart quickened.

'And there's some other barbarian children as well, a lass and a lad and an older lass,' the man continued counting, 'plus old Quartz. Did I say Quartz, already?'

'They should have sent word ahead,' Willie complained, rubbing his hands on his apron with nervous energy.

As the cook's agitation increased at the unexpected numbers, the housekeeper's calm grew. 'Something light,' he reminded Willie. 'And have it brought up to the summer parley room. They're about to start. The horse business. The Caballo Companion has landed her province's barbarians on the Wheat Companion's doorstep so there's bound to be a bit of horse trading,' the man laughed at his own joke. 'Yes, bound to be a few deals brokered.'

Willie turned to his apprentices and assistants who, sensing his need, had appeared out of nowhere. He pointed to four young men. 'Fruit and teas upstairs within six minutes.' He turned his attention to the next in line. 'And you lot get out our best selection of breads. I want the loaves sliced and buttered. Nice and thin the way the sorority always likes it. We don't know about young Talia's tastes yet, so we won't worry about that. But fruit, bread and teas should be enough. Then since the Wheat Companion will whisk everyone away, we can get on with preparing a big welcome dinner for when our lot return.'

The housekeeper stood up and brushed down his coat, preparing to leave. He began issuing instructions to his houseboys.

'I need to see my people,' Mica spoke softly, directing his voice toward the cook.

Willie shot Mica a cautionary glance, shaking his head.

The housekeeper clicked his fingers and his houseboys smartened up in front of him. He pointed to the youngest. 'You stay here. Carry cook's messages if he needs to send any.' With that, he turned toward the door, calling out over his shoulder, 'How long till you serve?'

'Four minutes and counting.' Willie glanced around the kitchen at the activity that was already under way.

Mica followed his gaze. The kitchen staff was hard at work. The benches sounded with the noise of rattling cutting boards as knives sliced through fruit. A long piece of orange peel fell to the floor beside Obsidian. His twin reached out and spun the rind on the floor with his index finger, but the movement lacked the rock man's usual enthusiasm and zest.

When Mica turned back, the housekeeper had already left. The wanderer could hear the man's fingers snapping, calling his lackeys to attention, and beneath his rock skin he could feel the hurry and excitement of the houseboys.

Mica spoke to the cook, 'I need to see Quartz.'

Willie looked stressed. 'Have you got standing in the province? Are you someone who should be up there too?' But he didn't wait for an answer. He bent down and began pulling platters from a cupboard.

'Yes,' Mica spoke to his back, 'but the Wheat Companion's no friend of mine. It's her who's behind the soldiers looking for me, so I need to get Quartz down here.'

'It's not as easy as you think.' Willie straightened up. 'None of my staff can go waltzing in there to fetch him. We're kitchen; not house.'

Mica nodded at the housekeeper's boy, sitting on his own in the kitchen corner as the hands hurried at their tasks. The wanderer lowered his voice, 'Could we use him?'

'To fetch someone? No,' the cook answered his own question and began lining up the platters on the serving table. His assistants stepped up and began filling the plates with fruit. 'A house like this has rules. The houseboy can carry messages to the housekeeper:

nothing more. Maybe I can ask to speak to Mother Talia after they all get back from lunch with the Wheat Companion.'

At the suggestion, Mica felt the urgent, cold, damp chill of his twin's thoughts. Obsidian didn't want him to wait. 'I need to speak with Quartz,' he pressed the cook. 'I need to see my brother wanderer before he leaves with the Wheat Companion. It's urgent. It's life and death.'

The cook clicked his tongue and waved toward two kitchen hands, sending them over to the kettles that were steaming on the stove. 'Two teas... No three. A bone tea for the old sisters. They'll need it. A summer tea for our people and grey tea for the horse people. No, scratch that.' He held up a hand. 'See if we've got any kumis in the back pantry. Hurry!'

Mica found that Obsidian was already standing beside him, ready to go. 'We'll have to take our chances in the house on our own.'

Willie motioned for Mica and Obsidian to sit back down. 'Wait. I'll help you. The parley has only just begun. There's no question of them leaving early for lunch. They'll be lucky to get out of the parley room in under two hours. Wait a little longer. Wait for the household to settle and I'll see what I can do.'

Obsidian moved over to the cook and leant his head against Willie's broad chest and somehow the air felt warmer and the cook looked younger, stronger, leaner, as though the gesture had the power to turn back time.

'There, there, Pet.' Willie patted him and then looked over at Mica. 'You must wait. Let the teas and other refreshments go up first; let my staff finish serving; let everyone become a little bored. Then your friends will rock sense you and they can slip out for a quick chat. But you must promise me,' he held up a finger, '*absolutely*, to behave yourself. I want no discredit brought on my kitchen.'

'All right,' Mica agreed. 'We'll wait.'

27

O ria stepped into the parley chamber in Oak House and gazed around her. From what she had gathered, the usurper Talia couldn't have been in charge for more than a couple of days and yet there already seemed to be signs of her hand at work.

They had ushered Oria and her party into the summer parley chamber, which was probably the best place in the house for all of them to gather. It made sense, not only because the season was right but also because the summer chamber was the largest. It could seat Oria's party and all the other people attracted to a gathering full of provincial drama and visiting Berans. But Oria noticed straight away that the blinds were lower than they should be, giving the room a sleepy energy at odds with its purpose. Even though she'd spent most of her life in the province, Oria's tastes and opinions had always reigned supreme in her house in Komey, with each detail of her domestic preferences understood and obeyed. When the weather was good, windows were open. When it was night, the blinds might close, but only on dark nights.

She frowned. It looked as though Talia had re-arranged the furniture too. Oria always kept a little irregularity in a parley chamber, let the chairs rest where they were, but someone had arranged these chairs in a semi-circle as though the parley members were about to watch a performance, not take part in good government. It didn't feel right. But what really upset her was the sight of the parley bed covered in the usurper's colours, an ostentatious bedspread with a working of irises and oak leaves. Talia's father had been an Iris; Talia's mother an Oak.

The anger Oria felt at seeing the girl's bedspread surprised her. It was all she could do not to rush forward and pull the thing off. Her rock skin prickled with discomfort. Doubt cast her a worried look, sensing her emotional signature. Two of the horse wanderers shifted in their chairs, looking at her with quizzical expressions. Rock skin and rock sense were all very well, but the connection they forged could be claustrophobic. She'd have to remember to dampen her emotions if she wanted to maintain any sort of privacy.

She took a deep breath, settled her inner state, smiled at Doubt to reassure him, then allowed herself to be ushered by a houseboy to a footstool at the rear of the room. He seated Doubt and Saury beside her. Clearly the houseboy thought she was young enough to be treated like a child. It was a bizarre position to find herself in: she who was so old, now considered young enough to be seated at the back of the room. But there it was. They would, all of them, have to rely on Fox to protect their interests in this parley. Unfortunately, the girl seemed to have lost confidence since their arrival in the city. She'd done nothing to press her claim and Oria couldn't help worrying about how Fox would behave in this setting.

Fox stood in the doorway. The stupid girl hesitated, dithered. Then a parley monitor spotted her and ushered her to a chair behind Aikin. Behind! The location was at odds with Fox's status as a birth-mother. And there was worse to come. When Talia walked into the room and sat on the foot of the bed, Fox did nothing. Not even a murmur of complaint or a haughty eyebrow or a shake of her head. There were many times Oria had wished Fox was more demure and obedient, but this wasn't one of them.

Oria's pulse raced. She wanted to walk over and speak to Fox before the rest of the room sat down, but that would draw attention, something she couldn't afford. Being unnoticed was important. It might help her find a quiet and unobtrusive way into the propagation room when the house asked Fox to prove her unborn child carried Oak's gravity. *If* Fox was asked... This business about Talia could ruin everything. It was all so worrying. Oria rubbed her arms to ease the unpleasant sensation in her rock skin that the thought of Talia had induced. There was a slight ripple of movement in the parley chamber as she did so. The Beranish guests shifted uneasily in their seats. Some even turned and cast curious glances in her direction. How odd. Rubbing her arms shouldn't influence her emotional signature and yet they'd seemed to notice the action. That hadn't happened when they were back in the province. And Doubt had said nothing about there being a physical connection between Berans: rock skin to rock skin. In fact, she was sure such a thing was impossible. Rock sensing between Berans was all about reading emotions, not bodies. She wondered if she was some sort of rare case and whether the day's tension had somehow triggered a new talent.

She ran a finger down her rock skin. Throughout the room, Berans shifted in their seats. But not Fox, not the one person Oria wanted to communicate with. The girl must be too nervous to notice the signal, that or her rock skin was still too immature. Oria suspected it was nerves. Fox looked preoccupied. Even from the back of the room Oria could see she was fidgeting in her seat like a child.

Aikin was relaxed in his chair. Oria glanced across at Whilomena. The woman looked and felt smug. Even Talia seemed more at ease than Fox. The pretender had a regal air about her, despite her youth. Not good. Not good at all. There had to be some way Oria could prompt Fox, get her to alter the power balance in the room. A thought niggled at the edge of Oria's mind. She wasn't the same as the other Berans. For a start, she was Companionari and an adept at managing her body. And Promise's body wasn't an ordinary Beranish body. It was old. Promise was from a different time. Her body's rock skin was more extensive than a modern Berans. Was there a possibility that she could use Promise's body in a more intentional manner? If rubbing her arms caught Beranish attention, could Oria get inside the rock skin and project a message? Communicate with Fox? It was worth trying. Fox would have no chance of claiming the Oak companionship sitting demurely behind Aikin.

Oria thought back to her exploration of Promise's body when she'd rested in the crater. She'd used her training to dip into the interior world of Promise, but there had seemed nothing special about her new body's rock skin apart from the fact that it had felt like bone and had resisted her mental penetration. Perhaps she'd overlooked something.

She closed her eyes and released the illusion of the external nature of her existence. She dropped her consciousness into her inner world. Immediately she felt the familiar harmony between her psyche and the interior of her body, albeit a still unfamiliar body. She paused and gave thanks to Promise before letting go of the notion of the strangeness of being in a new form. She moved her attention to her rock skin. It appeared as a bony cliff above the thin, sinewy aspect of her flesh.

Yes, it was just as she remembered from the last fleeting visit: her rock skin was an impenetrable wall of bone, resistant to her attention. She called up a more refined energy within her psyche as she examined the space beneath it, searching for the reputed seat of rock sense. And there it was! Well, there was something there: small and subtle, soft and pliant. It felt like a lake anchored to the base of her rock skin.

She moved her attention forward to penetrate the surface, but the lake flexed around her without admitting her. She tried again; again the membranous organ seemed to step around her, evading her attempt at penetration.

It occurred to her that her consciousness might be too large to penetrate the surface of her new organ. So she broke her attention up into smaller parts in a technique that was mastered by few, even among the most dedicated practitioners of body melding. It was hard to concentrate with such a scattering of attention. She resisted the natural urge to gather her thoughts, knowing it would only lead to a reassembly of her mind. Instead, she held onto something more sensual, on the urge to move against the soft membranous body below her rock skin. Blindly, with her broken and clouded mind, she obeyed a lingering urge to press forward. She moved: thinking of nothing; almost drifting. Then, stupidly, she found that her awareness that she was moving forward re-wove her scattered mind! The lake-like organ flexed around her, keeping her at bay.

She sighed and started again.

With an increasing loss of focus, she dissolved her attention into its infinitesimal parts until her consciousness was little more than a thread. She felt a chill slide over her as though she'd dived into a cold pool and then her consciousness snapped back together.

She was inside the organ of her new sixth sense, and there was noise everywhere. The thoughts and chattering feelings of every Beran in the parley room jostled for space, along with the blunt emotional signatures of the Companionaris. Other people's feelings filled her psyche, blustering, knocking against her consciousness. It was painful, intolerable. She fled backwards, trying to escape, but something barred her way. The same membrane that had blocked her psyche's admittance now blocked its retreat.

She panicked and threw herself against it, but it repelled her, landing her back in the emotional wind. The storm increased as she felt a sudden rush of concern from the other Berans in the room. She wondered what they were seeing. Promise unconscious or apparently dead? No, not dead because if they could sense her panic they would know she lived.

She tried to gather her thoughts, tried to gain some control, but her wholeness kept slipping away, blown apart by the emotional gale around her. Then, like a cave in a storm, she found Quartz. The wanderer's emotional signature was steady and familiar and she clung to it. She gripped the wanderer's certainty, and it allowed her to draw herself together again and to remember her skills. She calmed her mind then turned her attention to the surrounding signatures. Oria searched among the amplified emotions, looking for Fox. She found Doubt's worry and love, and Saury's excitement and hunger for Fox... No. She kept searching, ignoring the blunt sensation of the Companionaris in the room. She passed through the longings and fears of the horse wanderers, looking for Fox. And then she caught her! The girl was thin with uncertainty, her confidence in her purpose shattered by the reality of facing Talia and Aikin and Whilomena. Oria looked at the girl's signature. It had physical substance. The Oak Mother moved her psyche forward and took hold of her niece's emotional thread. Gently and carefully she entered it, pressing her thought message forward: *Don't let Talia*, she began.

There was a moment of clarity and relative silence within her rock sensing organ as every Beran in the parley room came to sudden attention. And then, just as suddenly, emotional chaos reigned as each of those listeners reacted to her psychic words. Overwhelmed, Oria lost consciousness.

Don't let Talia!

Fox shot out of her seat and knocked over her chair. Oria's voice shouted inside her head, the old woman's words crashing over Fox like a roaring wave. And then her rock sense felt the swamp and wash of a multitude of emotional signatures as the rest of the Berans in the room reacted. She looked around, half expecting to see Oria standing beside her, but there was no one at her shoulder. Instead, the Berans were rushing to the back of the room. Then she saw Oria lying on the floor with Doubt and Saury crouching over her. Fox rubbed her forehead. She frowned. She could still feel the companion's psychic voice: *Don't let Talia!* Fox put her hands into her pockets and felt for her rock children. As soon as she touched them, she felt calmer, more grounded, and the echo of Oria's voice receded to be replaced by the ordinary tones of surprised conversation in the room.

'What happened?' a Companionari woman asked Fox. 'Can you see something?'

'What's going on?' another echoed the question.

Fox didn't answer, but she glanced around the room. Most of the parley guests were out of their seats. Talia too. Talia had stood up and was craning her neck to see what was happening. Fox caught her eye and Talia spoke, 'I can't see. Can you see? Do you know what happened?'

'My handmaid,' Fox hesitated. 'I have to go.'

A look of worry crossed the pretender's face. 'Your handmaid?'

An Oak householder spoke before Fox could respond, 'It's one of the Berans fallen sick, Companion. A girl. She's fainted.'

Sousette's voice sounded from across the room. 'Has anyone called the nursing sister?' Fox turned and saw the Caballo Companion wave at a houseboy. 'You there... Call the housekeeper. A guest is unwell.'

Fox began moving. She stepped away from her chair, intent on making her way toward the back of the room. Then Aikin put a hand on her arm, halting her progress.

'It's nothing to worry about,' his voice seemed kindly, but she could feel something new in him, or maybe it was always there, but her growing rock skin meant she was seeing more of him. He felt like a hundred bees caught in a glass, like pure anticipation might feel. He felt as though he was hungering for something. She realised he was still speaking, '... after all, your party has walked a long way and no doubt hasn't eaten. Ah,' he nodded toward the door, 'here come the refreshments. This will help.'

Fox glanced across and saw that the food had indeed arrived. A succession of kitchen assistants carried plates piled with fruit and steaming pots of tea, all of which were placed on the long serving tables at the side of the room. She looked back at Oria, who was sitting up now, waving away offers of help. Aikin felt volatile, complex, and she knew he was dangerous, but he was right about the food. And Oria seemed to have recovered. Then the crowd shifted and she lost sight of the Oak Companion.

Fox pulled away from Aikin's hand, careful not to move too abruptly. She mustn't make an outright enemy of him. The negotiations in Komey would be complex enough.

Without intending to, she found she had put her hands into her pockets, was once again touching the warmth and comfort of her rock children. Something stirred within her and she thought about Oria's disembodied voice, *Don't let Talia....* The companion's message had been meant for Fox. Its meaning was plain enough. Don't let Talia take control. The broken instruction seemed to give her back a bit of confidence and strength. She stepped away from her adopted father. 'I'd better see to the food and the guests' needs.' She turned, not giving him a chance to object that the role belonged to Talia. She wouldn't allow him to undermine her new sense of purpose. Out of the corner of her eye, she saw him move to reach for her and then change his mind. She'd been right to keep relations cordial.

Talia had also begun moving and was heading toward the serving tables. Fox hurried, directing her steps so that she and Talia couldn't help halting as their paths intersected. The other woman blushed and then looked down at the carpet. Fox realised that Aikin or Whilomena must have had time to let the girl know of Fox's claim to be the new birthmother. She felt a shiver of betrayal, a reminder if she needed one that Aikin had shown no enthusiasm for her own claim.

'I hardly feel as though I belong in this role.' Talia glanced at Fox. 'Perhaps we both have legitimate claims.'

Fox looked around the room. They were unobserved. Sousette had Aikin and Whilomena locked in a conversation that Fox rock sensed was full of passion and sorrow and demands. The rest of the parley members seemed focused on the drama at the back of the room. And the Berans? They surrounded Oria, huddled in animated conversation. Fox turned to Talia. There was something she liked about the other girl, something honest and unassuming. Fox smiled. 'We haven't spoken about the odd circumstance we find ourselves in.'

Talia blushed again. 'Our circumstance *is* odd, isn't it? I don't quite know anymore what's best, what I should do. It seemed straight forward before... when the crossover failed... I didn't think I had any choice.'

Fox frowned, confused, then remembered that Aikin had said that Talia's companionship powers hadn't appeared immediately.

Talia continued speaking, 'When we thought the crossover had failed, I was worried... for everyone. About famine and displacement. Then I acquired my gravity. Then you arrived,' the words tumbled out, 'and I didn't know what to do. I'm still not sure about what's best.'

'Perhaps it would have been easier if we had met in private before the parley,' Fox said.

'Yes.' Talia nodded, looking relieved at the kindness in Fox's voice. 'Because I do so want to do the right thing. What's best for the province,' she spoke in a rush. 'I don't care about being the new Oak Companion. I never imagined... We should talk in private. But for now...' She glanced around the room, looking worried. 'Perhaps we could serve the guests together.'

Fox had expected hostility. Certainly, she'd expected competitiveness, but Talia's gaze was uncertain; fragile, even. So the girl didn't yet feel the Oak companionship was hers by rights, and she cared about the province. And Fox sensed there was something else disturbing Talia. She wished she knew Talia well enough to ask what was worrying her, aside from the obvious problem of there being two Oak claimants, a new mother and new birthmother. Talia's manner suggested there was room for compromise. Perhaps there was some way of maintaining Oria and Fox in Oak, and Talia in Komey? A dual companionship? Fox found she trusted the girl, wanted to tell her about Oria and the transformation. Perhaps she would. Fox spoke again, 'Do you think we should sit together after they've had their refreshments? Both parley from the bed?'

Talia nodded, looking relieved, her blush fading as her composure returned.

'And then later, perhaps we need to put our hearts together as good mother and good birthmother?' Fox smiled.

Talia nodded again. She took Fox's hand, squeezing it. A group of parley guests walked past, nodded, heading for the table. Talia released Fox's hand and spoke, 'We'd better do our duty then. The guests look hungry.'

They both stepped up to the table and began directing the service. Fox saw the teas went to the elderly first and also sent a bone tea to Oria. It would strengthen her; it would give her back some energy. Talia sent the fruit around the room. The Berans remained in close conversation, bunched together around Oria. None accepted refreshments.

'We should get the parley back on track,' Talia spoke to Fox.

Fox nodded and, side by side, they took their seats at the foot of the bed.

Talia and Fox clapped their hands in unison to signal the parley was open and everyone in the room turned at the unexpected doubling of the familiar sound. Normally, the parley members would have hurried back to their seats, but no one moved. They stood staring at the unprecedented sight of two young women on the parley bed, both assuming the companion's duties. Fox could see Aikin frowning, catching the corner of his lip, but he felt calmer, less volatile.

Talia clapped her hands once more and then nodded to Fox, urging her to speak.

'We...,' Fox hesitated. 'That is... Talia and I... Well, the Oak companionship is still unsettled, but this parley is urgent so we should get back to work. Sousette has a pressing problem and has come to Komey for succour.'

Talia nodded. 'And this parley is the first to talk through her needs. So, let's—'

'Just a minute,' Quartz spoke from the back of the room, cutting across the opening statement. 'I'm sorry to interrupt, but my brothers and sisters and I need to be excused. Something significant happened to Promise and we have urgent Beranish matters to discuss.'

'By the Back,' Sousette frowned, looking at Patience Learnt, the old, bow-legged Caballo keeper, 'what could be more urgent than the matter of our horses?'

Patience held up a warning hand to the Caballo Companion. 'I'm sorry, Mother, but we have to withdraw.'

She glared back. 'I know you hold our mares as dear as I do, but what could be more urgent than Caballo's need? We are paupers now.'

'Enough,' he spoke sternly. 'I can't discuss this with you. This is urgent and private, and another hour or two won't make any differ-ence to Caballo's fate.'

Sousette's dusty plait had come loose and her hair now fell across her horsehair cloak. She looked ready to offer further argu-ment, but Whilomena stepped forward and put her hand on the Horse Companion's arm.

'The parley can wait,' the Wheat Companion said. 'Of course it can. Let our guests retire to sort out their affairs. They can use my little mill house. It will give them some privacy.'

She turned to the Berans still clustered around Oria. 'I was going to host a lunch in your honour so your afternoon meal is already there, awaiting you. Make the place your own. There are plenty of guest rooms for you to sleep in. You can consider the mill a Beranish tent while you're in Komey. Take it with the compliments of Wheat house. I'll show you the way myself. Once you're settled, I'll give you my key and you can be confident that none will disturb you.'

Quartz nodded, but his voice contained no warmth when he spoke his thanks. 'We can return later to parley. And not just on the problems in Caballo. We want a say in the matter of the two new Oak mothers. And it's imperative that we talk about this rumour that some of our people have been enslaved. Your name was mentioned...' He held the Wheat Companion's eye.

Whilomena sighed, shook her head. 'Ah... now *that's* a misunderstanding.'

Patience Learnt turned to face the Wheat Companion. 'I hope so. I've heard nothing of this.'

'Because there is nothing to hear,' Whilomena spread her hands, palm up. Then she turned toward the door and swept an arm out, inviting the Berans to leave. 'Let's just get you down to the mill.' She gave a soft snort of laughter and shook her head in apparent disbelief at Komey's capacity to gossip. 'Enslavement...? Honestly, Komey is full of the most extraordinary rumours.' She shook her head once more and walked out of the room.

Fox wondered whether she should speak up, warn the Berans about the risks of following the Wheat Companion, but Quartz already knew them. He'd spoken the accusation in this very room and now he and the others were following Whilomena out of the parley. Well, there was strength in the Berans' numbers. She had to think they would be all right, that Quartz knew what he was doing, but she didn't like being separated from them.

'Perhaps I should go too.' Fox said to Talia.

'Must you?' Talia looked disappointed. 'I thought we might use this moment to speak in private. The parley seems to be over and we need to talk.'

Fox glanced around. Talia was right. The parley guests weren't lingering. With the loss of the exotic Berans and the Wheat Companion, and with the deferral of any decision on the Oak companionship, they had lost interest in the parley. Soon, Fox was sitting beside Talia in an empty room. 'Perhaps you're right. Let's find somewhere more comfortable to talk.'

Talia stood. 'There's that lovely sewing room under the attic roof, beyond the dress room. Always empty because no one wants to climb the stairs. Perhaps we could use that. It's private enough.'

Fox stood up too. 'Good idea. But... I... Well, I think I should warn you that some unusual things have been going on in the province. Not just the rebellion, but some stuff that doesn't make sense. Strange things.'

Talia had already begun moving, but she turned and looked at Fox, her emotional signature sharp and startled.

'Difficult to explain,' Fox said.

Talia was silent for a moment and Fox wondered whether she was right to feel she could trust the girl with the full story. Fox doubted Oria would approve and wondered whether it would even be possible to explain the new treaty to Talia in a way that made sense, let alone explain the reality of Oria's re-birth. Explain to a girl who had never left Komey, who knew nothing of Beranish culture and the world outside. She hoped she could because, despite what Oria might think, they had no choice but to include this second Oak Companion in their plans.

Talia looked nervous, as though she was worried about being overheard. 'There have been some strange things going on here, too. But I can't talk about it in the open like this. Let's save this for the sewing room. Let's leave while we can. We may not get another chance.'

Fox found that she, too, was eager to be gone. 'Yes, let's go.' Her hands felt for the stones in her pockets and she ran her fingers across their surface as they headed for the door. There was still some comfort in the sensation, but her unease continued as though she was missing something or someone, as though there was something more urgent that she should be doing. Instead, she turned and followed Talia into the hallway and together they headed for the stairs.

28

For the second time that day, Aikin walked toward Whilomena's little mill house. He brought up the rear of the party, as was fitting. Whilomena led, her chatter with the Berans drifting back to him in snatches.

Aikin examined his emotions and found them tolerable. Some unease about what was about to happen but no second thoughts. If he needed a sign about the rightness of his actions, he only had to look at what had already happened. Fate had conspired to ease the path: the parley breaking up; the Berans demanding time alone. It almost worried him, that confluence.

He looked to Whilomena. She was at ease with the Berans, her demeanour relaxed and innocent of any violent intent. A frightening woman if you didn't know her intelligence and didn't understand her patriotism. Irresistible when you did.

She reached the red front door, her beautiful face animated as she turned to check on his progress. She smiled at him but didn't halt the account she was giving of the landscaping principles that underlay Komey's central gardens. Patience, the dirty-looking Caballo keeper, seemed entranced.

Aikin found he was smiling back at her, the exchange helping to still his racing thoughts. He knew their guests couldn't rock sense his intent, but emotions were leaky things. He focused on Whilomena's smile, on the warmth in the air, on the sound of the Fraise River turning the mill wheel. Aikin recalled the joy of his successes with Talia and Glory. It helped. It was something he deserved to be proud of. Let kinetic energy do the work of reforming the world, let it rush the future into the present.

Whilomena had turned to face the door and was slipping the key into the lock as she continued her patter, 'There's so much of interest in Komey,' she said to their Beranish guests. 'When you've finished here, you must look around for yourselves.' She opened the door and then worked the key off the ring, holding it out to Patience. 'I want you to have this. Master Oak and I will just see you settled and then leave. The place is yours while you're in Komey. Take all the time you need. No one will bother you here. Komey respects Beranish concerns. We always have.'

The Caballo keeper took the key and smiled. Aikin glanced at the rest of the group. Quartz and his party hadn't warmed to Whilomena's charms in the way the horse wanderers had, but they followed Patience and the two other Caballo wanderers through the doorway. Aikin came after, pulling the door closed .

Inside, Whilomena continued to move with confidence and grace. She showed her guests around the facilities and then brought them back into the living room, where someone had already set out their lunch. The food was simple by Komey's standards, but Aikin appreciated the care that had gone into its preparation. There were several vegetarian tarts and some light salads. There was also bread and a glass pitcher on the table that was filled with poisoned kumis.

Whilomena poured the kumis into glasses. 'We won't stay,' she spoke lightly. 'Not longer than to drink to your health.'

Aikin picked up the tray and served the drinks. He thought that Quartz and his people still looked sour, as though they already suspected Whilomena was an enemy, but he smiled as he moved from guest to guest. There was no way they could know about the poison. He made himself meet each person's eye. By the time he reached the youngest in the group, the tray was empty.

The Wheat Companion held up the empty jug. 'None left for us. Should I send for more kumis? We're a little short.' Then she scanned the table and, for all the world, Aikin believed her, believed that she didn't know whether there was more fermented milk. 'Ah-ha!' She walked across the room and lifted a second jug from where it sat behind a vase on a side table. 'Plenty more.' She poured two more drinks, filled her and Aikin's glasses with the unadulterated mix. Aikin came forward, took his glass from her hand.

'To the treaty.' She held up her glass.

'To the treaty!' the Berans responded, lifting theirs.

'To the treaty,' Aikin echoed the toast.

Out of the corner of his eye, Aikin watched Quartz. The old man didn't seem very enthusiastic, but he held his glass up and then drank his kumis. Aikin finished his own drink, set it down on the table beside him.

Whilomena was already moving, preparing to go. 'Now we'll leave you in peace. Just open the door when you're ready to re-join us. I believe they're expecting all of you in Oak House for dinner tonight. In Komey, in summer, we eat late, so that's about ten o'clock. And do take a wander around Komey's gardens. They're worth the effort. There'll be someone from Beranish Affairs stationed right outside if you need anything.'

In a matter of moments, Aikin and Whilomena were outside the mill and Whilomena was closing the door. She pulled a different key from her pocket and locked it, using a second concealed keyhole.

Aikin's chest felt tight. He realised he was sweating. 'How long?' he asked.

'It's fast acting.' Whilomena caught up his hand, gave it a squeeze. 'Not more than a minute or two to knock them out cold. But we'll wait ten minutes before we try to collect the rocks. They all drank, didn't they? I didn't like to watch them too carefully in case I raised their suspicions.'

He nodded. 'Don't worry. No one opted out of the treaty toast. How could they? Not in mixed Companionari and Beranish company. That would have caused offence, and Berans are polite.'

'But you saw them do it?' she sounded anxious. 'They weren't just lifting their glasses?'

He nodded and then they fell silent as they waited. Aikin even opened his unfashionable, Galean-made, pocket timepiece and watched the second hand sweep around its face. After three turns he heard sounds from inside: muffled cries. Then there was a sudden thump against the door and he stepped back, as though it might spring open. Whilomena held her ground. The next six minutes passed slowly. Soon the silence was so strong it was hard to remember there ever had been any noises of struggle.

'I can't hear anything.' Even to his own ears, Aikin's voice sounded plaintive.

Whilomena reached up and stroked his hair. Her warm hand sent shivers down his body. He looked at his timepiece again and couldn't help noticing that his fingernails were immaculate today. He was glad he'd had the boy do them after he and Whilomena had arrived back from New Lytalia. Twelve minutes had passed.

'We should go in,' he said. 'More than enough time.'

She didn't take her hand from his head. Instead, she moved closer and pressed her lips against his. She pulled back and whispered, 'It's difficult. I know it's difficult for you, my brave darling. Don't think it's easy for me, either. But I know we're right. There's more at stake here than these few individual lives and our poor consciences.'

'Hard courage,' he said. 'That's what Dewy Powers called it. That's written on his tombstone. He lived in times like these, difficult times. I find the idea that we're part of a lineage comforting.'

She moved back a pace and looked at him. 'Yes. Hard courage. That describes it nicely. Our hard courage will save and improve thousands of lives.' She took a deep breath, asked him if he was ready. When he said he was, she waved a hand toward the river. 'I'll go around to the balcony. I can look through the window and check. Then I'll come back and we'll open the door. I just want to be sure that they're... down.'

'Dead.' He corrected her.

'Not yet. They won't be dead, not for a while yet. But down, yes. And beyond recovery, certainly.'

She turned away and started down the path, disappeared around the edge of the building. The light tap of her footsteps sounded on the wooden steps and across the balcony.

Aikin put his ear to the door. Still quiet. He ran through the details of their plan. Tonight, Birch and another guardswoman would bring up one of Whilomena's barges. They would take the bodies down the river and drop them into the Komic Sea. It was Whilomena's idea. No point in alarming Komey before the rock child harvest, but it meant that Birch hadn't been able to ride out with the other guardswomen. In the meantime, he and Whilomena would explain that the Berans had left Komey on some errand and who could argue with that, given their odd behaviour in the parley room earlier that day? No one. Everyone would believe that they'd taken off of their own accord. And that left Fox, but she wouldn't ask too many questions now that she had her claim as birthmother to protect.

Whilomena's voice startled him. 'They're all down. Move back and I'll unlock.'

He blushed, realising he hadn't moved, still had his ear pressed against the red door. He stepped away, watched as she turned the keys and tried the door. It didn't move. She put her shoulder to the wood and pushed. It opened fractionally.

'One of them must be blocking the way,' she said, and she grunted, pushing harder.

He reached over and lent a hand. This time, the door opened wide enough to let her squeeze through. He followed, stepping over a man on the floor. The air was foul with the smell of vomit. He hadn't quite expected that.

'Let's hurry,' Whilomena sounded nervous now. 'Go through this one's pouch and get him out of the doorway while you're at it.' She moved away, walked into the reception room, leaving Aikin on his own with the dying man.

Aikin shut the door behind him and then bent down, taking hold of the man's robes, suppressing his own urge to flee. He wondered if the poison could pass through his skin. Because his fingers felt numb. The thought made him want to drop the body, but he began pulling it away from the door. The man groaned beneath him and took a ragged breath.

'This one's still alive,' Aikin called out.

'I told you they'd still be alive,' Whilomena's voice carried through from the other room. 'Just hurry and check him for stones. It's awful in here and I need your help.'

'It stinks,' he agreed, glad he wasn't alone in this horrible place with the dying. Life to death, emptiness to life. It was all equal, he reminded himself. None of it mattered because energy could not be destroyed, only transformed. The beauty of that truth calmed him. He opened the man's cloak and pulled up his shirt to reveal a wanderer's pouch. Aikin fumbled with the knot and then remembered his knife. He opened it and cut the pouch from the man's body. There were five stones within. His heart soared.

'Have you got a sack or something?' he called out to her. 'To put the rock children in.'

'There are pillowcases in the bedrooms.'

Aikin hurried to the nearest room and fetched two strong linen cases embroidered with haystacks.

It took longer than he'd expected, but soon enough, they'd finished. Whilomena stood in the middle of the room and wiped her forehead with the back of her hand as she spoke, 'Should we drag the bodies to the balcony door?'

Aikin hefted a pillowslip over his shoulder. 'Leave the heavy work for Birch and her soldiers. Here,' he held out the second pillow-case, 'this one's light enough for you to carry.'

Whilomena shook her head, laughed. 'Best not. The Wheat Companion can't lug things around the place like a houseboy. It wouldn't look right.'

Aikin nodded and hefted the second sack.

Fox looked across at Talia. The other woman sat opposite her in the small sewing room under the attic roof of Oak house. It was hard to know whether she'd convinced Talia of the truth about Oria. Fox rock sensed some sort of response in the woman. Relief, but she also felt something akin to horror, which was confusing. But then again, she wasn't sure. Her own rock skin was so new. Maybe it was fear, not horror.

'You're sure?' Talia shifted in her seat, blinked. 'Promise is the Oak Companion reborn?'

Fox nodded.

Talia took a deep breath and looked away, then busied herself with the sewing basket beside her. 'And... and you?' She pulled out a lacemaking card and peered at it without seeming to see it. 'You've also got a companionship?'

'No. Just letting my rock skin grow.' Fox pulled back her sleeve and held out her arm. It took Talia a moment or two to look up, to look at Fox's arm. The younger woman leant forward and reached out a hand. She touched Fox's rock skin and then pulled her hand back. 'It's warm. I thought it would be cold, dead like stone.' She wiped a strand of hair that had fallen across her face, tucked it behind her ear. 'I don't know why I thought that.'

Fox pulled her sleeve down again, stopped trying to work out what was wrong with the other woman. There was no time, and she had so much to explain. 'So it's complex, this situation that you... that we're facing,' she corrected herself. 'The Oak Companion isn't dead. She's tied us, the Oak family, to a new treaty with our camp. Obviously, it's a sensitive situation and Oria wants some control over who is told and when. Now that you know, I hope you'll agree that we are both bound to her as daughters in the Oak family: for she's the true companion despite what's happened to you. I hope you'll agree that you mustn't—' She broke off, frowning as her rock skin prickled.

The sensation sharpened, urgent and painful. It almost felt as though someone had reached out two hands and had grabbed her. A desperate rock call. Then, abruptly, multiple calls hit her arms as though a crowd of stones was shouting at her. She found she was standing.

'What is it?' Talia asked.

'I felt something. I can feel something's wrong.'

Talia stared at her, mouth open, breathing hard.

The call pulled again, and Fox gasped. It felt indiscriminate, anonymous, as though any Beran would do. But surely Quartz would respond. The call couldn't be for Fox. It made no sense. Then another wave hit her, and she staggered forward, felt herself pulled toward the window. She hugged herself, shuddered, uncertain what to do.

'What's wrong?' Talia asked.

'I don't know.'

Fox looked out the dormer window. All was still. There was nothing to show any sort of desperate drama. Below, two garden girls picked roses and laid them in open baskets. Everything seemed slow. But not in her arms. They rippled with pain that seemed to emanate from somewhere east of Wheat house.

Talia joined Fox at the window and Fox tried to explain, 'I can feel something, but I can't see what's wrong. It's like someone walking over my grave, but worse. Like someone crying out for help... I...' she stopped, realising something. What if Quartz couldn't respond? What if he and the others were in trouble?

Talia began speaking as though she hadn't heard a word Fox had said, 'Are you sure Oria has kept her gravity in this... in this new body of hers?'

'Promise's body.' Fox nodded, still staring out the window.

'How do you know?' Talia asked.

'The trees responded to her. She's still the Oak Companion.' Fox turned to look at Talia, forcing herself to ignore the calls. This was important, too. They needed Talia's cooperation. But Fox was finding the younger woman's singular focus, somewhat bizarre.

'So, there's no need for me, then?' Talia sounded desolate.

Fox felt exasperated, couldn't help the impatient sigh that escaped her lips. No doubt Talia felt disappointed, but this was ridiculous.

Then Talia covered her face with her hands. 'What a waste,' she mumbled. 'What a terrible cost. What a crime. And I thought there was a point to all of this. I thought we had to...'

Fox frowned, rock sensing the girl's shame. She touched Talia's shoulder. 'I don't know what you're talking about, but if you're worried about there being two Oak companions... Well, the world is desperate for companions. Provinces are failing and people are hungry. Perhaps you could start growing oaks in one of the abandoned provinces, help some refugees start a new life on the Stone Body. Your gravity is a gift. Look at it like that.'

Talia lifted her face. She looked devastated. When she spoke, her voice was so halting that Fox had to strain to hear her, 'I only did it to save the province. I thought I was saving lives.'

'Did what?' Fox asked, struggling to stay with the conversation as the pain in her arms grew.

'I can't tell you.' Talia shook her head. 'I gave my word.'

Another call hit Fox, and she gasped at the weight of it. The urgency of it was beyond anything she'd felt already. It didn't matter that there were older and wiser wanderers in Komey. She had to respond.

She opened the casement window, leant out, looked east. A warm breeze blew in, but it brought a chill to the hot surface of Fox's rock skin. Talia stepped close, craned her neck to see what Fox was seeing. Trouble was, Fox couldn't see anything.

Talia looked down and then tugged at Fox's sleeve, pointed at the lawns below them. 'Look! Someone's running.'

Fox followed Talia's gaze. Beneath the window, a man was running away from Oak house. It was Mica! She'd know him anywhere. He was alive, as though the body they'd found in the trench had been nothing but a dream. Then he hesitated for a moment, scanning the horizon, as though listening. And before she could even make sense of what she was seeing, another man ran to his side. Another Mica. Two men. Two Micas.

'Brothers,' Fox whispered. 'Mica has brothers?' The realisation that there was a logical answer was almost more unbearable than the pain of the rock call. The rebellion in Oak, her disapproval of Mica's tactics. None of that mattered. How she longed for him; how she wished he were alive.

'Twins,' Talia said.

'No. Triplets.' Fox felt tears rolling down her cheeks. She'd not known. He'd not mentioned siblings. She'd been sure he'd said that he was an only child. Below her, Mica's brothers seemed to lock onto the call and suddenly they were running.

'Wait!' Fox called out.

One man hesitated. He looked up and saw her. She saw a flicker of what looked like recognition, but at that very moment she felt the rock calling rise again and this time it was so insistent that Fox had to grip the windowsill to keep from falling out. The man below spun like a top as he turned around and began running again.

Fox stepped away from the window. 'Rock children are calling,' she said to Talia. 'Something's wrong. And those men... I thought they were Mica's brothers, but the one who looked up... I think it was Mica, but Mica's supposed to be dead. I have to go.'

It wasn't until she was halfway through the dress room that she rock sensed Talia following her, the other woman's emotional signature full of dread and grief and need. 'Look, we'll talk later,' Fox spoke over her shoulder, maintaining her pace. 'None of this has anything to do with you, but I think the stones who are calling are in mortal danger.'

'Shamans' stones?' Talia said.

'Yes.'

Fox ran through the doorway to the landing and heard Talia behind her, whispering a line from the Turning:

The intimacy of childhood has passed. Now Man is alone, now Woman is alone: alone like God. Man must decide; Woman must decide: what is right and what is wrong; what is just and what is unjust; when to bend and when to stand.

'I'll help you.' Talia spoke as though it required some sort of decision. 'And then... and then... We'll have to warn all the wanderers...'

'What are you talking about?' Fox paused at the top of the stairs.

'Aikin found a secret in a book,' the other woman said. 'He made powder from a stone, rubbed it into cuts in my skin to turn me into a companion.' Talia pulled down her collar.

Fox looked at the patch of skin with its bluish coloured scars. The cry of the stones thumped in her chest, and there was some sort of banging noise coming from somewhere downstairs. She turned away from Talia, hurried down the steps, spoke over her shoulder, 'The stone must have been dead already. Aikin wouldn't kill a rock child.'

'I don't know if the stone he used on me was alive or dead,' Talia said. 'It was powder by the time I saw it. But they're going to get more stones to create more companions. Living stones. That's what they're doing right now.'

They reached the first floor. The pounding and banging was coming from Wren's room. Fox hesitated and then raced back down the corridor and opened Wren's door. Wren shot past her, startling two houseboys who were carrying a load of sheets. Fox followed, and Talia trailed Fox.

Fox spoke again, 'Who are *they*, these killers? Who else apart from my father?'

'The Wheat Mother,' Talia answered.

When they reached the ground floor, Talia spoke again, 'Your father and Whilomena said we had to take all the stones by force if we wanted the world to survive. They said it was a matter of *everyone's* life, of *everyone's* death, and we had to do it. Aikin said it would buy us another thousand years for Berans and for us. I'm sorry.'

Fox ran on, following Wren across the foyer. An elderly doorman rose to his feet, but Wren reached the front door before he could do his duty. Then they were running along the same path that Mica and his brother had used, if it was Mica. Talia kept pace, but she'd fallen silent now. New oaks and corks were sprouting around them, forming a wave of trees that threatened to overtake them. Fox didn't want to think about any of it. Couldn't afford to.

The rock calls, had moved, were moving. It meant the stones were travelling across the landscape. Alive but carried by whom? Not by the wanderers, because the stones' cry for help hadn't diminished. Whilomena and Aikin must be carrying them. Fox dreaded the implication. Her friends were likely dead.

She ran on. The three of them ran on. Gravel flying under their feet. Faster, she urged herself. Run.

29

Mica's lungs hurt with the effort of running. He hadn't stopped since he'd spotted Fox at the window, high in Oak House.

He turned his head. The rock man was at his shoulder, keeping pace. Obsidian seemed unaffected by the continuous clamour of the stone calls and the effort of running. Mica felt as though he couldn't take much more, that his chest would burst, and he was becoming increasingly worried about the fact that the calls were moving. Soon, Mica and Obsidian would need to leave the path to keep following them.

They should never have waited in the kitchen. He clung to the hope that Whilomena and her accomplices would feel safe enough to act slowly.

Ahead of him, the path swung left, but the stones were no longer calling from the east. The rock children were moving west and there was a high retaining wall barring the way. Mica rock sensed it: the grab points; the footholds, the weaknesses in the mortar; and above it all, a wheat field. He covered the distance in seconds and began ascending. It took him a moment to realise that Obsidian was no longer at his side. He looked back. His twin was standing on the bend in the path, clicking his tongue and shaking his head like a dog trying to lose a burr.

'This way,' Mica urged.

Obsidian didn't budge. His clicks became louder and more disapproving.

Fatigue had replaced Mica's adrenaline. He clung to the wall, feeling heavy, tired and old.

Obsidian turned his back on Mica. He walked off, slow insistent steps accompanied by a grown rock man's version of a stone call. Feelings, not words, but clear enough.

Mica resisted even though he felt his body thrum with the strength of Obsidian's will. His twin stopped, waited.

'This way,' Mica whispered.

The rock man sighed and turned back. But it wasn't a concession. When he reached Mica, he grabbed the wanderer's hand and pulled him off the wall. Mica scrambled to keep his feet. Obsidian drew Mica's hand to his chest.

For a moment, Mica imagined the rock man was apologising. Then he felt the beat of his twin's heart: slow with pauses that seemed to stretch beyond what was normal, what was healthy.

The rock thought in Mica's head pulsed in time with Obsidian's fragile and uncertain heartbeat. The combination was awful. Mica shuddered. Obsidian tightened his grip and began dragging Mica down the path.

Then the feeling of people and the sound of running feet intruded, halting their struggle. Not just people, there was also a familiar feeling of oaks, flourishing, of new forests emerging in the Komey landscape. Mica's heart lifted as he rock sensed the trees, but there was something else. And then he caught it, the beloved emotional signature that was Fox. She felt frantic, and she was with two other women, one brimming with shame, another so tangled Mica couldn't make sense of her.

The three of them rounded the bend, making a strange vision as trees sprouted in their wake.

Fox looked up, saw Mica and Obsidian, and her pace increased. Before he knew it, before there was time to speak, she was throwing her arms around him. Obsidian hooted and danced, his insistence that Mica follow him momentarily forgotten.

Fox spoke into his shoulder, 'We found your body. You were dead.' She pulled away from him and stared into his face. 'It is you, Mica, isn't it?'

He nodded, and the movement seemed to dislodge something, readmitting the distress calls and Obsidian's need and the strange presence of the trees. He needed to hurry. 'This is Obsidian, my obsidian, grown into a man. Everything grows for him. He is gravity itself. I have to go.' He pulled away. 'The stones are calling for help.'

'I can hear them,' Fox said. 'And Talia... This is Talia.' She waved at the younger of the two women accompanying her.

He looked at the woman and couldn't reconcile what he knew with what he saw and rock sensed. What he'd overhead in the kitchen meant this was the woman who had killed a rock child to satisfy her greed, but she felt young, confused, sorrowful. She was bent over catching her breath, looked dishevelled, felt ashamed. Then she stood up and Mica saw the intense concentration on her face, felt her struggling to manage the trees. It was something he'd felt Oria do, but Talia was out of her depth. Then, somehow, she managed it because the trees settled, stopped growing.

Fox continued speaking, 'And this is Wren.'

He looked at Fox's other companion. 'Wren? Your Wren?'

'Yes. Talia says that Whilomena and Aikin are about to kill the children and all the wanderers. Or have already killed them...'

Obsidian reached for Mica once more, snatched up his hand, tried to draw him down the path, away from the call.

Mica looked at Fox. 'It makes no sense. Obsidian wants me to go this way.'

Fox nodded. 'I suspect they've separated the wanderers from their stones. Go with Obsidian. Save them. We'll go after the stones.'

It was then Mica realised he hadn't felt the emotional signatures of his friends. He remembered the feel of Obsidian's strange heart-beat and understanding dawned on him. His twin was communicating the wanderers' fate, using the only means he had.

Obsidian pulled Mica's hand, and Mica spoke a last word to Fox as allowed himself to be led away, 'I'll come as soon as I can.'

Fox called out from behind him, 'I think we'll be in Wheat House. I think that's where they'll take them.'

Mica didn't bother answering, just waved as he ran.

Then the Companionari woman called out after him, 'They're in the mill. Don't bother with the door. It's locked. Break the windows overlooking the river.'

Mica rounded a corner and saw it, the pretty-looking mill and now he could feel them, the other Berans. Their emotional signatures were so dull that he couldn't discern one person from another. He ran faster. Soon, he could sense individuals ahead of him, but fading fast. He remembered the Companionari woman's advice and didn't pause at the door.

Mica took the steps to the balcony overhanging the river. He went straight to the picture window and rammed his rock skin against it, shattering it. He stepped into the room with Obsidian at his heels. There were bodies everywhere and the air stank of vomit. Oria was the closest. He felt for her pulse. It was horribly slow. He looked to see what they had done to her, looked for injuries, for bleeding that he might stop, for something: but there was nothing. He moved to a stranger, one of the horse wanderers, presumably. Mica bent down to examine him, but the man was dead. Mica looked around him, looked for life. There were bodies everywhere. He realised with an awful dread that it had to be poison, that he didn't know how to save them.

He let out a cry of fury and sorrow and immediately Obsidian was at his side, patting him on the arm. Mica tried to shake him off but Obsidian ignored him, stroked his hair, made kissing and crooning noises. Mica took a jagged breath and then thought of something. He looked at his twin, remembering the way the rock man had called Louis' compost to life.

'Can you help them?' He gestured at the bodies of the dying. The rock man stared at Oria and then tilted his head as though listening. Then he began making the same clicks and kissing noises he'd used to germinate the seeds in the compost. He bent and stroked Oria's face, and she stirred. He hummed a long, sweet note. She opened her eyes and coughed, sitting up.

'What happened?' she asked, then caught sight of Mica. 'You? But you're dead.'

Mica didn't answer. He was already moving past the horse wanderer, who was beyond help, to the next body. He recognised the Caballo keeper, Patience Learnt. The man was unmoving and Mica couldn't see any rise and fall in his chest, but there was a small thread in the wanderer's emotional signature. It was weaker than Oria's had been. 'Can you help him too?' He turned to his twin. For a moment, Obsidian looked a little unsteady on his feet, but he recovered himself and moved closer, crouched beside Patience. He tilted his head to listen to something only he could hear, then began calling. In moments, Patience roused.

Mica looked up and found Oria staring at him. 'See who else is alive,' he instructed. 'We can't waste a moment.'

Then Mica left the Caballo keeper to recover and followed Obsidian further into the room. They found a man on the floor behind the couch, but he was dead. Then the wanderer spotted Quartz and hurried over. He thought the old wanderer might be dead too because he felt nothing from him: no signature at all. But just as he was about to give up, Quartz's heart gave a beat and his signature fluttered. 'Try,' he urged his twin.

Obsidian's noises held a new intensity, as though he was calling to Quartz over a terrible distance. Mica held his breath and kept his fingers on the old wanderer's wrist.

'There's a dead man by the front door,' Oria's voice was full of panic. 'But I can't see the children. Where are the children?'

Mica looked around and saw that Patience had recovered sufficiently to be standing, if somewhat unsteadily. 'Help her look for them.'

And then he turned his attention back to Quartz as the senior wanderer's pulse throbbed under his fingers and his emotional signature surged and then fell again. Obsidian shifted slightly. Mica stole a quick glance at his twin. The rock man looked pale and almost dusty, his face lined with fatigue. Obsidian sang a few more notes. Quartz shifted but didn't open his eyes. Obsidian seemed to shudder, but he continued, calling to the old wanderer with melodic whistles and clicks. Finally, Quartz roused. He looked tired. He looked in need of a good meal and a long rest but strangely he appeared younger. It was as though Obsidian had restored him to a healthier version of himself. Quartz grasped Mica's shoulder. 'You're alive?'

'Later,' Mica said. 'I'll explain later.'

Quartz's hand dropped from Mica's shoulder, and he blanched. 'The stones,' his voice was harsh. 'They need us!'

Beside Mica, Obsidian slumped to the floor. Mica grabbed the rock man's hand. It was hot. He felt for his pulse. It felt weak and the rock man's eyes were closed.

And then Oria wailed.

Mica and Quartz stood up, moving toward the sound, but Obsidian didn't rouse. Mica hoped his twin wasn't dead, but there was no time to look.

They found Oria and Patience in the kitchen, bending over Saury and Doubt. The children were dead. Crumpled on the floor, their lips blue, their faces empty.

The shock of it felt like someone had taken a hammer to Mica's chest, and his hands shook. Doubt, his dear, sweet nephew; Saury, his earnest, passionate apprentice. He wanted to throw himself down beside them and never rise again, but the stones were still calling.

'They're dead,' he said, his voice sounded brittle, sharp. 'We have to leave. Save the rock children.'

'No.' Oria reached for Doubt, gathered him up, held him close. 'They can't be dead. They're young; they're strong.'

Quartz shook his head. 'No signature. No pulse. I'm sorry.'

Oria looked up at Mica. 'You have to do something! Get the other you to fix them like he fixed me.'

'I don't think even Obsidian can help the dead,' Mica said, his words full of regret.

Oria was crying now. Her voice shook when she spoke, 'You don't know that. They're not cold. See.' She held out Doubt's limp hand. 'They've only just left. Only just. Try. Get your twin to try.'

'What about the stones?' Quartz said. 'They are calling, and they are still alive. They need us.'

Oria caught hold of the elderly wanderer, pulled him down until his face was close. 'Are you forgetting that Promise was dead?' She let Quartz go, but she hadn't finished. She turned to Mica, shouting now, 'I was dead. You were dead. But you're trying to tell me you're not even going to try? Not even going to ask your twin to help.'

Mica looked into the parley room. Obsidian lay unmoving on the floor. 'Reviving Quartz took everything,' Mica said. 'He's unconscious, maybe in a coma. He can't save anyone.'

Quartz put a hand on Mica's shoulder. 'But you can try to wake him.'

Mica shook his head, but he was already moving, already conceding. 'If he wakes, you need to know he can't talk. Obsidian's different, not an ordinary man. He won't be able to tell us if it's possible.'

Mica knelt at Obsidian's side. He shook the rock man's shoulder and his twin opened his eyes, a soft smile breaking across his face. Mica felt relief sweep over him and he helped the rock man sit up. The effort of moving drained the colour from Obsidian's face. Mica could see his twin wouldn't be able to walk to the kitchen. He called for the others to carry Saury and Doubt into the parley room. They moved quickly, setting one child down on either side of the rock man.

'Can you bring them back?' Oria crouched down and looked into Obsidian's eyes.

Obsidian shook his head. He stroked one of Doubt's fingers and made a soft and sorrowful sound. He ruffled Saury's curly hair.

'Please!' Oria put her hand on Obsidian's arm.

Quartz reached for Oria's hand. 'We have other duties now. You asked Mica to try, and he tried. We need to focus on helping the rock children.'

'No!' Oria pulled her hand from his, turned to Obsidian, her face fierce. 'Please. I know you can do something. Please try.'

Obsidian looked up at Mica as though asking for his permission.

It was an impossible choice. Balancing his love for the children against Obsidian and all that his talents promised: the end of a famine. 'It's going to kill him, kill the first rock child who grew into a man, the only creature that can save us from hunger. He's the real companion to the land. Everything grows in his presence; everything flourishes when he calls.'

Oria turned to the rock man, took his chin in her hand, looked into his eyes. When she spoke, her voice was gentle, 'It's your choice, Obsidian.'

Obsidian smiled at her, and he reached up, pinching her cheek. Then he turned his attention to Doubt and Saury. This time there was no tilting of the head, no kissing noises. Instead, the rock man sang. The song was wordless and low, strong enough to rattle the ground under the mill house. Obsidian put one hand over Doubt's heart and the other over Saury's. He continued singing, and the notes dipped and wove until it made a complex, rumbling melody.

Mica saw Saury's eyelids flicker. Doubt's chest moved.

Out of the corner of his eye, Mica saw another movement, something odd. He turned to look at Obsidian. His twin's fingers seemed to fray. As Mica watched, the fraying grew, and Obsidian's fingers disintegrated. Tiny grains of sand fell onto the children's bodies and the surrounding floor.

'Stop!' Mica reached for Obsidian's arm. It disintegrated into a shower of rocks and stones. Then the rock man's body collapsed and all that remained was a pile of gritty sand and three small rocks.

Mica fell back. 'What have we done?' he groaned. 'Look what we've done. We've killed him. The first rock man we've ever known and we've killed him.'

Patience stared at the stones. The two children coughed.

The Horse keeper turned to Quartz. 'Can you feel that?'

Quartz shook his head.

'Can you?' Patience asked Mica.

Mica felt nothing. He stared at the pile without answering.

'They're calling,' Patience spoke again. 'Those stones are calling to me!'

'New rock children,' Mica spoke softly. 'Obsidian's children.'

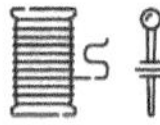

Fox ran into the wheat field on the northern edge of Whilomena's expansive grounds. The golden façade of the companion's house was visible in the distance and the calls were no longer moving. A horrible, obvious destination.

The wheat stems slapped Fox's thighs as she, Talia, and Wren raced over the ground. She glanced back. Oaks and corks continued to sprout in their wake, but the wheat seemed to resist them.

Fox had no plan. That worried her almost as much as the cry of the stones. Would she burst into Wheat House and demand the rock children? Hope that the house militia were elsewhere? Hope by some miracle that the household would support the three of them, not their own companion? Or would the three of them resort to creeping in? Fox couldn't imagine attacking Whilomena and Aikin, but they were unlikely to give up the stones without a fight. So she would do it; she would fight. But wasn't that the sort of decision she'd judged so harshly in Mica? And Wren and Talia were not the allies Fox would have chosen if there was to be a skirmish.

She stopped. They needed a moment to think. Talia pulled up short beside Fox, but Wren flew past, so that Fox had to take off again, grab hold of her, bring her back.

'Why are we stopping?' Talia asked. 'They're not dead, are they? Are we too late?'

'No,' Fox said, keeping hold of Wren. 'But we need a strategy, a way into the house.'

'I know a few ways in,' Talia said. 'I can help.'

Wren pulled at Fox's grip, yanked. 'Acerila, achroite, acmite,' she spoke under her breath. She waved a finger in the air, counting off the stones that only her mind could see. 'Actinolite, adamine, adularia, aegy... aegyrine.' She tried to pry Fox's hand from her forearm.

Talia spoke, 'I can lead us in and then you... then you grab the rock children while Wren and I distract Aikin and Whilomena.'

Wren was shaking Fox's arm now, trying to dislodge her. The list of stones growing louder, 'Agalmatolite, agate, alabaster....'

'Shush,' Fox said, but Wren continued speaking, 'Alacranite, alamandine, albite, alexandrite.'

'It's a good list,' Fox said. 'When we save them, you can make a new one.'

'Save them,' Wren whispered, relaxing. 'Then I'll make a new list.'

Fox's heart lifted at the ordinariness of the other woman's tone. 'Yes. Stay beside me. Talia and I will take care of everything.'

Fox checked the horizon for soldiersisters, but the grounds were empty. To one side, in the distance, she could see the rooftops of the Mint Gazette. The sight triggered something: a sense the place could help, but she couldn't catch hold of a solid idea. Wren stirred, shifted from foot to foot, then resumed speaking the names of stones. Was that it? A place to leave Wren? Fox felt a breeze pick up, heard the wheat rustle. The call of the stones was hurting her arms. She shut the feeling down, tucked it away.

Talia followed Fox's gaze, looked at the Mint Gazette's rooftops. 'You think they might help us?'

'With Wren? Yes. That's what I was thinking.'

'No. I meant with saving the rock children.'

Fox frowned.

'All those retired bureaucrats from the Department of Beranish Affairs, the Oak House domestic staff, the day workers: they live there,' Talia said. 'There are more Oaks in the gazette than Wheats. And even the wheats are traditionalists. They won't like the idea of Companionaris damaging rock children. I have a connection there, a family who might help.'

Stepping away from the direct route to Wheat House was hard. It intensified the ache in Fox's arms, and she had to coax Wren to follow her. And when they reached the settlement, Fox felt helpless. Too many houses. Too many winding streets, suddenly treed in Talia's presence.

'Don't look so worried. I know the way,' Talia said. 'I came here when I was Acacia's junior. We visited her family.'

Acacia. She'd helped Fox several times. If her family lived here, they might help too.

Talia led them through the gazette, down one street, then another and another. The call of the rock children worried at Fox, plaintive, desperate, breaking through her Companionari trained defences. As she followed Talia, she dropped a sliver of consciousness into her body and shut out the calls. In the sudden quiet, she realised what she'd been missing. The realisation hit her so hard that she grabbed Talia. 'You're the new Oak Companion.'

Talia blushed. 'I shouldn't be.' The trees surrounding them creaked and rattled, and saplings sprouted between the cobbles. It wouldn't be long before the oaks had them fenced in. 'Sorry,' Talia said. 'My concentration slipped.' She inhaled, held her breath for a moment, then released it and the growth halted.

'Whether you should or shouldn't be a companion isn't the point,' Fox said. 'We need to save the stones and the Mint Gazette could help us. You said it yourself; the place is full of families who work for the Department of Beranish Affairs. They might respect Aikin as its head, but they *revere* the Oak Companion. They'll listen to you. Every woman wants to be in your sorority; every man wants to be your husband or lover or the father of your babies. You've got everything we need to stop this.'

Talia blinked, opened her mouth to speak, closed it. But when she resumed her lead, she moved with purpose and there was a distinct absence of new oaks and corks in the gardens they passed.

Talia led them to a small home with green crippet cages hanging from its eaves and a garden filled with poppies and red peppers. Bird song sweetened the air. Acacia's was a purposeful, orderly house and that gave Fox hope.

The woman who opened the door, peered at them. Then her expression turned to amazement as she recognised Talia. She let out a long breath, 'Back and Path, it's the new companion.' She curtsied and then called out to those behind her, 'Quick, you lot. And get dad out of his chair.'

'You're Acacia's sister,' Talia said. 'She brought me here when I worked in household records.'

Acacia's sister stepped onto the verandah, began a second curtsy, then seemed to think better of it. She acknowledged Fox and Wren, but her attention returned to Talia. 'Mother, we're so relieved to have you, to have a new companion.'

'The thing is,' Fox interrupted, 'we need your help. There's something going on in Wheat House that's terribly wrong. Master Aikin and the Wheat Companion have stolen some rock children and they mean to crush them.'

'Crush Beranish treasures? Surely Master Aikin wouldn't be involved in something like that?'

'It's true,' Talia said. 'And we must stop them. Can you gather the gazette?'

Fox caught movement in the corner of her eye. The front door of the rather decrepit house next door opened, and a familiar and welcome figure emerged. 'Louis!' she said.

'Louis,' Wren echoed.

'Well, if it isn't my two favourite lovers,' the large man called out from his overgrown garden.

As Acacia's family emerged from the house to greet Talia, Fox and Wren crossed the yard, stepping over the low fence and into Louis' garden. He met them halfway and was soon making the somewhat ominous promise to rouse the low life in the gazette. As Fox and Wren made their way back to Talia, he left his house. The man moved quickly for someone who claimed to be unfit to walk.

It took about ten minutes for the people to gather in the street, pressing into Acacia's front garden. They spoke in quiet whispers, captivated by the novelty of an Oak Companion standing on a Mint Gazette verandah.

'Thank you for coming,' Talia said. 'Oak House is grateful to you. I need your help. But before I ask for it, I want to let you know about some worrying things that have been happening in Komey,' she paused, waited for the crowd to still. 'You remember when the cross-over failed? And I developed my gravity?'

'Strongest in a thousand years,' someone called out.

Fox wasn't sure where Talia was heading. They needed the crowd's support. They didn't need a public confession. If Talia was about to sully her own reputation, it was a risky move.

'Yes,' Talia said, 'but I'm afraid my gravity resulted from something terrible. Something I'm deeply ashamed of.'

The listeners shifted. Only Louis seemed at ease, sitting on an upturned barrow at the edge of the crowd.

'What are you talking about, Mother?' a woman called out. 'What are you saying?'

Talia looked to Fox, but it was too late for advice. If they'd had a wanderer with them, they could have framed this story, but it was loose now. The results were in the Stone Body's hands. Fox just hoped the land was paying attention.

'The crossover failed,' Talia said. 'We all felt desperate...'

Several listeners murmured in agreement.

'Thought we'd have to abandon Oak province,' someone called out.

'Master Aikin came to me with an idea about creating new companionships. I believed in him. I let him experiment on me. He rubbed crushed powder into cuts in my skin, powder made from rock children, and it created my gravity.' Talia lifted her blouse and exposed the scars on her stomach. Around them, the trees seemed to respond, leaves fluttering branches creaking.

The crowd was silent, but Fox could feel its unease.

'I didn't know at the time that Aikin was killing wanderers for their stones and I didn't understand that the stones are living beings. But I take responsibility for what I did. I accepted the life of a stone, took its body into mine. And I... I was part of a subversive parley where Aikin and Whilomena and some others decided it was necessary to take *all the stones* on the Stone Body, kill *all the wanderers* who carry them, that no other parley mattered. It's murder: nothing but murder.'

The crowd split, formed rivulets as people absorbed Talia's words. Some moved away from neighbours; others moved closer. Some leant in to whisper in an ear; others stepped back to shout an insult across a newly formed aisle. Fox found she could read the movements and her hopes rose. It wasn't just her rock sense telling her which parts of the crowd favoured Talia and which favoured Aikin and Whilomena. She'd always been good at seeing patterns, only now it was beginning to feel like a gift because she could see it in the movement of their feet, in the language of their stance. The tide was turning in their favour, but it was the minority who spoke up.

'We should trust the Wheat Mother,' a young woman called out, 'not this nonsense from an untried companion.'

Several people clapped, reminding Fox that the outcome was still uncertain.

A man stepped forward. 'Thing is, it's all very well not wanting to harm those wanderers. But if we need fetish stones to survive and it's us or them... Well, we can't sit and watch the provinces fail. If it costs a few wanderer's lives and a few stones, that's what it costs.'

'Shut up, you!' His neighbour elbowed him. 'Us that's worked in Beranish Affairs know what's right and what's wrong.'

'Barbarians and rocks,' a woman called out. 'That's what you're talking about. It's the Wheat Mother who's feeding everyone. My sympathy's with her and Master Aikin.'

Fox looked at the crowd. The words had altered the pattern. She crossed the verandah to stand beside Talia. It was time to speak up. 'Have any of you wondered how Berans survived before the settlers arrived?'

'Half starved probably,' someone called out and there were some embarrassed laughs, but no denials.

'There was a natural cycle that was interrupted when the Companionaris arrived on these shores. Rock children are meant to grow into adulthood. I've seen one: a rock man; a wanderer twin. I saw him today. *Everything grows for him,*' she repeated Mica's words. 'He's the adult form of a living stone and he and the others that will come, will grow things for us.'

The crowd was still now.

She took a deep breath, knew she was losing them, but pressed on regardless. 'Rock people are the Stone Body's natural companions. We need to work out what this means. But we'll never find out if we don't stop Aikin and Whilomena.'

'Stones as companions?' a woman cried out. 'What are you talking about?'

'If we let Aikin and the Wheat Mother kill those rock children, you'll never know, will you? You should have a say in what happens in Komey. The gazette's parleys are just as important as the parleys in the big houses.'

At the mention of the gazette's rights, Fox saw movement. A footstep here, a shoulder turned there. And though the listeners' signatures were still fearful and tangled, the threads also felt ripe with recognition. She just hoped she wasn't too late. Her arms throbbed with the stone calls.

'She's right,' a man called out, and several other people agreed.

'Hear! Hear!' Louis' voice boomed.

In the clamour of rock calls assailing Fox, one stopped. Fox gasped, grabbed hold of a verandah post as though an absence had more force than a presence.

'Are you all right, Little Fox?' Louis called out.

She waved away his concern. 'It's the stones. One has stopped. I can't feel it.' She pulled back her sleeves, no longer careful of the pretence she and Oria had agreed on, the lie that she was the bare-armed birthmother to a new Oak Companion. Her rock skin had grown since she'd last looked at it.

She held up her arms, scattering refracted light around her. 'These are magical times,' she spoke to the crowd. 'My Beranish rock skin has grown back. The stone calls are like children crying for help. Come to Wheat House. Have your say.'

It didn't take long after that and when Fox walked into the crowd, the only rivulet that existed was made by people making room for the three women to pass.

30

A couple of garden boys were the first to notice Fox and her companions as they approached Wheat House. Impossible not to with half the Mint Gazette following the three women. Talia hadn't spoken to anyone since she made her speech on the verandah. The dense wheat fields surrounding them seemed to have dampened her body's urge to grow trees, and she looked subdued. Wren, on the other hand, was looking better. She was lucid, talking about her children, asking Fox where they were. Fox should have been more careful with her answers, but the pleading feeling of the stone calls distracted her: needy, pitiful, desperate. She made promises to Wren that she hoped she could keep.

In front of Fox, two boys stood open-mouthed, rakes in hand. Their alarm prickled Fox's rock skin. She and her followers needed to get inside Wheat House before the house guards caught sight of them and called out the militia. Fox smiled at the boys. She just hoped the Stone Body was with her, that she looked reassuring, that no one was looking out the Wheat House windows, that the house guards and their soldiersisters were busy in a remote part of the building.

The stone calls drew them up the gravel path, past the open

gates and the great wooden doors. Wheat House looked relaxed and the gate mistress wasn't at her post. Fox didn't know whether it was the Stone Body's benevolence or blind luck. Probably the latter. Wheat House had never had a reason to worry about its security.

The party hurried down the arched carriageway into the trading room. Abruptly, they were among people, haggling traders. For a moment, the traders were oblivious to their presence. Then they caught sight of Fox and the others, and the noise in the hall collapsed. By the time Fox reached the centre of the room, there was silence all around and with it a spreading sense of fear.

The stone calls clamoured, pulled at Fox from every direction. Then she had it: they were beneath her feet. She turned full circle, looking for stairs, but couldn't see them.

A man accompanied by two house guards elbowed his way past the traders. His voice was tight with disapproval, 'Mistress Fox, Mother Talia, such an unexpected pleasure.' The golden sheaves on his frock coat marked him out as the housekeeper. 'I'll let Mother Wheat know that you're here. If you'd like to come with me, I'll take you upstairs.' He reached for Fox's elbow, gripped it, began pulling her.

She shook him off, grabbed him by his lapels, her rock skin bristling. 'Take me downstairs.'

One of the house guards took hold of Fox's arm. The other pulled at her shoulder.

Talia reached in to help and, in the tangle of arms, got an elbow in her face. The crowd gasped and the Mint Gazette's residents began demanding a parley, ordering the house guards to step back, insisting on seeing Whilomena in person, telling the guards they had no business touching the new Oak Companion.

A man's voice rang out above the noise, wheezy, more than a little breathless, but full of authority, 'You heard the new Oak Companion. Let Fox go. We've got business here, parley matters.' It sounded like Louis, but Fox couldn't see who had spoken.

The house guards looked from the crowd to the housekeeper and back again. They let Fox go.

'The door to the basement?' Fox said, her hands still gripping the housekeeper's lapels. 'Where is it?'

Beneath her feet, another rock child fell silent. Its absence felt like an ache in her soles.

The housekeeper pointed to a wheat-themed wall hanging. 'Behind there.'

Two of the gazette's residents ran over to the tapestry, pulled it aside, revealing an archway and a broad stone staircase.

Fox let go of the housekeeper and ran, almost tripping in her haste, the crowd on her heels. The steps led down to a large ante-room. Well furnished with silk rugs on the floor. There was a goods' lift and, beside it, a door. Probably the door to the original dry goods store, but the furnishings suggested the basement's function had changed. She hurried to the door, tried the handle, but it was locked.

The housekeeper spoke without being asked, 'Mother Wheat has the key.'

Fox banged her fist against the door. 'Open up!'

'We're not to be disturbed!' Whilomena's voice was sharp.

There was a slight easing of the calls, as though the stones knew help was at hand.

'Aikin! Father!' Fox called. 'Are you in there too? Let me in.'

'Go away,' he answered. 'Go home Fox. You shouldn't be here.'

Fox banged on the door again, but this time there was no response.

Talia joined Fox at the door. 'Open up.'

Fox turned to the crowd. 'Can anyone help?'

A man edged his way forward, ducked his head in greeting, and hurried over. He drew some tools from his pocket, and Fox and Talia stepped aside. He began working on the lock and then waved Fox forward. This time the handle turned, opening onto a beautiful room that smelt of flour and spices. It was decorated as a private suite.

The Wheat Companion stood beside Aikin, furious. 'You!' She

glared at Fox. 'How dare you! I've had just about enough of you. Never mind that your Aikin's—'

At the sound of his name, Aikin reached up, put a hand on her arm. He nodded at the crowd pushing its way into the room, and Whilomena's tirade broke off.

A long worktable stood between Whilomena and Aikin, and everyone else. It was covered in an assortment of oak jewellery boxes that looked to be lined with silver. Fox frowned, sensing something, seeing some sort of pattern, but there wasn't time to wonder what the boxes signified. She could feel the rock children, hidden behind some pillows on the bed in the far corner of the room.

Behind her, the room was filling with signatures that were full of worry, curiosity, fear, anger. In front of Fox, Whilomena's expression shifted as she took in the crowd's numbers. Rage turned to confusion, then to something that approximated mild affront.

'Talia, dear,' Whilomena said, 'what a surprise. And so many people with you and young Fox. Companions and birthmothers rarely call on each other like this, in such a public manner. I wish I'd known you were both so desperate to speak with me. I would have come to you.'

Fox was about to answer, but a familiar voice interrupted, 'We're here to parley.'

Fox turned and saw Louis pushing his way past the housekeeper and several traders.

'Is that you, Louis Oak?' Aikin sounded nervous. 'Not used to seeing you out and about. What are you doing here?'

'Same as all of us,' a woman called out. 'Maybe come to change your cause.'

'Our cause?' Whilomena arched an elegant eyebrow. 'I'm not sure I understand what you're talking about.'

'Killing wanderers,' Talia said.

'Killing stones,' Fox asserted.

Fox didn't need her rock skin to see Aikin was unnerved, but his voice was smooth, 'This is a private room. Mother Wheat and I have every right to be here. You people, however, do not. It's the height of bad manners.'

Fox moved quickly. She walked over to the bed and pulled the pillows away, revealing a cloth bundle. She opened it, exposing a pile of stones. 'These are rock children,' she said, 'living stones. And some are missing.' She turned to Aikin and Whilomena. 'Where are they? Have you killed them already?'

Then she realised the answer was right in front of her. She cradled the bundle of rock children in one arm and walked back to the table. Using her free hand, she began flipping open the lids of the boxes that were closed. The first four were empty. When she opened the fifth, she felt it before she saw it: a tiny rock child. Undamaged. Not dead, but silenced by the silver-lined boxes. She breathed easier as she continued searching. She found another rock child. Also undamaged.

'Rock children?' Aikin laughed. 'Don't be silly.' He turned and spoke to the crowd. 'My daughter's unwell. These are just stones. I enjoy the study of rocks. That's all this is.' He shook his head, shrugged, held out his hands. 'A small passion for geology and some lovely specimen boxes I ordered in Galea. Unfortunately, I ordered the wrong sizes. Too small to house my collection, hence the stones on the bed.'

Whilomena waved a hand at everyone in front of her, Fox included, 'You should be ashamed. I may be a companion mother, but I'm entitled to some privacy, some affairs of the heart.'

Uncertainty and shame fluttered through the emotional signatures around Fox, growing stronger by the minute. What had been believable in the Mint Gazette wasn't so easy to believe in the face of the Wheat Companion's outrage. Fox turned to face the crowd. Some people were staring at the ground; others were edging towards the door. 'They've been killing stones and murdering wanderers,' she said. 'You can stop them.'

Fox realised Wren had crept up beside her without her noticing.

The woman was leaning over the worktable. She pointed at the rock children, began whispering, 'Granite, kernite.'

'Not now, Wren.' Fox turned back to the crowd, tried again, knowing her voice sounded desperate, 'I was there when Malachite, the wanderer, was killed. I think… I believe Aikin is responsible.'

Aikin sighed, spread his hands, 'My daughter is unwell. Unfortunately, her delusions have entangled others. I blame myself for what's happening today. I took her on a field trip where a tragedy occurred and I should have known better. Adopted talents shouldn't leave the city. It unsettles fragile minds. She has misread the situation. It's possible her dust bush tea has slipped past her grip. Sadly, she's led others astray. Poor Wren is a case in point. Someone needs to take her back to her bedroom. Please,' he looked at the gazette locals, the traders and all the other on-lookers, 'please go home. Go back to work.'

Fox saw that her father's words were working. Several people had already left and more were leaving.

'Wait! There are wanderers here in Komey who can testify.'

'Wait!' Talia echoed Fox.

Their pleas had the opposite effect. People began jostling to get out the door.

Then the movement stopped. Fox stood on her toes and strained to see the reason. Several people were doing the same, craning their necks.

Then she felt them. Mica, Quartz, Oria, the children, and Patience. 'They're here,' she whispered.

'Let them through!' someone called out from the back of the crowd. 'They'll know their own stones.'

'It's the barbarians,' someone else called out. 'The wanderers. Let them in.'

This time, the crowd listened. First one and then another turned and began edging their way back into the room. They kept their eyes on the ground, unwilling to declare an open allegiance, but Fox could sense that it was Aikin's and Whilomena's gaze they were avoiding this time, not hers.

As the tide reversed, the room filled. Through the middle came the Berans. First Quartz, then Mica, then Oria holding Doubt's and Saury's hands, then Patience Learnt. It was a relief seeing the children, especially Saury. Fox looked for Obsidian, but couldn't see him. Nor could she see the other Caballo wanderers.

The newcomers walked over to the worktable. Oria reached for one of the small rock children in the jewellery boxes.

'Kernite,' Wren said.

Fox set down the bundle she'd been cradling, pulled back the cloth, exposing the stones.

As the wanderers claimed them, Wren spoke each rock child's name. Quartz gave Saury the piece of flint that had once favoured Mica and then Saury reached over to the table for her pebble, lifting it from the wooden box.

When every rock child had passed into wanderer hands, Quartz spoke, 'Until a few hours ago, I carried this dunite child. This other,' he held up a fist-sized bit of tiger's eye, 'was carried by a wanderer who's now dead. There are four stories in any truth. The first is mine: I am angry; I am bitter. I'm not willing to wait for a quieter time to share my knowledge.' He glared at the crowd, as though daring anyone to speak. The Companionaris in the room seemed to press back against the walls, but many nodded, acknowledging Quartz's right to anger. The other Berans were silent, waiting for Quartz to go on.

'The second story is also mine,' he said. 'My enemies,' he pointed to Aikin and Whilomena, 'these two, have the third story. And I'll ask my brother wanderer, Mica, to tell you the appropriate fourth story. I believe he knows it well. The elements of knowledge are here in this room. What you do with that knowledge is your own affair, but you will have to face up to the rot in your culture.'

Whilomena interrupted, 'All this quaint cultural chit chat is charming,' she gave Quartz the haughtiest of looks, 'but I'm not prepared to engage in it. I'm not prepared to be bailed up in my home by people who have no right to be here!'

Her words seemed to bring Patience Learnt to life. The Caballo keeper had been standing a little behind Mica. He stepped forward, stood in front of Whilomena and Aikin, the long work table between them. He lifted his grief-stricken face and stared at the Wheat Companion. 'I was *invited*,' he spat the words, 'and my dead friends were *invited*. By you.' He pointed at her and then lowered his arm again, turning his attention to the crowd. 'Let her speak or not, as she chooses. Him too. But I, Patience Learnt, keeper of Caballo and senior wanderer, have the right to be here: by the laws of hospitality; by the laws of treaty; by the right of grievance.'

'Well then,' Louis Oak spoke as he hobbled further into the room, 'Looks like this here is a proper parley and a parley has a right to be anywhere,' his voice still wheezed and he looked exhausted, but Fox could see that despite his frailty he carried weight with his neighbours. He headed towards Whilomena's enormous bed.

Without waiting for permission, he lowered himself onto the foot of the bed. 'And since I'm here on a bed resting my legs, I may as well host the parley. Welcome then.' He looked at the crowd. 'And welcome to our guests.' He acknowledged the Berans in the room. 'And welcome to the new Oak Companion, the Wheat Companion and to Master Oak. This parley's open,' he clapped his hands, 'so let's see what's been going on.' He looked at Quartz. 'Tell us, wanderer, and we'll listen.'

When Quartz started speaking, the weight of what he had to convey had replaced the fury in his voice, 'The second story then. This morning I was one of a party of people walking in from Oak province. The adopted Beran, Fox Oak, led our group,' he gestured at Fox with a sweep of his hand. 'We came to discuss the status of the Oak companionship. We met Patience and the Caballo Berans when we reached the banewood, just shy of Komey. The Caballos came to Komey to parley on the matter of the sudden failure of their province. Whilomena and Aikin were in the Horse Companion's tent when my party arrived at the trees. They urged us to walk with them into Komey to parley on the problems of Caballo and on the strange events surrounding the Oak companionship. And so we came.'

Quartz closed his eyes briefly, and Fox could feel him summoning up the details of the day.

'We went to Oak House,' he continued. 'A parley began, led by Talia Oak, the woman you know as the new Oak Companion, a woman whose gravity appeared seemingly from nowhere, and by Fox Oak. That parley broke up because this woman,' he waved at Oria, 'had fainted. The four stories invite us to testify to what we know to be true and so I must tell you a fraction of a longer knowledge, which touches this day,' Quartz paused and looked across at Oria in what, to Fox, looked like an apology. He pointed to Oria, and all eyes turned to look at the beautiful young Beran with her dark hair and exquisite rock skin.

'We introduced this woman to everyone who met her as a young Beran named Promise, but she is, in fact, Oria, the twenty-third Oak Companion, the old Oak Mother.'

There was a slight stirring in the crowd, more puzzlement than amazement. Several people giggled.

Quartz continued speaking, 'She is Oria, the twenty-third Oak Companion, given a second life in the exhumed body of Promise, a legendary but very real figure from the time of the treaty.'

Fox looked across at Aikin. He was frowning, but she could see his curiosity getting the better of him. 'And Fox?' her adopted father spoke. 'Is she yet another contender as the birthmother of an Oak companion? Do we have three claimants now?'

'Fox masqueraded as birthmother to secure Oria's continued governance of Oak.' Quartz became irritable. 'I'll talk about that later,' he snapped. 'The second story has its own shape and I'll tell it as I see it. Whilomena invited my people to her little mill house, her *folly*, under the guise of giving us some privacy to discuss Beranish affairs. Eight of us left Oak House alive: myself, Oria, Mica's nephew Doubt and his apprentice Saury, Patience Learnt and three of his fellow wanderers. We are now only five,' Quartz let his words sink into the silence in the room before continuing. 'Five left alive...'

He turned to Aikin and Whilomena. 'It was poison, wasn't it? I imagine the poison was in the kumis that you served us?'

Neither Aikin nor Whilomena responded, but Aikin looked uncomfortable. Not Whilomena, though. The Wheat Mother was as cold and immaculate as ever.

The wanderer shrugged. 'They'll tell their own tale, but I must tell mine. We drank. We collapsed.'

'Now I'm going to explain something of Mica's story. A week or so ago in Oak province, one of his stones, his piece of obsidian, called to him to climb down into a trench in the ground near the foundation oak.'

Someone in the crowd interrupted, 'In the ground? No self-respecting Beran would do that, break the taboo.'

Quartz shrugged. 'His rock child demanded that he do it. We came upon his body the next day. He was dead and his obsidian had disappeared.'

Several people in the crowd edged forward to get a better look at Mica.

'I can't tell you how he died and then appeared, alive, in Komey, how that could be possible. But when I was roused from my poisoned state, it was Mica who leant over me and with him was a magical being, a twin named Obsidian. A rock man. Obsidian rid my body of poison, rejuvenated me, made me feel about ten years younger. And he saved Oria and Patience too. Then we watched him pull Doubt and Saury back from the dead. The effort destroyed him, but his death showed me who he was even before Mica could tell me more. When he died, he changed. He literally fell to pieces, and in his place was a small pile of newborn rock children. Obsidian was a rock man, brought into adulthood through the Stone Body.'

Whilomena rolled her eyes and turned to Aikin. 'I thought they only used myths in fourth stories.'

Fox watched Aikin. There was a stillness about him that told her that Aikin believed what he was hearing.

Quartz continued, ignoring the interruption. 'The Beranish taboo about uncovering the earth and swimming in the sea looks suspiciously like something artificial, something devised to keep our stones in their infancy, to keep them from realising their potential. Because Obsidian could do more than call back the dead and cure me, make me younger and healthier than I've been in years. Mica tells me he could germinate seed, any seed, all seed.' Quartz paused for a moment. 'Obsidian was a Stone Body companion: a true companion. That is the second story.'

Louis sucked on his teeth and looked at the rest of the people in the room. Then he turned to Whilomena and Aikin. 'One of you can tell the third story if you like. If you don't like, the wanderer here will ask if anyone else has got an opposing account. What will you do: speak or not?'

'I'll speak.' Whilomena stepped forward, stood at the edge of the worktable. She ignored Aikin's attempt to interrupt her. She turned to give Quartz a look of complete hatred. 'Of course, I dispute all that nonsense about bringing people back from the dead. And as for that girl being Oria,' she pointed at Oria, 'I won't even bother you with what I think about that.' She sighed and shook her head, exasperated. 'The Berans are barbarians,' she appealed to the Companionaris in the crowd, waving her hand toward the wanderers. 'They believe all sorts of things. And they're entitled to. Who cares? I don't. It's Komey that's been keeping them alive. Our companionships. But the companionships are failing and we had to do something.'

Aikin reached out, placed a hand on Whilomena's arm as though it might halt the flow of words, but she ignored him.

'I admit we poisoned them,' she said, 'but it was for your benefit. We needed their rock children to create companionships and they won't share their stones. Killing wanderers was our last resort. I'm not ashamed to tell you I was prepared to kill a few barbarians to protect everyone from starvation. Everyone! Including their people.'

Her gaze raked across the room. 'Course, I regret the suffering,' she shrugged, 'but Komey needed leadership and I was brave enough to give it. There you are,' she turned to Louis, 'that's your third story.'

The old birthfather scratched at his head for a moment, then looked at Mica. 'Quartz seems to think you know a suitable fourth story.'

Mica nodded. He spoke slowly, his voice lacking the sing-song lilt that was employed for fourth stories, 'One day, Wanderer fell in love with the Stone Body and began dreaming of marriage. At first he wooed the Stone Body with flowers, but she turned him away, telling him to find a woman, not a creature of earth and mountains and rivers and oceans. But Wanderer wouldn't listen because his heart was set on having the Stone Body as his wife. He wooed her with arnuts, but the Stone Body wouldn't eat them. Next, he brought her tea and pleaded for her hand, promising his undying love. But the Stone Body said no. So Wanderer took a spade and dug a hole without the Stone Body's consent. And when the hole was deep enough, he lay with her against her will. Afterwards he slept. The Stone Body watched him sleeping within her and shuddered. She decided to kill all Berans in revenge. But then she caught sight of Mother and Father and saw that they were not to blame. Next she looked at Cook and at Child and at Huntress and Hunter, and saw the same. So the Stone Body satisfied herself by crushing Wanderer and she threw his bloodied corpse into Cook's fire as a warning to anyone who might try to dig more than a foot beneath her skin or delve too deeply into her waters.'

Mica looked up at the crowd and then turned back to Louis, addressing him directly. 'This is the story that we've always used as the fourth story for the knowledge about the death of the generation of wanderers who lived during the treaty wars. We thought it suggested those wanderers had deserved punishment, but we never understood why. I see the story for what it is: a cover up. Concocted by the first Companionaris after they killed our ancestors, stole all the rock children they could find, and then ground them into powder to fuel the first companionships.'

'When the Stone Body transported me to Komey, giving birth to the first rock man in living memory, Obsidian and I found a book.' Fox saw Aikin stiffen at Mica's words, but the wanderer continued without pause. 'The Book of Kinesis. It's a manual for cause and effect, a nonsense book, an exercise in Companionari vanity. But it also contained a ledger, a record about creating the first Companionari companions. I can only assume that Master Aikin stumbled upon it and used it to create Talia Oak's and Glory Bass' sudden gravities.'

Everyone in the room turned to look at Talia. Many had seen the scars when she'd spoken in the Mint Gazette, and knew the young wanderer was speaking the truth.

'There's nothing more to say.' Mica fell silent.

Louis sighed. 'A parley should focus on good causes. Not for their effects, what's good in itself. Well?' He looked around the room, seeking ideas. 'Anyone?'

'There isn't a cause that will repair this,' it was Patience Learnt who spoke. 'The treaty is broken. Berans and Companionaris are divided now. You live how you can. We shall thrive. We have what's ours: the key to Beranish companionships. Our only tasks now are to rescue our brothers and sisters, for I've heard the Wheat Mother's been enslaving people and now, seeing the worst of her, I know it must be true. And to find the Stone Body's portals.'

Oria stood up. 'Yes, of course. We must free the enslaved and we must find the portals, but I don't agree with you that our two peoples are divided. At least, not irrevocably. We can't just go our own way. It's too late. We're together on the Stone Body, and in body, too. Look at me, I'm Beranish and I'm a Companionari. Maybe my name should be Promise Ahead. I'm the link. I don't know what it means, but that's what I am, and the Stone Body was the one who chose me. I'm singular: a new life, a map for the future.'

A trader was the next to speak, 'We lived by the treaty for generations. We should acknowledge the harmony it brought.'

'Paid for by us,' Mica spoke. 'Brokered dishonestly.'

'That can change,' the woman held her ground. 'It's a good thing to know what happened, and it's a good thing to live honestly, but it's not a good thing to turn our backs on trade and the beauty of negotiations.'

'That's true,' Fox said. 'Perhaps we should treaty again.'

Heads nodded in agreement.

'Seems to me,' Louis spoke up, 'this is a matter for everyone: all the Companionaris; all the Berans. We shouldn't go deciding on our cause today. We should look to rescuing the enslaved Berans. And we should spread the news of these four stories. As for these two,' he gestured to Whilomena and Aikin, 'they can sit awhile in the Oak House cells until we can hold a parley that includes everyone, decide what to do with them.'

'Yes,' Fox agreed.

'Aye,' someone else seconded.

'Well, I don't agree!' Whilomena said.

'Don't need to,' Louis said. 'Majority rules in parleys, not gravity.' He got up from the bed, waved the house guards forward. They'd been keeping out of the fray, standing in the housekeeper's shadow. 'Come on, you two. Time to earn your keep. Take Master Aikin and the Wheat Companion into custody.'

The guards looked reluctant, but they came forward. The taller of the two pulled a leather thong from her pocket. She was hesitant about touching the Wheat Companion, but she obeyed Louis' directive, stepping behind Whilomena, looping the thong around one wrist and then another.

Fox frowned. Something wasn't right. Something niggled at her.

The other guard bound Aikin's hands with a lot less deference.

Her adopted father looked irritated, but the Wheat Mother's face was expressionless and her signature was bordering on smug. Why? Did she think someone would free her? Unlikely. Well, likely, but not immediately. There would be parleys upon parleys, but it wouldn't be easy to keep Whilomena incarcerated. The woman had too many allies. Something else then... And then it hit Fox. The answer was standing in front of her: there were two house guards.

Two guards and no sign of the Wheat House militia. Yet news of the altercation in the basement must have drifted beyond the trading room.

Fox spoke to the taller guard, 'Where are your military sisters? Why haven't they come to your aid?'

'They're not here.'

'Where are they?'

'They left the city,' the woman said.

'When?'

'A few hours ago. Just after the parley in Oak House.'

'Where were they going?' Fox asked. 'What were their orders?'

The woman looked uncomfortable. 'I'm sorry, Mistress Fox. You'd have to ask the Wheat Companion.'

'I'm asking you.'

'All I know is that they were carrying tents and packs. Some had horses. They left on the trains. I think some others went with them. Other militias.'

Whilomena looked at Fox, tilted her head, raised her eyebrows. The hint of a smile touched her lips.

Mica spoke, his voice low and certain, 'Gone to kill wanderers, to steal rock children. And we're too late to stop them.'

Quartz shook his head. 'Never say that. We must try.'

31

Fox felt as though Komey had been tipped upside down. The city had changed in the days since Aikin and Whilomena's arrest. Even the Oak House kitchen gardens had altered. Fox stood, watching Willie handing out food to impoverished Companionaris and hungry Berans. The hunger remained the same but the people in line were different. The Companionaris were subdued, the Berans more numerous. And the increase in the Berans' numbers wasn't because of new provincial failures. Komey had opened its gates to Beranish families. Not graciously, not happily, but the gates were open. And it was those families who had altered the landscape.

The grounds beyond the kitchen gardens were full of tents. Many were decorated with the running horses so beloved by the Caballos, but there were others too, and Mica's among them. And she had joined them. She'd moved most of her belongings out of Oak House and into Mica's tent. There were still a few books and precious pieces she hadn't found time to collect, but she'd moved most of her things.

Willie's voice interrupted her thoughts, 'Are you helping or just standing there?'

'Not today. Sorry.'

He grunted, but his voice was kindly when he spoke, 'Off to rescue another adoptee?'

'I'm trying.' She smiled, but knew it wouldn't fool him. There was no hiding her disappointment.

The cook handed some fruit and a bag of flour to a Companionari couple and reached into his barrow for another load as they moved on. 'Ah, don't blame yourself. You can only offer freedom. You can't make a person take it.'

Fox wanted to tell him it was more complicated than that, but Willie had his own worries. There were so many people to feed and Komey's houses were in uproar with many households refusing to help the Beranish families. Even Oak House, a house where both Oria and Talia were committed to the new way of life and a new treaty, had faced internal difficulties.

Willie handed a bag of flour and some onions to a Beranish family. 'So where to today?' he asked Fox.

'Mallow House.'

'Sneaking in or using the front door?'

'Acacia is coming with me so we won't be sneaking in, but probably the back door. An informal visit. At least we hope so.'

An hour later, as Fox and Acacia climbed the stairs inside Mallow House, Fox reminded herself that visitors behaved like visitors, not like uninvited guests preparing to be sent packing. She took a steadying breath, lifted her head and put a bit more confidence into her stride as the houseboy led them up another flight. Her efforts to free the other adoptees had been largely unsuccessful. It had surprised her how often her visits were received with hostility by the women. She'd been thrown out of several houses, but she told herself that today would be different.

Their reception at the back door of Mallow House wasn't auspicious. The housekeeper had looked startled by Fox's polite assertion that she and Acacia were making courtesy visits to all the adopted talents. Fox doubted she would have been admitted at all if she'd been on her own.

As it was, the housekeeper had stood in the kitchen doorway, blocking their way, his attention moving from Fox's eyes to her arms. Luckily, Acacia had proved her worth as Fox's unofficial diplomat. She'd voiced her sympathy for households coping with events in Komey when their companions were still in the provinces, and the housekeeper had softened. It wasn't long before the man admitted them, handing them off to the houseboy with all the courtesies a pair of Oak daughters could wish for.

They reached the landing on the second floor and the boy gestured to a door decorated with stylised cotton bolls. 'This is Lark's door, but she doesn't enjoy being disturbed in the mornings. Be careful.' He knocked on the door. 'Visitors, Mistress Lark.'

Be careful? The advice seemed a little extreme, but Fox remembered those times when Wren's confusion had led to violence. Perhaps Lark was similarly unsettled. As soon as the door opened, Fox saw she was wrong. The woman who greeted them was as golden-eyed as any Beran, as bare-armed as any Companionari, but her gaze was clear. She was busy working on a complex piece of lace. 'Yes?'

'Visitors,' the houseboy repeated, retreating, not waiting for a response. He closed the door behind him.

Acacia introduced herself, which did nothing to soften the woman's imperious manner. '... and this is Fox Oak.'

'Yes? And?'

Fox answered, 'We've come to check on your welfare.'

'Really?' Lark turned her attention to her lace. 'I don't recall asking for someone to check on my welfare, let alone strangers from other houses. And you've interrupted my morning's work.'

Fox would have spoken, explained more, but Acacia reached for her arm, held her back.

'Our apologies,' Acacia said. 'I take it you've heard about the Wheat House scandal and the breakdown of the treaty?'

'Wheat House *and Oak House.* Both were involved in the scandal.'

'True,' Acacia agreed. 'Aikin Oak shamed us. You've heard the detail, of course? Thought about the implications for your own position?'

Lark lifted her head, held Acacia's gaze. The woman's signature was brimming with certainty. Fox could feel something more, subtleties threaded underneath the certainty, but couldn't catch their meaning.

Lark set down her lacework. She stood, looked from Acacia to Fox and then back to Acacia. Her voice was formal when she spoke, her chin held high, 'Don't let me keep you.'

Fox couldn't help herself. 'You can leave here. You can come with us. Live anywhere. Return home.'

'Home? This is my home. I have seven children here, five grand-children. I see them most days. We are Mallows. They are Mallows. You want me to abandon them?'

'Bring them with you,' Fox said.

'Where? To live in a tent? I don't think so.'

Acacia tightened her grip on Fox's arm, tried to draw her back, but Fox held her ground.

'If you change your mind,' Fox said, 'ask for me.'

Lark gave a sniff, looked at the door in a not-so-subtle suggestion that they needed to leave.

Fox spoke again, 'You should have a say in the negotiations about the new treaty.'

'And you should mind your own business,' Lark said. 'As if I'd take advice from a girl who doesn't know how to dress for a house visit.'

Fox glanced down. Her tunic was unadorned and rather wrinkled and the long tips of the collar of her shirt were frayed. This time, when Acacia drew Fox back, Fox let her.

Outside, on the path beyond the Mallow House gardens, Fox began to cry. It had been a long few days. Her dream of liberating the other adoptees was falling apart and the tensions in Komey were worsening. It was so disappointing. The Companionari houses were consumed with forming and joining factions. Likewise, the Berans.

Some Companionaris wanted to liberate Aikin and Whilomena. Some Berans wanted to destroy Komey. Some people were committed to negotiating a new treaty and others argued for a separation.

Acacia put her arms around Fox, drew her close.

Fox's tears wet the other woman's collar. 'I wanted to save them'

'You saved Wren. She's free of her teas. She's living in Louis' house. She has her baby with her. The other children are visiting.'

'I know,' Fox sniffed, 'but none of the lucid adoptees want to leave their houses.'

'And why would they? It's different for you. You don't have children and you're younger than most of them. Women like Lark have a lot to lose. You need to be patient, Fox. Wait and see what the new treaty brings, wait until life becomes settled. The most important thing is, they have a choice.'

Fox lifted her head from Acacia's shoulder, took a step back. 'We forgot to tell Lark that she can stop drinking dust bush tea.'

'Do you think someone like Lark doesn't know that? She told us she'd heard about what happened. Lark will have heard the four stories. She knows about the theft and the deception.'

'Then why doesn't she stop drinking the tea?'

'Why would she rush to take sides when she doesn't have any difficulty managing the toxin? Be patient. The new treaty will ban dust bush tea or make it optional, and there won't be any new adoptees.'

'Then what are we doing here if everything is going to be all right?'

'Exactly what we told Lark we were doing: we're checking on the adoptees' welfare.'

Fox looked at the cotton bolls bobbing in the warm wind, reached out, broke one off. 'Maybe Lark will have something to say in the treaty parleys.'

Acacia shrugged. 'If she decides to speak.'

'I'll write to her,' Fox said. 'Maybe I should ask for her advice.'

'I think she would like that,' Acacia said. 'It's a good idea. So which house is next? You said the Mouflons have an adoptee…'

Fox started moving down the path. 'Yes, but I need to go home first, collect the rest of my things from Oak house. Talia's taking my suite and she wants to move in today.'

Acacia fell into step beside Fox. 'She should use the companion's suite. Oria won't need it. She's determined to live in the Oak province camp.'

Fox slipped the cotton boll's stem into the buttonhole on her lapel. She wished she could explain how she felt about Talia. She understood why the other woman preferred Fox's rooms to the companion's suite, but understanding Talia didn't mean Fox was ready to forgive her. 'Oria wants to send Talia to live in one of the failed provinces. She thinks Talia and some resettled Berans could form a new camp and grow timber.'

'Makes sense,' Acacia said. 'Until we find the portals, until there are stone men and women, we need to make the most of what we have.'

Two small figures came into view, heading towards them. There was no mistaking Saury and Doubt. Fox suspected cleaning out her rooms would have to wait because the children were bursting with excitement. Clearly, something had happened.

Saury reached them first and was already speaking before Doubt opened his mouth, 'Guess what? One of the trains has come back.'

'But I saw it first,' Doubt said. 'Not Saury. I was the one who was at the station, watching for the trains. It's the Persica train. I know all the trains. Fruit trees and birds, that's Persica.'

'Everybody knows that,' Saury said.

'But I know all thirty-seven provinces. Not everyone knows that.'

Fox interrupted, 'Were there any wanderers on board with the soldiersisters?'

Doubt and Saury both nodded, but it was Doubt who elaborated, 'The soldiersisters are from Persica House and they've brought Persica wanderers back with them.'

'But they're acting like friends.' Saury frowned. 'The soldiersisters and the wanderers.'

'And what about the Persica Companion?' Fox asked. 'Was she on board?'

'No,' Saury said. 'Just the wanderers and the Persica militia.'

Doubt looked up at Fox. 'Do you think it means everything is going to be all right?'

'I hope so,' Fox said, already hurrying towards Oak House. 'I hope so.'

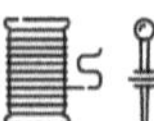

Mica watched the captain of the Persica House militia. She was an unassuming, kindly looking woman with a mop of unruly white hair that looked as though she'd cut it herself. Her appearance didn't fool him. There was a strategic mind behind her grandmotherly aspect.

They were in the Oak House trading room, and they weren't alone. The place was empty of trade but full of those professing their allegiance to finding a new path. Berans and Companionaris crowded in to listen to the captain explain why Persica House had initially decided to lend its soldiersisters to Wheat House and how Persica's decision had changed.

'We were wary, but we agreed in good faith. The Wheat Companion promised the Persica Companion better trading terms.'

Oria stood at the back of the room, at the edge of the circle of listeners, but it didn't stop her sharp comment from being heard by everyone, 'In good faith, you say? That just tells me that Persicans will trade lives in return for a better deal on their next bulk purchase of flour.'

The captain shook her woolly grey head, held up her hand. 'You're getting ahead of yourself. Listen. Persica agreed to encourage the province's wanderers to come to Komey. We agreed to tell them the city needed them for a new parley. That was all we were asked to do. Nothing dishonourable.'

Mica caught sight of Talia. Her lips were parted as she listened to the captain. Mica could see that she was desperate to hear that the situation wasn't as bad as they had feared. 'So they didn't send you to kill?' she said. 'By the Back, I'm glad. I'd feared... Well, it doesn't matter. The main thing is, your orders were to persuade.'

'I wouldn't assume everyone's orders were the same,' the captain said. 'We are not close allies of Wheat House. Persica has a complicated relationship with the Wheat Companion. Suffice to say, we had to take the deal Whilomena was offering, but Mother Persica told me to keep my eyes and ears open, to be careful and cautious, to do no harm. Persica's platform is near some of the southern provinces' platforms. We had some time together with the soldiers from the southern houses before we departed Komey on Whilomena's mission. There were whispers about different agendas, secret orders.'

Mica couldn't help himself, couldn't contain his dismay. 'You realised there were other agendas? And yet you went back to your province and persuaded our people to come to Komey even though you suspected a trap?'

The captain stiffened. 'I went to warn our camp, to warn our wanderers. To tell them what we knew, what we suspected. To take advice from Mother Persica.'

A wanderer, a tall lean Persican, came forward to stand shoulder to shoulder with the elderly Companionari captain. Mica didn't need rock skin to see that the Persica militia and the Persica Berans were close.

The wanderer continued the captain's story. 'When we heard about all the different militias being sent out to seek wanderers, we came here to see what was going on. To keep the peace, to help if help was needed, to collect stories. Always to collect stories. It must be done.' He looked at Mica. 'Even in the face of mortal danger.'

Oria spoke, 'We've been trying to send warnings, stone sendings with my new talent. Did you hear anything? Feel anything?'

Quartz spoke up, explained Oria's curious ability to speak through her rock skin.

The Persican wanderer looked uncertain. 'Perhaps,' he shrugged. 'An unease, but nothing more.'

'That tells us something,' Mica said. He unfurled a map of the Stone Body and laid it on the nearest trading table, smoothing it out. As usual, the Stone Body was depicted as a woman stepping across the Cotton Sea, her clothing a patchwork of provinces. The listeners crowded forwards, peering over each other's shoulders. Mica felt a frisson of fear that not all who were present were necessarily friends. He would watch his words, but some risks couldn't be avoided. Too many houses were reserving their positions, refusing to commit to new treaty negotiations, and yet there wasn't time to sort friends from those who might do harm.

He touched the map at the point where Persica Manor stood, then he turned to the Persican wanderer. 'That unease? How strong was the feeling?'

'Not compelling, but there was something of a stone call about it. Put it this way: I didn't feel comfortable staying in camp, but I wasn't sure where I should go, just a general sense that I might need to visit the city. No one else felt it.'

Mica looked at Quartz and saw that the senior wanderer's worry matched his own. Oria's message wouldn't be enough. 'In that case,' he said, 'we have to assume that none of the wanderers living below the Kelp River will have sensed Oria's call, let alone heard her words. We'd counted on her being heard. We thought that would be enough.'

There was movement in the back of the room as Fox arrived with the children and Acacia. She moved through the crowd, coming to rest beside him. His worries didn't ease but the welcome feeling of her presence was like a smile beneath his rock skin.

Oria was speaking, 'The Oak House soldiersisters have ridden out. I told them to head for the most distant camps on the Stone Body, just in case. But I can see we'll have to send out more people, not just soldiersisters. Otherwise we won't reach everyone.' She looked across the table to the head of the Department of Transport. 'And no other trains have returned?' The woman shook her head.

'And I'm afraid I sent ours back to Persica,' the captain said. 'Thought Mother Persica might need it. Should I call it back to Komey?'

Oria shook her head. 'It's not as though we can use it on anyone else's tracks. Yet another shortcoming of the parley system,' she sniffed. 'Different gauges for different provinces.' She bit her lip. 'Trains will start returning eventually, but can we wait?'

The Caballo wanderer, Patience Learnt, stepped forward, cleared his throat, 'Horses might be better anyway. For meeting wanderers in the field, they're much better. We can provide the mounts. Our entire herd is here. Some Berans will have to stay in Komey to protect any wanderers who arrive in the meantime, but we can fan out across the Stone Body, cover more ground.'

The Caballo Companion spoke up, her voice intense, her rheumy eyes impassioned, 'I will ride out myself.'

'I don't think that will be necessary, Sousette,' Oria said.

Doubt spoke up from the position he'd taken between Mica and Fox, 'I can help. I'm an excellent rider. I could take one of your horses. If you've got a spare pony, I'll warn a camp. I know the way to Kelp. I've been there before.'

'And it's my home,' Saury said. 'So, I should go too. Doubt and I could go together and if you think we're too young, then maybe Fox and Mica can come.'

Mica felt the children's longing: a tangle of youth, a wild wind of courage.

'This isn't a job for children,' Oria said.

Mica looked at Sousette, felt the energy bristling in the elderly horse companion, the yearning for action. 'Nor is it a job for companion mothers who are better placed to try and influence parleys in Komey,' he said. He turned to Patience Learnt. 'Or our most senior wanderers.' He shifted his gaze to include the tall Persican wanderer whose signature also spoke of a hunger for action. 'There's work here, duties, vital work for each of us who must remain in the city.'

Neither the adults nor the children looked or felt pleased, but Mica recognised their capitulation. He'd need to keep a close eye on Doubt and Saury, but hoped the example of their elders would hold some sway. No, the task of riding out would need to rest with the ordinary men and women camped in Komey.

The meeting broke up shortly after. Most of the people in the room followed Patience and Sousette out of the trading room and into the landscape, eager to watch Patience marshal the horses, eager to farewell those Berans and Oak soldiersisters who would ride out. Mica stayed where he was until they'd gone. He'd thought he might have trouble keeping Doubt and Saury with him, but they were waiting, trusting he would provide them with important work. Soon the only people remaining were his close allies: Berans from Oak province, Fox and the children, Talia, Oria and Acacia.

It was Fox who broke the silence. 'Caballo's horses will help but if we're to have a future, we must find the portals. Find them and use them.'

'We have to save the wanderers first,' Talia said. 'Save them and their stones.'

'And the slaves,' Acacia said. 'Let's not forget we need a force to travel to New Lytalia.'

'But Fox is right,' Oria said. 'The balance of power won't shift while Obsidian is just a story. Right now we have nothing, no evidence to sway the sororities.'

'And what news of the portal in Oak?' Acacia said. 'Still nothing?'

'It isn't calling anyone,' Quartz answered, tapping his finger on the approximate location of the portal on the map. 'The Oak train is at our disposal, for all it's worth. I've sent wanderers and rock children backwards and forwards, but we've had nothing from the Stone

Body. It hasn't called any of us. I've had wanderers try each of their stones. They all rested in Promise's grave to no end. Nothing seems to work.'

'All right,' Oria said, 'We don't understand why, but Oak's portal isn't calling. Perhaps it needs to rest before it can produce another transformation. But there must be others. Is there anything in the fourth stories about avoiding being underwater or underground in particular locations?'

'Anything?' Mica laughed, shook his head. 'There are too many.'

'I left Kelp when I was still a child,' Fox said, 'but even I can remember at least twenty of them.'

Oria sighed, 'I see. Of course. So we must find another way.' She looked up at Fox and frowned. 'I tested you for your potential talent as a birthmother, but I've noticed something else in you, a different sort of talent.'

Mica thought Oria was referring to Fox being a wanderer. It was unusual in a woman and with Saury also being stone called, it clearly ran in their family. Oria's next few words caught him by surprise.

'You see patterns,' she said to Fox. 'Mostly it's just something that seems to draw you into the middle of things, even when it's quite clear that you don't know what you're doing.'

Mica went to speak, to defend Fox, but Quartz lifted a hand, frowned in a silent urge for Mica to keep quiet. And truthfully, Fox didn't look as though she needed defending. She was listening, her head tilted, trying to make sense of the companion's words.

'But maybe you can see other patterns beyond people. Maybe you might see some pattern in the landscape. If you tried.'

'Patterns connected to the Stone Body?' Fox asked.

'There are patterns everywhere,' Oria nodded. 'And that's all we have. Patterns in stories, in people, in the world, in images. And we should all look for them.' She turned to the children. 'It might not be Fox who sees them. It might be you, Doubt, or you, Saury. Or one of us.' Her gaze swept the small group of allies.

Mica felt something shift. It was nebulous, uncertain, but they all seemed to feel it: there were portals to be found and Oria had suggested a means to find them.

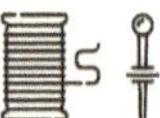

Fox pulled her bed away from the wall, exposing the dado panelling. Like almost everything else in Oak House, it was ornamented with acorns and oak leaves, hand carved and painted in the deep greens and browns of the forest. The dado was surprisingly dusty for a room tended by both houseboys and chamber girls, but a lifetime as an outsider in Oak House had its benefits. Fox had wanted privacy, and no one cared enough about her to interfere with her preferences. Her status as Aikin's daughter and Oria's talent had also helped. The household had never liked her, and likely loathed her now that the world had turned upside down, but her status had held her in good stead. The domestic staff mostly left her suite alone and its cleaning was cursory, and that hadn't changed.

She bent down, squatted on her heels and examined the panels. She was looking for the fault line that hid the cavity, the fault line she'd created when she'd first arrived and had needed a place for the meagre treasures she'd brought with her from Kelp. Fox had filched a carving knife from the dining room and had cut along and then across the panels. She'd worked by night, and when she'd removed a section of panel, she'd chipped away at the sandstone to create a cavity. She'd finished her hiding place by replacing the panel, hinging it with hardware she'd stolen from a disused secretaire. So much effort to protect her small treasures, but it had helped her cope with being alone and having no one. The thought that she had something hidden had comforted her.

It had been years since she'd looked in her hidey-hole and she couldn't help feeling proud that the fault line in the dado was diffi-cult to see.

She used her fingernails to pull at the edge of the panel. It opened onto a filthy, cobweb-laced space. She wiped the cobweb away, flicked it from her fingers and returned her attention to the cavity. The first thing she found was a bundle of her own letters home. She hadn't been able to send them, but that hadn't stopped her writing them. And behind the letters, she found what she'd been looking for. The parcel she'd carried with her when she arrived in Komey. Her grandmother had wrapped fish hooks and lines in a piece of old tent canvas. It was the images on the canvas she'd remembered when Oria had spoken about patterns.

Fox unfolded the package and several fish hooks fell to the floor with a soft clatter. But what she saw didn't make any sense. She'd come searching for a remembered drawing of the Stone Body as a woman, but the image on the canvas was nothing like she remem-bered it. Well, some of it was, but the rest looked absurd, almost as though someone had stolen into her room with a nib and a bottle of ink and a mind to prank her. She spread the canvas on her bent knees, ran her hand across it.

The drawing was a slightly naïve, black and white sketch of the Stone Body. That part was right. Likewise, the marks floating on the Komic Sea she'd always assumed were rust spots.

What was new... felt new, was the ornamentation on the woman's patchwork dress and the decorative border surrounding the map. The motifs suggested a Companionari hand: buttons added to the Stone Body's patchwork dress; and a border of needles and cotton reels crafted to look like dancing monsters.

Could someone have stolen in, found the map and changed it? To torment her? To frighten her? Would someone do that to her? Fox swallowed, her throat tight and painful. She lifted the canvas, exam-ined the drawings more closely, and the ache eased. The Compan-ionari ornamentation was definitely the work of a second hand, but it was old. Very old.

She sat back on her heels and tried to make sense of her failure to remember the image correctly. She'd poured over her treasures in those early weeks. Afterwards, they'd remained hidden and forgotten. For a while, she'd added the unsent letters, but she hadn't looked at the map. Back then, in the early days, she'd known nothing of Companionari culture. She must have remembered what she knew, what meant something to her: the Beranish woman and the rust spots left by the family's fish hooks. The rest, the cotton reels and buttons and needles... All that was alien.

Fox rubbed the edge of the fabric between her fingers. She'd always imagined it was a tent remnant, but it felt a little too thin for that. She sighed, wishing she could write home and ask. She wondered where the scrap had come from and how it had ended up with her grandmother. Had her grandmother ever worked in Kelp Manor? Could she and a sister have drawn it together? But it looked older than that. Way older.

Fox stood up, carried the canvas over to her desk where the light was better. Her surprise at the forgotten images changed nothing. The talk of the portals had brought back the memory of the rust spots, and that's why she was here. But looking at them now, her heart sank. They weren't suggestive of portals and their location in the middle of the Komic Sea wasn't promising. Worse still, there didn't seem to be any pattern. Not one that Fox could see. Some spots were lighter, some darker, some bigger, some smaller. There was even an outline of a fish hook. It had rained on that journey from Kelp to Komey, and her small bundle had been in an open wagon. Amazing that the hooks hadn't done more damage.

She bit the corner of her lip. Probably just rust then. She'd take the map to the camp, but she couldn't help feeling disappointed. She ran her fingers over the dots, and then hesitated. Did it again. Something felt odd. Some dots were flat, but others weren't. Fox felt a small stirring of hope. She put the map on the floor at her feet in case an overview helped. Nothing. She closed one eye, squinted. Nothing.

Oria said she was good at seeing patterns, but if she was, it wasn't working.

She sighed. She still needed to pack up the last of her belongings before heading to Mica's tent. She glanced at the map again, frowned, realised she'd been so focused on the marks and on the unfamiliar ornamentation that she hadn't really looked at the figure. The woman wore her patchwork dress. She always wore that dress. Even the Companionaris showed the Stone Body as this woman in that dress. Only...

Fox bent down.

When you looked past the Companionari buttons, the patches were a little off. They didn't match the provinces' boundaries.

She picked up the map, put it back on the desk. She felt it rather than saw it. There was a pattern. Not the dots, not the border, not the buttons. The patchwork suggested a folding pattern.

It took her twenty or more tries to find the right folding order, but in the end she had it. The portals lined up. The outline of the fish hook and the other genuine rust spots became obvious. What remained, was a series of seven dots, each a fingernail's width from the next.

She smiled. The precision was a message from the maker. She unfolded the map and looked at the seven dots, once more offset from one another. If she found the map's scale, it was likely the offset meant something, and Fox thought it suggested bearings. The artwork might be naive, but the maker's message was exact. It wasn't the whole story, but this relic represented hope. If they could find the scale, they'd find the portals and the famines would end. Then she and her allies would have the power to free the slaves, and the new treaty would have a future.

JOIN MY READING COMMUNITY

Thank you for reading *The Light Heart of Stone*.
If you enjoyed the book, please consider joining my reading community. You'll be the first to know about new releases.
Visit www.torroxburgh.com/join
When you join my reading community, you'll receive a free ebook short story: *The Tidings*.

About The Tidings
When a man is found dead in a quiet Australian town, Detective Senior Constable Romy DuBois finds an unlikely ally in her investigation - a territorial magpie who can speak to her in perfect Old Birdic. As they investigate a string of cockatoo murders and a human death, they discover that justice comes in many forms, and some crimes can only be solved when two species work together. But in a world where humans and birds see justice differently, can there ever truly be a perfect resolution?
The Tidings is a darkly humorous murder mystery that blends natural and human law, told through the sharp eyes of Australia's most vigilant bird.

PLEASE LEAVE A REVIEW

Enjoyed this book? Your opinion can make all the difference.
Your review can help other readers find their next book. Writing a review helps everyone, including me.
Please share your thoughts online. Whether it's a review at your favourite bookstore or on your reading app, or a quick post on social media, there is a beautiful wisdom of crowds when readers speak directly to readers.
Thank you.

ACKNOWLEDGMENTS

With two editions, there are lots of people who deserve my gratitude.
My thanks to June Wilson, Caspar Roxburgh, Ari Roxburgh, Nina Roxburgh, Velislav Georgiev, Tracey Taylor, Clifford Thurlow, Iris Gioia, Rosaleen Roxburgh, and the late Sam Roxburgh for reading various drafts of the first edition's manuscript. My thanks also to Michele Winsor, Helen Hunter, Nina Rootsey, and Patrick Bonello, who also extended their professional expertise.
My gratitude to Cathy and Henry Jelinek for helping me to understand the process of harvesting cork and for sending me their wonderful photographs of the cork harvest.
I am particularly grateful to Midnight Voss for her developmental edit for this revised edition, to Beauregard Furu for proofing the manuscript, to Stuart Bache for the new cover, and to Patrick and Robert at Bigger On The Inside Media for website and graphic design support. Likewise, a second thank you to June Wilson and my family for encouraging me to persist with the re-write, particularly Georgette Karvelas, Nina Roxburgh and Ari Roxburgh for chasing typos. Finally, I'd like to thank Norma and Lindsay Rose, the Falkiner-Rose family, and Leslie Falkiner-Rose for their hospitality in hosting the Retreaters on our periodic writing sojourns on the Mornington Peninsula.

BOOKS BY TOR ROXBURGH

Tor Roxburgh is an emerging epic fantasy author with over 30 years of professional writing experience. She has published 17 works across speculative fiction, young adult novels, non-fiction, and short stories. A multidisciplinary creator, she exhibits artwork internationally and co-hosts *OK Smart-Ass*, a technology podcast. Her love of crafting worlds extends beyond the page – when not writing or creating art, she can be found reupholstering furniture, tiling floors or building stone walls.

EPIC FANTASY

The Light Heart of Stone
The Rush of Stone

SHORT STORIES

The Tidings (enjoy reading the ebook for free by joining Tor's email list at www.torroxburgh.com/join or read the story in print in the *Who Sleuthed It?* anthology)
The Boudicca Society (read the story in print in the *And Then...* anthology)

You can listen to *Ok Smart-Ass* via your favourite podcasting service or at www.oksmartass.com.

Tor's books and stories have been published by William Heinemann Australia, Pan Macmillan, Pan UK, Australian Consolidated Press, Greenhouse Publications, The Federation Press, Curious Crow Books (her own imprint), and Clan Destine Press.

Tor's digital home is www.torroxburgh.com and her online socials include Instagram at *torroxburghwrites,* and Facebook and TikTok at *torwriting.*

1
The Galean colonists arrived on the Stone Body 1118 years ago.

2
More colonists followed.

3
The Stone Body experienced famine.

4
Galeans and Berans died during the Treaty Wars.

5
An anonymous Galean wrote The Book of Kinesis (Promise's era).

6
The first Galean talent affected horses. The Galean settlers renamed themselves the Companionaris.

7
Fifteen years after they arrived, the Companionaris signed a treaty with the Berans.

8
Provincial boundaries were drawn three years later.

9
Now, 1118 years later, famine returns.

A Galean History Of The Stone Body

www.ingramcontent.com/pod-product-compliance
Lightning Source LLC
Chambersburg PA
CBHW050110120726
47904CB00004B/1284